Praise for Suzanne Hudson's writing

"Hudson writes like a fallen angel. Her characters might have one foot in heaven and the other foot in hell, but she touches them with an ironic humor and a fiery grace."

~ William Gay, author, *Fugitives of the Heart*

"Suzanne Hudson's work is a raw, beautiful glimpse into the depth and humor of the human condition. A craftswoman of epic genius, she transforms the literary into an accessible art form, a delicate feast of impeccable truth and infinite grace."

~ Suzanne Kingsbury, author, and founder of Gateless Writing, Inc.

"Suzanne Hudson is a remarkable writer. Her short stories are perfection, and that's a difficult genre to excel in. To be honest, I would read anything she wrote. Take a minute and enjoy these stories. It's a journey you won't regret."

~ Carolyn Haines, author, and Harper Lee Award winner

"The ultimate question is this: Are these stories nothing but. . . pulp to titillate the peeping toms of the morally corrupt? Or, like Faulkner and Caldwell, is it art whose subject includes deprivation because to ignore it is to condone it? Suzanne Hudson should be read. The subject is low, the art is high."

~ Tom Hull, *The Education Digest*

"Bawdy, grotesque, beautiful, gruesome, ribald and sometimes laugh-out-loud funny. Such is the paradox . . . Hudson is fearless in confronting the awful verities of a past and present most would like to forget or ignore."

~ Brad Watson, author, and National Book Award finalist

"She is the best among us. Suzanne Hudson . . . brings together some of the finest short stories written in the South in the past decade or so. 'Opposable Thumbs' is fast becoming, like O'Connor's 'A Good Man is Hard to Find' and Welty's 'Why I Live at the P.O.,' a Southern classic."

~ William Cobb, author, and Harper Lee Award winner

"Suzanne Hudson writes about what Southerners do when faced with dire circumstances. It ain't always pretty, but sure as hell is readable. . . Hudson is like a tornado looking for a trailer. Look out! You might get blown away."

~ Marshall Chapman, author, *Good-bye, Little Rock and Roller*, and singer-songwriter

"Suzanne Hudson reminds us in blistering detail how strange people truly can be. She takes us on a stroll into that room on the other side of civility and carefully shows us ourselves."

~ Frank Turner Hollon, author

". . . if you should live to be a hundred, you're not likely to ever forget her words, her stories, or her characters. Quite a legacy."

~ Jill Connor Browne, author, and Sweet Potato Queen

"I'm a long-time admirer of Suzanne Hudson's work. She writes with great verve about people for whom the stakes are never trivial. Her stories matter, and they will stand the test of time."

~Steve Yarbrough, author, PEN/Faulkner Award finalist

"Hudson is capable of casting spells. She wields a power that renders readers breathless."

~Karen Spears Zacharias, Best in Appalachian Fiction Award winner

Deep Water, Dark Horizons
and other stories, plus

Suzanne Hudson
2025 Truman Capote Prize winner

Livingston Press
at
University of West Alabama

ISBN: 978-1-60489-396-0 trade paper
ISBN: 978-1-60489-397-7 e-book
ISBN: 978-1-60489-398-4 hardcover

1977 photo courtesy Walter Bower
Current author photo courtesy Kevin D'Amico
Book and cover design by Sonny Brewer

Other Books by Suzanne Hudson

Short Story Collections:
Opposable Thumbs / Finalist, John Gardner Fiction Book Award / Binghamton, NY
All the Way to Memphis and Other Stories

Novels:
In a Temple of Trees
In the Dark of the Moon
The Fall of the Nixon Administration

Memoir, "Fictional-ish":
Shoe Burnin' Season: A Womanifesto by pseudonym R.P. Saffire
Previously published and pulped as *Second Sluthood: A Manifesto for the Post-Menopausal, Pre-Senilic Matriarch* by Ruby Pearl Saffire

for Joe Formichella, of course

Contents

The author in her youth, when she won the *Penthouse* Fiction Award
photo: Walter Bower

Introduction

Toni Morrison and Kurt Vonnegut, Jr., were late to the party. The whole gang in our creative writing class knew Suzanne Hudson had a gift. No amount of writing practice or study or efforts at imitation could bring a new writer to that level of art and skill.

Our professor, John Craig Stewart, required a writing sample from any student who wanted into his program at the University of South Alabama. I can see him now as he removed pages from his faculty mailbox and went into his office on the second floor of the Humanities Building. Sitting heavily in his swivel chair, propping up his feet for a read of this latest sample. He sighed. How many timid submissions for a chair at his table? How many manuscripts from students who'd get a handwritten note, "I'm sorry . . ." Mr. Stewart was a kind man.

Walker Percy, in his introduction to *A Confederacy of Dunces*, confessed that reading a bad manuscript was the last thing he wanted to waste his time doing. And, further, he simply would stop, and sometimes with a single sentence. Writers would cringe knowing their blood and sweat to bring a story to life could be so grossly and easily rejected. But, like being offered a taste, say, of seafood gumbo for the very first time, you know *immediately* whether you like it. You don't need to keep chewing. It would only get worse. With John Kennedy Toole's manuscript, he knew in that first sentence as an author and editor of Louisiana State University

Press, he was in the company of something good. He didn't know it would win the Pulitzer Prize for the deceased writer.

Mr. Stewart's eyes would have brightened with that first line of Suzanne Hudson's sample story. A tilt of his head slightly forward, as if to get closer to the story, the words. With the last sentence, he'd keep holding the page. Maybe stare out the window, trying to picture the author. Bookish like Flannery O'Connor? She wrote that well. Tennessee writer William Gay, who Stephen King said, was "an American treasure laboring in obscurity in the hills of east Tennessee," would many years later tell her he found her writing like that of Flannery O'Connor minus God.

I was also similarly arrested when I first heard Suzanne read a story in his class.

We showed up on Wednesday afternoons for the three-hour, seminar-style class. Mr. Stewart sat at the head of a long rectangular table, something like you'd see in a corporate board room. His gaggle of hopefuls, these emerging authors, sat five on either side and two brave souls at the other end of the table facing him.

At the start of class, Mr. Stewart might say, "Today we'll start with stories from Kenny Hall and John Hoodless and Erin Kellen. After the break, we'll come back in for the second half of our class and hear Blake Savell and Sonny Brewer and Suzanne Hudson." Then he'd remind the class, as usual, when each reader finishes, "We will pause after each reading for ten seconds, and then offer comments and suggestions."

He'd lift his hands from the table in front of him and slap them down, but lightly.

"Let's get started. Are you ready Mr. Hall?"

"Mr. Stewart?"

"Yes, Mr. Brewer."

"There's this short story contest, for new writers only, sponsored by *Penthouse*."

After the initial and not unexpected snark about the magazine, I listed some of the authors who'd been published in its pages: "James Baldwin, Philip Roth, Gore Vidal, Paul Theroux, Isaac Asimov, T. C. Boyle, Harry Crews, Don DeLillo . . ."

And then I added, "The first prize is $5,000, plus a purchase fee of $500. And the winning story will be published in the magazine, so your name can be added to that list of literary lions."

Still, Erin Kellen protested, "There're no women on that list."

"So be the first," I told her.

Mr. Stewart took over. "What have you got to lose? Everyone should send in a story. Get with Brewer during the break or after class for the mailing address."

I got my story back within two weeks. Whichever of the team of freelance editors hired to read 7,500 submissions from all over the world read mine had a hangover, I'm sure, and didn't give my story a fair shake. But it was comforting to learn from my peers that their work, too, had been tossed aside.

All except for Suzanne Hudson.

Already that quarter, she'd won a contest sponsored by a New York-based literary magazine eponymously titled *New Writers*. Still, we were all shocked and maybe a little jealous when she brought in a letter from the *Penthouse* fiction editor, Paul Bresnick, saying her story "LaPrade" was one of a dozen semi-finalists. The letter also said that Toni Morrison had been one of the judges, and, further, that those twelve stories would be passed to Kurt Vonnegut, Jr., who would choose the overall winner.

"LaPrade" won. Suzanne was notified by a telegram she keeps to this day.

All in, she was paid $5,500 prize money and publication rights fee for "LaPrade," which appeared in the December, 1977, issue of *Penthouse*. It was our senior year. And we demanded she take the class and Mr. Stewart to Thirstie's Bar and Grill on Old Shell Road, just off campus, and treat us all to gallons of beer. She first bought a new washer and dryer. Then she bought rounds for whoever showed up that Wednesday night after class.

Our friend William Gay, that same writer, whose novel *Twilight* was selected by Stephen King as his favorite book of the year 2006, and who had two of his short stories made into movies, and who won a MacArthur Fellows Genius Grant, also entered the *Penthouse* magazine contest. He told Suzanne he was upset about losing. "Until I saw your picture," he confessed.

"Yeah, she might be pretty," I said to William, "but she didn't shave her legs or under her arms." Which didn't bother him. They became dear friends. And he showed up for her, joining Suzanne and Frank Turner Hollon and me for a reading panel at Agnes Scott College. He never passed up a chance to boast about her writing, nor to confessing that Toni Morrison and Kurt Vonnegut, Jr., favored her writing over his.

Suzanne and I both wish William were with us still, for he would likely join her when she accepts the Truman Capote Prize from the Monroeville Literary Festival in the spring of 2025. This collection of stories, *Deep Water, Dark Horizons*, commemorates that event. It gives strong testimony to the power of Suzanne Hudson's writing art and the literary career that I had the pleasure to watch grow from its bright beginning into her shining legacy of Alabama letters, as conveyed in her bibliography following the stories in this collection.

The crush I had on Suzanne during our days seated around Mr. Stewart's table is none of your business.

Sonny Brewer,
Waterhole Branch, Alabama

LaPrade

The man rolled over on the ground, a patch of dirt on the left side of his face. Anyone could see that he had been crying, and he brought his fists up to rub the tears away, just as a child might. He made no move to untie the rope around his neck.

The sun was just coming up—edging its way through the ribbon of haze separating earth from sky. The haziness played tricks on the old man, mixing the greenery of spring with the blue that was always above it—or did it surround it? He heaved himself into a sitting position to watch the rusted Studebaker raised on concrete blocks, a monument to a past he only remembered in distorted snippets. "Charmaine?" he whispered, then looked away, recognition lost.

The night's quiet still settled over the rotting wood and tarpaper shack, but soon he would hear Missy shuffling about, doing those things he imagined other women did in the morning. Boards would creak, then she would appear at the door. She would look at him and say, "You know you done bad, LaPrade." He would nod yes. Next she would put on the faded blue-and-red plaid dress that hung on the doorknob every night, walk over to the car, squat down beside it, and pee, holding onto the door handle to keep her balance. Finally she would come and untie the rope around his neck. He would promise to do better.

Missy was a lightly freckled mixture of child and woman, almost pretty when the light filtered just so. That same light, strained through a honey jar, birthed the color of her eyes—an eerie echo of amber. Although her hair was brown, the light sometimes found a reddish tint, and the thick waves that spread out from a ponytail hanging down her back turned auburn at sunset.

She watched as LaPrade pulled some radishes for breakfast. She wore the green plastic bandeau he bought for her at the Dollar Store in Isabella. It had a flower design cut into it. That made it extra special. Over the last couple of years LaPrade had bought her more things than ever—a pop bead necklace and bracelet kit, some Romantique perfume, a ballerina pin (that was her favorite), comic books—"Archie," "Heart Throbs," "Richie Rich," and lots more. Every Saturday he walked the twelve miles into the little valley community of Isabella, bringing back some small treasure to occupy her for a while. Still, she knew that one swoop of his eyelid could reveal a soul unredeemed and threatening.

Missy didn't go into town with him often—people stared so—but once in a while she would go with him to the picture show, or the Farmer's Exchange, or to a drawing at the Sheriff's Office. And the Dollar Store. Now that the child had come, trips to town were rare. The welfare check had to go less for Dollar Store perfume and more for baby things. Missy slid the green-flowered headband off, then on again, combing a few loose strands of hair back with its plastic teeth. "You know why I done it, don't you, LaPrade?"

The man straightened up, motions slow and deliberate, as was his speech. "It makes me sad when you tie me out like that, Missy." LaPrade put the radishes in a metal pail and carried it towards the car.

"You was pinching the baby. I seen you do it. That ain't right. And the rope's your doing, too. Always has been."

LaPrade set the pail on the ground by the old car, sat down in a splintery, straw-bottomed chair, and began to lick the dirt off the radishes, spitting and scraping in the cracks with his fingernails. Finally he spoke. "I believe you care more for that young'un than you do for me." The tears came again, just as they had the day before.

Missy put her arms around him, holding his face close to her chest. "I do so care for you," she said. "And you ought to care for that young'un, but I got to purnish you if you do it harm. I just got to." She did love him, she reckoned. She knew how to read him and how to tend to him, and he had needed tending ever since her mother died three years earlier—ran the car into the river and killed herself. LaPrade had borrowed a truck and pulled the wreck out of the water, but he never found a body, and he hadn't been the same since.

She loved her six-month-old child, too—no reckoning about it. So she took care of them both, in spite of instinctual uncertainty. At first she was sure that LaPrade would get over his jealousy of the baby, but the jealousy was fading into harsh resentment now, and what might it become next? She thought more and more often of how her father used to be, back before her mother died.

"I ain't bad," the man sobbed.

"No, you're good, real good." Missy stroked his bald head, unconsciously avoiding the newborn soft spot.

The man turned, studied the car with a confused grimace, then reached out and ran his hand over the hood. Some rust stuck to his wet palm. He slowly brought the palm to his mouth and began to lick the rust, to make his hand clean, but he stopped abruptly with Missy's "I got to go see about the young'un." The man's sixty-some-year-old eyes followed the sway of the girl's hips, shrouded in red-and-blue plaid. His lips settled into a childlike pout.

When she returned, the baby was at her breast. "LaPrade? You know tomorrow's Easter Sunday?" Missy was smiling. She always looked forward to Easter, when LaPrade would wake up before dawn to hide eggs. Exactly two hours later she would follow, dressed in her prettiest Dollar Store things, and begin to hunt. They would play hide-the-egg for days after, until the smell of rotten eggs, whose hiding places LaPrade had forgotten, filled the house and yard.

His pout became a gap-toothed grin. "What do you want me to get you for Easter, Missy? I'm going into Isabella today."

"Get some of them plastic eggs—them kind that don't go rotten," Missy said. "I seen them at the Dollar Store. They're all colors. And you can take them apart and put other surprises in them. And we can play hide-the-egg all the time 'cause they won't go rotten!"

"What color eggs you want?"

"Green," Missy said. "And pink, too. I'm going to wear my pink pop beads and my pink socks tomorrow, so get pink!"

LaPrade stood up, stretched, then began to unsnap his overalls. "Missy, do you reckon we can do business now? Hit's been a spell." His eyes showed her the shadow of malevolence that lived behind them if she refused.

The woman nodded yes, put the baby in a cardboard box next to the car, and lay on the ground. It wouldn't take long. No. Not long at all. It never did.

***

The red clay road wove its way down the side of the mountain for five miles before it turned into pavement. Missy always said the county road to Isabella was ugly—no good scenery to look at—but LaPrade loved it. So skinny and gray without any of those white lines down the middle to bother a person's eyes. The way the trees coiled themselves over the strip of concrete gave him a sense of being sheltered from the rest of the world. It was rare that a car passed, and even less often that anyone offered him a ride, but he didn't mind. He didn't feel at ease with people—not even the few kin he had scattered across the county. Only Missy gave him comfort now. He loved his daughter. She takes good care of me, he thought, watching with fascination as a small brown rabbit shot across the road, disappearing in the dark mass of trees and dank earth. "Yep, she shore does that. Takes real good care of me," he said aloud.

Green scents, black-eyed Susans along the edge of the road, and a feeling of Easter crept into LaPrade. Going to be a good walk, he told himself, just as he heard the soft sputtering of an engine from the hills to his back. Panic, as the old body jerked, trying to move in several directions at once; knees hitting hard on the pavement as he fell. LaPrade wanted to hide—run deep into the trees like that rabbit and hide. If only he could get far enough from the road before—but the black pickup was already in sight, beginning to slow down. Dammit, he thought, rising into a stumble. Don't want no ride.

"How you doing there, LaPrade? Want a lift?"

LaPrade grimaced, rubbing nervous palms over worn denim thighs. "Well, McCall, I just—"

"Oh, come on," the voice from the truck interrupted. "Hop in. No sense in you walking the whole way." McCall slapped the seat on the passenger's side.

They rode in silence for a long time, LaPrade staring down at his hands, strong hands in spite of age, resting on his thighs. He would hurt McCall if he had to, if the man got too much into LaPrade's business. A car passed, heading in the opposite direction.

"Welfare lady," McCall noted, craning his neck to watch the blue convertible in the rear-view mirror. "Going to your place, you reckon?"

No answer. Missy will take care of it, LaPrade thought. She always did. Smart as a whip, that girl.

More silence; but finally McCall cleared his throat. "So tell me there, LaPrade—how's everything at your place?"

"Fine," he mumbled, without looking up.

"And your girl Missy?"

"Fine. Missy's just—well—" He rubbed his hands together. "Missy's just fine," he blurted.

Silence, except for the sputtering truck, as green scents and sunshine blew through the window against LaPrade's face, black-eyed Susans blurring along the roadside. McCall again cleared his throat. "To tell you the truth, LaPrade, I was hoping to catch you today. There's something—well, I figure we're neighbors and all, even if we don't live close by and don't talk much."

LaPrade could hear the blood pumping through his ears, a clock ticking, low and loud.

"Is it so that Missy's done had her a baby? There's been talk of it."

LaPrade stiffened. There it was. The baby. He tried not to give McCall any sign of the hate he felt for the child. The hate he kept hidden from Missy. Maybe if it weren't an arm baby it would be different, but the child wouldn't be ready for the ground for a long while. He could not stand to see Missy give her touch and time to anyone other than himself, but he did not dare change expression or McCall might suspect. We're kin, LaPrade told himself. We got our way of doing things. Why does anybody have to bother it? All because of that goddamn baby.

"All right," McCall sighed. "I just wanted you to know that there's talk. And there's going to be people looking into some things. Thought you ought to know. Is this okay?" he asked, stopping his truck in front of Stoner's Hardware Store.

LaPrade looked at his interrogator for the first time, mumbling a thank-you, ducking out the door, and began his attempt to blend into the little town of Isabella, Georgia. He didn't see McCall staring after him, puzzling over such a crazy old man.

LaPrade chuckled at his reflection in the window of Stoner's Hardware. I'm going to do real good today. I been bad. I know it. But tomorrow's hide-the-egg. Out of the corner of his eye, the man could see a young woman walking beside and a little behind him. She was pretty, he suspected, because she wore a pink dress—Missy's favorite color—and she had red hair. LaPrade stopped walking as recognition came for the second time that day. Charmaine's hair had been red. Is it you? I done it. Done drove you away. You come back, you hear? Ain't going to do it no more. Ain't going to hurt you no more.

The roar of a cattle truck startled LaPrade. He felt perspiration on his forehead, the stares of passing people, and drew in his breath. Charmaine didn't enter his mind very often anymore; it was a jolt when he did think of her.

The Dollar Store loomed before him, the words "Clary's Five & Dime" still stenciled across plate-glass windows, even though five-and-dimes were obsolete. Familiar smells hung over the store like the past it represented—month-old popcorn, stale chocolate and coconut, plastic things. The occasional ring of the antique cash register. The whir of the drawer shooting out. Wooden floor boards creaked as he made his way to the back left-hand corner where the toys were. Polka-dot balls, Yo-Yos, and hideously grinning dolls cluttered the glass shelves. Dolls. Baby dolls. Babies. Their plastic eyes laughed down at him, and he glared back.

"Can I help you?" An elderly saleslady was beside him, smiling.

"Yes'm. I want to buy some Easter eggs."

"Easter eggs."

"Um, yes'm. Them kind that don't go rotten?"

"I don't think I understand," her smile at once artificial.

LaPrade exhaled a nervous whimper. "Them kind you can put other surprises in. Them—"

"Oh," her true smile back again. "Straight that way and to the right." She pointed to a large Easter display.

He stared at the pyramid of stuffed rabbits, yellow-and-blue baskets full of shiny artificial grass, marshmallow chicks, and candy—every kind of candy—and cardboard fans proclaiming, "He Is Risen!" LaPrade wished that he could take it all to Missy—make her forget about the baby.

He picked up some of the plastic eggs. Twenty cents a package. He could get two green packs, two pink ones, and still have enough left for a chocolate rabbit—a little one, framed in a box with clear windows. Missy'd be happy with that surprise especially.

Once outside again, the sun was bright, reflecting off the pavement in glittering patterns. He squinted, feeling very proud carrying the big green bag with "Bill's Dollar Store" printed across it, couldn't resist peeking inside the bag several times during his walk home. The chocolate bunny stared back from the green paper prison, from its cellophane cage. The orange candy eyes put him in mind of a demon, like the picture show scary movies, werewolf demon eyes. But knowing what a treasure he had was all anticipation, for Easter morning.

***

Missy heard the automobile approaching long before it arrived. Now she and Mrs. Owens sat in the front seat. It was a convertible, looking brand-new. Missy loved the feeling of sitting in such a fancy car—even if it wasn't going anywhere.

"That sure is a pretty dress you got on, Miz Owens."

The middle-aged woman smiled. "Well, thank you, Missy. Now if we can—"

"And that perfume smells real nice, too. LaPrade buys me perfume sometimes. I got some Romantique and—"

"Now Missy, stop all this." The woman leaned forward. "You know I didn't come here to chitchat about clothes and perfume and nonsense."

"Well, that's what ladies talk about, ain't it?" Missy whined.

"Stop it now. You're trying to keep us off the subject. Now behave." She paused, lighting a cigarette. Then, in a gentler tone, "I'd like to see your baby. Where is it? May I look?"

"No?" It was a half question. Mrs. Owens touched Missy's shoulder.

"Oh, Missy, honey, did it die?"

"No'm."

"You've got to show me sooner or later. You can get aid, you know."

"My baby don't need nothing from nobody."

"Is it a boy or a girl? And is it healthy? You know, childbirth is not without hazard if you do it alone, especially at your age. And if this is your father's—"

"It ain't his," was the calm reply, but the green-flowered bandeau was coming off and going on again nervously. "Can't you mind your own business, please, Miz Owens?"

"Missy, you *are* my business. And I know you aren't stupid—you could do so much better for yourself. The most important thing is for you to be honest with me."

"Yes'm."

The older woman took a deep breath. "Now, I must ask you this question again. I'm just as tired of it as you are. But please. Please answer it honestly this time. All right?"

"Yes'm."

"Has your father ever raped you?"

"No!" The tiny voice began to rise. "He ain't never done that! And I told you—it ain't his!"

"Missy, you never cease to amaze me." Mrs. Owens exhaled cigarette smoke through her nose, a menacing dragon with dyed hair. "Now listen to me. I may be fairly new on your case, but I've learned quite a bit, so don't think you can fool me. I know you've not socialized with anyone or attended school for years. And your former teachers say what a good student you were, what an imagination you had. Even used words like 'bright' and 'more than capable.' I just don't understand why you pretend otherwise. Could it be all these years of playing along with your father?"

Missy said nothing.

"Why did you quit going to school when your mother left? You really were such a good student. Did he make you? Did he beat you? I certainly don't doubt that he beat your mother."

"Miz Owens, Brother Claud told you them things, but he don't know. I swear he don't. We quit the Church a long time ago."

"You'd like to go back to the Church, wouldn't you?"

"Yes. I mean—no! They talk about me and LaPrade. I hate Brother Claud." Then she felt guilty, as if she had professed hate for Jesus. "But I don't hate Jesus, " she said aloud, tearful now.

Mrs. Owens touched her shoulder. "It's not your fault. Don't you see he's always been a disturbed man? And he's getting old before his years, Missy. Feeble-minded. Could be serious mental illness, or even dementia. But we can deal with that. There are—places that we could—"

"You leave! Right now!" The bandeau was moving on and off more rapidly as Missy sobbed. "Why can't you people just leave us alone? We do just fine." She leaned onto the car door. This was different. Mrs. Owens had never insisted that Missy should change everything.

The woman pulled Missy close to her. "Honey"—her voice became softer again—"honey, if you're doing just fine here, then why are you so upset?"

"You can't have my baby," Missy hiccupped, disentangling, reaching for the door. "And you can't—well, you can't take LaPrade and send him away from me nowhere."

"Don't you worry about that yet, honey. But do you think that he might mistreat the child?" She rested her head on the steering wheel, then raised it, looking, Missy thought, very sad. "Let me tell you one more thing, Missy." There was a small silence, then, "We think your mother is alive. It's not certain, of course, but she may be in Atlanta, using the name Charlotte Spurlynne. Here. I've written it down for you. Now why would your mother want to run away, do you think?"

Missy wondered why she wasn't surprised, and spoke without emotion. "Well, she always liked Atlanta. And she was pretty. Real pretty. Lots of boys liked her, but there weren't nothing to it."

"Your daddy didn't like that, did he? Especially since he was so much older than your mother. It made him mad, didn't it?"

"Sometimes. Sometimes he was mean to her, and sometimes she was mean. Sometimes LaPrade called her bad things. But she was a good Christian. Brother Claud said so at the memorial service. He said she was washed in the blood of the lamb," pushing the door open. "And LaPrade he ain't mean no more," she lied.

"How was he mean? I mean, years ago. Did he beat her?"

"I don't remember. Can't you just leave? He ain't mean!"

Mrs. Owens flicked her cigarette to the ground. "All right. I'm leaving—for now, anyway. I think we've actually made progress today, but, Missy, if you just think about that baby of yours. Think about your mother. There's a lot we can do for all of you. Think about that, all right?"

The blue convertible soon disappeared down the red clay road. It didn't even take much time for the cloud of dust left behind to disintegrate. She went into the house to tend to her child.

It wasn't the house she had grown up in with Charmaine. That house was further up above the creek that fed into the river. There had been a kitchen table, some nice furniture, and pictures of Jesus on the walls. After Charmaine died, LaPrade boarded up the windows, padlocked the door, and forbade Missy to set foot in it again—even though he visited it every once in a while. She had not allowed herself to miss it much until now.

Their present home was an abandoned shack with a sparse kitchen, a crude shower, and a shithouse down a trail near the creek. But it was enough for LaPrade. She knew to go along with him over the years, keep him from turning on her. Be a good daughter. But I'm fifteen now—like Mama when I was born. And now I'm a mama, too. Missy sat in the doorway of the shack, the baby at her breast. She could see LaPrade walking toward her about half a mile down the road. "Yonder he comes, baby. Bringing Easter eggs. You like that?"

The child replied with passive sucking noises. "He's a good man," she said. Then whispered, "Oh, I know he's bad from time to time—like pinching you. He just needs to be took care of." She reached up, touched her bandeau, and thought about how nice

LaPrade was to buy her pretty things. She didn't like to punish him. It wasn't any easier now than it had been the first time—the day after he had given up the search for her mother's body. She had been twelve then, confused by the man her father was becoming and the strange changes in her parents over the years. But he had begged her. "I thought some lies about Charmaine," he had whined, like a little boy. "I'm bad. You got to purnish me, Missy."

She had been frightened. He had always done the punishing, the beating, the deciding of everything. But he was handing her a rope, begging to be punished for his wife's death. At first Missy thought he wanted to be hanged, but she couldn't do it, and he didn't have enough left within him to do it himself. She'd solved the problem only by using the first thing she noticed—an old, but sturdy, fence post. One end of the rope around the post, the other around her father's neck. Missy's night, alone in the house, was filled with intermittent sounds of LaPrade's guilt, occasional thuds, and cries of pain as he ran out the length of the rope and was thrown to the ground.

"Charmaine, you can't be dead!" he would scream. "You come back here! I ain't going to say no more! Nothing about Fred Culver or Adon McCall or none of the others! I ain't! I swear to God I ain't!"

It felt like forever for the night to dissolve into dawn. Finally she had crept out of the house and held him next to her—pitied him—done business with him. It was her obligation. She was kin. She accepted it. It was a sacrifice—a Christian sacrifice. Any guilt that reared up she learned to dissolve like the night. It was a matter of survival.

"Baby, you sure are pretty." Missy spoke aloud again. "Just like my ballerina pin. Sort of hard to tell you two apart."

The screen door squenched, slamming behind her father. "Wait'll you see!" LaPrade cried, laughing. "Wait'll you see!" he sang over and over, dangling the sack in front of Missy's excited face, dancing around in crazy circles.

"Give it, give it!" she squealed, laying the baby on the floor, chasing LaPrade outside and the fifty yards to the creek, where he collapsed in the weeds, hugging the bag to his chest.

"You know you can't see till tomorrow."

"Well, I reckon I *will* see tomorrow," too out of breath to play any longer.

"You take care of that welfare lady today?"

"Told her to let us be," she answered, wondering if she should try to share her thoughts with him. No, she decided, I ain't going to spoil no Easter Sunday. I can let him have that, at least.

"I thought about Charmaine today," LaPrade said. "There was a red-haired woman looked just like her in Isabella." He scratched his elbow. "Missy? What you reckon made me call her all them names? She didn't—"

"Now don't you go feeling bad, and don't you go crying. Tomorrow's hide-the-egg."

He nodded, looked to the creek, mumbling in that helpless way of his. So different from the angry, accusing father of her childhood, who drew blood and defiance from her mother as Missy huddled in corners praying for God to make him stop. Missy shivered as a phantom rabbit scooted across her grave, reminding her not to think forbidden thoughts, but getting to know her mother, as a mother.

"Come on, LaPrade." Missy took his hand and led him back to the house; she would cheer him up. They would giggle and tease one another, plan for hours about Easter. Then she noticed the baby on the floor, felt the uneasiness again, and made to comfort it.

***

A good day for hide-the-egg, LaPrade thought. He stole out of the little house, careful not to disturb Missy. The mist took on a yellowish cast, sun shining through greenery. Fresh dew on clumps of grass made it look like the artificial Easter kind at the Dollar Store. Pretty, he told himself, reaching for the packages in the big green bag. Missy'll be happy.

He carried some pink eggs over to the old automobile, a perfect hiding place—one egg behind a concrete block supporting the vehicle, another under the front seat. "She'll never find that one," he whispered. He dotted the plot of land with the plastic eggs. A green egg was situated in a clump of grass by the house, and he was proud of himself for being so smart about mixing the colors.

LaPrade stood still for a long time, thoughtfully searching out a hiding place for the last egg. I done good, he told himself, wedging the egg behind a flap of tarpaper.

"You just can't figure out what that big old green thing is, can you?" LaPrade said to the termites there. "Well, this is the best hiding place ever, so don't you go messing with it." He laughed at himself. "Talking to bugs," he muttered.

Now it was time for the real treasure, the ceremony. He took the chocolate rabbit out of the cellophane-windowed box. He set the candy treat with the orange demon eyes in the radish patch, where a real rabbit might be.

She'll be awake soon, he thought, almost tripping over the baby. The child gazed up at him, not making a sound. LaPrade had a sudden urge to crush it—place his foot on the child's tiny body until all life was gone. No, he told himself, that would be bad, and Missy likes it. Likes to play with it. Suddenly, LaPrade had a wonderful idea. I'll hide the baby. He began to get more excited. Missy's gon' love this game. He lifted the child, stiff-armed. It still didn't make a sound—but then, it hardly ever cried.

By the time he returned, the woman was standing in the doorway—all blue-and-red plaid and pink.

"I never seen you looking so pretty, Missy."

"You think so? You think my pop beads look good? I was going to mix some blue in with them, but pink's such a pretty color all by itself."

"It's fine, Missy. You're prettier'n ever."

"LaPrade?" Missy walked toward him and touched his elbow. "Where's the baby? I couldn't find it when I waked up." She must not show anger, must not confuse him or rile him.

He smiled. "Don't you worry. I done moved it. Right now you got to hunt the eggs!" he exclaimed.

The woman hesitated, then giggled, knowing that she must, and immediately ran toward the car. "You always hide some here, fool." Laughter. Green and yellow sunshine. It went by much too quickly to suit LaPrade. He was disappointed when, after the last egg was found, Missy again asked about the baby.

"Missy, I can't tell. You got to find it—like the eggs. It'll be fun!" But Missy wasn't smiling. That wasn't supposed to happen.

She was supposed to be pleased.

"You better not've hurt it, LaPrade."

"Missy, don't be mad. It's a game. It's—" He stopped. Her face wore an unfamiliar expression.

"You tell me where it is. Right now, you hear me?"

The man turned his face toward the car, then the creek, then back to Missy. He began to cry. "I done forgot," he sobbed.

"No," she whispered, then screamed, "What did you do to it?"

"Don't worry, Missy. She ain't dead. I seen her in Isabella yesterday, remember?"

But Missy was running—running hard, pushing through morning-moist leaves, head whipping left and right, searching. Where you at, baby? Under that old car? LaPrade, he ain't right, Mama, but you lied and I need my young'un. Panting, running from car to house to clumps of trees and back again. There was not enough of her to get to all the places the baby might be.

She lifted the hinged door set in the floor of the shack where LaPrade stored potatoes and moonshine. But at once she realized she had already looked here, panic pushing her into a randomly repetitious search of only the most obvious places: the shithouse, the old car trunk, a kudzu-covered aluminum boat, the washtub where she had bathed her doll babies only a few months before.

Frantic phrases of thought flashes kept time with her movement. *Baby ain't no doll. Baby's real. Ain't no plastic toy. Baby can die. LaPrade killed it? No, please. Need my young'un. Got to be it. Mama. Mama.*

"Mama!"

At once she knew, began to run the fifty yards towards the creek, the word *mama, mama, mama* drumming through her head.

She saw it as she approached the water. A tiny, mud-caked child, making strange little choking sounds. "Oh, baby," she whispered, gently picking it up. "Baby, poor baby," she cooed over and over, as she walked toward the house. Mizres Owens must be right. It must be so. Wiping mud from her baby's face, she knew.

LaPrade was exactly where she had left him, only he was sitting now, rocking back and forth, crying, "My fault, my fault."

"You could've kilt it!"

"Oh, Missy, I ain't—"

"You could've kilt it! Just like—well, just like you could've kilt Mama."

"But she ain't dead," LaPrade said. "I seen her in Isabella."

Missy sighed. "You just ain't right, LaPrade. Now you know what I got to do?"

The man, all obedience, walked over to the fence post and allowed Missy to tie the rope around his neck. She sat in the doorway of the shack and stared at her father for a long time, sometimes glancing at the rusty automobile. She held her child close, reaching up every now and then to comb loose strands of hair back with the plastic headband. "You know what we got to do, baby?" she whispered. The child gazed up at her, some dark mud still ringed around its neck. The woman sighed, stood up, and went to LaPrade. She gently kissed the top of his head. "Goodbye, Daddy." She stroked his cheek. "I got to do it. I just got to."

"Where you going, Missy?"

She stopped. Turned around. "Leaving." Tears touched the faint freckles on her cheeks.

"You cain't!" LaPrade screamed. "Where you going?"

"Don't know," she sobbed. "To see Miz Owens. Maybe to Atlanta."

"You don't know what you're doing!" The man called out. "Look here, Missy. Look here what I got you. In the radish patch! Look here. A candy rabbit!"

She hesitated, then continued walking. "Done made my mind up, baby. Ain't no candy rabbit going to change it," she mumbled.

"Missy!" he yelled, running out the length of the rope, feet rushing from under him, falling hard against the dirt. "I ain't going do it no more!" he yelled louder, pounding his fists in the dirt. "I promise! You don't care nothing about that young'un. It ain't even got no name! Missy!"

The woman stopped, motionless except for her shoulders rising, falling, rising.

She turned one last time and screamed, "William! Its name's William!"

The man lay in the dirt. She was out of sight now, had been

for quite a while. He stared at the chocolate rabbit. It was melting, in the morning's full sunlight, and those orange demon eyes had gone lower, going down to hell, he figured. He would not move, he decided, drooling a pool of spit in the dirt, thought-cursing the nothingness of the high noon and the nothingness that was him. By mid-afternoon the demon eyes were gone, the Easter confection swarming with ants and flies and even a few yellow jackets.

The Thing with Feathers

She didn't meet her stepfather until she was five, having lived with a cousin of her mother's in Beaumont, Texas, since she was born, having been ensconced in the womb during the marriage ceremony. An apathetic judge of probate oversaw the wedding, a hasty, desperate ritual her mother rushed at, in order to find legitimacy for herself and, by default, her daughter. In 1950, the world of small town Alabama did not look kindly upon unwed mothers, and her own mother thought it best to spend some time alone with this man who was now a husband, would be a husband for the next thirteen years, until he shot himself in the head on a creek bank—accidentally, some said; on purpose, said others.

The relative who brought her up to the age of five was sometimes affectionate but many times harsh, tugging at the child's clothing in frustration as she dressed her, brushing, too hard, at the tangles in the child's hair, impatient and full of spat-out sighs, like the sounds of an angry cat. Still, there were storybooks read in drowsy snuggles on the relative's bed when it was time for a nap. There were stories the relative told for truth, about God and Jesus and arks and healings; but mostly there were fairy tales: "Snow White and Rose Red," "Jack and the Beanstalk," "Rapunzel." The toddler, the child, did not understand all the words, the intricacies of plot, but the soothing sound of her surrogate mother's voice spun silky tendrils of hope, though she couldn't name it at the time, around her soul.

Her mother visited her on her birthdays, sent her packages at Christmas time, doll babies in shiny wrapping paper tied up in fumbled ribbon, shipped in boxes all bumped and scarred by errant postmasters. The child played with the dolls in the floor of the relative's kitchen while boiling cabbage eked its humid, acrid scent into the walls, the curtains; cheap furniture disemboweling brown-flecked stuffing across the linoleum. Then one day she was told it was time to go and meet her stepfather.

She remembered hanging back, there in the doorway of her new parents' house, dropping her eyes from his overpowering form. He was all plaid flannel shirts, khaki work pants, and heavy boots that seemed to shake the earth, like the giant in "Jack and the Beanstalk." And he worked to win her over, his fingers nibbling at her ribs, games played until he drew her in to the fun he concocted, though she always glanced away, holding back a bit of herself. "She's shy," her mother said, but she wasn't. So he called her "Sugar Bugger" and "Baby Doll" and "Dipsey Doodle." When he came in from work he would throw her in the air and the world would blur and the colors would bleed into each other and she would shriek with delighted laughter, even though there was that quick moment of terror, breath sucked back and where was Jesus?

Her stepfather had a shotgun for killing deer, limp brown forms laid blood-spotted in the bed of his truck on autumn evenings. He had a thick-handled, thin-bladed silver knife for slitting through the skins of squirrels and catfish, or carving through the meat of an apple to offer her a small slice: "Eat it down, Sugar Bugger. An apple a day keeps the doctor away." He had a pistol he would use sometimes at night, to shoot at the raccoons that dug in the garbage, crashing her awake, sending her screaming and crying to her mother, who would say, "Don't be a silly girl. Go back to sleep. Your mama's tired as the devil."

He had a collection of fishing lures—rubber worms in purple and orange, golden spinners shimmering, enticing her—a kaleidoscope's colors, some like feathered jewels in the hinged, top-handled treasure chest he carried.

"Show me the thing with feathers, Daddy," she would say, for he had insisted, insisted that she call him "Daddy," and she, who had never had one, tried the word on and enjoyed the way the sound of it wrapped her in the feel of a safe-layered warmth.

"They ain't feathers," he would say, pulling out the Shyster lure, letting her tickle it with the soft tips of her fingers. "Fish don't eat nothing with feathers."

He drank beer most of the time—like water, her mama said—and whiskey of an evening, and if the child was up too late, or lucky enough to be invited to sleep in the big bed next to her mama, she would sometimes see the other man emerge, the one who was much more unpredictable, the stumbling one, who mumbled curses and kicked her mother's bedroom door when she shut him out.

"Don't want no drunk slobbering over me," her mother would say.

He finally took her fishing when she was six, a special day, just the two of them, to a pond that pooled a blue stain in the woods, where he cast into the weeds, building a mound of empty cans, with each toss of a can a glance at her, going from strange into threatening into frightening and where was Jesus? Then, the pile of cans grown to maturity, when the sun caved in to the horizon, he twirled her hair around his fingers, stroked her face, her little arms without recourse because she didn't understand. And when he put his hand to her panties, the soft white cotton ones her mother hung out on the line each week to dry, the ones he would throw into the blue pond going all deep-colored as the sun withdrew, tears streaked trails of salt down her cheeks because it hurt and she wanted her mama.

In elementary school the child was not especially noticeable, moving at an average pace, producing average work, sometimes pushing at the rules, as children will do, seeming good natured, even charming at times. She raised her hand, walked single file, clattered her green plastic tray along stainless steel bars in the lunch line, flew in circles around the metal-chained maypole, ran in games of tag on a playground dusted with dirt. But at home she had grown tense and vigilant, keeping alert, watching doorknobs, listening for the pad of feet down the hall, in the night, while her mama slept. She had to be aware, stay keen to the barometric changes in the atmosphere of the little house, because she knew that darkness held the thick, syrupy smell of whiskey riding warm breaths across the slurred dreams of a girl now eight years old—when her only father would stand beside her bed and put her small palm to the thing that lived there beneath the hairy curve of his belly.

She would try to shove pictures into the grainy dark, try not to see him, not feel the mash of her tiny hand into his, but she could not pretend his looming form away or conjure anything that would color the dim shadows of her bedroom, not while she looked into the dark. So she shut her eyes tight, so tight it hurt, sending bursts of light against her clenched lids. And all the while, as he moved her palm along the creature he coaxed with his own, she would see nothing but the black-eyed Susans growing along the highway, or yellow buttercups at Easter, or her mother's azalea bushes, hot pink and white against green. She would bathe herself in floral colors, fending off the dark and the molding of her fingers to the creature taking shape there, boozy breaths—all laced with the harsh, hot scent of the Camels he smoked—bearing down on her small body. She strung the flowers into garlands spiraling out around the little bed until his breaths hit hard and the thing spat venom across the pistils and velvet petals she had laced through the thick layers of the night.

When she was nine, ten, eleven, he would take her on long rides in the game preserve, slits in the rough-trunked horizon strobing sunlight into the periphery of her vision, where he lived, on the edge of a look, a quick cut of an eye, never full-on and vulnerable, never a challenging stare. She would lean her chin on her hand and hang her arm out the open window, trying to catch and hold the air, pushing her palm against the gale. Just the two of them, away from the house, furtive, like lovers trysting and traveling across the borders of contexts and closed-off emotions. He would find hidden, high-walled creek banks, where he would fire his pistol at the empty beer cans that forever clattered across the bed of his pickup. He taught her how to shoot, wrapped her small fingers around the butt of the Ruger and helped her support the weight of it, showed her how to hold it, palm cupping wrist, breathe in, let out slowly, and as shoulders drop, squeeze—no, no, squeeze, real slow, Baby Doll. That's it, that's it.

The noise of it, set off from her own thin fingers, crashed booming into the wild silence of the forest, an ear-ringing power of more dimension than she could have ever imagined, and its echo cracked and cracked its fade into a silence. And she liked it. So she practiced, asked him to teach her how to load, clean and care for the thing, squealed with the thrill of firing it, exhilarated by its deafening blasts, those sounds that had more than once chased her from her little bed. She made secret dares, vows to herself to get better, be the best, know it like an intimate friend, a confidante. In time she began to practice with even more determination, with the grim focus of a guerilla warrior, whenever he took her out for one of their rides down the red clay roads curling through the wooded, forested walls that hid them. She put aim at beer cans and milk cartons and squares of cardboard with bull's-eyes drawn on them. She exploded an olive green wine bottle she had found under her mother's bed, sending a spray of glass bits sparkling like emeralds scattered to the sky.

"Got him!" her stepfather grunted.

And she smiled at him, a coy one, the one she had learned to use early on, to maneuver him there in the unpopulated margins of her life. She could force an advantage, she had gradually discovered, could write a tune without words and suspend him in a dance. A lift of her chin, a pout of her lip, an inflection, a glance—she had found where the lines could be, if she wanted them there. She could change the course of a day with the bat of a lash, the turn of a wrist, the knowledge she had gathered and filed away during those solitary moments at his side. She could finally see who might really hold the cards, and where his weaknesses resided, and get the true lay of the land he had hidden for so many years without her ever suspecting. She squeezed the trigger.

"Got him!"

And she knew she had. Even at the age of eleven, twelve, and then, thirteen, she knew she had "got him," would get him, eventually, Jesus or no. She would take it upon herself, still a child but not a child—never, really, a child. She would take herself up on her secret dare and look at him directly, for once, eyes focused hard down the barrel of a gun, silver and straight, its lines looming outward from her fixed gaze like railroad tracks, parallel until she inched it down, real slow, breathing out, the squares of the sights put to the target at the end of her vision. She would meet him on a riverbank and burn him red, his work boots all slogged in the slick mud. She would get him and reclaim herself, take herself by her little girl's hand, dimpled and unscarred, to the place where her soul was hidden. And then, finally, the two of them would blend into each other, into the notes of the music, notes in chromatic half-steps and notes of modulation, staves winding around and nestling against the warm skin of the relative in Beaumont, Texas, where the thing with feathers could sit unabashed on its perch, reach into its sweet, sweet depths, and sing.

Yes, Ginny

Ginny Widdamacher's stepdaddy, Johnny Lee Fowler, went missing sometime Christmas Day, though no one could be sure when. After all, there were friends and relatives in and out, gift-wrapped boxes blotting out some of the routine family scenes, ripped paper tearing sheared holes in the underlying goings-on of the place and its blurred boundaries. A spirited din of raucous voices and laughter buzzed through the holiday pretend play of the children in the ramshackle trailer.

Johnny Lee's absence was first mentioned around mid-afternoon, and the family was hard pressed to remember when, exactly, they had last noticed him, passed out in his perpetually-worn purple and gold plaid pajamas. As always, the LSU cap was turned sideways on his head in a way that annoyed Ginny's mama to no end. Everyone agreed that he had spent at least some of Christmas Day there in the La-Z-Boy recliner like the lump that he was, deaf and numb from the Old Charter. Ginny's relatives, a collective noun of arms and legs and faces, whose conversations writhed in and around one another's like reptilian hissings in a pit of stranded snakes, offered theory after theory about where Johnny Lee Fowler had got off to, suggesting such offerings as:

He went to the A&P to buy cigarettes and watch folks come in for batteries for their bawling kids' toys

He went to the bowling alley that never closed to drink and

shoot pool with Pete and Bootie and Killer Jones, derelicts all, who were surely there, as they were every other day of the year, listening to Johnny Cash on the jukebox and swapping lies

He went to harass and romance Connie Babb, that skank of an ex-girlfriend of his, the one he went to prison over, for slicing her across the cheekbone with a switchblade knife

He went outside to take a leak and passed out in the woods

He went somewhere, anywhere, driving his muffler-loud Chevy, with a belly full of booze and an attitude, and got himself locked up. Again.

But Ginny, six years old and swept up in the magic of Christmas, didn't care where he was or where he might be. She didn't like Johnny Lee Fowler. He was mean to her mama and mean to her brothers and mean to her. He sat in her real daddy's burnt-orange recliner and yelled to be waited on by her mama, bossed her brothers to do their chores, and squint-watched her for the least little mistake so he could call her a doofus or a retard or a maggot-head. And when he got up from that chair, he staggered and stumbled and shoved and slapped and punched. Sometimes he fell out in the floor and the family would step over him as if he were not there, mouth gapped open, drooling saliva, a cigarette's dying glow clamped between his hairy knuckles. So Ginny was nothing but glad that he had disappeared.

She spent the day rearranging the cardboard furniture in her Barbie Dream House, making up pretend dramas with Barbie and Ken and Skipper: Skipper running away from home and becoming a trapeze artist; Barbie kissing Ken because he saved her from a thing kind of like The Blob; Barbie throwing furniture at Ken because he liked Skipper better than her. In between conjured-up dramas, she played languid games of Candy Land and Chutes and Ladders with her older brothers, bent the wrists and joints of her brothers' G.I. Joe dolls, and pretended to be a majorette in the uniform Santa Claus had brought her. The relatives spent the day cooking and talking and laughing and bickering and cursing and drinking and, later in the day, wondering, though only in spurts, just where the hell Johnny Lee Fowler was.

"That's a stupid damn thing," Johnny Lee had said to her, early that morning when the light was dim, his hangover thick, when she ran her little-girl-smooth palm over the Dream House, awed and proud. "Ain't nothing but a cardboard box. And somebody's hand-me-down, too."

She didn't answer back. She never did. She already knew the Santa who visited her got his toys from the Fire Department. The Fire Department had a used toy drive every fall, toys they painted and repaired for the poor kids, the non-discriminating children they thought wouldn't notice a nick here or a ding there or a scratch underneath. When Ginny took one of her Santa presents, a Tiny Tears doll, to show-and-tell in first grade, another little girl, Glendaline Moorer, came up to her afterward and said, "That's my old doll I gave to the firemen. That right there's where I stuck push-pins in her leg." And she pointed to the scattering of bore holes, the pricked, pink-plastic flesh, the pattern of dots Ginny had already noticed, been suspicious of, and now had confirmed as the mark of a cast-off.

Less than a month later Johnny Lee Fowler moved in, loving on her mama, pretending to like Ginny and her brothers, doing little odd jobs around the trailer, calling their home a tin can and calling himself a stepdaddy. He worked at the paper mill until summer, when he claimed he hurt his back, then badgered Ginny's mama into quitting her job at the Ben Franklin and going to work at the mill herself, working the night shift, making better money, enough to barely pay the bills, but not enough to entice the Santa who delivered brand-new toys. That Santa visited the other side of the creek, where Glendaline Moorer lived, where the little girls wore shiny hair ribbons and pressed pinafores with white eyelet ruffles.

For his part, Johnny Lee collected a government check, every cent of which went to the liquor store in town or for Alpine cigarettes or for bets on games of pool, or, as her mother accused from time to time, for other women. He planted himself in the burnt-orange recliner and looked at the TV when he wasn't out with his running buddies. He entombed himself in that recliner for hours on end, thumping cigarette ashes into the honey-colored glass receptacle on the TV tray at his right side, reaching for the bottle of amber liquid on the floor at his left, anchored to the spot by the whiskey and the fuzzy glow from the television screen. "Turn that damn hat around," her mama would say to him. But Johnny Lee just sneered, "Can't see the TV good enough with the bill out front," and the only time he turned his hat frontwards was when he made to leave the house. Ginny loved to see his hat turned frontwards.

Ginny and her brothers were allowed to sit in the living room with Johnny Lee in the evenings, in front of the television that glowed fantasies into the shabby little trailer home. They were not allowed to pick any programs, but watched whatever Johnny Lee Fowler wanted to watch—*The Ed Sullivan Show, Alfred Hitchcock Presents, Perry Mason, The Twilight Zone*—until he ordered them to bed. They knew not to argue, knew not to dispute or resist or offer up any evidence that they had anything like thoughts and feelings of their own.

Ginny shared a tiny room beside the bathroom with two of her four brothers, usually sleeping wedged against their calves and heels at the foot of the bed. Whenever she couldn't sleep, she listened to the night, to her brothers' snores, to the television until it signed off with the crescendoing strains of "The Star-Spangled Banner" and turned into hissing gray snow, to the uneven steps of Johnny Lee's bare soles against the linoleum as he stumbled for the bathroom, invading the dimness in the hall. She listened to the wall groan as he leaned his palm against its opposite side while he used the toilet, trickling his imprint into those spaces in the little trailer where her own wishes and dreams resided, and she began to wish on him, on his intrusion. She began to wish him away and into thin air, like that magician did the lady in the box on Ed Sullivan's show; she wished him broken down on the stand, like Perry Mason always did the guilty people; she wished him into a suspense-filled fantasy, into the twilight zone of no logical explanation. And all that wishing, it seemed, had all of a sudden paid off, because now, on Christmas Day, he had vanished.

As the afternoon dimmed, the relatives fretted and frothed and stewed and railed about that sorry Johnny Lee Fowler, to skip out on his family on such a day, to rise up out of his drunken wallow to go and do something else, something he deemed more important than the day Jesus was born. They demanded answers of his empty chair. What about the children? Wasn't this *their* day, the children's? Didn't he realize how disappointed the little ones were? But, most of all, wouldn't he catch it when he got back home! And they offered Ginny's mama advice and admonishments and ultimatums about how to adequately punish Johnny Lee for his holiday-season sins. They rolled their eyes and ate more turkey and drank more beer and vodka and gin and whiskey, while Ginny and her brothers played in their walled-off worlds of pretend, the living room a sprawl of toys and dime store candies and nuts and apples, the hot-bulbed lights on the four-foot-tall tree burning her brothers' skin whenever they wrestled each other into its artificial branches.

Ginny sashayed in her majorette uniform, though there were some frayed places along the hem. Every once in a while she would catch the pattern of Johnny Lee's purple and gold pajamas in the corner of her eye, see the sideways-turned LSU cap that made her mama so mad, and feel a small tickle of a shudder at the nape of her neck. She would cut her eyes to the place where his whisper of a presence tried to break through, seeing—nothing. So she dismissed the fear and grounded herself in imagination. Instead of worrying over the possibility of his return, she pretended to twirl the flaking silver baton, its marshmallow-knobs at the ends now dull from being dropped. She wished for white boots with big red tassels, just like the majorettes at the high school wore when they pranced out ahead of the marching band, which formed and re-formed itself into shapes as it marched, reconfiguring itself into a drum, a star, into loops and interlacing circles before dissolving into another set of lines, marching to the stands, leaving the field empty and green and waiting for the game to proceed.

After the sunlight died, the relatives drifted out into the night, back to their own homes. The friends, though, still came and went while her mama fumed and sighed and sobbed over where Johnny Lee might be. Had that slutty ex-girlfriend picked him up at the foot of the dirt road, out of the family's line of vision? How had he managed to slip through the crowd? Her mama blew her nose a lot and smoked cigarette after cigarette while her best friend cursed Johnny Lee Fowler for a low-life piece of nothing that meant nothing but misery. "But I love him," Ginny's mama said, as if that answered all arguments.

Her mama had loved Ginny's real daddy, too, even though he

was not a nice man, either. Ginny had vague memories of a shotgun trained on them all, of her mother leaning over the sink while her busted nose bled a slick sheet of red to the porcelain, of her oldest brother screaming with the sting of a leather belt. She remembered wishing her daddy away, wishing him dead. And it had worked, when her daddy was killed in an automobile accident on Highway 59, exactly one summer before Johnny Lee took up with them.

Late that night, Ginny sat on the floor beside Barbie's Dream House, the heavy cardboard case open to reveal upstairs and downstairs rooms full of colorful, modern, clean-lined furniture, though the cardboard was bent in at a table corner here, torn on a chair leg there. She imagined Barbie as a beautiful majorette in a satin uniform, and marched the doll naked across the floor of the Dream House, Barbie's plastic feet perpetually arched for stilettos, black eyelashes forever swooped up solid, mounded breasts fixed, unmoving, and devoid of nipples. Barbie marched across the scatter of toys on the floor, to the beat of a marching song, and up and over the arm of the empty chair, then up and across its back to the other arm. "It's time to go to sleep, Virginia Anne," her mama slurred and sighed, laying her head down on her own arms as she sat at the kitchen table, while her best friend made a pot of coffee.

Ginny closed the Dream House—Barbie, Ken, Skipper, and all their furniture tucked away for the night—and stood, and stretched, and yawned, but as she turned to the hall, to go to bed with her brothers' calves and ankles, she noticed something very, very odd. It was something that certainly would have been noticed earlier, in all the uproar surrounding Johnny Lee's mysterious absence. It would have been noticed by now had it been present before now, but it seemed to have simply dropped from thin air, from a hole torn in the ether, from a place of no logical explanation.

It was a cap—the purple and gold LSU cap—the one he wore always, turned to the side for TV and to the front for leaving. At this moment it was turned to the front, in the very middle of the seat of the La-Z-Boy recliner. Ginny walked over to the burnt-orange chair, eyes wide, full of the kind of astonished surprise brought by Christmas gifts anticipated in dreams but not truly expected in reality. She picked up the cap, drawing in a breath, then set it back down and fingered the rough fabric that covered the chair, let her touch go to some of the places where a lit cigarette had left circles of melted black enmeshed in the material. There were burned marks on the TV table beside the chair as well, and a mound of butts in the honey-colored ashtray. The Old Charter bottle sat on the floor where he had left it, a strange sight to see it left there, as the bottle always went wherever Johnny Lee went. Ginny nudged it with her big toe, sliding it closer to the chair, smiling, gazing at the empty chair, at where the indentation of him was still pressed into the coarse, rumply upholstery.

She turned, but, one more time, in the corner of her eye, came the pattern of plaid that was him, there in the dented foam where his body had born down, where the LSU cap now sat, facing front. She leaned close, and still closer to the cushioned seat where he had lounged, day in and day out, barking insults, picking at weaknesses, stick-poking at hidden angers, cementing insecurities. She looked into the weave of the fabric, deep into the threads loomed into one another, and a separate weave began to emerge. She squinted, adjusted, aligned her vision. There it was. There, within the pattern of burnt-orange, the solid color of the chair, came another color, then another, as a new pattern emerged, though melded deep within the recliner's thick covering. It was the purple and gold plaid of his pajamas, forever imbedded in the depths of that chair, the place where, in selfish ignorance, he strode on the edge of a lost child's reconfiguration, the transcendence of her dreams. Johnny Lee Fowler's presence had given Virginia a wish, and the ripening of that child's fresh wish had taken him into thin air, into the kind of forever where faith danced in the yellow satin slippers of sugar plum fairies.

from *In the Dark of the Moon* / Novel

Royce Fitzhugh was feeling pretty good for a change, knowing there would be a way out soon, away from Sumner, Georgia, away from his slut of a mother, and out into the world, a world that was lining up for war, he hoped. The only sad thing about leaving was that he wouldn't see Elizabeth Lacey, who was finally, at twelve, coming into her own, in exactly the way he predicted to her at a political rally, a little over two years earlier.

Royce had always been curious about Elizabeth, ever since the days when she visited Chen Ling and the three of them would toss horseshoes in the Chinaman's backyard or play dominoes on the porch. But now Royce was seventeen years old, a frustrated pursuer of girls, still watching Elizabeth, ever and always miles ahead of the other girls her own age, but never more than now. What he saw in Elizabeth these days promised to overtake even the girls *his* age, girls already three, four, five years older than she, girls who criticized her while they vied for her attention, hoping some of the mystique might rub off on them. These days, when Elizabeth visited the Chinaman, Chen Ling blushed and looked down with increasing frequency. These days, Royce felt a shift in the repartee—both spoken and unspoken—between himself and Elizabeth. These days, boys in the upper grades were mentioning her name, looking at Royce with a new respect, keenly aware of his access to her. Royce knew what she promised to represent for the boys in town: the magnetic force in their tiny universe, the sun at the center of their solar system, already exemplified by their willingness to take up one, just one, of Lizzie's dares, win her delight when, the task complete, she charged over to offer a hug, a kiss, or, for himself, Royce hoped, someday, that confection of a galaxy between her legs.

At only twelve years of age Elizabeth was getting noticed.

But Royce also knew that Elizabeth had something much more than extraordinary good looks, something not as obvious as overly developed curves and thick, wavy hair and sapphire blue eyes; but something subtle and stinging and sensual, some kind of musky certainty that promised to intimidate as it beckoned, overlaid with the ripening glaze of potential, just on the verge, poised there, on the sweet verge of something he sensed in the most primal way. Hell, she was just a kid, on paper; but he could always see that those blue eyes knew things, that she was watching far into some peripheral kind of anticipation and had the carnal capacity to wash over men with the pull of a rip current, carrying them out to sea on a sweet, rough-and-tumble tide. It was the precursor of swollen flesh and hidden renderings of sexuality, the burst of an egg through a Fallopian bloom, the sigh of a scent of that first heat, folds of skin pushed out, making ready, waiting for the lunar signal to set it all in motion.

"You've been bruised, on the inside, like me," Elizabeth said to him from time to time.

"Why do you think that?"

"I've seen it in your mama's eyes," she'd say, and her own eyes would fill with tears, but only for a second.

Bruised on the inside? It seemed to make her feel tender and kindly toward him, so he let her believe it was true. Hell, he would let her believe anything as long as it gave him an edge, a shot at being the one who would get close, who would conquer that sweet, rich part of her. If she wanted him to be bruised, by god, she could have him that way, though he was anything but bruised.

Royce had, in fact, calloused over so many times he was hard as stone by the time he was twelve. His daddy was long gone, had spent only five years as a fixture in Royce's life, a presence that reminded him daily how worthless and stupid he was, welting

Royce's back with a razor strop or a buggy whip, wrenching his little arm in its socket in order to lay into his bare buttocks with one of his brogans, snatched in anger from beneath the sofa. Royce hated him, resented his mother's silence, her tacit approval of Lucas Fitzhugh's brand of discipline. The only days his daddy missed out on administering a beating were those welcome periods when he disappeared for weeks at a time, on a drinking and cheating tear, his mama said, seeming relieved that her husband was at the moment not a presence in her life, a relief that gave way to fear and fretting over money, which gave way to nights out, away from Royce, when she stayed out late, sometimes overnight. Royce had vague memories of playing in his crib in the dark, in the silence, having cried himself spent, and without anyone coming to see to him.

The Chinaman came, though, from next door, every so often, when he heard Royce screaming for a mama who was not there. On those nights Chen Ling would sit by his crib and tell stories half in English, half in Chinese, until Royce fell asleep. By the time he was three, Royce knew not to mention Chen Ling's presence in their home—his mother had gone next door one Sunday and railed at Ling for meddling, screaming and cussing so loud the law had to come—and by the time Royce was four, he began to notice that his mama had grocery money on those mornings after she had stayed out all night.

His daddy would finally come home and there would be cursing accusations and arguments and his mother thrown into walls or slapped around or punched. "You need to sport a shiner for a while behind that shit," Lucas sometimes said. Then he proceeded to give her one while Royce looked on, at once both afraid for her and glad she was getting what she allowed Royce to get with brutal regularity.

Finally, one day when Royce was five years old, perhaps after weighing the solitary freedom Lucas's absences afforded her against the misery and cruelty he brought, his mama finally stood up for her son. His daddy had just cussed him and slid the belt out of his pants, whipping through the loops, a quick leather snake to accompany the venom of his words: "You goddamn idiot. Why you want to be such a goddamn idiot, boy?"

But on this day his mama stepped forward with a Colt .45, a gift from one of her man friends, leveled at Lucas Fitzhugh, a gesture that said, without hesitation, Stop. It was the first time Royce had ever seen that side of his mother, the reservoir of determination, the certainty that acted in this brief battle as the element of surprise.

Lucas let go of his arm as an expression of shock took his face. "Woman, have you gone around the bend?"

"You ain't going to do him that way," she said. "It will come to your fists by the time he's eight, and then what? Either you'll kill him or he'll get growed up and kill you. Best for you to get on gone, right now, before I kill you instead."

Royce always thought it strange how quickly his daddy left, and how permanently, too. Royce never laid eyes on him again, and if his mama did, well, she never let on. His daddy didn't even pack up his clothes. Lucas Fitzhugh offered up no argument, no inclination to compromise, just a sneer of a snarl at Royce's mama, with the words, "He ain't none of mine noway."

The boy watched him walk away, the back of his neck wearing the 'V' of dark hair that curled all the way down his back, beneath the work shirt, arms bowed out at his sides, fists balled up, itching for a fight. It was only a few months later that the implications of his daddy's last words began to sink in, when his ears picked up on the whispers of the decent folks of the town, how Mona Anne Fitzhugh was a two-dollar whore for sale down by the tracks, down near nigger town. And, even though Royce could not fully comprehend—not yet—what a "two-dollar whore" was, he could not help but notice that, once Lucas was gone for good, the men began to trickle in to the little shack, for drinks and laughter, until his mother's bedroom door swung shut and the bedsprings squawked out a rhythm picking up faster and faster. Sometimes the boy heard mumbled curses or loud moans, even shouts that startled him out of his slumber and into those provinces of the man-woman world he was only beginning to fathom, and much too early.

When he was six, seven, eight, he wandered out on the back porch when the bedsprings started screeching. He lay on the glider and waited for trains to roar past and drown out the sounds. Sometimes the Chinaman stepped out on his own porch, saw the boy lying there, and whispered, "Come here, Roy Fitz. Come play domino Chen." And they would steal into the Chinaman's little shotgun house and play rounds of dominoes until Royce was sleepy enough to go home and crawl into bed.

"You stay night if want," the Chinaman always said.

But Royce never stayed. He asked his mother, once, if he could stay overnight with the Chinaman, but she squashed the idea fast. "Hell no, you can't sleep over there with that slanty-eyed devil. He ain't like us," she said. "He's a foreigner. They got strange ways that you ain't liable to know what he might be up to. Worser than a nigger. Now go on and don't ask me about that Chinaman again."

So Royce continued, when he was eight, nine, to sleep on the glider some nights, play dominoes at the Chinaman's house other nights, and feel relief on the nights when his mama did not have company. It was the late nights that got him, though, when he heard a knock at the door around midnight, the swish of his mama's bare feet against linoleum, a hushed, murmured conversation ending with his mama's, "Okay. Come on in." Then muted words from the front room, the room next to his, followed by his mother's moans and the uneven squeak of the bedsprings, the sound that drove into him like a jackhammer, stirred in him the suspicion that his mama could not be okay, not with that racket going on, yet the human sounds he heard seemed to be expressions of pleasure. It did not make sense, and so finally, at ten, Royce slipped to her cracked bedroom door one late night, just past midnight, just as the mattress began to squawk. He put his face to the doorway's opening and let his eyes adjust to the dark, making out a man's bare backside, that bare backside moving toward and away from the bed. And then he realized it was his mama the man was moving onto, and her knees were drawn up and he heard her say, "That's good, Daddy. Do it like that. Show me." Then the man moved faster and Royce was afraid to stay there, afraid of what he would see next that he did not understand.

He tried, in his child's way, to get the Chinaman to explain it over dominoes one night.

"Ah, no," Chen said. He seemed embarrassed and just as awkward as Royce had felt in asking, the Chinaman's English breaking up even more from the awkwardness. "No say much. Maybe say too much. Mama no make fuck. Now you play domino."

By the time he was eleven, Royce had figured out what the man was doing to his mother, there on the bed with her knees drawn up, and he had figured out some of the other things she probably did with them, things he heard older boys bragging about. And it was around the same time that some of the boys at school began to taunt him once in a while on the playground, where they played baseball to the peripheral squeals of the smaller children and thick ropes dangling tire swings groaned their deep-toned rhythms.

"Know where we can get a piece of tail, Fitzhugh?"

"A piece of tail for sale?"

"Who can pleasure many a man?" one rhyme went. "Go see moaning Mona Anne."

Royce knew he was fated to be either a sissy or a scrapper, with no in-between. He chose to be a scrapper, to be Lucas Fitzhugh's son, whether or not he was claimed as a son, and beat the shit out of anybody who teased him, and then some, serving up preemptive beatings before the other boys had the chance to think. Sometimes he lost the fight, but most times he won, getting a meaner and meaner reputation that eventually silenced those inclined to say anything about Mona Anne—to his face, anyway.

So it was that, as Royce entered adolescence, his already muted love for his mother had gown tainted with disgust, and he spent more and more time away from the shack and the men and the woman who spread her legs to keep him in milk and eggs and corn meal and shame. He never mentioned her to his friends in high school and they were by then mature enough and kind enough not to mention her, either, even though there was the occasional rumor that some of the athletes were going to go visit Mona Anne this night or that one. The bitter taste of her name in its carnal contexts slid down his throat and deep into his gut, eating away any kind of respect or caring he might have been able to conjure up for her. Finally, in the months leading up to his seventeenth year, he began to see a way out.

The Germans were all over Europe and folks claimed it wouldn't be long before Roosevelt went on and committed to helping out, running the Krauts back to Berlin, and Royce aimed to be signed up and in on that detail if it happened. He even began to hope for it, in spite of the fact that the popular sentiment in Blackshear County was that Roosevelt had no business even thinking about sending troops. Royce didn't care whose opinion was right; he only wanted to get the hell away from his whore of a mama, away from the stares of the church folks, and maybe even come back a hero in the process. He already had a career for himself in mind. He had taken to killing time around the sheriff's office, talking tough with the High Sheriff, sometimes running errands for him and Deputy Jack, Elizabeth's father, cleaning up for a tip or two. Old Man Lacey seemed to like him, telling him more than a few times, "You got a hard edge to you, Royce, and I guess you come by it honest. You ought to get into law enforcement."

"Would you take me on?"

"You just a pup. I need me a full-growed feist. Get out in the world and get some experience. Then we'll take another look."

It was during his days as a hanger-on at the sheriff's office that he began to plot an attempt to worm his way into Elizabeth's heart in earnest. She was young, certainly, but it was not uncommon for girls of twelve, thirteen, fourteen, to be married, here in the rural part of the state. Maybe he could rescue her from her burgeoning reputation as a flirt—she was, after all, coming out of her social seclusion, and dramatically, to amuse herself with the antics of a few of the boys around town—and make a war bride of her, or at least make an engagement come about.

He knew it was a long shot, though, knew she had a flip attitude about having and keeping a boyfriend, pronounced it "a bore." Moreover, she did not even seem to care that there were social codes demanding adherence or that folks looked to judge the missteps of others on an hourly basis. The gossip about Mona Anne's and his low-level social status always ate at him; Elizabeth cared not one whit about the talk she generated with her wild actions as well as her simple ones, such as strolling through town with Hotshot trailing after. Hotshot had been orphaned over to the jailhouse, certainly—and as a young boy— becoming Elizabeth's childhood playmate, but she took no note of his skillet-black skin or his simple-minded demeanor. She cast thoughts of propriety to the side, in most matters, like the day she confirmed her sexual confidence, just strolled right into the sheriff's office, where Royce sat alone doing some filing for Mr. Jack.

"Where's Josephine?" she asked, referring to one of a couple of courthouse cats that roamed in and out of the sheriff's office, the office of the judge of probate, the county clerk's office, animals who served as pets for those county employees who took the time to feed them. Long blonde braids hung down her back, brushing at her tiny waist.

"I don't know," he said, rolling his eyes as Hotshot followed her into the room. He couldn't for the life of him understand Elizabeth's willingness to put up with Hotshot's idiot ways.

"Oh, but I want to pet her," Elizabeth said.

"She's probably off somewhere getting knocked up again. I think she's about ready to be. Again. Why don't you send the nigger to find her?"

"Shut up, Royce," she said. "Hey," she said, sitting on the sill of the open window, turning sideward, propping her feet on the sill as well, "you think you'll ever get sent to go fight those Germans?"

It was an autumn afternoon. She wore a light green shirtwaist dress, patterned with cherries, apples, and grapes across thin cotton, thin enough for Royce to know the new secrets her body was keeping, the fresh, rounded rises at her chest, unencumbered by a second dressing of an undershirt or even, he suspected, step-ins; and the juncture of her thighs, the slope of those very thighs set off by the sun spilling its light through the open window. Hell, she was just twelve years old, but she did something to him.

"If I do, you're going to see some flat-out dead Germans," Royce said, thinking how that would sure as hell give him some experience in the world to put before Campbell Lacey.

"My grandmother says they're running crazy all over Europe."

"Well, that's a fact. Crazy as hell. Done took Poland, France, coming right at England."

"My daddy said I was crazy as a one-eyed dog." This came from Hotshot, who was standing at the bulletin board, staring at "Wanted" posters.

Royce could hardly abide Hotshot, with his stupid sayings and his gappy-toothed grin. He was close to Royce in age but acted like a little kid, had been a fixture at the jailhouse for years, had become a source of amusement for the townspeople who threw him change when he sang and danced on the street.

"You aren't crazy, Hotshot," Elizabeth said. "You're original."

"Why you got to carry him around everywhere you go?" Royce chewed on a toothpick he took from Jack Lacey's desk drawer.

"I don't 'carry' him anywhere. He's my shadow. That's what my daddy says."

Royce rolled his eyes again, not believing Mr. Jack condoned his daughter running all over creation with a nigger that was probably up to no good, putting on an act for the white folks. "Well, you ought to be careful. Do you even know what people think about it and what they say?"

"Why would I care?"

"Well, because of your reputation, I reckon."

"Who am I trying to impress? The people who think they are so good and then talk bad about other people? I don't care about any of what anybody says."

"Not even about what they say he done on that train that time?"

"Shh!"

Hotshot whirled around. "I didn't, I didn't, I didn't," he said.

Elizabeth got up and took Hotshot by the arm. "It's okay, now. Stop that." She led him to a chair by the door.

"He ain't going to get that gun. Is he? I didn't," Hotshot said, eyes large and fearful, looking for the weapon associated with that specific time and place and incident.

"No gun," Elizabeth said. "Don't worry, Hotshot."

"I can get you a gun," Royce grinned. "Does your shadow want a gun?"

"Shut up, Royce," she said, and he kind of liked the way she said it, so he did.

"I didn't, I didn't, I didn't," Hotshot whimpered.

"Wait here," she said, stepping out into the hallway, turning back to Royce. "Don't get him scared any more than he is," she said, "or I'll …"

"Or you'll what?"

"Just don't!"

"Yes, sir!" he said, saluting her, playing at being a soldier.

Royce glared at the boy sitting opposite him. Hotshot did not look up, only rubbed his palms back and forth across his thighs, staring down at the backs of his black hands.

Goddamn retard, Royce thought. One day he's going to do something crazy, hurt somebody, and then what? Those Laceys were loony as hell, letting a girl like Elizabeth—just now coming into a more inviting kind of womanhood than most, a rare kind, even—take up with a nigger who was bound to step over the line, would have to step over it, being grown, if he—and here was a thought that made the blood burn through Royce's veins: if he hadn't already.

When Elizabeth returned she was carrying Josephine, a gray and orange tabby with honey-colored eyes. "Here, Hotshot," she said, laying the cat in his lap.

Hotshot rubbed the cat's back. "Josephine's a crazy cat," he said. The animal mewed a guttural sound and writhed against Hotshot's palm.

"You really don't care what folks think about you? Royce asked.

"No, I don't," Elizabeth said. "The Bible's full of warnings about gossip and judgment."

"Still and all, you ought to know folks don't think a girl your age should be roaming the streets with a grown nigger."

"He's not grown," Elizabeth said. "My Aunt Frances says he'll never be grown in his mind. And even if he was, I would still take up time with him, even more, because he would be more like a friend and not a shadow."

"A friend?"

"Yes."

"Well you better be goddamn glad he ain't grown in the head, then, 'cause you ain't got no business, at your age, taking up with a nigger friend."

"That's all you know," Elizabeth said, as Josephine mewed in agreement, wallowing against Hotshot's thighs.

"Yeah, I do know," he said. "You need yourself a big brother kind of guy, to look out for you." He grinned, letting his gaze glide down her body.

"I'll never need a boy to look out for me," Elizabeth said.

The cat mewed another deep-noted sound.

"Oh, yes, you will," Royce said. "Believe me. I know. You're turning into something that's going to need a lot of looking out for."

"Says who?"

"Says me. I hear things."

"Like what?"

"Like how you smoke cigarettes on the street."

"So?"

"I bet you already been into the brandy, just like your mama."

Elizabeth shrugged.

"Well, have you?" It was appealing, Royce thought, the picture of a liquored-up Elizabeth with her braids down, lying on top of him, loose hair hanging down across her face and into his.

She smiled. "Maybe."

Royce laughed. "I heard how you dared Bobby Dees to steal a pack of his daddy's Picayunes, how the preacher caught y'all smoking on the front steps of the church."

"I'll say it again." She flipped one braid back. "So?"

"And I heard you got Stew Weatherall to steal all the ladies' corsets from the Empire department store round the corner."

Elizabeth broke into laughter herself then. "We had the best time lacing them onto the pine trees by the picnic grounds!"

"Yeah, I heard old Stew got a whipping from his daddy behind that."

Elizabeth rolled her eyes. "I'm afraid so," she sighed with exaggerated drama.

"I don't reckon anybody whipped you?"

She laughed again, and the sound melted over him.

"You didn't get in no kind of trouble?"

"Well, my mama got drunk and my grandmamma fussed, but my daddy just had to laugh. It was a funny prank, that's all."

"What about your granddaddy?"

She bit her lip and her eyes shadowed over with a kind of angry sadness. "He did *his* usual prank with his pistol and—"

A sudden screech and the pop of a hiss came from the cat.

"Josephine, what?" Hotshot shouted.

The cat had leapt from his lap and lay writhing and growl-mewing on the floor. Then she rolled over, the front half of her body in a crouch, her hind end raised, twisting at her rib cage, making more feral sounds, long, drawn-out groans.

Hotshot stood, agitated. "What you doing, crazy cat?"

"It's all right," Elizabeth said, and Royce winced at the calming effect of her words on the solidly muscled, solidly black teenager. She got up and squatted down next to the cat, her dress sliding up over her knees. Royce wanted to be in front of her, getting a look up that thin dress.

"She's in heat again," Elizabeth said. "Remember the last batch of kittens, Hotshot? Remember I told you she had a litter once or twice a year, spring and fall?"

"She ain't hot," he said, kneeling, putting his hand on the cat's haunches. Josephine wriggled against his touch.

Royce stood, thinking how Elizabeth had not one whit of shame in her, to be squatting down watching a needing-to-be-fucked cat with a horny nigger.

"She wants a boy cat," Elizabeth said, pointing to a place beneath the cat's tail, where its fur made a deep black 'Y' shape, "to put it in her."

"Like them dogs at Miss Martha and them's house," Hotshot said.

"Yes, like that. But cats have really vicious fights, the boys against the boys, and even the girl fights it. And when the boy cat finally gets on her, she makes all kinds of racket, like she is now."

Royce had maneuvered around to the chair in front of Elizabeth, who had dropped back on her rear, sitting with her knees drawn up now, ankles crossed, not caring, enthralled as she was with watching the cat, that her dress crept further up her thighs. Royce glanced at Hotshot, to see if he was looking up that dress, but the ungrown boy was only studying the cat's rolling, writhing motions along with Elizabeth.

"Poor thing," Elizabeth said. "She wants a boy cat really bad."

"Just what we need around here," Royce said. "Another mess of kittens for me to have to carry off and drown." He let his eyes take in the flesh of her thighs, already promising himself he would touch them one day.

"No! Don't talk about things like that! And don't you dare hurt her babies," Elizabeth said. "Ever." She scratched Josephine's head.

Royce did not tell her that it was her own grandfather who routinely gave him the order to execute the kittens no one cared to adopt from the courthouse grounds. Usually he carried them in a croaker sack to Cane Creek on the edge of town, weighted the sack down and chunked it under the bridge. Sometimes, though, he would wring their necks or pound their skulls with a heavy rock before throwing them in the water, but that was only if there weren't too many of them and he didn't need a sack to carry them all.

"Do you see how puffy it gets?" she said. "And sometimes the way they carry on is like they're really hurting."

As if in response, Josephine let howl an even longer cat moan, flipping to her back, twisting back and forth sideways against the floor. Royce let his eyes find the place, the white cotton of her step-ins, and stay there a while, wondering what she looked like, right—there, thinking it would maybe be smooth and pink and sweet, not like the overused, worn-out one that certainly resided between his mother's routinely pounded thighs. He conjured up the image of Elizabeth's flesh, where his gaze rested, shucking the undergarment from his vision, seeing it there, waiting for him. Then he noticed the silence in the room, save for the cat's fevered growls, and he glanced up. Elizabeth was watching him, a knowing smirk on her face.

Royce looked at Hotshot but the boy was focused on the cat's contortions. "You ought not to go letting your skirt up," he said.

"Do you think I give a care if you look at my underdrawers?"

"Well, you should," he said. "Look at you. You ain't even trying to cover up."

"You're pretty stupid," she said, scratching Josephine's head. "You really think I care if you see."

"You know what the Bible says about modesty, don't you?"

"How do you know what it says?" she countered.

"Because the Primitive Baptists are all the time hauling me to Sunday school, trying to make me out a lost lamb."

"Are you a lost lamb?"

He liked the way she looked at him in that moment, all concern and tenderness, so he replied, "Maybe I am," before adding, "but hadn't you better cover up your drawers?"

She smiled. "Maybe you better read more Bible verses if you're so concerned about my drawers."

"What the hell more I got to learn from the Bible?" She still had not moved, and his eyes kept making fleeting returns to the white cotton underwear.

"Well, for one thing, the Bible says, 'Flee also youthful lusts'. That's Second Timothy." And she giggled as Royce's face went red. "Let's go, Hotshot. We'll go find Josephine a boyfriend. Pull me up."

Royce watched Hotshot take her hand and bring her to her feet, hating the boy's familiarity with her, the ease with which she cared for the jailhouse orphan. He sat for a long time after they left, watching goddamned Josephine carrying on like a cathouse whore, growling and gyrating. He thought of the untouched place between Elizabeth's legs. He hoped like hell it was soft as a hen's feather, pristine, that the whispers of speculation about Hotshot and the long-ago train ride were just rumors. Was that place she had just shown him really untouched, unlike the one used so regularly by Moaning Mona Anne? Elizabeth sure acted like she knew more than other girls her age. He stared at the cat, struck again by how Elizabeth had described Josephine's estrous with such utter unselfconsciousness, just as she refused to feel embarrassed to have him studying her underwear, imagining her flesh. Shit, she would probably describe the fine details of her own body with an equal absence of shame, a thought which teased excitement into him. He put his hand to his crotch. Maybe she would do that sometime, tell him what she saw when she looked at herself.

Josephine let out a piercing wail that droned into a groan and lifted her haunches again, curving her backbone downward, amber eyes pupil-dilated with a primal, wild look, and his mind took a turn. Maybe she would tell him what she really saw when she looked at that ungrown nigger. He imagined Elizabeth and Hotshot sitting side by side on the floor of a boxcar. They were watching a coupling of cats, to a quickening rattle of the rails and blows of a train whistle. Swallowed up by the motion and the rhythm, they were fascinated by the orgasmic tenor of it all, maybe even aroused by it. Maybe they had felt it before. Josephine rolled over again on the office floor, pawing her feet at the air, then over again, to raise the vulval offering high as she mewed, deep and long. He stood, leaned over her, reaching with both hands, getting both hands around her neck, squeezing tight and lifting fast. And just as fast, before the animal could get claw the first in him, Royce flip-flopped her body over with a circular swing of his arms, feeling the snap of the spine's crack from the cat's skull, Josephine limp and heavy in his grasp, dead weight hitting the floor. He walked into the bathroom and opened a cabinet beneath the sink. He found a croaker sack there and raked the lifeless feline into it, unapologetic, unsympathetic, and unaware of the lifelessness within himself.

He wasn't sorry for his mama, "Moaning Mona Anne," never for one second bought her story that she had to get money to support him, that there was no other way when times were so bad for everybody. He wasn't sorry for Hotshot. Lost from his daddy? It was probably more like his daddy lost him on purpose, saw through that retard act and knew he was a lunatic likely to do somebody in one day. And Josephine? He wasn't one bit sorry that goddamn cat was dead. Elizabeth would sure as hell never have to know and if the sheriff ever figured out what he did, well, Old Man Lacey would probably thank him for solving the population problem. Royce smiled and reached down to grasp the rough weave of the fabric into a tight bunch, bringing it up off the deep brown hardwood floor, straightening his body and his sense of purpose. He slung the sack over his shoulder and headed for the bridge over Cane Creek.

Opposable Thumbs

Kansas Lacey was twelve years old the summer Leo Tolbert carelessly took up a sharp hatchet, chopped off his five-year-old brother Cooter's thumb, and threw it up on the sloping tin roof of the jailhouse. Over the sweltering days that followed, Kansas, Leo, and his twin sister Roxy watched the tiny appendage go from orange to blue-green to black against hot silver, swirling small currents and sprinklings of decaying scents down to the scrubby back yard of the Blackshear County Jail. It was on a Thursday. It was 1962.

Leo was the jailer's boy, pudgy, pork-fed, and red-headed with freckles all over; Roxy was more angular, rust-haired and speckle-flecked as well, but pretty to Leo's plain. They lived in the house attached to the front of the jail, a dungeonesque Victorian structure with steep brick stairs and dark, barred windows that glared down at the back yards and alleys where they played. Victor Tolbert, the jailer, spent his days visiting a cold-edged humor on the inmates he kept, sometimes turning hard taunts at his wife, Joleen. When this happened and when stabbing words or the muffled pounding of a fist to a wall drifted from the open windows of the front rooms, the Tolbert children scurried like mice to Kansas's yard to create games and stay out of their daddy's way.

Next to the jailhouse was the office of the *Sumner Local*, serving the small town with church notes, wedding pieces, and farm news. Next to it was Kansas's grandparents' and great-grandmother's house, where Kansas had lived for the seven years since her mother's death.

The Lacey home stood crisp and white, jalousied windows across its face, looking out over the main street of town. Across the side alley, the courthouse loomed like the Acropolis, its huge domed clock chiming out increments of childhood in surreal crescendos of hours and half-hours building to sultry noons and coarse midnights.

***

The day of the thumb-chopping, Kansas spent the morning helping Great-Grandemona and LittleBit, the cook, make dinner for her grandfather and the prisoners. When Kansas had been orphaned at five, she had desperately insisted on calling her grandfather "Daddy."

"It's Grandfather," his wife, Miss Pearl, would correct her.

"Daddy," Kansas would stubbornly volley.

"Grandfather," came the return, until the bastardized moniker finally stuck, becoming ingrained in the fabric of the familial landscape.

Daddy would walk over from his office at the courthouse every day with the twelve o'clock chimes to have dinner with Kansas, Grandemona, and Miss Pearl. The dining room table would be set with silver and starched linen in his honor, and dotted with dishes of barefoot LittleBit's ham-juiced, fatback cooking, and syrupy sweet tea. After dinner, the ritual would move to the living room, where Daddy would knock back a shot of Early Times, then savor a second shot, slowly, inhaling a Camel as he watched the midday news on the TV. After a fifteen-minute nap, he would walk back over to the sheriff's office, leaving his wife to her soaps and peach brandy.

Kansas stirred the amber liquid in the yellow ceramic pitcher, the wooden spoon clicking at ice cubes. "Our prisoners sure do eat good, don't they? Mr. Hooker over at the hardware store says they ought to get bread and water is all." She dipped her little finger into the liquid and sucked a sugary drop from the improvised teat.

Grandemona's deft white hands carved at a tomato, unwinding its skin into one languid serpentine strand. "Anybody can wind up in a jail," she said. "Imagine if it was one of your people. Cane Hooker is just a mean old man."

"I can never get skins off in one piece," Kansas said, watching the red-orange tomato strip coil snake-like on the white metal tabletop as her Grandemona slid the tiny paring knife between skin and meaty pulp. The old woman twirled the fruit between thumb and palm as she peeled, mucus-pouched seeds sliding across her thumbnail. "You will with practice."

Kansas walked over to the sink and looked out over the back yard to where coal-black Pruella sat on the porch of Pinky's shotgun house, fanning herself with a cardboard funeral parlor fan. Both LittleBit and her sister Pruella now lived in the Quarter across the railroad tracks, but they had grown up in the Laceys' backyard. Their mother Pinky had been nursemaid to Miss Pearl, to Kansas's mother Ruby Elizabeth, and to Kansas herself for a time. Now she lay dying of cancer, so her daughters took turns staying with her. Kansas would sneak and visit her, too, even though her grandmother did not want her entering colored folks' houses. Not anymore.

Visiting Pinky had been just fine when she was five, her mother freshly packed beneath fertile South Georgia soil. In fact, Pinky's granddaughter, Bernice, was her primary childhood playmate, giggling with her at tea parties held on rainy days underneath Pinky's house, where they exchanged doll-babies of opposite hues. But Miss Pearl no longer welcomed Bernice once Kansas turned ten.

***

Kansas's kinship with Pinky grew out of penetrating black nights in the aftermath of her mother's death, when Kansas crept from the big house to Pinky's bed, nestling against the old woman's flannel gown in a curled, soothing sleep.

"You ingrown, child. Ingrown like a toenail, into me," Pinky would laugh, "because I tended your mama, all through her growing up, put my soul into her when she just a baby. Then her soul go into you. Miss Pearl always be a cold woman; now she cold and lifeless, too, since her baby be dead. You come to Pinky when you want the truth. Pinky can't lie."

And Kansas did seek Pinky's truth over the years, the implicit understanding between them that their shared truth was not to be undressed before the family, mired as her folks were in ritual and propriety.

"Why do you reckon Mama killed herself?" Kansas asked in her eighth summer. She and Pinky sat at the metal table in Pinky's tiny kitchen, no wall separating it from the rest of the miniature house. Butter beans thumped into aluminum pots as they splayed the green sheaths, zipping thumbnails through thin, moist membranes.

"She took a fit is all," was the matter-of-fact reply. "She were always one or the other. High up in the trees or low down on the floor. She put that rope round her neck when she down on the floor. Just couldn't stand what all come behind her dealings with your daddy."

"Tell that part of the story," Kansas had urged, biting on a raw butter bean, sending a waxy singe to the back of her tongue.

"Yes, Lord. Your mama Elizabeth thought Eddie Frye was about the handsomest thing on the world. He give you that dark hair of yours. He were a traveling salesman she met over to the Bye and Bye Club in Albany. From Topeka, Kansas, your daddy was."

"And that's how I got my name," the girl recited.

"Only cause your mama sneaked it up on her Daddy, is how."

"Sneaked it?" This was a new part of the story, and Kansas's ears tingled with curiosity.

"Yes, Lord. Your sneakin'-around mama went and sneaked you a name." Pinky fumbled through the butterbeans to find those still sheathed and hiding on the bottom of the pot, lying low beneath fallen kin.

"Sneaked how?"

"Well, when your mama told that Eddie Frye she were with child, he cut and run. He weren't a damn bit of good, just like I knew. He left some hurt folks in Blackshear County, hurt to the bone. Your Daddy had all the deputy sheriffs and state police from here to Dothan chasing him down. They got him this side of the Chattahoochee. They must have worked him over real good, too, cause that handsome face of his was sure enough swole up when they brought him back. Took him to the courthouse with a cocked shotgun to his head. Had him say 'I do' and then run him straight back out of town again." She took the pot of beans to the rust-stained sink and began rinsing them.

"But what about the name?" Kansas reminded her.

"Oh. Miss Elizabeth's daddy said the courthouse wedding made you legitimate—not a bastard child—but the sorry name of Eddie Frye weren't good enough for his grandchild. That's why you took the Lacey name. Then, when you was birthed and your mama said, 'I think I'm going to call her Kansas,' Daddy went on and on about what a pretty name it was. I don't reckon he knew where that man was from and don't still to this day."

And Kansas wrapped herself within the folds of this one sharp secret, watching her features in mirrors over the years for the developing imprint of her no-good daddy—the olive skin, brown eyes, and ink-black hair that lived in her mother's last thoughts, as she swung gently from a pine limb near Scratchy Branch.

***

Kansas vaulted herself to the countertop where she sat by the eight-eyed, double-ovened gas stove watching LittleBit stir corn meal and water in a thick mixing bowl. "Did you know," she said, "that you'd have an awful time stirring and Grandemona peeling if y'all didn't have opposable thumbs? I read it in *National Geographic*."

"You a reading somebody," LittleBit said.

"It's true," Kansas went on. "When the monkeys and all sprouted a thumb, it got to where they could peel food like bananas and open nuts and all kinds of other things. And just look at us humans. When the apes turned to cave men and our brains got big, we could do all sorts of stuff, like art, because of our thumbs."

"You saying we come from apes?" LittleBit asked sharply. "'Cause that's evil talk." She poured the corn meal mixture into a flat iron skillet over a gas flame. Then she placed a large kitchen match between her teeth to suck up the stinging fumes of the white onion her knife pierced.

Kansas wiggled and curled the fingers of both hands into each other, then apart, then close to the eyes of LittleBit, who swatted them away. "Look how beautiful they are," Kansas insisted. She cupped them together in a gesture of prayer. "The Methodist preacher says God's hand hath wrought the Creation. Well I say the human hand hath wrought even more. Like the cathedral at Aachen. I saw it in *National Geographic*, too. Those Germans are some building folks."

"You go on, now," LittleBit turned the corn meal pie in the skillet. "Done wrought a mess," she muttered.

"Kansas, stop talking in riddles and don't contradict Brother Altman," Grandemona ordered.

"Yes'm." Kansas again looked out the window. Pruella had gone back inside the shack. The courthouse clock struck eleven-thirty.

"Yonder comes Sampson," Grandemona said as LittleBit placed triangles of hoecake into the tins that the trusty would carry over to the jail on large, stacking trays. Today there were nine tins of snap beans, fried chicken and mashed potatoes. The squeal and smack of the screen door and a rhythmic jangling of steel keys up the hall to the kitchen announced a short, stocky man, the color of an aging copper penny. He lifted the trays as they exchanged brief pleasantries.

"I'm going with him," Kansas announced, following the man in the white pants, a black stripe running up the outside of either leg. Then she thought to add, "Don't tell Miss Pearl."

As Kansas passed through puberty, Miss Pearl was less inclined to allow her to roam the jailhouse as she had in childhood. And it was common knowledge that her grandmother judged the Tolberts to be pure trash, so sometimes she did not even want Kansas playing in the jailhouse yard. "But they are the only children nearby," she would sigh. "Well, at least they are white."

"You be back by noon," Grandemona called after her.

Kansas knew not to talk to Sampson, though she had done enough of it over the months to learn that he was in jail for stealing a car, that his wife was a friend of LittleBit's, and that he spent most of his time washing Daddy's sheriff car or doing yard work around the jail or the courthouse. He spoke with a soft, muffly voice, and didn't seem like a thief when he warned the prisoners not to cuss or talk nasty around Kansas.

She followed him past Grandemona's flower garden and the big-leafed bouquet of a fig tree that Kansas often hid beneath, peering out at her world, at Pinky's house, enveloped in the harsh smell of sun-dappled black dirt and juices of roly-poly bugs and rotten figs. In the fecund cave formed by the fig tree, Kansas would marvel at the notion of Grandemona turning the hard, velvety-skinned fruit into shimmering preserves that wetly sugared LittleBit's buttermilk biscuits.

Today Leo was at the tree stump behind the jail with a hatchet, passing the time hacking sticks into smaller sticks, destroying things the way only boys could. Cooter sat in the dirt, picking at scabbed-over mosquito bites, tempting impetigo. Roxy was nowhere in sight, probably inside reading a Cheryl Ames, R.N., novel, feeding her interest in all things medical. She had read *Not as a Stranger* four times already this summer.

Once, she and Roxy had hidden beneath the fig tree in a night game of hide-and-seek with Leo. The two girls crouched motionless, muddy-toed and sliding sweat, for a short forever; thighs, shoulders, forearms touching and electric, shallow breaths filling the dampness with summer. Roxy's deep-red hair caught slips of moonglow oozing between the leaves, her eyes wide with childish fear, and Kansas suddenly wanted to kiss her. She leaned in, imperceptibly, drawn to the lips that panted swift currents in and out, under the shield of midnight green. When she was close enough to see, even in the earthen darkness, Roxy's front teeth gently working her lower lip the way she always did when she was nervous, Leo screamed. He snatched back a limb to expose them, making Kansas feel naked and ashamed of the mystifying urges taking her to places she dared not share with anyone, not even Pinky.

***

Kansas followed Sampson into the jail, the six-inch skeleton key making hollow clicks and rattles in the metal locks. They walked down a corridor of cells, the concrete floor stained with years of tobacco juice, amber imprints of time served, prisoners' voices echoing across the divide to one another. Each cell door had a rectangular port in the bars large enough to pass through the meal tins, and Sampson always let Kansas deliver them.

"Mmmmmm. I smell me some fried bird," the one called Joseph said.

Another one, called Gabe, said, "Tell Miss LittleBit she sure do some fine cooking. I'm going to send my wife by to get her recipe for hoecake."

And they all thanked her and didn't seem like criminals at all.

White prisoners were put on the far end of the corridor, but there were no white prisoners today. There was, however, a woman prisoner on the second-floor corridor whom Kansas did not want to see. Her name was Angel and she had been in the county jail for five months already, charged with attempted murder for dousing her husband with gasoline and setting him afire. Both of them had been badly burned, and one side of Angel's face and both hands and forearms were grotesquely scarred.

Kansas had only taken Angel's meal to her once, whistling her way up the narrow steps to a cell stacked with packs of Alpine cigarettes and movie magazines, where its occupant sat and puffed the days away to the dazzling lives of the stars. Angel had not praised the food or thanked anyone; she only looked at Kansas with her one good eye, the other draped in scarred flesh scythed like slick satin across the mahogany face.

"A whistlin' woman and a crowin' hen be sure to come to no good end," Angel had recited, her eye finding secrets in the skinny white girl bearing food.

Kansas had been ashamed and afraid to return. So when Sampson headed up the steps with Angel's tray, Kansas went out to where Leo was still producing piles of sticks with his hatchet.

"You are one big, sure-enough time waster," Kansas said, as the hatchet came down with another loud thwack.

"I'm going to build a fort for my army men," he said, indicating two cellophane bags of soldiers, Confederate and Union, battle flags and artillery lined up across the ash-gray dirt. "Go on, Cooter," he said to his little brother, who laid his hand on the chopping stump and drew it away in a taunt.

"Cooter, quit!" Leo demanded.

But Cooter repeated the motion as the hatchet came down,

before Leo's brain registered it, and the thwack reverberated with the pained shriek of the child and Kansas' scream of revulsion.

The child lay writhing on the ground, squalling an ear-piercing wail, clutching his bloodied fist. Leo could only move slowly toward the chopping stump, repeating a mantra of "Don't tell Daddy, don't tell Daddy, don't tell Daddy." Suddenly, with a rush of nerve, he picked up the amputated digit and hurled it blindly as far and as hard as he could. Then he bolted, never looking back.

A crash of iron announced Sampson, jingling and clanking from the jailhouse. He pulled off his tee shirt and scooped the boy up just as Mrs. Tolbert and Roxy rounded the side of the building. Kansas could only stagger, heaving through the chain-link gate, horrified by a gore—the like of which she had never before witnessed. The leaves of the fig tree slapped at her face and arm as she passed, bound for her own back door, above which an industrial kitchen fan blasted a typhoon of noontime smells into the August heat.

***

Miss Pearl sat tall at the dining room table, attentive only to Daddy, her husband since she was fifteen. She was a remote, delicate woman who barely haunted the house where Kansas grew up. She sipped peach brandy in the early afternoons and spent days at a time in bed, yet always appeared for meals. "She hasn't been the same since your mama died" was all Kansas ever heard by way of explanation, so her faint presence was accepted, and everyone, including her family, referred to her as "Miss Pearl."

"The nigrahs over in Albany are getting all tore up," Daddy was saying. "It's likely there'll be some trouble downtown this weekend. State police'll be there. Our office is to be on call."

"Why anybody would want to go where they aren't wanted I'll never understand," Miss Pearl said to her husband. "I wouldn't go within a mile of where I wasn't wanted."

"It's a damn mess, is all," Daddy said.

"You can't believe how Cooter hollered when Leo chopped his thumb off," Kansas said. "There was blood all over—"

"Not at the dinner table," Grandemona interjected.

"Yes'm."

"It's the goddamn federal government taking over how we do things," Daddy said.

"Thank goodness the nigrahs in Sumner don't carry on that way," Miss Pearl said.

Kansas thought about Pinky, how she used to keep her money folded in her sock and a can of snuff deep in her bra. Her skin was like black leather; her arms must have been sinewy and sure as they held the Lacey babies she had tended alongside her own.

"What would be wrong with Pinky or LittleBit going to the Walgreen's for a CoCola, Daddy?" Kansas asked.

"Kansas!" Miss Pearl hissed.

But Daddy was laughing. "It's a lot more complicated than that, and it's something you don't have to worry about. But if it's thumbs you want to know about, just ask Royce over at my office to show you the one he's got. Keeps it in a jar of alcohol down in his desk drawer. I'm surprised you've never seen it."

"That is enough," Grandemona snapped, "about body parts and race relations. I want a civilized conversation at my dinner table."

The exhaust fan in the kitchen hummed deeply to the swish-swishing as LittleBit scrubbed pots. The grown-ups chatted an effortlessly empty chat, but all the while Kansas felt awed by the happenstance appearance of two severed thumbs in the midst of her thirteenth summer.

***

Royce Fitzhugh grinned as he held the small jar up to his desk lamp, Leo, Roxy and Kansas mesmerized by the gherkin-sized object floating in the chemical wash. The sheriff's office in and of itself was a mysteriously fascinating place. Kansas spent storm-gusty summer afternoons poring over the Wanted files and photographs of dangerous criminals, talking to state troopers riding the southwest Georgia highways, creating patterns of numbers on the ciphering machine, or typing notes to Leo and Roxy on the big black Royal typewriter on Daddy's desk.

Every great once in a while, she would talk Daddy into opening up the evidence closet to show her guns, knives, and tire irons, instruments of assaults and occasional murders being tried in the upstairs courtroom. Once he had let her sample a sip of shinny that had been tested clean by state experts; it ran a trail of fire down her throat, sending her coughing and gagging out to the water fountain in the cavernous hallway. "Whites Only" the sign above the fountain had said, and she was grateful at that moment to be white.

"I got it from Victor Tolbert, your very own daddy," he said to Leo. "Vic said he found it in a fox trap, like some poor fellow had a tragic accident, kind of like Cooter, I hear."

Leo looked down sheepishly.

"Can I hold the jar?" Kansas asked.

"Sure thing, girl," Royce grinned.

It was translucent almost, veins and muscle like dwarfed spaghetti tubes inside the larger tube of the thumb, lightly spotted in places like some strange bruised fruit. The thumbnail had settled on the bottom of the jar, but the place it had once grown upon was definable, and Kansas felt a shudder rip through her as she realized there had been an actual person attached to this tiny bit of flesh and bone.

Royce laughed. "You got to have a stomach for it, I reckon. But a sweet little girl like you ain't never got to worry over seeing such as this."

"I'm going to be a doctor," Roxy said, "so I'll see dead people all the time."

Royce laughed harder. "Ain't no such of a thing."

"She will, too," Kansas insisted. "She's going to Emory and be a baby doctor."

The deputy chuckled them out the door. "Ain't no girl going to be no doctor. Especially not no jailer's girl. Get on, now."

Two curved wooden staircases led up to the courtroom, where they regularly played Perry Mason, acting out bizarre murder trials concocted from the thick summer air. The trio sat on the bottom step.

"Where's Cooter's thumb?" Roxy asked. "I want to cut it open and see what's inside." The younger boy was still at the hospital in Albany, his parents yet to come home; Sampson was in charge of the jailhouse.

"Don't know," Leo said, glancing a warning at Kansas.

"I looked all around the chopping stump. It would've been there, so don't be stupid. Kansas?"

Kansas spread out her hands and shrugged. "Maybe a squirrel ate it," she offered.

"Daddy's going to be mad as hell," Roxy said. "I'm just trying to help you." She gazed into her brother's brown eyes, her gold-flecked ones looking deeper until he buckled.

"I was scared of what Daddy would do, so I threw it away. I don't know where."

"You thought you could cover the whole thing up?" Roxy's eyes grew larger. "Are you a retard?"

"He panicked, is all," Kansas said. "Let's go hunt the thumb."

The grounds of the courthouse were greenly manicured, sidewalks bordered with monkey grass. At the northwest and southeast diagonal corners of the lawn were steps leading down to recessed toilet areas for coloreds. Leo spat into the stairwell as they walked past it. "Nigger shit," he mumbled.

It was only after a half-hour search of the back yard of the jailhouse that Kansas caught the glint of the sunset on the high tin roof of the jail. The thumb lay where it had been pitched. They could make out the meaty end bearing blackened blood, and reasoned that it must be wedged on a bent nail or a stob in the tin that prevented it from following gravity to the ground. They took an oath to keep its location a secret, to gather to view its decomposition each day, and to never tease Cooter about his missing thumb or make him feel freakish in any way.

***

LittleBit sat in the dark on the porch of Pinky's shack, barefoot, smoking her Salem, a small lamp from a bedside table within drawing moths to the screen. Pruella had gone back across the tracks to see to her children; LittleBit, who had no children, only a husband long dead, now spent the nights with her dying mother. She wiped at her sweaty neck with her palm, and Kansas thought her face, light cocoa glazed with acorn-hued freckles, was unusually strong and beautiful.

"I'll sit with her if you want to walk over to the Blue Goose," Kansas said. She knew LittleBit liked to visit the club just across the tracks, come back all giggly with beer and flirtation.

"You'd better get on, before Miss Pearl sees you out here."

"It's okay. I told them Roxy and Leo and me were going on a playout. We go all over town on a playout, and I don't have to go in until Daddy turns on the siren."

The town that was their playground was a two-block-square expanse of narrow alleys and stone buildings: the Feed and Seed, the Five and Dime, Mason's Drug Store, Hooker's Hardware, and others that lined the streets, their granite faces inscrutable. The bank's front was shiny black marble, cool and rich; Dougie Moore's Furniture Store had swing sets and yard chairs along the sidewalk, their own private park. On summer evenings the three of them would do night dances across sidewalk fields of darting palmetto bugs and moribund cigarettes, finding adventures in store window displays, climbing the fire escape to the courtroom's open windows, filling it with new dramas.

"I won't be but a little while," LittleBit said as the wood steps groaned under her callused feet. Her thin yellow dress, held together at the waist with a safety pin, framed the sturdy form beneath it as she stepped through the hazy glow of a street lamp into the dimness on its other side.

***

"I'll have me a shot now," Pinky said as Kansas entered.

"You hurting?"

"It's Satan's own fire," Pinky said.

Kansas opened the cigar box that held several syringes and vials, plus the mysterious white powder brought from Albany by a friend of Sampson's. Kansas smiled, thinking how jealous Roxy had been to know Kansas had a patient in her back yard. She held the spoon over a kitchen match until the liquid was ready. She tourniquetted Pinky's arm, then pricked the vial, drawing back the plunger, carefully, to the mark LittleBit and Pruella had shown her. The vein easily took the pop and gentle slide of the needle's point. Pinky's eyes rolled back, black lids falling almost the whole way, pulling her into an abbreviated sleep while a solemn cadence of crickets and humming bugs droned dirges in the dark.

❊❊❊

Kansas sat on the edge of Pinky's bed, the old woman just awake after a short drowse. Pinky was alert now, pain muffled enough for company, so Kansas launched into her tales of severed thumbs, the habits of the apes, and the trouble in Albany. When she turned to Pinky for a comment she drew back instinctively. The old woman's black eyes, expressive of a sudden shock, surrounded as they were by the dark circles of illness, gave her face the ghoulish look of a deep brown skull. Pinky reached out to touch her forearm. "It's all right," she said. "It's only Pinky." She gave a deep sigh that caught in her neck and became a wrenching cough. She spat in a Maxwell House coffee tin she kept on the bedside table. "You done said a heap just now. And a heap more to come, I bet. You be wanting the truth, just ask. I won't be dying with a lie on my lips."

"Do you think it's wrong not to tell where Cooter's thumb is? So his mama can maybe bury it?" Kansas asked.

"No, baby. Cooter's thumb ain't got no spirit in it. It's just a old shell, just like the ones them biddies leaves in your Grandemona's chicken coop. Just like Pinky going to be real soon. 'Course, some of Cooter's spirit might be done leaked out of that hole in his hand before they got it all sewed up. But he'll be all right."

"Leo's mostly scared of what his daddy's going to do," Kansas said.

"Well, them children ought to be scared of they daddy. You stay slap away from him. He's a evil somebody. He's done busted many a nigger's head, plus his woman's. And that girl child of his better be sly cause he humps the woman prisoners, white and colored."

Kansas's face grew hot at the reference to sexual intercourse, a term Roxy had once shared with her along with the stark details.

Pinky chuckled. "You old enough. Ain't no sense in keeping them thoughts away from Pinky. You be doin' it your ownself before too long."

"It's nasty!" Kansas spat out. Roxy had told her about the milky stuff that would fire out of the man's penis and into the woman.

"Well, it's how we all come to be," Pinky said. "It's how you come to be."

"How come LittleBit didn't do it with her husband?"

Pinky laughed with all the energy she could muster. "You don't get no baby every time. Some folks never get no baby. Folks do it 'cause they like it. You'll see one day."

They talked on for a while, Pinky allowing that the trouble in Albany was bound to come and right as rain, allowing that she liked doing it with her husband, even though he left her when LittleBit was born, allowing that she was not afraid to die. Kansas put out the light when Pinky finally slept again, just as LittleBit's bare soles slapped against the steps.

***

Friday afternoon found Kansas, Leo, and Roxy sitting around the chopping stump gazing up at the thumb, still perched imperiously on the tin stob. It had not changed much, but it was quite high up; subtle colorations could not be noted yet. Cooter had come home during the morning but was to mend indoors for a few days lest he infect his stitches.

"I don't think Daddy and Miss Pearl do it," Kansas said, shuddering at the image.

"Sure they do," Roxy said. "All men do, anyway. Who else could he do it with?"

"I want to do it," Leo said. "And I will."

The courthouse clock chimed out four-thirty, sending droves of sparrows out from under the dome in a frenzied flapping.

"Y'all want to play out tonight?" Kansas asked.

"Sure." Leo drew circles in the dirt with one of his chopped sticks, the Civil War fort still only a vague intention. Kansas reached over and touched the swollen bruise on his left cheekbone with her fingertips.

"Does it hurt?"

"No."

"I can't play out at night anymore. Daddy thinks I'm off with boys," Roxy said.

"But that's crazy!" Kansas kicked at some of the sticks. "You're with us. We're your witnesses."

"Daddy says we're all liars," Roxy said.

"To hell with Daddy!" Leo strode across the yard and began banging at the chain-link fence with a baseball bat, sending rattling shocks all the way down its length.

Roxy gazed down at her hands, tucking her left thumb under as though imagining what Cooter's life might feel like from here on out. "It'll be strange," she said. "The three of us going to Blackshear County High School next month, being the youngest class. Seventh graders."

"You think any coloreds will ever try to come? Folks keep saying so."

"Not as long as my daddy has a gun, they won't." Leo had tired of bludgeoning the fence and joined back in the talk. "And I'll personally kill any nigger that thinks he's going to sit in a class with me." The rawness of his anger shoved itself into the words.

"Daddy feels the same way, I think," Kansas sighed. "I don't know, though."

Leo threw the bat hard into the fence. "I'm going to go look at Royce's thumb again," he called over his shoulder as he walked away.

"Do you think we'll stay friends?" Roxy asked, and her gold-flecked eyes were incredibly sad. "It's such a big school. All those older boys."

"Since when were you scared of anybody?" Kansas asked.

"Since forever." She stood. "I'll tell Leo to meet you at the fig tree at dark."

Kansas watched her step through the chain-link gate and walk up the side yard of the jailhouse, the afternoon sun playing the rich red of her hair beneath its glow into muted flames. She stopped abruptly at the corner of the front porch, took a deep breath and forged ahead, her delicate hands coiled into tense, knotted fists at her sides.

***

"I want to show you something." Leo caught her hands, pulling her from where she sat beneath the fig leaves.

"What?"

"Just be quiet," he snapped. "And do what I say."

They crept through the dark that was just past dusk, toward the jailhouse yard.

"Where—" Kansas breathed.

"Shhh!" He motioned her to follow as he entered the back stairwell of the jail through the door that remained open during the summer's hottest heat. A few steps up to the first barred door, and the male prisoners' conversations hummed and lilted through the iron slats. Leo flattened his back against the opposite wall of the stairwell, easing up the brick steps. He put a finger to his lips and she followed his lead. The stairs zigged, then zagged toward the second floor. Just as they zagged she could hear it, a heavy, rhythmic, grunting exhalation as if one were being punched repeatedly in the stomach, and a slapping, sucking sound. She hesitated, but Leo clutched her wrist, eyes warning her not to cry out. The grunting came louder and quicker now. They stepped up the last increments of the bricks.

Angel's cell was angularly framed by the doorway, steel bars slashing the picture into six-inch segments. Yet the picture they saw was clear: Angel naked on her back on the unyielding bunk. Victor Tolbert on top of her, knees cocked, pounding into her with all his strength and speed, groaning raspy growls into her neck. And all the while, Angel's arm, draped over the side of the bunk, a burning cigarette clamped between two fingers, never lifted to her lips. And her one good eye, the other being scarred into blindness, riveted into a blank nothingness from an expressionless face.

When Leo and Kansas emerged from the jail, she punched him three times in the back with her fist and ran for Pinky's house, where the lights were unusually bright and a small knot of ladies from Pinky's church whispered to Pruella.

"Pinky gone, child," Pruella said gently. "Gone home to Jesus. LittleBit inside tending her."

Kansas gazed at a girl on the porch she knew to be the Bernice of her childhood, blood kin to Pinky. Kansas nodded and turned toward Miss Pearl's big white house, itself a crypt for the lifeless.

***

On Saturday afternoon she watched the paddy wagons roll in from Albany, loaded down with black folks who sat down in the middle of the city because they wanted a CoCola. The county jail in Albany was packed, so the surrounding counties took on the overflow. Miss Pearl was worried that LittleBit wouldn't be able to find a cook to replace her as she mourned her mama, but LittleBit surprised them all by announcing she would spend the next few days, twenty-four hours per if need be, in the kitchen cooking for the Albany folks. Pinky would want her to, she said.

It was during that marathon cooking session in the Lacey kitchen, late in the evening when the family slept under humming air conditioners, that LittleBit told Kansas a story. It was about how her husband, Ned, went fishing up Scratchy Branch one warm autumn night some fourteen years earlier. It was only about a mile up the branch that he stumbled upon a white couple having sex on the bank, the glare of the moon against their skin turning them the color of catfish bellies. The man spied him before he could slip off and ran him down. By the time the rumor ran its course, the tale had LittleBit's husband deliberately sneaking up to watch, "just to see a naked white lady get her eyes fucked out," LittleBit said.

Ned went into thin air, but they found him a week later, strung up from a longleaf. Nobody was ever charged, and nobody ever took credit for it, but it was said to be Klan. Ned had been beaten, hanged, and castrated. Strangest of all, every one of his fingers and toes was missing, and some said they were passed out amongst the Klansmen as souvenirs. Meantime, the white man on the creek bank didn't have the decency to marry the white woman and save her reputation, even when, not long after, she turned up pregnant.

Kansas listened as Pinky's truth came full circle. Faint traces of her mother's anguish made futile stabs at her memory, but Kansas did not want to comprehend the rippled effects ringing her conception in the gravelly sand alongside Scratchy Branch. She thought of the shell of Pinky's body, lying out back in her tiny shotgun last night while LittleBit bathed her for the colored folks' undertaker. She wondered if the worn flannel gown was still in Pinky's bureau. There was no one to be ingrown with, and she dreaded what was to come.

She observed Cooter's thumb a few more times, perfunctorily, never looking Leo in the eye, unable to reveal the truth to Roxy. Then one day it was gone, perhaps carried off by a scavenging rat or an errant blue jay, so there was no longer the pretense of a reason to visit the jail yard. Instead, Kansas crouched beneath the fig tree for quarter-hours at a time, studying Pinky's empty house and Miss Pearl's equally empty one.

In the late afternoons leading to September, Leo, Kansas, and Roxy roamed Sumner's streets and alleys, kicking rocks and bottle caps into the silence growing between them, serenaded only by the chimes of the courthouse clock. One desolate Sunday, Kansas and Roxy put pennies on the railroad tracks, and, while a thundering string of freight cars mashed the money into thin copper puddles, Leo tossed slurs and track gravel toward the rows of shacks beyond the Blue Goose. The bank's black marble facade threw reflections of the three of them behind the Feed and Seed, Leo poking poultry corpses with a sharp stick, the girls shuddering at the odor of stale chicken droppings, feathered carcasses, and the decaying eggshells of newly-hatched biddies. And while Roxy hung back, shoulders hunched with a splintering spirit, Kansas stomped the mounds of shells with her bare feet. The drying embryonic spittle stuck bits of eggshells to the summer-toughened skin of her soles, and razor-thin shavings zipped stinging slices into the tender, untouched secrets between her toes.

Chilling Out

School had been out for only a week, and Zack was spending his fourteenth summer doing little other than sleeping and watching the adults go at each other. It was just about his only entertainment, plus it helped pass the time while he was on restriction for his last quarter's grades: two F's, four D's, and a C in PE. A side benefit to all the confusion was that Zack had ceased—temporarily, at least—to be the source of everyone's anger. He was not even the cause of his stepmother's headaches, for now—the coat was.

The fully-lined (all silk), knee-length, sable coat had arrived via UPS on Saturday—just four days ago—and all hell had broken loose since, leaving the coat to be held accountable for each of the following events: Zack's Aunt Bunny and Uncle Voncille had arrived on Sunday to lay claim to the coat, which was not granted; Aunt Bunny had swallowed a handful of her reducing pills Sunday evening in a bogus suicide attempt; on Monday morning Uncle Voncille had come just so close to announcing to the News 12 Live Eye that he could cure AIDS and erectile dysfunction with his TRU-FLO water purifying pump (all diseases and disorders, he was convinced, were spread by pollution in city water systems, and the coat was to be cashed in for the capital he needed—unless Bunny got her way—to get the project off the ground); and by Monday night, Zack's daddy, Big (short for "Big Boy," the nickname that had stuck to distinguish him from "Little Boy," his twin brother, deceased at age two) had vowed to move to the Australian outback to "raise kangaroos or something" unless Nedra decided to be reasonable and let him buy himself a new truck.

Zack's stepmother, however, was standing firm. Nedra wasn't one to budge when she felt endowed with the moral upper hand, the hand she always held (having dealt it from the bottom of the deck, Zack thought) very close to her pretty chest. She had not been around luxury since she lived with her mother and father, she said, and Big was not the sort of man who would attain luxury. Not that she didn't admire Big for that. She didn't value luxury, either—she just missed the feel of it every now and again. Big was a good man, she said—a man of principle who helped keep her honest. So what if Voncille had bought the tickets? It was *her* ticket—#0482—that was drawn the winner, so the coat was legally and, more important, morally hers. Vonnie and Bunny had simply wasted the trip they made from Tallahassee because she wasn't about to compromise her principles. Furthermore, if Bunny thought she would get the coat out of sympathy over a fake suicide attempt, she was sadly mistaken. You see, it was the *principle* of the thing.

Then, when Big had pointed out that, principles aside, Nedra had no use at all for a fur in the Mobile, Alabama, humidity, while he could certainly use an air-conditioned truck, Nedra had put her fingers in her ears and hummed "Summertime" for three and a half minutes. Solid. Zack timed it.

Now Zack rolled into a sitting position on the edge of his bed. The Budweiser tee-shirt he wore was stretched out at the neck; his shorts were too small. He lifted the right side of his behind and tugged at the material, then picked at a scab on his knee, yawned, and thought about brushing his teeth. "Hey man," he said out loud to the posters on the walls. Limp Bizkit, Korn, and Tool all gazed back at him in punked-out petulance. The collage posters he had made from pages torn out of *Metal Mania* and *Spin* flashed pieces of images—defiant ones: Rage Against the Machine, Metallica, Helmet—dozens of hard-core, heavy metal heroes. Above the door to his closet was a glow-paint sign he made when he was twelve, shortly after his daddy's third remarriage: ZACK'S LAIR/ BEWARE/ SOCIAL MISFITS ON PARADE followed by an Anarchy symbol. He posted it outside his room, but his new stepmother—stepmother number three—made him move it because it gave her sick headaches. That was two years ago and her migraines weren't cured yet.

Zack leaned down between his knees and groped under the bed. He came up with a pair of dusty socks. He put them to his nose—once, then twice, shrugged, and slipped them on. Nedra did not like to see him barefoot. "Parasites!" she would shudder. "You'll be just like those little cousin creatures of yours who had tape worms that time!"

The red-lit numbers on the clock radio said it was 5:14 p.m. Good. Nedra rarely let him sleep past 1:00, so this was a kind of victory, at least. Actually, though, he'd been up twice today, so maybe he hadn't gotten the one hundred percent best of her.

The first time, he was shaken awake by Uncle Voncille poking him in the ribs. He had just kept on and on, laughing that goose-honking laugh of his, poking at Zack. "Get up, boy. You're wasting away."

Zack's eyelids lifted to the over-fed, gap-toothed grin of his least favorite uncle. Voncille was nothing like Big. Where Big was quiet, thoughtful, and steady, his older brother Vonnie was loud, stupid, and hyper at times. Like now. He was the kind of man who would wake a person up at 9:00 a.m. and not even be ashamed. "You gonna lay around all summer? You need to sweat some, boy!" Uncle Vonnie had bellowed.

Zack had groaned. He'd been awake until 4:00 a.m. alternately watching MTV and playing video games because his days and nights were getting all mixed up, reversed. He hiked up into a sitting position, giving Vonnie a mean look.

"Look here." Vonnie sat on the edge of the bed, which dipped into a big 'U' with his weight. Both he and his wife were big people—round people. Lardasses, in some circles. They reminded him of Weebles. "Look—I want to talk serious to you. Sort of man to man."

Jesus, Zack thought. "Man to man" sounded like something Dennis the Menace's father would say. Zack watched Dennis most afternoons on Nickelodeon. He kind of felt for a kid who always screwed up, but sometimes he wished Dennis would just get a backbone and tell everybody to fuck off.

Vonnie clasped his hands together in front of his mouth, tapping at his lips. He wore several oversized gold and diamond rings; they winked sleazy secrets at Zack. "I was hell when I was your age," Vonnie had begun. "Always looking for a good time, you know—partying, going after the women—had a lot of that stuff, too—still do."

Zack rolled his eyes. So predictable. Next Vonnie would be riding his ass about school.

"And if you want to make it graduation—high school, that is—you've got to buckle down. Hell don't you want to put on the ol' mortarboard with the class of '96? Your buddies, your homies, your—"

Zack thought about his few friends, fellow freaks and outcasts whose day-to-day time was occupied by first finding, then smoking as much pot as they could get their hands on. Any balance of the day was devoted to disdain—for brown-nosers who tap danced for good grades, for loud-mouthed-smart-ass jocks, for well-meaning teachers who likely feigned all their earnest concern, for the disjointed family units they credited with fostering the grievance they wore like badges of honor.

Vonnie was in the middle of a story about a beer joint brawl when his wife poked her head in the door. Her eyes slightly crossed, so Zack never knew exactly where she was looking; to her back Nedra called her the "Wall-Eyed Witch" and sometimes mocked the off-center gaze when Bunny was not looking. Zack thought that was over the line, though, and noticed that Big never laughed when she did it. "Now, Vonnie, don't bore the poor child to death," Aunt Bunny had giggled.

You must've been lurking out there in the hall, you old wart hog of a Weeble, Zack thought, and grinned, which Bunny mistook for an invitation. She joined her husband on Zack's bed, creating another 'U' to hook up with Vonnie's to become a 'W'.

"All I was saying," Vonnie went on, "was how valuable a little hard work can be. Hey, boy—what you gonna do after high school?"

Zack shrugged. He never had understood why adults kept telling you: (a) This is the best time of your life! Enjoy! and (b) What are you going to do about your future?

"Ever think about learning a trade? Like plumbing? Hey, guess who could teach you everything he knows?" Vonnie winked at him. "And I mean everything!"

"I haven't decided what to do," Zack said, yawning on purpose.

Aunt Bunny suddenly leaned over and hugged him, pressing his face to her doughy bosom. "He doesn't know!" she exclaimed, voice breaking with pity. She could cry at anything, just like Nedra. Zack's body went rigid next to her smothering embrace. He had a mental snapshot of a pig in a blanket.

"You don't go to church much, do you?" Aunt Bunny asked after releasing him from the headlock.

"No." Zack took the rude approach, hoping they would take a hint, knowing they would not.

"Plumbing has some real good money in it," Vonnie said.

"You know, Zack," Aunt Bunny whispered, "some of these groups on your posters are Satanic. It's proven."

"No, sir, you don't need no college diploma to get on good in the world," Vonnie went on.

"A lady in our church had a son to join a satanic cult. It was right after he watched MTV. That Marilyn Manson. He is Lucifer himself, you know."

"Hell, I make sixty dollars an hour sometimes. I don't have no diploma."

Zack sighed, just like Big did when he was totally bored or frustrated. "Can I go back to sleep now?" He slid back down under the sheet. As his aunt and uncle were leaving the room, he heard Bunny whisper, "It's no wonder he's always in trouble. With that woman raising him. It's understandable."

It had all been too totally strange, Zack thought, and he sleepily puzzled over the conversation several times throughout the day. He tugged at his socks again. From back in the kitchen he could hear adult voices: Uncle Vonnie's loud, know-it-all one; Aunt Bunny's nasal drawl—whiny, holier than thou; and Nedra's—clipped, condescending, haughtily polite.

Zack thought about joining them and smiled, visualizing the shocked looks he would get—particularly from Nedra—if he went back there, opened a beer, and just joined right in on the coat argument. Not a bad idea. He could—no. That was where he made his big mistake earlier today—he expressed an opinion about the coat, and wound up in his room all afternoon.

It was around 11:00 a.m. the second time Zack awakened, this time on his own. He shuffled toward the kitchen to the repeated revolutionary rap rhythm of Zack DeLaRocha throbbing through the earphones of his Walkman. The house seemed deserted. Good. Nobody to mess with him.

But Nedra was at her heirloom oak table, in the den just before the kitchen door. A burning cigarette rested on an ashtray at her elbow sending a snaking 'S' of smoke slithering to the ceiling. The little crescent of pink on the filter went contrary to her claim that she never wore makeup. She glanced up, then down. Too late. She had seen him. He couldn't retreat to his room, so he decided to be cool.

Nedra was sketching a still life of some grapes, onions, and a bottle of wine she had arranged on the table before her. When she wasn't having her artsy-fartsy friends over for brunch, or talking about the supposed blue of her family's blood, or going to meetings with the ladies of the Garden Society, she fancied herself a great unknown artist. That, she insisted, was what caused her headaches, fits of temper, and inability to finish college. She just couldn't concentrate, she said, for all the creative clutter in her head.

Yet there were times she would focus for days on one thing—an item in the paper, maybe, or a remark someone, usually her mother, had made in passing—and it would be analyzed, bisected, and dissected until no other angle could be found to satisfy her quest to find its true meaning. These were the days Zack's internal radar steered him away from her and he silently questioned her sanity. Now her lips were moving wordlessly, so Zack pulled one side of his headset out from his ear.

"I said, turn it down!" she shouted. "And I said, 'good morning'!" Her skin was fine and white, eyes as green as they wanted to be. Zack had to admit she was pretty—small, delicate. He even harbored a crush when he was eleven—often thought of her late in the evenings, then felt an awful guilt and disloyalty to his daddy.

"Morning," Zack mumbled, easing down the volume while he poured a glass of Coke. He spilled some on the counter. Nedra pointed at the paper towels, nose crinkled with disgust.

"Where's everybody?" he said. He wiped up the spill—but not too quickly. He got what he missed with the edge of his Budweiser shirt. Nedra's left eyebrow lifted, a tic of disapproval.

"They went for a walk—Vonnie and Bunny. To take some air. Bunny's claiming heart palpitations now." She looked at Zack as if she wanted him to join her in running down the relatives. "Of course," she went on, "we all know what she's feeling in her heart—avarice. Over that coat. She can't stand that I won it. And Vonnie—that man has lost the last bit of what little mind he had. I mean, a news conference? A cure for AIDS?"

Zack didn't responded. Tom Morello, he could hear faintly, was seriously jamming down on guitar. He picked up an apple. Nedra pointed at the sink. The boy rinsed the fruit, but slowly.

"Oh—and your father has gone to look at a job this morning—a nice, big house on the bay. They're planning a huge addition. Oh, I hope he gets it. We could use the money."

"He could use a new truck," Zack had mumbled, before he thought.

"I beg your pardon?" Her eyebrow arched higher.

"Nothing." Zack knew the eyebrow could only reach a certain height before her mood would dissolve into what had the potential to be just this side of crazy.

Nedra's back was properly perpendicular to the chair seat. She put a dramatic little scribble on one of her onions, then studied the sketchpad. "You didn't edge the sidewalks yesterday," she said with rehearsed nonchalance.

"You didn't say nothing about that."

"Anything," she corrected.

"Anything." He added a faint touch of sarcasm.

"Now, Zack," she sighed, calmly, sketching on. "Edging is always part of mowing."

Sure, Zack thought, ever since you won Yard of the Month back in May, you've been trying to win it again. Only *I'm* the one that does all the work.

She held the pad at arm's length in front of her, squinting. "Besides, if the job isn't finished, I can't pay you. You know that."

"Bull," he muttered, knowing he was getting into it, knowing the game was fixed. He went ahead and sneered, though, curling his upper lip the way she hated.

"Excuse me?" Her eyes widened with a look of practiced propriety. The argument was old. The expressions and angry words simply fell into place.

"That ain't right," Zack had said. "You didn't say nothing—"

"Ain't? Fine. Forget it. We'll speak with your father. He would not approve of this behavior one tiny bit."

There it was: the challenge Zack could never meet. She had known Big for four years and Zack had known him for fourteen, yet she thought she knew him better, that he would always back her up. Zack felt nothing but stammering rage at her clipped confidence, her pretty green eyes, her "polite" expressions: "Excuse me?" or "I beg your pardon?" in place of "What?" "Father" in place of "Daddy." Zack began to sputter. "I—I ain't got to do nothin' to your damn yard."

"You may not curse at me, Zachary."

"Okay. Your *darn* yard can kiss my behind." He hated himself for being sucked into the same old rigged game, but he could see that he had pushed her just beyond her composure, emotions were about to turn, and he would be the cool one next.

She threw down the sketchpad, which skidded into the onions, which sent grapes scuttling across the hardwood floor. Her face was suddenly hard. Ugly. Just that fast. "That's it!" she shrieked. "I cannot do it! I try and try and—you set out to upset me every single day! Nothing, but nothing, will ever change your trashy attitude!"

He stared, fiddled with the tone knob on his cassette player.

"You're on restriction!" she yelled. "Do you hear me?"

"Huh! I'm already on restriction."

Her hand trembled as she reached for the cigarette. "For how long, then?"

"One week," he answered, full of the cockiness that came with knowing something she did not know.

"Make it two, then."

"No, hell. Make it three," he countered.

"Get out of my sight!" she screamed. Louder than usual. The grooves in her forehead were deep, but Zack knew she would not lose it completely with Vonnie and Bunny in the vicinity. He sauntered back to his room. Very slow. Very cool. Chilling out.

Zack picked at the scab again, still sitting on the edge of his bed, still trying to decide what kind of nothing to do next. The adult voices still floated up from the kitchen. Maybe he should go back there. Besides, he was getting hungry, and the large bag of Bar-B-Q potato chips he kept under his bed was empty.

Zack rubbed the bright orange hair that was spiked in a dozen different directions and shaded with red, then carefully poked three little gold balls into the holes that lined his left ear lobe. From beneath his pillow came a jumble of shrill, tinny sounds. He fished out his earphones ("They miss me already," he whispered) and listened to a Jethro Tull oldie on RK100. Bad. After a while he flipped off the radio, sending "Aqualung" back into electronic purgatory. He fumbled for a tape. A little Metallica? "Freak on a Leash?" No, not in the mood. Some blues? Stones? Never. Nedra might think he was listening to something worthwhile. He snapped in a classic, Pink Floyd, took a deep breath, and headed for the den and the TV.

The coat lay in an open box on a low Parson's table just outside Zack's room. It *did* look expensive and fine, sleek, chocolate-colored. "Genuine sable," the label read, and Zack ran his palm across the slick-soft fur. He tried to conjure an image of the doomed creatures that went into the making of the coat, then chuckled at the thought of some animal rights freak dousing Nedra with red paint. As he turned down the hallway he stumbled over his aunt and uncle's suitcases in a neat line, ready to go. A good sign, no doubt about it.

The adults did not notice the boy when he sprawled out on the sofa, draping his right leg up over the back cushions. They did not even notice when he flipped the TV's remote control to a "Brady Bunch" rerun. Zack took off the headphones and wore them loosely about his neck, shifting on the sofa so that he could see both the TV and the adults through the kitchen door. It was a familiar feeling—watching the adults through doorways, listening around dim corners. But he wasn't disappointed at not being asked to join them—not really. Besides, he thought, what do you say to those people?

He thought about his mother, the phantom who had dissolved from his life before she was even a presence, hung out in bars with him when he was four and five, called him every so often with promises he could never trust, though he grasped at trust anyway. Stepmother number one was another drunk, who left Zack alone on a dark afternoon that crackled with summer lightning and thunder that shook the house like the angry giant in his child's mind. She lasted only two months before Big ran her off, the only woman he had actively ejected from his life. Stepmother number two had come along a year later, when Zack was seven. She was nice enough, when she wasn't taking out her moodiness and unhappiness on him; she lasted four years, and Zack saw her once in a while after the divorce. Then came Nedra, a princess until she married Big and turned into a frog. She banished stepmother number two from Zack's life; if a birthday card or a Christmas gift arrived, she would dissect the motive for days, then finally conclude that stepmother number two was determined to destroy her family, tossing the offending gift or card into the trash. Big would only shake his head and sigh.

Throughout the dizzying cacophony that was Zack's life, his father was a steady presence, a physical presence, reassurance that there was no bodily danger threatening his son. But the mangled emotions Zack held in check, triaged and tourniquetted, only evoked a nervous glance from Big on those isolated evenings when they made stumbling attempts to talk to one another.

"I'm feeling so much better now." Aunt Bunny was rambling the way only she could. Probably to keep Vonnie quiet. "I had to be pumped out, don't you know, and it was just *so* embarrassing. Now that I think of it, I believe those palpitations I had this morning were embarrassment flutters."

"Well, Bunny," Nedra said sweetly. "Those little old Dexatrims never did anybody in. You'd have to swallow a truckload. I don't think you have to worry that you were ever in any *real* danger. But I guess it is embarrassing to have picked such an ineffectual kind of pill."

Zack wondered a moment what "ineffectual" meant. Then it occurred to him that Bunny did not know either. This was another of Nedra's tricks: talk over their heads to put them in their place. It worked, too; Bunny had shut up.

"Got to have a truck to make a load," Big's ironic voice came from off to the side, steady and slow. His father's tone never changed much, no matter what. Once, when Nedra was having an artistic fit, she had smashed four African violets and six potted geraniums against the fireplace brickwork. "Woman, your mind's gone," was all Big said before he turned on the TV to watch a Braves game. Nedra had gaped at him. Zack even felt her frustration, a twisted kinship gnawing at him out of nowhere. All she could do was throw her arms up over her head and scream at the top of her voice until Big threatened to put her in a straitjacket. For some reason, that shut her up.

"Think of it." Aunt Bunny whined. "All those strangers seeing all that mushed up food and those teeny-tiny gas bubbles coming up that squiggly little transparent tube. The contents of *my* stomach! I liked to have went through the floor."

Zack saw his stepmother roll her eyes at the description. It was no secret that Nedra considered her brother-in-law and his wife only slightly better than trash, regardless of how much money they had. "So what if plumbers make good money?" she would say. "You have to work on people's toilets. Let's face it, now. That's low."

"Baby, you've got to try to not be so sensitive," Uncle Voncille said, reaching across the table to pat his wife's bloated little hand. "She's always taken things too much to heart," he explained, glancing meaningfully at Nedra, who merely flicked back her wavy blonde hair, tilting her pretty face, presumably, at Zack's father.

"Let's don't argue," Big said, coming into Zack's line of vision to sit in the empty chair, his back to his son. "Nedra and I will work out what's to be done."

Nedra smiled up at Big, and Big probably smiled back, but Zack imagined it was his daddy's male version of a Mona Lisa smile—the one that seemed kind of lonely and laughing at the same time. Nedra's face, though, had "I win" written all over it.

Zack thought of the time when he was twelve and his stepmother accused him of taking twenty dollars out of her purse. Zack denied it repeatedly, to her face and to his father's face, but she insisted that he must have done it. After all, the money was gone and Zack was the only one who had been in the room. It was the lowest thing he had ever been accused of, and, couched in confidence, he waited as his father took one of those long, thoughtful looks at him.

"You oughtn't to have done it, boy," Big finally told him, and Nedra smiled that same smile—victory written all over it. The next day Zack dyed his hair bright orange and poked three holes in his left ear lobe with an unsterilized needle. Nedra screamed that he looked like every piece of white trash she had seen in her life, all rolled up into one subhuman, and that he was mentally disturbed, besides. But Big only said, "You oughtn't to have done it, boy." That night Zack cried for four hours in helpless frustration and fastidious secrecy.

"Well, it's got to be settled," Aunt Bunny was saying. "And we have to all be Christian enough to put aside our greed."

"Greed?" Nedra was sitting her straight-backed, indignant way, left eyebrow raised. "It's greedy to adhere to principle?"

Bunny wore her wounded look, and she let her eyes fill to go along with it. "I just don't understand why you have to keep it all to yourself." She blew her nose into a dinner napkin while Nedra cringed.

"Maybe we can work out a compromise, Big said. "Divvy up the money some way. Then we could all spend a little. I'll get tickets to a Braves game." Zack knew Big was now smiling another kind of half smile—the one he smiled when he was really laughing hard at someone, everyone, on the inside. Zack smiled back, at the back of his daddy's head.

"But—the coat," Bunny said.

Nedra looked puzzled. "I really don't understand, Bunny. Didn't you say Vonnie just bought you a cyclonic vacuum cleaner?"

"Well, yes, but—"

"And a Jacuzzi? I mean—I'm not prying, I hope, but it seems to me that you all could probably afford. . . " she let her voice trail off, for effect.

"Sure! Sure!" Voncille, who had been staring down at his diamond rings, perked up and laughed, too loud. "Well, hell, yeah, I could buy Baby a coat. Thing is, it was my money that bought the ticket in the first place," he pointed out for the eighty-eighth time.

"Which you gave to me," Nedra said for the eighty-eighth time back at him.

"Compromise," Big said quietly.

There was a fair-sized lull in the conversation. Zack waited. Finally, Vonnie cleared his throat. Here it comes, Zack thought, the big pitch.

"You know, that TRU-FLO system diagram I drew is something, boy. Hell, I got several investors already. Shoot, they're falling all over theirselves." Vonnie waited, but no one spoke. "There's money to be made, yeah, money to be made. Hey, do you know how many folks has got the AIDS? Right this minute? A million, I bet. Multiply a million times 50, for the 50 investors. And—"

"I'm sure you're very clever with plungers and drain traps, Vonnie," Nedra dripped. "I just think that it would have been unwise to share this—fantasy of yours with a TV reporter. I mean, think of your family. Think of how people would react to such overblown claims."

"Vonnie knows that," Aunt Bunny put in. "And he is not scared of being laughed at, which is what everybody here is scared of."

"Bunny!" Nedra put on her scandalized face.

"Do you know," Bunny said, "that inventors have been laughed at all down through history? Like—well, Ben Franklin. They laughed at him all the time."

"I forget, Bunny." Nedra picked up a cigarette. "What did Franklin invent?"

Bunny's face went white. Nedra shot Big a conspiring look, but Zack could tell just from the back of his daddy's neck that Big was not comfortable. "Just think," Nedra said. "Vonnie could win a Nobel Prize!"

Suddenly Zack laughed. He could not help it. It was Aunt Bunny's face. It had gone completely blank. She probably thought the Nobel Prize was handed out by Mr. Nobles who ran the Bay Street Fish Market. An image of Uncle Voncille accepting a bronze mullet flashed through his mind and he laughed out loud from the sofa. The kitchen went silent. All but his daddy's eyes turned to him. Nedra leaned over to whisper something to Big, then to Vonnie and Bunny, who nodded solemnly. All but Zack's daddy left the room, resuming their argument as their yapping little voices faded down the hall like a protesting pack of Chihuahuas.

Big allowed his son to stare at his back for a long time, until his shoulders rose in a great sigh and he stood. When he was seated next to Zack, his eyes were on his hands, cupped awkwardly over khaki-covered knees. He lived up to his name. He stood nearly 6 feet 6 inches, and he even sat tall. Two decades in the construction/contracting business had kept him solid, muscular—but his voice always held that remote, terrified calm.

"Nedra tells me you're back-talking again."

Zack said nothing. His leg was still draped over the back of the sofa, so he traced on the wall with his big toe.

"We can't keep on with this."

Zack watched him. Funny, whenever he looked at his father, his father looked away. As if he were being chased.

"Well, what's wrong with you, boy? What do you have to say for yourself?"

Plenty, Zack thought, but having already quit, merely shrugged.

Big sighed. Zack picked at his scab some more. A pinpoint of blood appeared. The boy wet his finger with spit and dabbed at it.

"You don't have to like her, but by god you can keep things peaceful around here."

Again Zack dabbed spit on his knee.

"She tries," Big said. "It's not easy for her. You don't know what she's been through with that crazy family of hers. She's insecure. She's—I don't know, she gets—" he looked helpless. "She cares about you," he said, with sudden certainty.

Zack snorted. His father looked away, a scamper of guilt taking his eyes.

"Well, I don't know what you'd have me do," Big said. Then he cleared his throat. "Vonnie says you can go stay in Tallahassee for a while with him and Bunny. You want to try that?"

Zack fiddled with the dials on his Walkman. So that explained the strange bedroom conversation he had with his aunt and uncle this morning. Sure. He could just see himself plunging out toilets and picking people's pubic hairs out of drains and—oh no, going to church with Aunt Bunny, and choir practice—Zack turned up the volume so that the earphones squealed into his neck. Big made an angry motion, as if he were going to yank the cassette player from the boy. But he stopped short. Instead, he stood, ran his hand over his face, through his hair. Then he reached down uncertainly to pat his son's knee. Zack felt strange in his throat; it seemed to double in size, and the back of his head tingled.

"We'll think about it," Big said. He looked at the boy, eye to eye, for what seemed a long time, then away, fast. "We'll think about it, then," he said again, and he sighed one really huge sigh—the biggest Zack had heard in a while—as he left the room.

Zack lay numbly still for a long time, listening to the arguing voices rise and fall. He sensed that they were arguing about him, now, but they seemed so far away. The faces of the adults intruded occasionally—they all visited him on the sofa until he felt like a corpse laid out at the funeral home. Bunny came to tell him that she had always wanted a child even though God had not blessed her with one; Vonnie came to punch his arm—playfully, of course—and tell him he'd be okay once he learned how to sweat a little bit; Big's sighs echoed through it all like a desert wind.

Finally Nedra came to him, as she did from time to time, talking very sweetly, gently, almost real-sounding—the voice she had wooed him with when he was eleven. "I love you," she said before she began attaching qualifiers to her love. "I care what happens to you, but you just don't try at all. Can't you just try?"

But you're a liar, Zack thought, and glared her back into the kitchen. He could hear her sniffling pathetically while she cleared the table. He watched her pick up Aunt Bunny's dinner napkin, gingerly. She held it out from her body, between thumb and forefinger, as she walked to the washing machine. When she was finished, she came to Zack once more. This time she had her hands on her hips, her very proper, enunciated, witheringly sweet tone of voice. "Zack? You're bleeding all over the sofa, sugar," she said, and walked away.

Zack went to get a Band-Aid for his knee.

The street light outside bathed Lars and Tom and the other musicians on Zack's walls in a stage-like glow. From the bedside table the clock radio clicked—4:18 a.m., the red lights said.

Zack sat cross-legged on the floor, shoulders curved, skinny knees pointed outward, orange-red head bowed in fierce concentration. Surrounded by tangled strips of deep brown fluff, he resembled some kind of nesting tropical bird.

His right fist gripped his father's linoleum knife. He made a firm incision where the left sleeve had been joined, then pulled downward, leaving a rough groove in the hardwood floor, beneath the material he had cut. That made twenty-eight strips of fur, varying in length, to work with. Zack stroked the last strip. Yeah, it did have a nice, rich feel to it. $6,800 the radio promo had said.

They had been asleep for hours, having pretty much decided to let Nedra keep the coat until she was ready to compromise. Still, Zack was careful not to make a sound when he eased through the front door, arms full of cascading pieces of sable. Quiet. His whole head was quiet, earphones still dangling around his neck.

The small hatchet lay near the front steps, where he had left it earlier in the night. Little mounds of dirt and grass roots were strewn about the sidewalk. But the crickets that had kept him company earlier were silent now, and in a while the birds would begin to wake up.

He picked up the broom, which also lay across the sidewalk, and swept the dirt and grass debris to the end of the pavement, over the curb, and onto the street. Then he set to work, arranging the strips of fur along the neatly edged concrete. Whenever a strip did not line up properly, he used the linoleum knife to slice it to specification—patiently, quickly, methodically.

Finally he could step back to admire his work. It was surprising how far a fur coat could go—he had even been able to edge some of the rose bushes with the leftover pieces. Now the deep brown took on a dewy, shimmering sheen next to the moist green of the grass. Damn fine job, he told himself, silently using his father's words.

Suddenly Zack was truly tired—an honest kind of tired, born of real work, not like the exhaustion that came with sleeping all day. He sat at the foot of the sidewalk, leaning against a fire hydrant. The effect his handiwork lent to the lawn, he thought, would really come out against the sunrise.

Zack squirmed his back uncomfortably next to the metal, surprised by the strange ache that once again settled in his throat. He wished he had some weed. The thing about being on restriction was you had to be without your dope for so long. And there was so much time to kill.

He automatically reached for his headphones. Pink Floyd. The Final Cut. Bad. That Roger Waters dude could really mess around on some nasty-smooth lead guitar. He turned the volume way, way up and waited.

The Good Sister

She was the eldest of nine and therefore the substitute mother to many, those in the middle in particular, beginning when she was barely seven. And of course the middle shifted pretty much yearly, or whenever her mother's belly grew round and ripe. They lived in a four bedroom two story with a dog and a cat, a washing machine that seemed to never stop washing, one bathroom for all the children, and another for parents only. There had to be blood or imminent vomiting or diarrhea for that rule to be relaxed. Otherwise, urges were to be controlled and the mandate was clear that the children's bathroom was to be used efficiently. That is, with no shut door and multiple users at different tasks, as necessary.

She was happy to help out because the nuns at St. Mary's Catholic Girls' School said that faith without good works was a dead and useless faith. The parable of the Good Samaritan was one of her favorites; it made perfect sense to a child with a pure heart. And she was happy to do unto others, following The Golden Rule that hung in every classroom.

St. Mary's was her favorite place, the one place she could really and truly be a child—or rather, attempt to be one. But even as she grabbed onto the steel clutch at the end of a chain, and ran to gather enough speed to fly around the maypole, even as she roamed the monkey bars, jumping from square to square, her squeals of laughter and her giggles bore tonal differences—varying octaves, underlying melodies, odd rest notes, something very unlike the delightful sounds of other children. If one of the boys skinned a knee or fell from a tree limb on the playground only to come up with a gashed forehead, she was the one who comforted him and took him to the nuns, walked with them to the school nurse, her arm curled around his shoulder. If one of the girls became ill in class, she was the one who helped her to the restroom and held back her hair, saying soothing words while the girl threw up into the tiny toilet. Her experiences had evolved into a demeanor, a carriage, that said she was already wired to be a mother, after hours upon hours of diaper changing, rash nursing, nose wiping, book reading, stroller rolling, lullaby singing, bottle warming, rattle shaking and all things infant, toddler, little one.

And she loved her siblings, every one of them, though like any honest mother she had to admit she played favorites. She grew automatically partial to the newest born, each and every time, could not resist the petal-soft skin, Gerber-baby mouths, scents of Johnson's Powder and Baby Oil, and the innocent, sweet eyes that gazed deep into hers. Of course, she could offer no real competition to the one who gave birth and was always relegated to second-degree mom status, herding and tending as much of the brood as her young years allowed. Aside from the newborns, her favorite was the Fifth Born, the third amongst the boys, who were of a different class than the girls, but not in the early years, when they had to mind her and the other surrogates. She could only guess, as she grew up, as to why her strongest affection leaned toward the Fifth Born of nine, the third of five boys. Maybe it was the endearing way he sucked his thumb, self-comforting in the din of child sounds. Maybe it was because he seemed the most lost and unnoticed within the herd, although by the time he was four he had figured out how to demand notice by making mischief. He pranked, provoked, finagled and weaseled his way into more, she figured, than a few harsh punishments, more than the other boys combined. Her mother's wrath fell upon the Fifth Born, with his practical jokester ways, and wrapped it up in one word: deceit.

Over the years, this label officially stamped the Fifth Born a liar. So the Good Sister made extra efforts to tend to him, extra time with books, with toys on the floor, playing games. She taught him to draw using the "Peanuts" comic strips from the funny papers every Sunday afternoon, Snoopy and Charlie Brown and Linus with his blue blanket taking shape on lined spiral notebook paper. Bonus hugs were bestowed upon him, attempts at inoculating him with a vaccine to prevent, she must have felt on a primal gut level, self-loathing, a word she could not have known.

It was not too difficult to make extra hours for the Fifth Born. By the time she was eleven and he six, there were third- and fourth-degree moms to do her bidding. Three girls, woven in amongst the first four boys, upon whom the family's real hopes were pegged. Her parents expected that all of their sons would be altar boys and that at least one, or more, please God, would follow destiny when called to the priesthood. She knew that there were no expectations that she would be an altar girl, though; there were no such things. The highest expectation of her and her sisters was that they be good surrogate mothers, get postsecondary educations, marry well, marry within The Church of course, and have their own broods of babies bred of good stock and righteous faith.

When her mother was not rigidly barking orders and keeping schedules and administering punishments, she was distant and aloof, although her husband brought laughter and music and dance into the family realm, entertaining the brood by firing up the Zenith Hi-Fi Stereo, putting on record after record, and performing ballroom dances like the waltz and the cha-cha and the tango with his bride. "She could have been a Rockette!" he would exclaim, a puff of pride in his cry. His wife rolled her eyes and blushed, but followed that with a faraway gaze that watched well past the modestly furnished living room where the threadbare wool rug had been rolled back for the frivolity. "Yes," the look appeared to say, "I could have." And it seemed to the Good Sister that her mother's distance grew after each of these infrequent courtings by her father, as he tried to draw a bit of joy from the woman he clearly loved but who, though she must have loved him back, could not let loose with those tender emotions as easily as he.

Even though *Time* had recently declared that God was dead, the Good Sister clung to the teachings of the nuns, prayed the Rosary every day, and attended weekly Mass with her entire family, knowing that God was, indeed, real, and that she would be with Jesus in Heaven one day. She would also be there with the one baby sister who died, who could not stay in her mother's belly long enough to grow. Angela.

The Good Sister imagined Angela with long golden hair and large green eyes, with soft little palms and ticklish toes. She had cast her unborn sister in the role of princess among the angels, decreed to be eternally four years old, because that seemed a magical age.

All the girls in the family attended St. Mary's Catholic Girls' School while the boys attended the prestigious St. Ignatius Catholic Boys' School, all on scholarship, sporting button-down shirts, khaki pants, navy coats and ties. It was an honor, their mother said, and would get them into good colleges one day. "You mind the Brothers and keep out of trouble. Do not bring shame on this family."

The Fifth Born presumably tried but found himself in front of the Headmaster often, for silly pranks or scorning authority or failing to do homework, so he was often banned from family nights of TV, often not allowed to play outdoors with neighborhood children in the hours after school.

Approaching the age of twelve, the Good Sister attended Catechism classes to prepare for her Confirmation. There she learned more about the Saints and the Miracles and the mysterious logic of the Holy Trinity. For the grand rite of passage, her mother sewed a beautiful white cotton eyelet empire dress with bell sleeves over silk, bought her a luxurious French lace veil that they could barely afford, her mother reminded her, but it was for the church. The Good Sister carried a white bible beneath her rosary beads and felt a sense of pomp and grandness when she filed into the cathedral with the other girls. And the scapula she would wear, always, bore the countenance and name of Saint Margaret, patron saint of pregnant women, for the fathers and the nuns thought it genuine and kind that she would honor Angela in such a way.

The white bible and French lace would become the standard confirmation gifts for each succeeding daughter, since it would not be fair to favor one child over another. The boys got standard issue black bibles, which made the Good Sister feel special, as if there were something girls had over the opposite sex. In this way she felt she was more of an intimate with the Holy Mother Mary, something a boy could never truly be.

The next three boys, including the Fifth Born, were also confirmed and did, indeed, become altar boys by the time she was seventeen. She was proud of them as they rang and dampened the bells during the Latin service, or held the gold tray of wafers beneath the congregants' chins, mouths of the faithful gaping open like hungry baby birds. "May the body of Christ be with you," the priest would murmur, initiating the response ritual. She loved the way the Fifth Born, especially, looked so somber and holy in his long black cassock with the surplus on top, pouring water and wine into the elaborate gold chalice held by the Monsignor. She got goose bumps when the boys chanted in Latin, their innocent sing-song voices a stark contrast to the deep voices of the men who called to them, and she was happy that her family's congregation was bound and determined to defy Vatican II and conduct the Mass just as it had for centuries. And they would also refuse to eat meat on any Friday, thank you very much.

The Good Sister knew it was a joke among her brothers and the other altar boys that when it came time to fill the chalice the Monsignor would have one of them pour wine and a seeming forever would pass before the cleric would give the ever so subtle signal to stop, by raising the vessel just a hair. Then the bearer of the water decanter would begin, only to get the signal to stop after a mere splash. They all knew that the priests had to drain the chalice of all that was left after communion, that none of it could be reused and that the two church leaders were likely tipsy enough after that.

The two priests at St. Ignatius Cathedral were a younger one, fresh from the seminary, who was serious but not standoffish, and The Old Father, the Monsignor, who laughed large and tickled the girls and mussed the boys' hair, and made funny faces at the toddlers to the delight of their mothers. As they approached adolescence, though, he was more hands-off as he guided them toward confirmation and the true gravity of being a faithful congregant. It was not to be taken lightly, he said, and he conferred with the boys privately, while the nuns took individual girls under their counsel.

Sometimes the Good Sister thought how wonderful it would be to become a nun, married to the Lord, wearing the billowing habit, the beautiful gold cross at her hip. Some of the sisters at St. Mary's were very stern, though most seemed kind enough, and a few were even beautiful, like the one in that Haley Mills movie, *The Trouble With Angels*. They were all, however, mysterious, with their private rituals, spiritual wedding bands, and secretive airs. But as much as the Good Sister wished to marry the Mystery, be as pure as they, she knew in her heart that she wanted to be a mother, always, and if she were ever to go into a convent as a novice she would surely be wooed away by some handsome man, as Julie Andrews was in *The Sound of Music*.

Sundays were a rambunctious time, before and after Mass, the rounding up of bibles and rosaries, making sure all the children's feet were shrouded in matching socks and dress shoes, petticoats in stiff silhouettes, neckties and hair bows and finery as if in preparation for a pilgrimage to Rome. And once the service was over, a flurry of undoing, the three boys, including the Fifth Born, wresting free of their full skirts in the anteroom of the Old Father's sanctuary. It was on such a typical Sunday that the family station wagon was found light of one sibling, the Fifth Born--not an unusual thing for this particular brother, free of spirit, with a tendency to roam the hallways and balconies of the huge building, to go missing. He was off with friends, wrestling on the back lawn, or exploring what might be hidden passages full of ancient treasures, or plundering the wine and wafers.

The Good Sister immediately attended to the task of gathering up one of her lost biddies. She went directly to the Old Father's sanctuary, fully expecting to find it empty of anyone, but as she entered she felt an oddness in the air, and her body willed her to slow down, to be quiet, the instinct of a lioness welling up, unconsciously uneasy. She approached the heavy oak door of the sacristy, where the accouterments and unsanctified communion wafers were kept. Ornately carved with cherubs and rosebuds, the door was chained on the other side, but carelessly, enough that it was caught open, the doorknob latch disengaged. It was open enough for her to hear, and then to see, through the sliver of access. And then to scream to the emptiness of the building, to push against the door, to hear the fumblings and murmurs and rushing of the Old Father, the clattering of the chain that echoed and held, it seemed, forever.

When the chain latch was finally released, the stark white

collar hung in the air above her head like a guillotine's blade, as if it could slice all of her spirit and comforts to shreds, but she felt strangely apathetic about that, and her claws must have been bared in her expression. Because the Old Father said nothing when she snatched the Fifth Born by the arm and spirited him away to the family coach, holding in, holding in, until she could stand before her parents, alone, and sob out what she had witnessed. Was she sure? Yes. How could she know? Because she was almost eighteen, ready to leave for nursing school and didn't they know teenage girls talked? Didn't they know teenage boys lusted and that she had been privy to some limited experience with that? Didn't they know how different the world was now, after The Pill and free love? Which turned their rage upon her. What did she know about The Pill? She knew some girls who took it but she would never, ever. What had she been up to? Nothing serious, just silly dates. Anyway, she was committed to chastity and what about the Fifth Born?

The Fifth Born was then brought in to that inner sanctum that was his parents' bedroom, where the whole lot of them had supposedly been conceived in mysterious intimacy that yielded miracles of life. Her brother was closely questioned, was vague in his responses, confused, ashamed, tearful, having neither the vocabulary, at thirteen years of age, nor the inclination to delve into what all the fuss was. And the Good Sister looked on, feeling she should have done something sooner, wondering why she had not prevented it, certain she was at fault, but that she alone could not be to blame, could she? She closed her eyes to attempt an escape from racing thoughts, but that white collar flashed into the darkness, so stark and unyielding, that she opened them for relief, only to find her brother's vacant gaze. She wanted to hold him, beg his forgiveness, do some kind of penance, and believe that she could hope to regain a sense of peace.

The first three, now four, brothers were abruptly withdrawn from St. Ignatius Catholic Boys' School and enrolled in public school, and the siblings found themselves deposited in a new church, St. Mary's. No explanations were ever offered, and the Good Sister never broke that implied vow of silence. She did not even have to be given that directive.

She left home for nursing school, studying human anatomy, physiology, and infection control, attending the small Catholic church in the little college town. She thought to speak to the priest about what had happened, make confession about her lack of diligence and the shattering repercussions of that failure. There were many evenings when she would stand before her dresser mirror, practicing what she would say. "Forgive me Father, for I have sinned." And she would piece together any number of awkward words, cobble together enough phrasings that would get out the gist of it, and even though she ended up in tears, she would promise herself that next Sunday would be the day. Instead, she could never scrape up the nerve to face her sins and always, of any Sunday, felt queasy and clammy and inadequate upon entering the foyer of the church.

When she visited home during breaks and for holidays, she was greeted with elaborately drawn posters made by the Fifth Born, featuring Charlie Brown, Snoopy and the gang, meticulously colored, with "WELCOME HOME!" in all caps and dedication. She knew he must have spent hours on the detail, was proud that he was such a fine artist, hoped that he would find solace someday, in art. She always made a big fuss over his efforts and made a point of taking the posters back to school, to hang them in her dorm room.

"I wish he would put as much effort into his school work," his mother said.

But the whimsical images of the "Peanuts" gang gradually began to close in on her—Linus with that thumb to his mouth, Pigpen shrouded in a billowing cloud of dirt, Lucy with her vicious football, forever betraying good ol' Charlie Brown's trust, and Snoopy doing his famous "happy dance" amidst it all. With her dorm room covered over in the colorful Lost Children, for the adults were never anywhere to be seen in the "Peanuts" strips, she slipped into an emptiness that must, she thought, feel like the death of a child. She developed migraine headaches that threw her into a fetal position every time, and she feared her skull would break wide open and ooze its contents onto the bed. She withdrew from school and informed her parents that she wanted to come home.

Her mother and father drove to the little college and confronted her. This was unacceptable. They were simply not having it, they told her, asking her what kind of trouble she had fallen into. Was she failing? No, although her heart told her she was. Was she giving in to poor peer influences? No, she told them, she did not socialize much. Then why? Oh no, Holy Mother of Jesus, was she pregnant? And that drove the Good Sister into a sudden gale of laughter, so much laughter that she had trouble stopping, even as her parents demanded it.

How could she laugh in the face of such a situation?

She was sorry, she told them.

They were terribly disappointed in her, they said. What about the family expectation of a postsecondary education? Sorry. How would they explain it to their friends? Sorry. How would they bear the shame? Sorry. They did not want apologies, they wanted explanations, and she had better offer one right this minute, young lady. To which the Good Sister lay down on the bed in her dorm room, on her back, hands crossed at her breast, like a corpse, eyes closed, and whispered repeatedly that she could not be in that room another minute, confounding them with such uncharacteristically odd and rebellious behavior. They loaded her into the station wagon and drove her home.

As the Good Sister unpacked her suitcases in her new old bedroom, the Fifth Born flipped through the old posters he had made. She complimented him, again, on his talent, but turned to him with tears and a look of defeat on her face. "I know this is you," she said, pointing to Linus. "And this," pointing to Pig Pen, and on through the other symbols that had seeped into her consciousness over the months. "But this," and she pulled a happy-dancing Snoopy out of the stack. "I have to know. Is this who you wish you were?"

He could only look down at his hands and shrug. "I'm fine," he said.

It wasn't long before her mother was happy to have the Good Sister's help once again, with the stair steps that now ranged from her eldest, at nineteen, all the way down to a surprise, pre-menopausal infant of eighteen months. That Ninth Child stirred real physical murmurings, hormonal sea-changes, even uterine contractions, and when she found the menstrual excretions, she wondered if she were really fit to be a mother. She wondered even more as she watched the Fifth Child, with his glib attitude, his academic laziness, his eyes red and puffy from the pot he smoked as often as he and his friends could get it, which was pretty much continuously. Their parents, though, were oblivious to anything but the superficial, such as poor grades. So the Good Sister tried to talk to him, not about the past, but the present and his future. She loved him, she said, and was worried. To which he would each time and always ever after respond by giving her a bear hug, a cheek kiss, and saying "Don't worry about me. I'm just fine."

But the Good Sister did not believe him, and that "I'm just fine," became a humming buzz in her head, which grew into a migraine until she had to take the pills that had been prescribed by the campus physician back at the little college. She would go to bed, blotting out the light with a sleep mask, the cacophonous family sounds with the white noise of an oscillating fan, hoping for sleep to keep her shame at bay. She would emerge to only repeat the cycle—the holding of the Ninth Born, the subsequent maternal yearnings, and then the doubt and self-hatred and feelings of loss, until she decided to lock herself in the bathroom, a bathroom whose door was never closed, for in a household of nine children modesty could have no purchase. And she lit a candle and swallowed all that remained in the bottle of prescription migraine pills along with some sweet red wine in her own private communion.

At the hospital, her parents told her how the door had to be battered in, how the ambulance had to deliver her to the ER to get her stomach pumped, and how could she? Didn't she know it was a mortal sin? Whatever could have driven her to do this to the family? But the Fifth Born held her hand and squeezed it and told her everything would be okay, and she almost found herself believing him. "I love you," she said, and he gifted her with a smile.

A church deacon was sent to counsel her, to reassure her that she was not a fallen soul, that God truly did have the grace to forgive, that she could repent and reclaim her salvation. He was stoic but kind, several years older, but very young for a deacon so he must be a good Catholic. He did not press her for details when she told him the church had failed her and she had failed her brother and hinted at the details. They talked in a strange kind of code, as if not daring to lay too much bare, needing to keep it in some subterraneous place, where secrets were at bay but living, some place like purgatory, she thought. The Deacon convinced her that with effort and prayer she could separate the church from any bad apple of a priest, and it ultimately made sense to her, for it was never fair to lump all good in with the bad, was it? By the following spring the two were wed and she was commencing to give birth to her first child.

The Fifth Born would continue to blunder his way through high school, often in trouble, worrying his father and being berated by his mother with more and more vitriol, enough so that The Good Sister, upon witnessing the public shamings at family gatherings, cried for him many nights, but what could she do?

The Deacon had the answer, as always. "Pray," he said, "for his mortal soul."

The day her favorite brother turned eighteen, two months after his high school graduation, her mother ordered him out of the house, to go and make something of himself. For a few nights he slept in the car of his brother, the Fourth Born. When the Good Sister discovered this she fetched him into her own home, but after a couple of days the Deacon put his foot down. The Fifth Born was disrespectful, to him, he said, to the church, to any authority, and his rebellious nature would likely land him in jail, and he was a damn fool to think anything different would come to pass.

The Fifth Born smiled. "Fools are free," he said.

The Fifth Born found his way to the only place that made immediate sense, into the air force, Vietnam or no. He served his time without seeing combat and went to college on the GI Bill, having discovered a love of literature in the service, where he thoroughly enjoyed reading books he wasn't forced to read. He spoke with the Good Sister from time to time, giving fair reports of his job as a university instructor, his own family, and any other newsy items of interest, speaking of his love of James Baldwin, John Irving, among many others; but he had little to do with reunions, or baptisms, or family weddings, or confirmations, and kept far from his home town and even farther from the church. "I'm just fine," he would say.

The Good Sister had married well, indeed. The Deacon was

a rigid defender of the faith, enforcer of church law, pillar of the congregation. He was a good provider, too, having shrewdly risen through the ranks of a national insurance company. With him she would bear eight children and order the infrastructure of her life toward being a Good Mother, successfully so, by all accounts. She was patient, loving, firm but understanding, and always quick to laugh, even though the Deacon did not share her joyous nature, that shining veneer of her desperation for a peaceful spirit.

When the Fifth Born gave her the news of his divorce, the Good Sister was sorrowful and appalled that her brother's soul was in such grave jeopardy, although the Deacon seemed perfectly smug in informing her that excommunication was a done deal. She did some research and inquiry, however, and learned that the Fifth Born could take a class in the church and ask for special dispensation for good works. It was a chance, at least.

The Fifth Born laughed when she gave him that option. He hadn't been to church since leaving home, which she already knew, of course, and he wondered aloud at her attempt to coax him back into the fold but she pretended not to hear. Sometimes she envied him his freedom, although she was certain the two of them were haunted by shared ghosts and always would be.

The Fifth Born was kind enough not to mention the twisted irony when the Deacon left her. The Deacon's promotion within his company required a move across the country. The Good Sister, though, could not bear to leave her extended family, thought it much too important for her own children to be near them. And that was that. The cold reality that he could so easily leave, however, gnawed at her heart. Her emotions took her to the cusp of that evening when she performed her Holy Communion in the bathroom with the never-closed door shut and locked. But even in the devastating wreckage of marital failure, her children came first, and she would as always tend to them with affection and warmth and humorous support.

She would seek the advice of the Young Father at St. Mary's, attend Mass, volunteer, and kiss her Rosary beads as she dutifully prayed her "Our Fathers" and "Hail Marys." And she would find her way into the confessional booth, curtains drawn, and pour out her petty flaws and dismal failures and any mortal sins that might be obstacles on her path to penance. But she could never, ever, put into words how she had forsaken her beloved Fifth Born, the mischievous boy of her heart. He was a stubborn reminder that this shoddy faith of hers hung on a clerical collar blackened with abandonment, deceit, and the kind of hollow lies she told herself every day, a solitary Mobius Strip of penitence that was destined to spiral on, into the Mysterious Forever.

See Ruby Falls

At the periphery of Eustace Bland's vision, his sister-in-law Marble unbuttoned her blue polyester Hawaiian-print blouse and unsnapped the cup of her nursing bra. "I thought I'd make it a little further," she sighed, "but Crystal wants her ninny right now." The baby had been fussing for twenty miles; Marble had been fussing for the entire trip.

A flash of palm trees and pineapples on aqua reflected at Eustace, who continued to stare out the window from the passenger seat of the two-tone brown LTD. He knew, though, that she was looking at him. He could feel her look, had known it all the while Marble had nursed her other three. "You like what you see?" the look said, and: "You better not like it too much or I'll tell Jole." Eustace wished he had brought along a book to read. A book would let him lose the Marble-clutter in his brain and push her miles away. He smiled at his reflection in the window glass at the thought of losing his marbles.

"You think this'll satisfy her long enough?" she asked, turning her head left toward her husband. "Lord, I just know she's going to be fussing again by the time we get there. Then I'll have to find a ladies' room. I don't know why I never switched over to no bottles."

"Well, they don't make no sense." This came from Helen, the mother-in-law in the middle of the back seat, surrounded by Jole's and Marble's three other children. "Why folks want to fool with bottles when they can just unbutton the lunch counter is a mystery to me. Too many complications in this world." She stroked the matted hair of four-year-old Amber Dawn, who was sleepily drooling a wet spot on the old lady's pantsuit.

"Why does she get to lay down?" Pauline whined. "Why do I got to always hold her old nasty feet?"

"Cause you're twelve, baby, and a good sweet sister to this child," the grandmother explained.

"She's done told you that two hundred times," Jole Junior, ten, hollered from the other side of the back seat. "Foot holder."

"Shut up, stupid," Pauline said.

"Nasty foot holder," her brother repeated.

"Hush up, the both of you," the grandmother hissed. "You'll wake your sister. Get back to counting billboards."

"I don't really see what's so wonderful about breast feeding," Marble said. "Some people just don't change with the times. Some people spend a whole life in the past." She glanced again at Eustace, who continued to ignore her.

"How many billboards has there been?" Jole called out.

"I got twelve," Jole Jr. said.

"You got the best side," Pauline said. "It ain't fair!"

"Shh! You can switch sides in a minute, when we're halfway," the grandmother said. It had been her idea to have the children count the signs for Ruby Falls on either side of the interstate all the way from Jenkin-Jones, West Virginia, to Chattanooga, Tennessee. They could count barn roofs, bumper stickers—anything advertising the tourist spot where Helen and her late husband, Carliss, had spent their honeymoon.

"Yep," Jole said. "All this advertising pays good. They sure make theyselves some money."

"And all from a hole in the ground." Marble tugged at her bra again as the baby made slobbery sounds against her breast. "Tell you what, Jole. Since folks crave theirselves a hole in the ground, why don't you take folks down the mine, charge five dollars a head, and we'll get rich."

"Aw, come on, Marble honey."

"No, I mean it," Marble tuned up. "Dig a hole and call it 'Marble Caverns.' Let Eustace here be a tour guide. Lord knows he needs a job."

Eustace went on studying the countryside.

"Are you going to complain the whole second half of the trip?" Helen asked. "You done complained up the first half of it."

"I just don't see what's so fascinating about a durned hole in the ground. Jole goes in one every day to work. Hell, Granddaddy Carliss *died* from breathing the air in a hole in the ground, and now we got to take a dad-burned vacation to a hole named Ruby Falls."

"Take some pride in having a vacation of any calling, then," the old lady said.

"Well it's a far cry from Myrtle Beach," Marble insisted. "Now there's a vacation spot! The ocean and a motel—and the children could get some of them shells. You can use them for ashtrays, you know. Grace Repass has them all over. *Her* husband took *her* to Florida." She squinted her blue-shadowed eyes at the dusty, insectified windshield. "Wouldn't I like a trip to Florida! Granny Helen, you can't say you wouldn't like no trip to Florida!"

"It'd be nice, I admit," the old lady said. "But I carry nothing in my heart for Florida. Carliss took me to Ruby Falls. I'm a old woman. I've wanted to see it again ever since he passed."

"Florida's better," Pauline said.

"Ha! You missed a bumper sticker," Jole Jr. taunted. "I seen it when you wasn't looking. I got thirteen!"

Pauline pouted out the window.

"Thank the Lord Jole took me on a decent honeymoon. Niagara Falls! Now there's a waterfall!" Marble nuzzled her husband's shoulder. "Thank you, baby, for giving your wife such a nice trip."

Jole grinned.

"It ain't the place I'm wanting to go back to so much as the feeling," Helen said.

"But Granny Helen!" Marble attempted to turn her head toward the back seat. "What feeling comes from a hole in the ground? Granddaddy Carliss spent his life under the ground. He couldn't of cared for no Ruby Falls."

"Anyway, we couldn't afford no long car trip," Helen said, gently.

Marble sighed. She nuzzled Jole's shoulder again, sat up and brooded, then, not quite under her breath, "A lot of good that union did Carliss."

For the first time in a long while, Eustace glanced at his sister-in-law. At twenty-nine she looked thirty-nine, aged by children, discontent, and greed. Her frosted hair was layered like that of one of her favorite soap stars, moussed into a cap that defied the wind, held in place by bronze-colored bobby pins festooned with suns and quarter-moons, cheap baubles glancing the glare like pyrite. Her face had once been pretty enough to coax Eustace into the back seat of a GTO. One year later it was Jole, and seven months later a marriage shortly before Pauline was born. Marble's face was now hard, embroidered by lines of bitterness. Frosty pink toenails popped from blue sandals below her jeans, matching the sculpted fingernails she paid for twice a month. There was an indefinable whisper of harsh hunger about her, a craving for all the things life had told her she could not have.

Eustace was amazed at the energy Marble put into grooming herself, yet her children were always sprinkled with a layer of dirt, scabby Band-Aids, and crusty upper lips—dried milk, or snot, or whatever they had eaten in the course of a day. And they all whined, just like Marble, with the exception of Crystal, who had not yet learned how. He glanced at the baby. The long, brown nipple popped from her tiny pink mouth. When Marble was seventeen, she had used those breasts to tease; now he watched a droplet of milk ooze from the same place his own tongue had touched and enjoyed until she decided that Jole would be the more malleable brother.

Marble was ever vigilant. "Getting a eyeful?" she asked. "Jole, tell your brother to quit eyeing my ninny."

"Aw, Marble, he ain't—"

"Is too! Ain't it bad enough I got to go to a hole in the ground? Now Eustace is giving me looks."

"Marble," Eustace said.

"Praise the Lord, he can talk. And don't you look mean at me." Marble snapped her bra cup and buttoned her blouse, slowly. She tilted her face at him—the look of one of her selfish children hoarding cookies.

"Daddy did the best he could for Mama," Eustace said with

forced calm.

"Well who says he didn't? I swear I don't know why you have to jump all over me ever' time I mention your daddy. I loved that old man too! Lord knows when he died he left a pair of shoes you won't never be able to fill."

Eustace felt icy anger in his stomach, the way he always did when Marble used the word "love," as if that word could cancel out all the dank words that came before and after it.

"Mama, I got to pee," Jole Jr. said.

"Oh, shoot," Marble spat out an irritated sigh. "Well, you're just going to have to wait. Sign said there's a Stuckey's in ten miles."

"I can't, Mama. I got to pee now!"

"Let the boy pee, Marble," Helen said.

Marble rolled her eyes. "Jole, baby, pull over. Wait—" She craned her neck around. "Right lane's clear. Get over now. Watch that transfer truck coming up behind. Use the blinker, baby! Lord, this highway's scary."

Marble continued to ramble while the boy peed. "There wasn't no finer man than Carliss Bland. Everybody says so. Him and that Fox man. What was—?"

"George," Eustace set his teeth hard, as he had come to do whenever she spoke of his father, whenever she spoke of George, his father's best friend and partner in building the union, whenever she spoke of anything he associated with that word she threw about—"love." It was impossible to tune her out when they were cooped up in a car together, but he had not had it out with her in over a year, and he didn't mean to start up again now, not on his mother's trip.

"But him and that George got to where everything was the union. Everything," Marble was saying. "The union this and the union that." She seemed determined to goad him into something, though he was not sure what.

"And that's why folks admired them," Helen said. "Still do, to this day."

"Oh, Granny Helen, I know. Believe me, I do. It's just that—"

"Peed on a big old ant," Jole Jr. announced, as he squeezed in beside his grandmother. "Drownded him."

"That's stupid," Pauline said.

"Shut up, foot holder."

"Mama!" the girl moaned.

"This car don't move until you two are quiet," Jole said.

"Foot holder," Jole Jr. said softly. He leaned across the grandmother to whisper in his sister's ear, "You ain't nothing but a nasty foot holder and you'll be a foot holder all your natural life."

Traffic began to pick up. Soon the Stuckey's exit flashed by. The hum of the air conditioner lulled the Blands into a traveler's stupor. Children dozed. Marble fiddled with the radio, then turned it off. Eustace smoked a Pall Mall, enjoying the relative quiet of the steady whistle of air from the window vent. He thought of the books he had left behind. He was right in the middle of a spy novel but was anxious to finish it and get back to the biographies he enjoyed. The trip would have been perfect for reading, but he chose instead to humor his mother, who insisted that Marble would accuse him of ignoring the family if he put his face behind a book.

"Carliss and me had a whole two days and a night," Helen said. "We stayed at a motel in Chattanooga and rode up the mountain both days. We saved Ruby Falls till the last. Remember, Eustace? I sent you that post card?"

"Yes'm."

"But Granny Helen," Marble said, "I thought it was a honeymoon. Was baby Eustace a love child?"

The old woman twisted her wedding band in slow circles upon the arthritic finger. "Oh, we never had no honeymoon after the wedding. And then Carliss worked so hard, put all his spare time and most money into union business we just never got around to it."

"Oh, a *late* honeymoon," Marble mused, as if there were something vaguely distasteful about this whole notion. "Well, that's just my point, Helen. Just think of all the time Granddaddy Carliss could of spent with you if he hadn't give off so much time to them union people."

"Daddy never did anything halfway," Eustace said, before he realized his mouth was open.

"Like father like son?" she said brightly. "Eustace sure goes whole hog at doing nothing."

"Marble, there ain't no call for—"

"Well look at him, Jole! He ain't worked in twelve years! At least you work, put food on the table. He just mopes around them old cars in Granny Helen's yard and reads them books all the dad-burned time!"

"Let him be, Marble Bland," the old woman said.

"It don't matter, Mama," Eustace said. "Let Marble do her bitchin'. She'd be miserable if she couldn't bitch at anybody."

"Jole, did you hear your brother? You tell him to shut up. Right this minute! I know what he thinks of you. He's said it outright about you working in a scab mine. About Carliss turning in his grave! And you just sit there and let him run us both in the ground. Be a man!"

Eustace heard the same raw edge of anger her voice had held when he rejected her the first time after she'd married Jole. That one scarlet vein of fury, so easily struck at times, let him know he was getting the best of her, but he was not yet finished. "You got to give him his balls back first, Marble," Eustace said, lighting another cigarette. Inside he was roiling, but outside he would not give her the satisfaction. . . .

"Whoa, now, Eustace," Jole said.

"Look!" Helen shifted forward. "We're getting almost there!" She squeezed Eustace's shoulder, a subtle act of allegiance, and he put his concentration, once again, upon ignoring Marble Bland.

The Blands washed up in the restrooms off the Ruby Falls reception area. Marble even put a rag to the children's nasty faces. Helen was beside herself, dragging Amber-Dawn from one souvenir display to the next, rushing to the observation decks, pointing out the exact spot where she and Carliss had shared a grilled cheese sandwich. While Pauline and Jole Jr. begged their parents to buy every trinket they saw, Eustace sat in the coffee shop to wait for their tour group to be called.

There was an uneasiness in the waiting, sipping hot coffee. It was like the hospital lounge where he and George had sat while his father coughed out the last of his spent lungs nearly fifteen years before. At twenty-five, Eustace had been angry at his father's death—at the strong, wiry man rendered helpless, the determined spirit turned impotent, the scarlet life's blood spat upon sterile cloths. But at the funeral his anger began to subside even as daunting, oversized expectations rushed in on him like an avalanche of stones.

Over six hundred people turned out that day. George delivered a eulogy of strength and new resolve. Eustace had felt a pull of pride in the gathering, in remembrances of battles waged: the '62 strike, the time Carliss whipped four scabs who jumped him at Bear Waller, the beginning of the Black Lung. As the casket was lowered, Eustace had felt the eyes upon him, silently urging him to step into place, filling his father's dreams.

"Look, Uncle Eustace!" Jole Jr. stood before him. In spite of the fact that Eustace's brother had laid down the law against buying "souvenir shit," the boy wore a tee-shirt that proclaimed 'See 7 states/Lookout Mt., Tenn' and a red sun visor with 'Ruby Falls' printed in white across the bill. He wanted to slap the child's cocky little jaw. "Come on, Uncle Eustace. It's time to go down!"

It was a slow day on the mountain. The tour group was small, but large enough to fill the elevator with a nauseating stuffiness that was too familiar. Eustace suddenly realized that he had not been in an elevator shaft since he quit his job, three years after his father's death.

Solid rock was visible through the elevator grillwork. The air cooled rapidly as they descended, swirling damp smells about the group.

"I'm scared," Pauline whined.

"Aw, it's just like a little old mine. Sort of like where I work," Jole said, proudly.

"But I ain't never been in no mine," Pauline said.

"Me neither," Jole Jr. said, wide-eyed. "What if it caves in on us?"

The door slid open; they stepped out into a cave of solid limestone and were herded into a line: a fat Yankee couple followed by two Yankee children; a teenaged girl with tattooed ankles; the girl's boyfriend, sporting a buzzed head and an attitude; two elderly couples laden with cameras slung like weapons over Bermuda shorts; an Asian man with a little boy; a well-dressed professional-looking couple. The Blands brought up the rear. Cameras clicked. Eyes glanced with uncertainty at the low rock ceiling.

Marble was visibly nervous, fidgeting the baby from hip to hip. "Lord," she said. "It's right close in here, ain't it?"

"Give me the baby," Helen said. "Y'all don't be so squeamish. Ain't it pretty? I reckon that's why Carliss liked it. It's pretty, for folks to come and enjoy. Ain't like a coal mine that folks go to 'cause they have to."

"I flat sure wouldn't be up in here unless I had to," Marble said.

Eustace was on the verge of telling her to just shut her mouth, just shut the fuck up, when the guide launched into a patter of rote facts and forced jokes. He was goddamn fed up with her dragging up all the union shit. Again. And again, and again. Then the crowd he was enfolded by began to move, making its way through the two-mile tunnel that would lead to the underground falls. As it narrowed they fell into single file, Eustace dipping his head instinctively under overhanging rocks. It was a clean, ornamental underground world, unlike the dusty monotony of the mines. Colored lights dotted the passageway and the highlighted formations bore names: "Cactus and Candle," "Mirror Lake," "Onyx Jungle." Water dripped echoes into hidden pools. The cool, cool air heightened his senses.

"Ain't it pretty?" Helen said.

"Oh, it's pretty, all right," Marble answered behind her mother-in-law. "Pretty narrow. Them lights is pretty, though. Hey, Jole!" she called to her husband. "Start saving up for some colored lights for your mine, okay, baby?"

"Daddy, I want to go back and buy one of them Chattanooga Choo-Choos up in the silveneer shop," Jole Jr. begged.

Eustace ground his back teeth together. He had been in and out of the mines with his father ever since he was old enough to walk, but he was not his father, and these children of Marble's did not have the connection to their grandfather that was their birthright.

In their world, yesterday meant nothing, if you were old you did not count, and if you were dead you were not even a ghost. Marble's words bit at his brain: Like father like son? No, he thought, not even close. His own failing had worn down the family's keen sense of history.

Soon after Eustace was elected president of WMA Local 660, the call for a strike was clear. The company had begun to mechanize, was demanding concessions, and was threatening to close down. Carliss's work was being undone before he was cold in the ground. Eustace had failed to move people the way his father had done so easily.

Eustace had watched his father go through strikes, knew the sacrifice. What he had not known was that the company would manage to hold on, that his friends would be out for ten months, then eighteen, then had to move on or give in. By that time another thing had become clear: things were coming apart so fast Eustace did not have enough hands to keep them together. Just as one thing was replaced, two or three others would come undone, until he began to think of the union as some ancient grandfather clock that had exploded. His arms were full of blackened springs and gears and he had no idea where they went anymore.

Finally, he, too, went back to work, and it was shameful. It wasn't that he had ever loved his job; it was not the sort of job anyone loved. There had been pride, though, in the strength he and the others felt standing together. Now they were broken apart, and there was no pride in a broken spirit. He quit after two days, spending his time with books, reading the lives of people long dead; or with cars, rebuilding the engines and transmissions of vehicles no one would ever drive. He knew that he had descended into yet another tunnel, just as dark and dangerous as a coal mine, but every time he looked up, thought to drag himself out, the shadow of his father loomed over him, impossibly tall. Still, it might have been manageable if not for Marble's braying criticisms.

"You ain't nothing but a foot holder," Jole Jr. had said. "You'll be a foot holder all your natural life."

The shadow of a roar loomed ahead. "I hear it," Helen whispered. The air was going from cool to cold; Eustace shivered, yet there was something warm uncurling in his belly. A mustache of sweat erupted on his upper lip and he wiped at it impatiently.

"Goody gumdrops," Marble said. "We hear it."

Eustace followed behind his sister-in-law, watching the way

her jeans drew up into the crack of her broad ass. The bottoms of her sandals were slippery; she lost her balance several times.

Eustace wished she would slip into one of the small tunnels branching out from the main one. The limestone would shake loose and come crushing down upon her precious breasts, searing deep faults into her skull, pulverizing her ribs into sharp pebbles. He would stand and do nothing while she suffocated under the rocks. Only with her graveyard dead was there hope that he could ever get back his family history, his honor, and his brother.

When Jole went to work in a scab mine his mother had cried for four days, begging him and Marble to move, cart the shame away, to Jewel Ridge or Richlands, but Marble would have none of it. Jenkin-Jones was home. She would not budge. There was already a down payment on a plot of land next to Helen's. Besides, unions meant strikes that would interfere with the house trailer she and Jole planned to buy. Her man would work steady. Her man would cooperate. Jole would never be a troublemaker.

Eustace ran his palm across a glassy rock. It felt clean and pristine, not at all like the soft coal that had turned his skin black and his father's lungs blacker still, filling them until there was no room for anything else.

Up ahead, the children begged for souvenirs, their demanding little voices filling cold rushes of air. His mother shivered and pulled the baby close. Her face, when she turned the profile to him, was set in the prideful way he had cherished as a boy.

"We paid upwards of thirty dollars to walk all this way up under a dad-blamed mountain?" Marble muttered. She stopped, reached behind her, yanked at the jeans that bunched into her rear, and turned to Eustace. "I bet you're having just the best time," she said.

Had she only known how pathetic she seemed to him. Marble's trailer was a clutter of knick-knacks, supermarket tabloids, and the smell of a child's week-old urine. With each of Jole's paychecks came a new J. C. Penney order: a blue polyester Hawaiian-print blouse, a square of mustard-yellow carpet, a pedicure kit, a La-Z-Boy recliner, a food processor to sit, untouched, upon the kitchen counter, processing nothing save Marble's need to own it. And with every acquisition, as though ascending to a higher moral plain, came more yammering and bitching and chastisement of Eustace. "Books and cars, Granny Helen," Marble would say. "Books and cars. When is he going to finish fixing just one of them cars junking up your yard? Shoot, whenever he gets just a little money, he spends it on more dad-blamed books and auto parts. When you going to take all that book learning and get a real job, Eustace? When you going to marry up and live out from up under your mama, Eustace? When you going be a real man, like Jole?"

Once, only two years earlier, he had backhanded her in the mouth. She had wallowed, half-naked, against him with the selfish confidence of an unimaginative woman. When he pushed her away she screeched, "You think Carliss rolls over in his tomb at the idea of Jole in that mine? Well look at you! You think Carliss would live up under his mama and be dumb enough to turn down a good-looking woman? Jole's his daddy's son but you're a dad-blamed pussy!" As far as Eustace knew, Marble had never attempted to explain the angry bruise that kissed her upper lip for days afterward. She had even held her tongue for a time.

The rushing sound was tremendous now, as the group stepped into a dark chamber, cold air thick with moisture from the spray of the falls. Eustace still rubbed at beads of perspiration that gathered on his neck; he chewed at the side of his tongue, the water's roar matching the angry rumble now rising from his belly to his chest.

"I'm scared," Pauline said. "Tell them to turn on the lights."

"Hush baby," he heard Helen say. "It ain't a frightful place."

Marble made a disgusted noise that was drowned out by music. It overtook the water's roar from several loudspeakers, as the theme from *2001* bounced across the rock walls, built, then crescendoed. *Thus Spake Zarathustra*. Just as it seemed Elvis was about to emerge from the darkness, spotlights poured out from all directions.

People whispered and "oohed" in reverent awe. Cameras flashed. Eustace edged over beside his mother and wrapped an arm about her curved shoulders.

"It's just the same," Helen breathed. "The music's been added, a-course, but it's—" her eyes began to water. "He was a fine man."

"Yes'm," Eustace said.

Marble pouted as the music concluded. "Ain't this been a lot of dad-burned sugar for a nickel," she muttered.

The narrow falls dropped 145 feet, powerfully, into a clear pool surrounded by a railed path. The guide began leading them, single file, along the path, under the falls, and out the other side. The three older Bland children raced to break in ahead of tourists who threw disapproving looks at Jole. Jole Jr. spat into the pool and his sisters followed suit.

"Take the baby from your mama, Jole. She's plumb wore out. And get the young'uns. Don't just stand there," Marble said. "There ain't a whole lot for kids to do down here, is it," she observed, as her husband wandered behind his brood.

Helen dabbed at her eyes. "You know, the Local paid for our trip. Sort of in appreciation after we won the strike. They knew your daddy was sickly. Knew we never had no wedding trip. They took up a collection," she sniffed. "Don't it fill your heart?"

"Yes'm," Eustace said, but the rumbling inside him would not be still. He wanted a cigarette. He wanted out of the tunnel; it had long since turned into an incomprehensible maze.

"Well, if they was going to give off a trip, why'd they pick this?" Marble said.

"Carliss picked it," Helen set her jaw.

"Well, all I can say is it ain't no Niagara," Marble muttered as she began to walk the path beside the falling water.

"Come on, Mama." Eustace led the old woman along behind his sister-in-law.

The force of the water created a windy effect in the cavern, blowing at his hair. Orange lights illuminated the fierce liquid that spilled above their heads. It was a show, all right, Eustace thought, all glamorized for the tourists, but there was a very real, raw, and unending power behind it. He gazed up at the ripples in the stone, set by centuries of continuous action, set in a pattern that would forever, but glacially, be moving. Sure, they could use it, make money off it, just like they did a coal mine, but they could never start it or stop it or control it. It belonged only to itself. He reached again for a Pall Mall, then shoved his hand into his pants pocket, fingers twitching, an underground habit.

Marble stood directly behind the falls, head thrown back, staring up into the push of water. "Lord, this is about the puniest waterfall I've ever seen," she said. "It ain't no Niagara. Shoot, Niagara makes this look like a garden hose." She prissed herself further behind the spray. "I'm going to have to tell Jole to hook up a garden hose down in the mine. We'll make us a mint."

Eustace approached her, clenching his fist tightly in his pocket, her voice rushing through his brain with the fierceness of the water dropping out, over, down. He could smell her on the cold mist—sickly-sweet cheap perfume mixed with sweat.

She turned to him. "Don't worry, Eustace. You can have a job—you can spray the hose through a hole in the rock. Oh—and play a cassette tape when I throw on the lights." She caught the look Helen gave her. "Well, it is right puny for all that build-up, Granny Helen. A-course, the lights is nice. Decorative, kinda."

Droplets of mist had settled upon Marble's stiff, unmoving hair; the blue eye shadow took on a garish purple cast in the orange light. She turned as the grandmother moved on around her, then leaned over the railing, admiring the reflection that watched her from the pond's surface. "It just ain't that big of a deal," she continued to no one in particular. "You wouldn't see Jole bringing me here for no romantic trip. That old man had to of been crazy."

It came out. The fist emerged from the pocket where he had confined it so steadily. Eustace stared down at it, slowly uncurling the fingers until it ceased to be a weapon, becoming just a hand, like anyone's. He placed it, and the other, both palms, on Marble's waist, softly, thumbs upward, little fingers against the first swell of her hips, seeing his hands as if far down a musky, fetid tunnel.

When her body twisted and her face turned to him the expression was an odd mix of surprise, satisfaction, and something he had not seen since the high school days they had spent sliding and pushing against each other in back seats, on riverbanks, on the altar of a Pentecostal church deep in the woods. It was the unmistakable look, sinister now, couched in greed, of a conspirator, as though the two of them shared some promise one to the other that the rest of the world did not know about. She jerked her head almost imperceptibly toward Jole's direction. Her mouth formed a silent word: *wait*.

When she made to turn back to her deception in a rush, a sandaled foot slipped, her legs flying up as she levered over. Her hands clutched at him, and a blue sandal kicked airborne past him. Maybe he could have grabbed her, but he did not, and she went over so quickly she didn't even draw in a breath, exhaling a sharp cry that disappeared beneath the water. Heads turned. He thought he heard a hard thud below the falls, as if her skull had struck some rocky underwater ledge. He wasn't certain, though, bringing his palms in to the railing, leaning, looking.

People called out. His mother ran to him. Children screamed. More cameras clicked, numbers intensifying as if this were the penultimate moment of the show and there must be something to remember it by. The Asian man jumped into the far side of the pool and swam toward the blue form illuminated by yellow lights beneath the shiny surface of wet.

Her frosty pink toenails and sculpted fingernails waved at him with the current below the ripples, distorted by gaudy reflections and the crashing sound of ancient rage. The falls pounded the water's surface, making it seem to hiss and boil with Marble's silent fury, unspent vitriol. Then, somewhere near the jumble of spray feeding the pond, a delicate line of warm, swaying red swirled through the cold, winding ribbon-like into deep scarlet. An aqua blur of palm trees and pineapples seemed to roll with the push of the water, gathering more color, rising. Eustace pulled a Pall Mall from his shirt pocket and let it hang, unlit, from his lips.

Bonita Street Bridge Club

Maggie watched him from the other side of the Formica table, careful to turn only her eyes toward him, aiming her face slightly away, toward the window over the kitchen sink, as her husband crunched through his morning toast. He stopped to take a deep, slurping sip of his heavily creamed and sugared coffee, a jiggling double chin, two rolls of flesh curving in one another, puckering in and out, in and out, a silent rhythm of consumption. She imagined that he could actually inhale his coffee, and had a flashing cartoon image of a giant half-man, half-vacuum cleaner moving around the table toward her to suck away the final bits of her spirit.

A small shudder crossed her shoulders as she looked away, through the spotless window of the immaculate blue kitchen—out to where the dying farm community of Warwick, Georgia, sauntered beneath cool, tall oaks and sweet gums. Each chalk-white house was nestled symmetrically among greenery and hot pink azaleas that were a reflection—of what she was not sure—but the soothing quality of the blue kitchen fell in step alongside an illusion. Order. Perfection, even. She had always taken solace in the façade, right down to scrupulously Windexed glass, inside and out. The effect of the blue-framed window was an idyllic vision of a world through a looking glass—beckoning, fantastical, with a trace of fear.

It was the world of her friend Missanne, the princess who had taken Maggie the Toad into her enchanted sphere. Missanne lived in an antebellum palace and did just as she pleased, as she had for a lifetime. Her father, a gentleman who had cradled, courted, and defended her over the years, now spent the days abed, yellowed with bourbon, an amber gaze fixed on the flirtatious approach of Death. Two maids saw to his care in the oak-paneled room while his daughter danced, partied, and slept it off. Missanne, ever the cruel coquette, would breeze in to kiss his forehead, say something a shade emasculating, then mercilessly regale him with stories of used and discarded men, while Maggie hung back by the door, intimidated by money and perverse affection. The magnetic, frenetic hours spent with her friend, in spite of the dangerous fact that Dunbar had forbidden it, put Maggie on the flesh-slicing edge of an enticing razor. Quiet cuts tapped faint wellsprings of emotions she had never suspected were there, flaws she dared not reveal in the perfected secrecy that was her life.

Dunbar continued to crunch. A stubby, bewhiskered backhand swiped at a trickle of Welch's grape jelly, burying the purple slug deep into the crease of his chin. Maggie watched it disappear. Yes, he could certainly devour things. But when he met Missanne for the first time it was clear that he could never devour her. The gauntlet of her aristocratic beauty and feisty nature told him she could indeed win, and, even though he smiled and seemed genuinely taken in by her flirtation, he later made it clear that he hated her through and through. She was a psychotic drunken whore, he said, and, aside from her bridge group, Maggie was to have nothing to do with her.

Her husband's gaze remained on the plate until every trace of fluid yolk had been sponged away by the biscuit remains that were eventually shoved into his mouth. Maggie wondered at the sameness of it, the uncanny routine, and again her eyes went to the window and outside order. It was—it had to be—the setting of some sort of fairytale, all pastel and elf-like, beads of emerald moisture dangling from the tips of the monkey grass. Before she could conjure a vision of animated Disney butterflies and bluebirds and dancing rabbits, a motion across the Formica caught her attention. She settled back in her chair to watch as Dunbar ceremoniously raised the "Back To Work" coffee mug to his baby-fat face. More predictable twinges tickled at the base of her neck. He would put away the remainder of his cold coffee in exactly four gulps. One gulp, Maggie counted to herself, two gulps, three—

"Goddammit!"

She flinched. Black glass shattered across the table, streams of cold coffee wiggling down the light blue wall. "What the hell are you staring at me for?"

"I'm sorry, Dunbar. I didn't realize—" Maggie's hands began to sweat the way they always did when he got started.

"I didn't realize, I didn't realize," he mimicked, standing, looming. "You know I hate people staring at me."

"I know. Really," her mouth soothed. "I'm sorry. I was daydreaming, I guess."

"Like hell you were. You were staring at me." Dunbar glared. Such tiny eyes, but they swallowed her with huge gulps, and the sensation was one of being pulled, like the time the undertow caught her at Panama City Beach. She took a breath, carefully. "I was only—" The deep purple of the grape jelly flickered at her from the fold of her husband's chins.

"Only what?" He challenged.

"Only thinking," Maggie answered too quickly, cupping a napkin in the damp of her palms, urging herself on. Another breath. Air. "I was only wishing we could talk some mornings. Like I imagine other people are doing when I look through the window." The napkin wandered to and fro in her tiny hands. She knew she was talking too much, too fast, but she knew, also, that she could not stop until he decreed it. "Sometimes I look through the window," she rambled, "and I try to see inside each blue kitchen or yellow kitchen or green kitchen—although I imagine them all to be blue—and the people, they—"

"Don't have anything to say," he glared, placing a white hard-hat on the peak of his bald head. Today he would scale telephone poles to repair problems in the lines so that thousands of people could do what he did not even believe in—communicate.

"Why are you so—" Maggie began, before she could think how to finish. Why are you so—what? Hateful? Cold? He was waiting. Maggie forced a giggle. "Why do you rub jelly on your face? Here—" she held out the sweaty napkin. "Let me get you cleaned up."

Dunbar caught her wrist, pulling her up and around the table, close to him. "Lick it off," he demanded.

She hesitated, felt the wrist being turned in its socket as she was submerged in cool salt water swirling about her neck. So perversely comforting. She knew she would be swallowed, murky blue water closing above her somewhere, and she lunged in a panic at the fleshy chin, breaths hard and quick, smelling him and tasting him and trying not to gag. Welch's grape jelly, she told herself. Welch's grape jelly.

"That's a good baby," he stroked her hair and loosened his grip. "That's a real good baby." He smiled, hugged her, and pulled her into his pillow-soft belly. She hated him by the ounce and the pound. "Now I'll talk to you. Are you ready?" She nodded from somewhere beneath the salt water. "All right. You'll like this." His tone told her she probably wouldn't like it at all. "I'll be home early today—maybe before four. You be ready, now, because you've got me all worked up for it. We'll go into Albany to the movies and—"

"But today's my bridge club day and we're playing here," Maggie said, in the forced, childlike whine she had perfected.

"Jesus! Why've you gotta do all that crap? You know how much I hate it."

She felt relieved, knowing that the promise of kiddie-fied sex was usually enough to prevent the tirade. "Oh, come on, Dunbar," she teased. "I'll make it up to you later. And we agreed on the bridge club a long time ago. As long as I keep my end of the bargain. And I have, haven't I?" She cocked her head down and sideways, looking up at him like a penitent little girl.

"That goddamned Missanne is going to be here again. I'll have to smell her when I get home. Her goddamned bitch-in-heat smell."

"Oh, baby, it's my only social life," Maggie whined, stroking his shoulder.

"Social life," he muttered, ambling his slow-moving woolly-mammoth body towards the back door. "A senile old lady, an apple-pie Jew, and a whorey alcoholic lunatic. Some social life." The slamming door was echoed by Dunbar's obese laughter, and Maggie watched the bobbing white bulb disappear down the alleyway, a garish buoy near the ocean's edge. She sighed. At least she had completed the ritual and put him in a good mood. She walked over to the sink. It was bound to hit her any time now. Yes—there it was. Maggie leaned over, watching her reflection in the stainless steel shine. She turned on the water and vomited. She didn't straighten up until every particle had been carried away in dizzying circles and there was only a silver-ringed black hole and clear water echoing through it.

Maggie arranged her freshly cut zinnias with precision—red surrounded by orange surrounded by yellow. Yes, the centerpiece makes all the difference, she thought, just like it says in *Better Homes and Gardens*. She checked her watch: 12:48 and everything was perfect, from shining silverware resting on shining wood down to the last cherry exactly centered on the last piece of cheesecake. Dunbar would have a field day with this, she mused, then chastised herself for allowing his name to enter this moment that belonged only to her.

She admired the table some more, gaining the inexplicable strength that came on these days spent with friends, inside the shiny atmosphere of a magazine's party layout. Annie Louise, Missanne and Marti had become an essential presence in her life, and she realized that moments of strength had been coming closer together lately, like the late stages of labor Marti talked about so breathlessly. Maggie had always considered strength a stranger, the ugly little girl within her never daring to step out and own up.

She narrowed her eyes at the table one last time and it became a four-legged food monster with glowering little pops of light—hundreds of them throwing reflections—a murderous scarlet hole in its head. For a moment, she wondered if she were insane. Over the years she had considered writing a letter to "Dear Abby," but she already knew the answer. *Leave*. Yes, Abby was always right, but her answers were so difficult in their simplicity. I don't care, Maggie told herself. Today's my day to be normal. My bridge clubs are always the best.

The Bonita Street Bridge Club (or B.S.B.C. as the members cliquishly referred to it) met at 1:00 p.m. every other Tuesday at alternating homes and was Maggie's refuge, thanks to Missanne. When Maggie and Dunbar had moved to Warwick two years earlier, it had been Missanne who initiated friendship and offered a spot in the B.S.B.C. "Hell's bells, Maggie," Missanne had laughed. We've finally got a fourth! Didn't you know that there's not another soul in this scrap of a town who knows, or cares to learn, how to play bridge? God help us if Annie Louise kicks off!" And they had laughed and become friends—confidantes, but only up to a point. Missanne's eyes showed a cold understanding of Dunbar, but Maggie would not dare reveal their secrets. It would be too humiliating.

Of course, a deal had to be struck with Dunbar. After much haggling, he gave in to bribery, and Maggie found herself bound to a promise of specified sex for bridge and a nauseating sense of dread before and disgust afterwards. But it's worth it, she thought, as the doorbell played out its three notes and the members of the B.S.B.C. descended upon the stillness of her home like a welcome plague of butterflies.

"Well, I swanee, just look at—Maggie I swear I don't know how you do it. Annie Louise, how do you s'pose she does this?" It was Marti Lazarus, Dunbar's "apple-pie Jew," the frantically vivacious one, the one who told breathless stories about her wonderful husband, David, and the antics of their five equally wonderful children. Maggie sometimes thought she glimpsed a shadowy, desperate edge to Marti, and felt a quietly confusing kinship with the woman with the hoarse laugh and the perfect life.

"Must be some little brownies livin' under the sink for sure," Annie Louise replied, brushing by the dining room table, sending one of the plates of cheesecake to the floor, china disintegrating into the panic that rushed over Maggie.

"Lawsy, I am so sorry," Annie Louise said. "I will replace it, of course. I am such an oaf!"

"No," Maggie replied. "Everything is just fine." And her stomach would not be still until the last smear had been buffed from the hardwood floor so that its sheen was consistent with the rest.

By the time Maggie's world was put right, Annie Louise had begun fumbling through her gargantuan handbag for the cards, the rings on each finger throwing off light, bracelets and necklaces jangling like some vagrant gypsy fortune teller. Annie Louise was approaching eighty, chain-smoked Camel non-filters, and always brought the cards, supposedly the same two decks she had first learned to play bridge with some sixty years earlier, never mind that they all knew such a claim to be false. Still, the cards were next to impossible to shuffle, the edges badly worn, and it was customary for at least one member to complain about it at each meeting.

Sometimes Marti would say, "Annie Louise, I swear, if these cards get shuffled too many more times, they're gonna just fray at the edges 'til they disappear into nothin'." Then Missanne would shroud her face in a let's-get-Marti look and whisper, "Of course you know what would happen then. We would just have to pretend the cards were still here to pacify Annie Louise, and somebody's bound to cheat if we just pretend, right, old woman?"And Marti would gaze decipheringly at Annie Louise's ghoulish, leathery face while the old woman launched into the story of Aunt Ethna's cards, embellished with a little variation each time: "Watch yourself, girl. My Aunt Ethna gave me these cards in 1936." She enunciated each digit. "That's when she taught me the game, and you won't find any cards prettier in any store." She would point a loose-skinned, blue-veined hand to the design on the backs of the cards, a cameo-like head and shoulders of a young girl dressed in the fashion of the 1920s. "You see that? That's Aunt Ethna. She had these hand-drawn from a picture of her, and nobody can tell one picture from the next. Nobody but me. I can see how her expression changes." And since Annie Louise was old and slightly senile, and since no one else in Warwick knew how to play bridge, her idiosyncrasies and tall tales were tolerated.

"I can't wait to have some of that divine homemade cheesecake, Maggie," Marti said as she eased her eight-month pregnant frame into one of the chairs around the card table. "I swear I wish I had time to make things like that. You're so lucky not to have children underfoot."

Annie Louise coughed a laugh at Marti's unintentional irony and lit a cigarette.

"So why do you keep having babies, then?" Maggie asked, trying to hide her envy. "I thought that was the Catholic way, not Jewish."

"Oh, goodness, I'm not—I didn't mean to sound like I'm complaining," Marti laughed. "My children are wonderful."

"Bunch of brats," Annie Louise muttered, but Marti went on. "And I guess I'll keep having babies as long as David wants me to. He's so wonderful about it all. Do you know he brought me a bunch of azaleas this morning in a fruit jar and told me I was beautiful?"

The old lady laughed a cloud of smoke at the remark. "Lord have mercy," she cackled, thick white face powder cracking around the already cracked red lips. "You are the ninny, aren't you? See, David just doesn't want to boodle, and when you have that big old ugly pooch stickin' out—well, he doesn't have to boodle, so he keeps you pooched out all the time. He's doing what a many a man has done to get out of the whole damn business so he can boodle some teenage Lolita."

"Oh, hush up, Annie Louise," Marti said in pretended indignation. "You talk too much about things that shouldn't be talked about. Actually, Maggie, I might have to pass on the cheesecake after all—the diet, you know." She patted her stomach as if she were actually burping a baby.

More intersecting cracks branched out across Annie Louise's face. "Marti's diets are all in her head, just like her ideas about my fine deck of cards—conjured up nonsense." There was a sudden tinkling and flashing as the old woman sucked on her cigarette, then, "Where the hell is Missanne? She's always late, I know, but not like this."

"I'm sure it won't be long." Maggie felt the old woman's edge of unease, calming her own as she poured coffee into the four spotless china cups she had washed twice each.

"She's not doing so good lately," the old woman insisted ominously, and Maggie thought the cups made too much noise as she clattered them to the table. No. Everything was fine. Life was good. The ritual chitchat must not include serious concerns.

Marti had put on her frozen face, the one of concocted enthusiasm, surreal exuberance, but when she shrilled, "Oh, she's fine," Maggie thanked her with her eyes, in spite of the nausea that told her Annie Louise was not going to be quiet, finally, about Missanne.

"Fine, hell. You don't see her these days without a bottle in one hand and some man on the other arm. Or running the roads with

Maggie of a day. She's probably sloppy drunk somewhere even as I speak." And Annie Louise lit another cigarette even though she still had the previous one. Just to prove her point.

"No!" Maggie breathed out in a half-whisper. No one had ever mentioned Missanne's drinking, outside of a joke or two—never come right out with it so bluntly. The stillness of the polished room yielded sounds that weren't there, tinkling silverware and crystal; Maggie knew it was only the old woman's jewelry. The refrigerator came on, back in the blue kitchen, and they all winced on cue.

"Well, we all know what goes on, Maggie," Marti said finally, feebly surrendering. "Sometimes I think she isn't right. You know. In the head."

"No," Maggie breathed again.

But Annie Louise was indignant. "You're damn right she's a loony one," she pronounced. "But she came by it honest. Her mama killed herself, you know. Put a sawed-off shotgun in her mouth out back of the Baptist church. Blowed the back of her head away with buckshot. They say she probably had enough of that husband of hers, him with his whore-mongerin' ways."

"She never mentioned—" Maggie said.

The old woman slapped a palm on the table. "I've been in this town all my life. I knew Valera well. She was a weak-willed, straight-backed little church mouse and she stuck the barrel of that gun in her mouth to punish that husband of hers and maybe Missanne, too—punish them the only way she knew how. Missanne and her daddy are too much alike for one person to take. They run over people, drain all the spirit out of them. And I'll tell you another thing." She leaned in. "There's something unnatural about that whole relationship. Missanne and her daddy. It gives me the heebie-jeebies."

"I won't listen to that kind of sick talk," Marti interjected. "But I do admit she's getting carried away with the drinking and all. And you are her best friend, Maggie. Maybe you should try to talk to her?"

A skeptical sound rumbled in Annie Louise's throat. "What Maggie ought to do is give her a wide way to go or she'll get the life sucked out of her, too. Lie down with dogs and you get fleas, you know."

"I couldn't." Maggie's voice still would only whisper. "I couldn't let her down." Cornered, she thought of the evolution of their friendship, how uncomfortable she had been at first with Missanne's fierce, dark prettiness and hyper-defiant talk of husbands and lovers and botched suicide attempts. Maggie had soon caught on to the fact that Missanne was tolerated by Warwick's solidly Baptist community only because her father was wealthy enough to have a new wing built onto the church after his wife's death, a fact Missanne verified when she confided: "A Baptist doesn't hate anybody for too long who will give money to the Glory of God. Hell—Daddy screwed everything he could get to—including the preacher's albino cook. That church is his insurance for Heaven." They had both laughed into coffee cups, conspirators in the fact of the prominence-payoff for Missanne. Maggie felt honored by Missanne's friendship and did not dare risk crossing the line by pointing out flaws.

"Well, somebody ought to mention something," Annie Louise insisted. "The way she carries on is shameful. Running around with Lord knows who. Hell, I went to see her the other day—three o'clock in the afternoon, mind you—found her silly drunk, talking out of her head about some man being after her and how she was gonna save somebody or something. Liked to have give me a coronary, the way she was carrying on."

Marti shook her head while Maggie's panic grew more intense. This wasn't supposed to happen, not at bridge club.

"And I'll tell you another thing," Annie Louise began.

"Shhh!" Marti broke in, motioning to the door and the sound of muffled humming.

Maggie never failed to be surprised at Missanne's beauty, always thinking of their friendship as physically ironic, and she unconsciously fingered the acne scars on her left cheek. In high school Missanne would have never entered the world of losers that Maggie had barely occupied.

"London Bridge is falling down!" Missanne shouted, then furrowed her forehead. "No, that's not it."" She thought for a moment. "I know! The sky is falling!" She dropped her purse on the floor and collapsed into the vacant chair at the card table. "God, I'm tired." The acutely blue eyes went from one woman to the next, and Maggie thought she saw a slight movement in Missanne's jaw—a twitching, framed by curly black wisps of hair.

"God, you're drunk," Annie Louise snapped. The back of Maggie's neck tingled in its nervously familiar way. Not now, she thought. Please, not now. Not today.

"What on earth—" Marti began.

"Wait just a minute," Maggie interrupted, determined to smooth things over. "You look so nice, Missanne. How about some coffee?"

"Lovely," was the sarcastic reply. "And I am not drunk, *Miss* Annie Louise Cameron. Not today. Really—today of all days. You should know better."

"It's true," Marti observed, sniffing. "She's not drunk. I can always smell the first teeny-tiny drop—even vodka. Some people say vodka doesn't smell." She giggled. "David—he's so funny—well, David says I must have a regular radar system running through my—"

"Oh, Missanne," Maggie babbled nervously. "You've just got to hear about the new diet Marti's on. Annie Louise, why don't you deal?"

The old woman shrugged and became absorbed in shuffling the worn cards, her jewelry-laden hands and arms morphing into a wrinkled, flashy rhythm band.

"Oh, my, yes!" Marti gushed. "I swanee I feel one hundred percent better."

"You look the same," Missanne smirked. "Pregnant. Like a bloated goddamn frog."

This brought approval from Annie Louise, but Marti went on, oblivious to insult. "Oh, well, it takes time. I've only been on it for a week, but I really—"

"Never mind," Missanne snapped, lighting a cigarette.

"Here we are," Maggie said with forced enthusiasm as the cards were dealt. Her nerves were raw and she wiped her damp palms on her favorite bridge club skirt, the one with little hearts, diamonds, clubs and spades scattered across crisp white cotton.

"One diamond?" It came out as a question from Marti, watching Missanne across the table.

"Let's see—let's see—" Maggie began. "Oh, I'll—I'll—I believe

I'll pass. Missanne?"

"Pass."

Annie Louise chuckled. "Six hearts—and y'all better watch out. This is my best hand in thirty years."

Missanne began to rap her long red fingernails on the tabletop, staring at each woman in turn. The silence was too eerie, closing in. Maggie's cards stuck together in her perspiring hands.

"Missanne!" Marti finally demanded. "What in God's name is wrong? What are you doing?"

"Actin' like a damn fool," Annie Louise sniffed. "Probably about to have another one of her fool breakdowns. She's about due for one."

Missanne rolled her eyes. "Quite right, Miss Cameron. I *am* due for one. Only this time I might just save myself the trouble and blow my brains out like my fool mama did. How would you like that?"

"Seems to me you've tried that before and aimed at your gut by mistake. Never could get it done right. Now my Uncle Nathan—there's a man who knew what he was doing. Went plumb crazy, rantin' and ravin' and carryin' on. Let me tell you—Aunt Eva Belle had to hide the shotgun and lock him in the tool shed, but that sure didn't stop him. No, sir. He just grabbed himself an axe and commenced to choppin' away at his limbs. Aunt Eva Belle didn't even hear him holler. Just found him all hacked up. Bled to death." She cackled, delighted with her story. "Of course, some say Aunt Eva Belle got away with murder."

Marti was holding her stomach. "I feel sick."

"Shut up!" Missanne snapped. "Annie Louise is right. That takes some kind of guts." Then, with molasses-sweet sarcasm, "If all you ladies really want to know what's bothering me, I'll tell you. And it's such a little thing, too. I just know you'll be disappointed."

Were they all conspiring against her? Maggie wondered how far the plot would go. And why today? Anger and fear kept rolling back and forth through her, like the winter waves in the Gulf of Mexico "It's all right, Missanne," she said. "You don't have to tell if you don't want to. Why don't we—well, let's just all go home and things will be better at the next bridge club meeting. You'll all see."

"Good Lord, Maggie!" Marti put her cards down and reached

across the table for Missanne's hand. "Can't you see something's wrong? Come on, Missanne," she coaxed. "You know you can tell us. We're your friends."

"Okay," then an ironic, "Friends. It's just this: I'm pregnant." She chuckled. "So you see—the sky *is* falling." She began to laugh, harder, louder.

Marti gasped. Maggie felt her body going numb. "Had it comin'," Annie Louise smirked. "Let's get on with this game. Best hand I've had in a 'coon's age."

But Marti kept prodding. "Well, whose is it?"

The laughter stopped. It was eerie, Maggie thought, the way Missanne's moods were changing from moment to moment. She was usually in a continuous state of white-hot energy, and on those infrequent occasions when she was low, she might spend hour upon hour in bed, refusing to let Maggie open the drapes to the sun. "Mine," was the harsh answer.

"No—who's the father?"

"How the hell would I know?"

"My God!" Marti exclaimed. "What kind of a—How many men do you sleep with?"

"Oh, really, Marti, must we cast stones?" Missanne giggled. "I will tell you this, Marti, honey—I won't be a bit surprised if the little bastard's first language is Yiddish." The hysterical laughter came again. Maggie's cards slipped from her fingers and slapped to the table.

Marti stood up and Maggie thought she saw a flicker of a new expression, something genuine, a glimpse of a maelstrom beneath the perfect life. Maggie drew in her breath. "I don't have to listen to this. David would never—you just—" Marti stammered, tears beginning to show. "I'm sorry, Maggie. I'm sure it would have been absolutely wonderful," she sniffed. "But some people just don't know when to shut their—"

"Some people are so stupid they won't look at the truth when it's staring them in the face," Missanne broke in.

"To hell with you all!" Annie Louise's jewelry jangled furiously. "This was my best hand in Lord knows when and y'all have to carp, carp, carp about who's playing with whose husband. That's old hat to me. I've been living here for most of my life and I've seen it all. I've seen deacons at the church lying with the trash that works the peaches. And you come along with your trashy self and make up some lie about this woman's husband. You're full of lies and meanness and trash. Maggie's welcome to you. Hell, she doesn't have the nerve to call your lies." She took Marti's arm. "Come on, honey. I'll walk you home." Stones and silver and pieces of gold flashed as Annie Louise muttered their way out the front door, an angry cloud of smoke trailing behind. "Carp, carp, carp. Can't even come up with something new. Same old song and dance."

The slamming door startled Maggie into the realization that she was left alone to cope with Missanne and the wreckage of the bridge club. How could they do this to her? All of them. Why had the words changed when the script had been so routinely rehearsed?

Missanne laughed. "That gullible idiot will believe anything."

"Then you didn't—"

"Hell, no! Look. I just wanted to get rid of them. Besides, I may be immoral, but I do draw the line at my own friends' husbands—even when those husbands come after me. Well, most of the time."

"Then you're not—"

"Pregnant? Come on, Maggie. I'm a big girl. I know all about birth control. Unlike Marti the multiplication table."

"Then why?"

"For you, my dear. My friend. For you. The sky is falling and I have come to give warning. Perhaps save you in the process."

Maggie sighed, puzzled by Missanne's cryptic words. "Bridge club will never be the same. And it's been so—such a relief. So important," she fumbled.

Missanne raised one eyebrow meaningfully. "Too important." There was a long pause, then, "Got any whiskey?"

"Oh, Missanne, do you think you should? I mean, you're upset and all."

"Get the whiskey." It wasn't a command—more of a tired insistence. "We'll sit on the sofa, preferably drunk, and talk. You know, we've never really talked. Not *really*."

Hadn't they? Maggie was startled, then remembered the line

and all the other lines that bordered her life—the one she could not cross with Dunbar and the line of a pane of glass between her kitchen and the world. For a second Maggie wanted everything—B.S.B.C. and all—to go away. She wasn't sure where. All there was to find was Dunbar, and he was no longer enough. She felt the familiar boundaries locking into place, felt herself going into the kitchen, all obedience. She saw herself reaching for the bottle while a tiny voice somewhere in her head reminded her that Dunbar would be especially angry if they drank all of his good whiskey. She managed to dismiss the rote sound, but tried to remain wary of her willingness to be led.

"So," Missanne began. "What do you think? Do you think I'm a nut?"

Maggie was shocked by the blunt question, recovered, and, with her breath high and tight in her chest, "How could I say?" She took a drink and the liquid warmth soothed her. "I mean—I'm no expert. And like you said," she hesitated, then, "we've never really talked." Her breakfast conversation with Dunbar rushed back at her, a dizzying pull of sand and bits of shell at her feet, water rushing in two directions at once.

Missanne held up her glass in a mock toast. "So I'll tell you what the experts say. Actually, I believe they're full of shit, but I'll tell you anyway."

"Look, Missanne, you don't have to—"

"First there was that quack in Albany. Said I was a nymphomaniac—but that was fifteen years ago, so I guess I'll forgive him his stupidity. And when my second husband committed me to Milledgeville they said I was schizo—utterly gone. Then they turned around and said: 'Uh-oh—we goofed—you're only—'" Missanne took on a posture of reading from a book, "'manic-depressive with suicidal ideation.' Bunch of bullshit, right?" She didn't wait for an answer but went on in the same bored tone of voice. "Another guy—I think it was the one in Macon—said I was just faking the whole act. You get the idea. For every doctor, I've had a new disease. And that's too many times to count. All because I like to drink and screw and attempt suicide every now and then. Don't you like those things?"

Maggie laughed, surprised at her ability to take it all so lightly, the way Missanne did. The tension ebbed for a moment. "Don't know about—" The word hung in her throat for a second. Foul language was not a part of her order, yet it wanted presence. "—Screwing." There it was. "Don't know about screwing, but I'm beginning to enjoy the whiskey more than I thought I would. Dunbar doesn't let me drink very often."

"Let you? Mother Mary, he's an ass," Missanne said between gulps. "I've been married three times and had any number of lovers, but never an ass like Dunbar. A lot of them have come pretty close, but your husband is—well, I know him, believe me. I knew him before he ever said a word to me."

"When has he ever talked with you?" Dunbar did not socialize, Maggie knew. "How could you know so much about him?"

Missanne brushed her lips along the edge of the glass. "Let's just say I'm perceptive. I can read men. It's easy, really. Tell me, Maggie—do you do everything your precious Dunbar tells you to? Is he your misguided shrink? Now don't make a face at me, Maggie Boone. I hated him on sight and it was mutual, and you know it."

"Of course I know it." Maggie smiled. "Dunbar isn't very likeable, I know. People just—don't like him. When we first met I thought he was so—well, charming. He wasn't so huge and overpowering then—and he was considerate of me. Really." Maggie stopped, thinking of the elation she had felt—the ugly girl—"pit face" was the unimaginative nickname that stuck—being swept off her feet by a tall man with dimples and sincerity oozing from a smile full of white teeth. The flattery she had experienced from the attention of any man had barricaded her foresight. But on this particular bridge club day she was beginning to see how the Dunbar who sat with her in the blue kitchen contrasted with the fantasy she had created through the spotless windowpane, how deliberate his choosing her had been.

"Don't underestimate me," Missanne was saying. "I've been with plenty of strange people. After all, I lived in Atlanta for a few years," she said with mock sophistication. "Anyway, I just don't understand. You're nice looking, and there just may be a personality somewhere underneath all that timidity. Why the hell do you stay with him?"

They giggled at the absurdity of it. "That's a good question." Maggie was feeling light-headed. Nice . . . she poured them another glass. "I guess I'm just—I just don't have the—"

"Right," Missanne interrupted harshly. "You don't have the guts to do anything about it. You really should grow up and get on with it."

Maggie tingled with the betrayal. That wasn't the kind of thing a friend said. Was it? But Missanne didn't stop. "Don't give me that martyr look—that's for Dunbar, remember? Jesus! You have to be the most complete coward I've ever known. All the way Sometimes I wonder if you even exist."

How like Dunbar's accusations. It had started with minor criticisms, taken to heart by Maggie's determination to please, her conviction that it was her responsibility to conform and shape herself to Dunbar's wishes. But criticisms gave way to belittlement, then harassment, and finally the hidden bruises that completed her reduction all the way down to nothing. Nothing. Missanne was right. She allowed herself to be formed by him—sometimes the benevolent dictator, other times the punitive monarch. It had been such a gradual change that what little control she had in the beginning was usurped before she caught on to his distorted idea of marriage. By that time she had been swallowed whole by the self-imposed solitary confinement within the blue kitchen and the purple jelly that glistened in the crease of Dunbar's chin.

"Really, Missanne, we're fine," she whispered, on automatic.

"No. You're not. You're not fine at all, and no amount of Windex slathered on your windows can make your twisted little life look cleaner."

Maggie felt her body jerking, sticky wetness around her nose and cheeks, then realized that she had not cried in years. It made her chest ache, like it did every time she bartered sex with Dunbar and threw up afterwards. Missanne pulled her friend next to her. "It's going to be all right. You do have it in you to change things. You'll see," she said gently, after a time lifting her chin, soft palms against her face, down her neck, fingertips dancing across her collarbones. She put a red fingernail to Maggie's lips, tracing a soft outline, over, again, then placed her own lips on the flesh she had touched. When Maggie questioned with her glance, Missanne whispered, "Trust me. I understand you." And she put her lips to Maggie's neck, the red nails disappearing beneath the hearts and spades on her bridge club skirt, hands turning, slick polish smooth against her thighs, leaving her will to fresh secrets.

They sat for a long time afterwards, Maggie wrapped against Missanne like a child, sobbing, occasionally breathing out fragments of her life with Dunbar. The perverted, painful, sickening things she did to maintain the sacred veneer. The lack of a backbone that held her down while he consumed her, sometimes even using her own father's childhood nickname for her, "Maggie the Toad." The words would send her heart reeling back in time, to those furtive moments with her father, those dusky, shame-shadowed moments she hid from her mother, who would never give a glance anyway.

Maggie's head rested in the curve of Missanne's neck and shoulder. It was warm. Nice smells, the feel of combed cotton against her cheek as her friend made soothing, strengthening sounds. Maggie began to perceive some new resolve radiating into her, up through Missanne's soft orange shirt, something long dormant, perhaps always dormant, though now it could never be still even if she wanted it to be. It rose on steady legs, stood with feet apart, reached down and cupped her chin.

Missanne spoke as she stroked Maggie's hair. "My daddy named me 'Missanne.' Mama wanted the name 'Anne.' Just Anne. But he insisted on putting the 'Miss' in front of it and Mama always minded him. It kept a kind of phony formality between us, like I was an acquaintance instead of a daughter. Very calculated. From the time I was born—hell, before I was born—that man had me pegged as his mistress. Now he's dying of cirrhosis and he wants a daughter. And I'll be goddamned if I will be one."

Maggie sat up and stared into the vibrant eyes. "I really can't do this anymore," she whispered. "I do know that. I just don't know how to do anything else."

"Oh, shit, Maggie!" Missanne pushed her away, clutching her shoulders, looked at her with such empathy and enthusiasm that the exhilaration rushed up and down the length of Maggie's body. "Do you know I can help? Do you realize?" Missanne demanded. "Do you?"

"Yes!" And they began to giggle again, first like two little girls with a secret, then the loud, purposeful laughter of comrades, as they clicked glasses of Dunbar's whiskey together.

"To my freedom!" Maggie yelled.

"To your freedom!" Then, in an almost inaudible tone, "Hey, when's Dunbar coming home? Maybe I'd better run." She began fumbling through her purse.

"You don't have to go. I'm free, remember?"

Missanne stood up. "Free, yes. But only by your own proclamation. It's not much good unless the Boss-Man knows it, right?" Missanne's pampered, freshly manicured hand withdrew from the purse and Maggie was startled by the sight of a small gun, a silver accessory to go with the sterling on the table. The hand disappeared again, coming out with a clip, and Maggie's bewilderment faded as she watched her new ally click it in as though she had done it after every bridge club of her pretty life.

"Don't worry," Missanne said, placing the weapon on the coffee table next to Dunbar's almost-empty bottle. "It won't bite. It's quite a friend to have, really. I just want you to keep it for—well, however long you think is best."Missanne bent to kiss her forehead.

"But Missanne, I've never—"

"Just keep it a while. Trust me. I know Dunbar. Whatever you do will have to be final." The beautiful eyes reassured as she lowered herself to the sofa. "Hell, trust yourself. You know the bastard." And she leaned her lips into Maggie's once again, this time sending the lines crashing in upon themselves, the two of them relaxing into the soft cushions of the living room couch. The refrigerator cut on, and the steady hum surrounded Maggie; she felt herself letting go of hesitation's remnants, feeling, hearing, being only in this one moment. The shadows lengthened unnaturally fast in the face of perfection, and they carried that perfection into the dimness of the late afternoon.

"Jesus fucking Christ!" Dunbar's voice burst across the dusky room, as the two women jerked up from the cushions, Maggie rigid with terror, Missanne giggling lightly. "Jesus mother-fucking Christ!" He crossed the floor in what seemed to be one movement, grabbing Maggie's forearm to pull her up into his fat face. "What the fuck are you doing? Are you crazy?" The eyes, more intense than she had ever seen them, pushed into her spirit once again. She could sense Missanne moving slowly to her left.

"Dunbar, I—I drank too much I think. I don't know—"

With one hard pull, he sent her pirouetting crazily onto the table opposite her, crashing across china bearing uneaten cheese-cake, sterling fork tines raking at her arms. But there was no pain. Oddly, Maggie only felt herself sitting at the edge of a gentle bay, clear salt water hypnotically lapping at her toes. She had to see him, though, to determine where the lines lay now, between dictator and insurgent, master and slave, consumer and consumed. When she stood and looked into his eyes again, they were like the soulless eyes of a dead shark, and an image of a giant gray fish hanging by its tail at the marina in Panama City careened at her. She was certain now.

"'I was drunk, I was drunk,'" he mocked. "Well you don't get to use that old excuse for wallowing around with a goddamned lesbo-whore in our own goddamned house. Are you crazy or just plain stupid?" He raised his arm in a backhand, sending her father's shadow up the wall and across the ceiling, coming down across her jaw; she felt herself hit the polished wood floor just as the blast of the gun sent a shock to her ears, glass and cheesecake spraying against the disinfected walls.

Dunbar turned to face Missanne, who purposefully and calmly leveled the gun at him. "I'm kind of drunk," she said, "but you are one big-assed target."

"You goddamned whore." Dunbar moved toward her, hesitation showing in his eyes, fixed on the small gun.

"Sit, Dunbar," Missanne said, and he withdrew. "Maggie, get up."

Dunbar eased himself into the chair opposite the sofa as Maggie pulled herself up by clutching the edge of her once perfectly set table. Missanne sat casually on the sofa, legs crossed, foot swinging, hands perched on her pretty knee and curled about the gun that promised its cargo to Dunbar. "You know, a whole hell of a lot happened at Maggie's bridge party today," Missanne said. "We figure you're just dying to hear all about it, so settle back. You are not going to believe the day we have had."

Dunbar winced, shrank back next to the right arm of the chair, and Maggie gazed at him, all the while straightening her table by second nature. She lined up forks, dabbed at cheesecake splashes on linen, re-folded mangled napkins, all the while staring at the pathetic form that would not meet her eyes. She imagined his sex shrinking as from a cold splash to the crotch. She visualized a daddy long-legs dropped into a sizzling skillet. Her chance at freedom burned hot, like the sun's light caught in a child's magnifying glass and dead-aimed at an ant, finding its mark on a faint patch of sticky purple on Dunbar's chin. She smiled, hoping that was where Missanne would aim when she fired.

Jesus, Sex and Sweet Tea

I. That Funky, Monkey Pentecostal Love Thing

Ain't nothing like it—I mean nothing. You get that preachment a-cascading down from the pulpit, just a-throbbing with the pulse of the Holy Ghost. You throw in a tambourine to beat out the rhythm of the preacher's anointed breaths while his voice rises, falls, rises, gets down in your soul and warms you with the sweet sweat of salvation, and when he goes to hollering and driving that rhythm right into your very spirit—well, any woman that says it don't make her moist in the panties is a damn lie.

I was twelve years old when I first accepted the Lord Jesus Christ as my personal Savior. It was at the New Hope Pentecostal Church of the Divine Advent, and old greasy-headed, borrowed-from-the-back-haired Brother Vastine Dupree, the regular preacher, had invited this guest preacher to give a talk who was some kind of fine. He was real young and sort of looked like Herman out of Herman's Hermits, and his name was Brother Rex.

Like I said, I was twelve, and I hadn't never thought serious about getting saved, but Brother Rex had that crooked-toothed smile—the spit of Herman—and it was like he was looking right square at me, smiling—at me in particular. It made me all tingly in the stomach, you know? My friend Reba-Jean was sitting next to me and she kept poking me in the arm with her elbow, a-whisper-ing stuff like "He's hot for you" and "He wants your body," but I couldn't hardly notice her. All I could do was stare at Brother Rex's Herman-blue eyes and wait for the times his eyes would see mine, and that tingle in my stomach got bigger and bigger 'til I thought if that altar call didn't come on, I was gonna bust. Just the idea of his hands on my forehead, purifying the sin I was born in, had me all beside myself. I hadn't never felt thataway, that kind of craving—I was only twelve, remember—and it was all wrapped up in that tingly feeling that had done by now took over my whole entire body.

Well, when I finally went up before God, the congregation, and Reba-Jean to accept Jesus Christ, Brother Rex gave me that Herman-like grin, looked deep down in my eyes, and put his hands on the willing flesh of my forehead while he prayed over me. I like to died, and finally my knees went all weak and I fell out in the floor kind of like Miss Clariselle does when she gets the Holy Ghost only without all the twitching and moaning.

When it was over I had such a feeling of spiritual bliss all mixed in with some kind of carnal ache that it left me with the most satisfied and most uncomplete feeling I'd ever knew. That evening, a-laying in my bed, listening to "Mrs. Brown, You've Got a Lovely Daughter," I—well, I guess you could say that was when I begun to backslide into several years of lust and depravity.

By the time I was fifteen, I had done give the flower of my purity to three different boys: Johnny Lee Dupree, the preacher's boy who picked his ear wax and who I went with from twelve to thirteen; Reba-Jean's stupid brother Claude Parker, my boyfriend from thirteen to fourteen; and Gordon Pugh, the one that drove me back to the Lord with his two-timing, whore-hopping, blue-ball-bellyaching self.

I knew I was wrong to be carrying on thataway, but once you step down the path of sexual sin it's mighty hard to get back right with the Lord. I done it, though. I stood before the congregation on my fifteenth birthday and confessed my sins to Miss Clariselle, who fell out in the floor, and Brother Vastine, who always wants you to tell everything, and the whole, entire congregation, right on up to God. I seen real clear right then that no matter how dark a stain my sins would ever get to be, the Blood of Jesus could wash me clean.

My mama was so proud she cried, and I taught vacation Bible

school that summer. But by the fall my feet was sticking out the side window of Gordon Pugh's pickup—again—only this time the Lord saw fit to bless us with a young'un, a shotgun wedding, and a used mobile home. A-course I had to get back right with God—again.

Three young'uns later, I was ass deep in the Holy Ghost, but without no more sizzling hot sin. It's a awful thing but it's bound to happen, and it had done happened to me. I had begun to wither on the vine. And once that thing starts to drawing up on you it's near impossible to get it juiced up without a whole lot of effort—and Gordon Pugh got to where he was taking less and less time on account of he'd go to drawing up, too. So he'd go to jabbing at me for fear of losing what he had, which didn't do much for me. I'd go to hollering 'cause the thing felt chapped like all my innards was going in the wrong direction, which would make him cuss and stomp off to the bathroom and—you know. Our sex life ain't been much ever since.

A married couple has to weather the storm, like Brother Vastine used to say. So even with his sorry ways and half-assed lovemaking I decided Gordon Pugh was my man and I made a promise to Jesus to hold onto him no matter what it took. Won't nothing or nobody ever come in the way of that.

As it stands now, thirty years, a total of five babies, and forty-two pounds later, I have done come into my own as a woman of the New Hope Pentecostal Church of the Divine Advent. Gordon Pugh is still a son of a bitch at times, and he will get drunk every now and again, but he ain't going nowhere in that pickup of his. I done laid down the law and I'll kill any bitch that messes with my man.

See, he give up his two-timing ways five years ago when I caught him red-handed with this slut Cecilia in the back seat of a Honda Civic. It was in front of God and everybody in the parking lot of a beer joint on the causeway. So I rammed her rear bumper with the Mustang Gordon give me for our anniversary, I shot out all her tires with the pistol I keep in my purse, and I would of shot her bony white ass, too, but the cops come and throwed me up under the jail.

Later on, when I told Gordon Pugh I'd leave his sorry ass and take all his money if he was to cheat on me again, he went and got saved. Just like that. Born again. He put a bumper sticker on his pickup and goes to church with me most every Sunday. Every great long once in a while, when he's behaving hisself of a evening, I give him some, best as I can, but aside from that I mostly do church work. A-course, you'll find me at every single service, prayer meeting, homecoming, and revival. I hope maybe Gordon'll even make a Sunday school teacher so we can be a real Christian couple.

I admit I get a suspicion about Gordon sometimes. Like today. He called to say he can't come home for lunch. Doing a job for somebody on Georgia Street. Well, he ain't one to get no jobs in that snootified neighborhood. Them rich people hire your big-name contractors. And on top, that man don't never give up his lunchtime groceries for nothing. Plus, he says ain't no tea as sweet as the tea I got. So I'm thinking about driving down to Georgia Street—just to see for myself. If his pickup ain't there I'll know he's back to his two-timing ways. If his truck is there, I'll tote him some Kentucky Fried and a Thermos full of tea, iced.

Some things just don't change. Like a low-down man. Like a woman's desires. Like that funky, monkey, Pentecostal love thing. I just can't get enough of it. I take my spiritual hungerings to those services and soothe my vine-withered needs in the blessed anointment of the Holy Ghost. I reckon it's true about your first time—you just can't leave it go and you're forever going back for more.

Even when I fall from grace, I know Jesus is one man who will take me back. And even after all these years, I still get moist in the drawers.

II. Episcopalian Sex

My church bridge club, along with the Ladies' Circle, will undoubtedly be appalled when they learn of my plans, but I am at a veritable crossroads. Besides, I *was* originally brought up in the Catholic Church, and my deep affection for the Pope is thoroughly ingrained and sincere. I only joined the Episcopal Church during my engagement to my husband, as his family had been influential members for eons. Nonetheless, I worked like a Trojan in the

Episcopal Church throughout our marriage, tirelessly, uncomplaining, just as my mother would have done, Christian martyr and *grande dame* that she was. So if I do not have a catastrophic nervous breakdown over this it will be a miracle, and none of it would have happened if not for that perfectly hideous bumper sticker.

You see, I arose at 6:00 a.m., as usual. My colored woman, Mattie, came in at 6:30 to start breakfast and to complain, yet again, that the screen door was just about off its hinges and was bound to fall off soon and knock her half silly. As usual, I let her histrionics roll off my back and by 6:45 I was, as usual, having my Café Vienna and my daily devotional out on the patio, absolutely swathed in that luscious scent of sweet olive and camellias in the garden. Psalms! Such poetry! Such a mighty preponderance of beauty in which to bathe the spirit.

I carried this devotion in my heart throughout the morning as I tended my prize roses, vigilant in my wide-brimmed hat where the sun is concerned, as we Bondurants have fair skin that absolutely roasts in the morning hours. Anyway, the Psalms kept my spirit impeccably serene right up until the very instant I laid my eyes on that dreadful, hideously tasteless bumper sticker on my way to the Piggly Wiggly.

Before I go any further, I must make it abundantly clear that I find certain topics truly offensive. I was just brought up that way. One's income, for example, is not a topic fit for polite conversation, as it is extremely personal in nature. One does not make a show, unless one is tragically nouveau, of one's wealth, nor does one reveal what lever one has pulled in the voting booth or proclaim one's party affiliation on the chrome of one's automobile. And one certainly never, ever, in this world, publicly advertises one's religious faith in any way, shape, or form. One simply goes, without fail, to Sunday school and church (always stylishly yet tastefully clothed), tithes the appropriate percentage of one's income, and belongs to the socially correct Ladies' Circle. Those poor, pathetic, bicycle-riding Jehovah's Witnesses and Mormons and other such creatures who roam the streets witnessing to their faith reach boundless heights of rude behavior that is the undoing of proper society. And to plaster one's vehicle with words praising the Lord or with those tacky little chrome fishes is beyond the peripheral limit taste allows. So when I saw the bumper sticker on the truck in front of me I was beyond appalled.

I was on my way, as I said, to the Piggly Wiggly for sweet milk and Fancy Feast for Mr. Monsieur, my blue-ribbon tabby, when I saw the words in front of me, adhered to the bumper of one of those abominable eyesores of a pickup, all covered in lumber, a ladder, and heaven knows what all else. I noticed it at an interminably long red light. "Got Jesus?" That was it. "Got Jesus?" My serenity dissolved and I was livid.

You can imagine the extent of my chagrin when this pick-up-driving cretin turned into the Piggly Wiggly parking lot and, as if manipulated by the hand of God, into the parking space right beside my own powder-blue Lincoln Town Car. Yet it was that precise millisecond when a powerful urge swept over my very spirit, a resolve to confront him regarding such unforgivably poor taste. Momentarily I found myself full of searing, passionate outrage and face to face with a rather scruffy, middle-aged, self-described carpenter's helper. The irony was certainly not lost on me.

I must pause here to explain that my beloved husband of twenty years, Wickham, passed away a full year ago, and I have not been touched by another man in my entire life as I was chaste at our candlelight wedding service. I do, however, acknowledge the urges one has from time to time, and part of my morning devotional is always a prayer to hold true to the Holy Spirit. So you can imagine how mortified I was to find my eyes on this—*person's*—nude chest and shoulders. The heat had apparently rendered him shirtless, and trickles of perspiration were literally racing down his body, patched with sawdust here and there, the dark hair of his chest all moist and curled, sweat coursing down to his unbelted jeans.

Years of manual labor had been kind to this man's body, and the muscles in his chest and arms were solid and practically shimmering like morning dew in the sun's first light. Poor Wickham was a sedentary banker and became quite rotund over the years. Why, I sometimes had full-blown panic attacks, lying there beneath dear Wickham, who, gentleman that he was, always did the honorable thing and graciously rolled off so that I could collect myself. This perspiring man, however, struck me as one who would never, ever, roll off—would, in fact, push harder, finding depths of pleasure, untapped reservoirs of glorious exhilaration, driving, driving—well, let us simply say that my spiritual center had shifted.

I was breathless, all hot in the face, but I managed to explain that I needed some work done and thought it fortuitous that I would find my vehicle beside that of a carpenter's helper in the parking lot of the Piggly Wiggly. He was my *savior*, I told him, and I would be devastated, absolutely prostrate, if he did not come to my home immediately, this instant, to look at a door that was bound to knock my maid silly. And heaven knows my very life would be in dire peril without my maid.

He seemed quite understanding for a working man and was most agreeable about doing this job for me with all due speed. I confess I forgot all about Mr. Monsieur's Fancy Feast cat food. I confess I went straight home, gave Mattie the remainder of the day off, and soaked in a hot tub full of English Lavender bubbles and Estée Lauder bath beads. I confess that, as I drowsed in the heated jets and the candlelit glow of the master bath, sipping sweet tea and counting my blessings, I could not help visualizing certain sensual renderings upon the canvas of that laborer's physique.

I am an Episcopalian, as you know, and the Episcopalian union and intimacy I had with Wickham was blessed by God. I do confess that I find my faith leaning more in the direction of Catholicism at this stage of my life. Actually, I believe I could be a most devout, upstanding member of the appropriate Catholic Church—one in a nice neighborhood where my late mother's garnet and pearl rosary would be appreciated.

I do confess.

III. The Sweet, Sweet Love of Jesus

I done had the love of a good man. A man of God. Can't nobody give a woman the kind of loving a preacher man can, and can't nobody take my man's place. That's why I don't be studying getting me no man now. What I'm going to do with a man? Old as I am? Shoot. But I can do one thing. I can tell when a man's done caught the scent. I can tell when can't nobody else. Once you done had a preacher man you can see them kinds of things in folks.

I met Pastor Henry Johnson, Jr., back in 1942 when I was seventeen and he was thirty-three. I was visiting my cousin Eula near Warm Springs, Georgia, and she took me to her church. The Mount of Olives Free Will Baptist Church. Child, it was packed like sardines full of soldiers from over to Fort Benning, and I ain't going to lie. After the service we had dinner on the ground—fried chicken, greens, and gallons of sweet, sweet tea with lemon. Them boys was looking fine in their uniforms, cutting the fool and trying to get us girls to go to the clubs over by Phenix City. But they was boys, and Pastor Johnson was a man. He was a man with a gift of The Word *and* a pretty face. I'd be grouped in amongst them soldiers but all the time giving a look, sideways like, at Pastor Johnson, and I'm here to tell you I opened up that man's nose. Then here I go home to Acree, down in Southwest Georgia.

Two weeks and three days later that man—the Most Right Reverend Henry Thomas Johnson, Jr.—took a bus from Columbus to Albany, Georgia, got drove by a friend to a crossroads, and walked—I mean to tell you he *walked*—twelve miles out to where we cropped, nose wide open the whole way. I spent the next eighteen years with him as his wife and helpmate, and he kept me satisfied the way a real man can. So I'm here to tell you I know when a man's done caught the scent and I can take one look at a woman and know has she done been satisfied.

The Lord didn't bless us with no children, but Henry and me had the church and our mission work and the civil rights over the years, so we praised Him. And I still praise Him for the eighteen years I had with my man. Then he was gone, and when Henry went to Glory back in 1960 I had to make me a decision. Oh, I prayed about it and prayed about it because I ain't too crazy about no white folks. But my daddy was a sharecropper and my mama took in laundry, so I know hard work ain't a shameful thing at all. Living off the government is the shame, and Henry Johnson, Jr., would turn over five times in his grave if I was to do that. So I took me a big old deep breath, went to live with my cousin Brenda in Mobile, and went to work for some high-class white folks.

Now, it's a fact that white folks ain't right in the head, but the family I ended up with for the next forty years was crazier even than most. I spent me a lot of time talking to the Lord behind them people—still do. When you get around folks that ain't got no sense about how the Lord means for his children to live, all the time worrying over what kind of show they're putting on and thinking up ways to spend up a bunch of money, well—it could make your heart harden up with bitterness and eat your soul up like a cancer. So I just think about what my man said when we done met our trials over the years. Henry said forget everything—even everything wrote down in the Bible—everything except what comes out of Jesus' mouth and that bitterness ain't going to happen. And it's the Gospel truth because I done tested it and tested it.

Miss Lucille was a club woman—bridge club, Garden Club, Art Club, Literary Club, Mardi Gras Society, you name it—and she had more silver for me to polish and more gatherings in a year than Henry and me went to all the time we was married. If things didn't go full tilt her way, she'd go to throwing china and screaming that she's a *grande dame* just like her mama and ought to be treated like one. Then she'd take to the bed for days on end and I'd have to go to toting her meals up to her. She'd say I was the only one who understood her because I was from the old school. I'd just smile and say yes ma'am and go to thinking she's nothing but a crazy old Scarlett O'Hara big-eye bitch. It beat the band what all went on in that house.

Her husband was rich for a living so he stayed half-drunk most of the time. Then she'd get a bate of it and go to dog-cussing him, accuse him of having girlfriends up to his hunting camp in Lowndes County. Next thing you know he'd buy her some jewelry and things would settle down again. Every few years she'd have herself a breakdown and go away for a month or two to rest and I'd tend her baby. A girl child named Precious. I reckon I tended that child over the years ten times what her mama done. I told you the Lord didn't see fit to bless Henry and me with no children, so I took me some time and care with Miss Precious. I tried to teach her how to live right and love the Lord behind all the Catholic voodoo her mama was giving her. I tried to show her how to be blessed with a happy heart.

But the apple don't fall far from the tree because Miss Precious was every bit as crazy and ill-tempered as her mama. She grew up to be queen of the Mardi Gras, found a rich man to marry, and you would've thought the Queen of England herself was getting married for all the carrying on her mama did. Throwed the biggest candlelight wedding this town done ever seen, with more dressed up white folks and black folks in aprons than you could shake a stick at. And do you know what that crazy woman give her daughter for a wedding present? Me.

I know you're thinking: Slave times is over. That's what my cousin Brenda said. All I could say was, I need to have a talk with the Lord. So I went to services and clapped my hands and stomped my feet and called out to Glory and swayed and sang and gave my meanness to Jesus. Then I went to work for Miss Precious. I watched her get older and eat up with clubs and boss that prissy husband of hers right smack into his grave. And I can tell you this: that woman ain't only crazy; she ain't never been satisfied by no man to boot.

Brenda says white folks is poison and maybe she's right. But as long as I got the Lord, my memories of Henry Johnson, Jr., and a place to go to three times a week for satisfaction of the spirit, then that poison ain't going to do me in. I can look them in the eye when they go to gushing about how I'm one of the family and keep a straight face. I can laugh on the inside when they're saying something about niggah this or niggah that and then get all hushed up when I come up in the room. I can watch Miss Precious bring them rich club women that call theirself Christian into her dead husband's house and know their faith in God is just an excuse to have a club meeting. If I'm right with Jesus, I can just shake my head and say ain't it a shame. But you know what the biggest shame is? Ain't none of them satisfied in the bedroom, that's what.

I told you I know when a man's done took the scent. Well, when I was leaving out of Miss Precious' house today here comes a man in a pickup. Says he's Gordon Pugh, come to do some carpentry work for her. I could see right then his nose had done been opened up, and Miss Precious upstairs in that jacuzzi whirlpool tub, with them candles lit and nekkid as a jaybird, just a-waitin'. I asked him did he love the Lord and he said, Yes ma'am.

I walked down towards the bus stop on Government Street and stopped to visit with Cletus Mitchell while he worked on the

Beauchamps' flowerbeds. He's old and bent over from working in the white folks' yards, but he does cut the fool for me. He says, "Let me give you just a little sweet stuff, Miss Mattie."

I'm laughing because, like I say, I ain't studying no man. He says, "The Ladies call me 'Sweet-Sweet' 'cause I got me some sweet, sweet love."

I say, "Go on, niggah, you crazy." And we laughed and carried on like that for a spell.

In a while, Cletus and me went round to the kitchen to get a glass of sweet tea from my girlfriend Lois. She works for the Beauchamps and we take the bus together every day from out by where we stay. I told her I ain't going to be at the stop this evening that I had done got the day off. We laughed for a while about how much money them crazy white folks throw out on their jacuzzi whirlpool tubs and their parties, and about how Miss Precious sure does need satisfying, then I walked on down to the corner stop.

'Bout that time here comes some fool white woman whipping round the corner in a dented-up Mustang convertible riding a box of Kentucky Fried on the dash. She's got the radio full blast and she liked to hit the curb and me, so I waved. She hollered, "Jesus loves you!"

And I hollered, "Amen!" And that big old city bus opened up its doors to tote me back to Brenda and them.

The Reverend Johnson could make me scream with his lovin' and the Good Lord can make me scream with jubilation. I know I'm satisfied. Maybe Miss Precious will be, too. One thing for real sure: All I got to do is take one good look at her in the morning and I'll be knowing the answer.

The Seamstress

"Well, all I can say about that," Mrs. Clark Hogan Wilson pronounced, with the bearing of a robed, gaveled judge, and even more of the authority, "is that Sarah Jo Cooper never had any inkling about how to keep herself a cut above the riff-raff."

Mrs. Wilson, "Francie" to her most bosom of friends, lifted a dimpled little hand to brush a puff of parlor-dyed curls back from her forehead, revealing grooved wrinkles born of brow-knitting and, on a typical day, glaring as she sulked. Today, however, she was not sulking, riding instead the crest of an exhilarating wave of self-importance while she engaged in the gossip that nourished her. She stood on a four-by-four raised platform, feeling that much higher than her handmaidens, while a seamstress altered the ball gown she was to wear a week from Friday.

She had just been regaled with the tale of Sarah Jo Cooper, who had left her husband of thirty-two years to ride off into the sunset with a drywall hanger who was renovating the antebellum home said husband had bought for her only a month prior. "Once trash, always trash," Mrs. Wilson said. "I believe I pointed that out to you at Mitzi Stanton's last dinner party if you'll recall. Do you recall that? Do you?"

"I most certainly do," her most recent best friend Camilla, Mrs. James Cunningham Dixon, replied, as the seamstress worked at pinning Mrs. Wilson's hem.

The seamstress, Celeste, had observed this cannibalistic

friendship over the previous weeks of fittings and alterations as she constructed Mrs. Wilson's Mardi Gras gown. She had noted that Mrs. Dixon was tenacious about doing her duty as a hanger-on, bearing platters of giddy gossip for her mentor to consume. Gifted with an encyclopedic knowledge of maiden names and double first cousins, Mrs. Dixon could sniff out vague ancestral connections to any scandal and find genealogical secrets that would horrify the sensibility of a St. Louis streetwalker. She had even prodded Celeste, a deliberately private soul, for personal information, for a family history from which to gain a point of reference. She had been delighted when she discovered that Celeste had grown up with her own maternal third cousin, Martha Sams, in Brannon, Mississippi, south and west of Columbus, immediately seeing that cousin Martha could offer the lowdown on Celeste.

In addition to her role as Troubador of Troubles, Purveyor of Peccadilloes, Mrs. Dixon also undertook her task of Flatterer-in-Chief to Mrs. Wilson with an effusive fervor. "You are an excellent judge of character, Francie. It's pure power of perception. You simply *know* people through and through, and I do recall that you pointed that out to me about Sarah Jo Cooper. Saw right clear through her. I swear, you don't miss a beat," she gushed.

Mrs. Wilson picked a piece of lint from the velvet skirt of her gown and flicked it into the air. It dipped and danced like dwarfed confetti. "Of course you also recall that it was at Mitzi's tacky little dinner party," she said. "Do you recall that embarrassing nightmare of a party?"

"Absolutely do," Mrs. Dixon said. "It was right there at that selfsame party that you pointed out to me about Sarah Jo's flawed character. You pointed out to me how cozy she was with the help. How she had her head leaned in to that college boy bartender who—"

"The one in the tiki hut," Mrs. Wilson said. "Do you recall that tacky little tiki hut Mitzi had set up by the pool as an island bar?"

"Well of course. How could I not? It was the one with the young college boy bartending in it. A medical student, I think."

"It was a Hawaiian luau theme you see, Celeste. A luau is a Hawaiian feast, did you know?" Mrs. Wilson spoke down to the woman at her feet. "All of our parties—well, the very best ones, anyway—they all have a theme. You know, the creation of a tableau, a setting, a dramatic flair."

"My, how elegant." Celeste, the seamstress, pulled another straight pin from her wrist cushion, working with the gold net material bunched at Mrs. Wilson's waist, draped down around the rich, deep purple velvet gown, the tips of her nimble fingers aware of little sausage-like rolls of fatty flesh beneath the clingy fabric. "Now, Mrs. Wilson, it's important that you bring those shoes you plan to wear with this when you come for your next fitting. This netting is very tricky to hem and—"

"Yes-yes-yes," Mrs. Wilson said in her hurried, impatient voice. "But as I was saying just now, the theme is what makes the party, if you have the flair to make it work. Believe you me, there is nothing more pitiful than a flopped theme."

"Well you wouldn't know about that, Francie," Mrs. Dixon said, rummaging through an oversized handbag. "I'm telling you, Celeste, there is nothing like one of Francie's parties. They are the best, bar none. You should get to see one before you die, my hand to God. Do you want a Life Saver?" she held out the roll of candy, its foil wrapper peeled and hanging like tossed serpentine.

"No, thank you," Celeste said. The gold netting was stiff and unwieldy next to the supple purple velvet. "Would you lift your arm, please?"

Mrs. Wilson complied, sending the sprung flesh on the underside of her arm into a series of jiggles. "Like last August. I had an all-black party last August. Not black *people*, you know, but a black décor, like a wake or a funeral, for Hogie's fiftieth birthday party. And he's way older than me, so don't you even think it. Do you recall that party, Camilla?"

"It was only the be-all end-all of birthday parties," Camilla gushed. Celeste pulled another straight pin from the red satin wrist cushion. Her own husband had not seen fifty, had died instead, at twenty-eight, leaving her with four small children, a Singer sewing machine, and an avalanche of debt, estranged from the family that could have helped her.

"And the all-black party was such a hit that on New Year's I had an all-white party, just like those jet setter folks do. You know, everything white—white food, like sour cream and cream cheese dips, and vanilla cakes and this divine, frothy white wine punch. Oh—and white flowers. You know, floating camellias and such. And white candles—white everything."

"It was nothing short of fabulous, Celeste," Mrs. Dixon, ever the sycophant, effused. "Francie throws the best parties of anyone in our circle, and you don't even get into our circle unless you know how to throw a grand party. Well, except for Mitzi Stanton, I guess."

"*Our* circle?" Mrs. Wilson lifted one eyebrow with arch indictment and let it soak in for a moment. Then she smiled with forced benevolence. "At any rate, it is no small feat to be a successful hostess, I am here to tell you. It takes quite a lot of thought and creativity. You can't believe all the little details you have to be mindful of. Just one tiny thing can cause a huge flop."

"My," Celeste said again.

"Right down to the guests," Mrs. Wilson went on. "You have to take care to have a complementary mix of temperaments and a code of dress. Of course, the guests at my white party were all required to wear white, so as not to disturb the theme. You have to be very specific on what to wear. Some people just don't have any finesse. Lord, my arm is tired. Can't I put it down?"

"Yes, ma'm." Celeste drew back and studied the netting she was attempting to drape as per instructions from Mrs. Wilson, who continued her pontification on the art of hostessing a successful party.

"If just one guest breaks the dress code, well, it simply sticks out like a sore thumb. It ruins the larger picture—the canvas, if you will. Anyway, I imagine I have just about done it all, party theme-wise."

"But whenever we think she's outdone herself, she comes up with a brand new twist. It's a flair, that's all. It's an inborn talent." Mrs. Dixon took a compact out of her purse and powdered down her nose. "I declare, I shine like a lighthouse beacon. And I don't have the first idea how to have my hair done for the ball." She scrutinized the stiffly layered flaps of frosty blonde, turning her head at sharp angles. "Good night alive, these highlights are all wrong."

Mrs. Dixon was in the process of moving from a social stratum just beneath that of Mrs. Wilson and into the one Mrs. Wilson presided over, so well done highlights were of utmost importance. Mrs. Wilson herself was hoping to be elected president of her Mardi Gras society the next time around, poised to launch up to the next social level, the one that every great once in a while pierced the true aristocracy of coastal Alabama.

Mrs. Dixon snapped the compact shut. "I do know one thing, though. Even a magnificent Mardi Gras ball hasn't got much on one of Francie's parties. Go on, Francie, and try to tell Celeste all the themes you've done just this past year," Mrs. Dixon urged.

"Well, let's see," Mrs. Wilson said. "I've done a Roaring Twenties party and a Screen Siren—that's where you come as a movie star. Hogie and I were Liz and Dick. Anyway, a Screen Siren party, a Beach Blanket Bingo party over the bay, a Monaco Casino party at the country club. Gosh, it must be a half dozen. And I'm here to tell the both of you that a Hawaiian luau with a tiki hut bar, a bunch of plastic leis, and Don Ho ukulele music comes a dime a dozen."

"Isn't that the gospel," Mrs. Dixon chimed in. "It's practically one of the commandments: 'Thou shalt not throw a Hawaiian luau.' But then, Mitzi Stanton has nothing near your sense of style, Francie. On top of that, she's a Jew. I don't think they even believe in the Ten Commandments, do they?"

"Yes," the seamstress said. "They do."

"Anyway, that was just fluff about the commandments," Mrs. Dixon said. "My main point was about Francie having oodles of style and Mitzi having not one blessed drop."

"Well at the risk of seeming big-headed, I certainly won't contradict that," Mrs. Wilson said. "And that is why I was elected parliamentarian and historian of the Merry Makers over Mitzi Stanton. The only reason we let her join in the first place was because her husband is Methodist and the premiere auto salesman in Mobile. A Jew and Mardi Gras is oil and water, so she had no business being an officer. The gall. But after that tacky little luau of hers, she might as well have just put a sign on wheels out front of her house saying, 'Mitzi Stanton has no flair whatsoever'. There was no way she could have avoided me beating her in that election."

"It was a landslide, Celeste," Mrs. Dixon said to the seamstress. "It was practically a unanimous mandate."

"Goodness." Celeste walked a slow circle around Mrs. Wilson, studying the fit of the sequined bodice. Mardi Gras sparkles of purple and gold winked promises from the roly-poly pudge of Mrs. Clark Hogan Wilson.

"Oh, absolutely. A landslide," Mrs. Wilson reiterated. "And an honor, of course. A position of leadership, which is where you ought to be if you have flair and a keen sense of style. I mean, the business of the Merry Makers is to have party after party. Leading up to the big party during Mardi Gras, of course. It takes a keen sense of style."

"Well, honey, that is you. That is just you all over," Mrs. Dixon cooed, retrieving an emery board from the handbag and commencing to sand the edges of her fingernails. "I swanee, my nails look like a scrub woman's." The scritch of the emery board punctuated a short silence before Mrs. Dixon remembered to re-focus on her friend. "Like I say, Francie, style is simply your calling card. You could have stepped right out of *Cosmopolitan* or *Vogue*." She craned her neck to see the seamstress, who again worked on the netting at Mrs. Wilson's back. "I'm sure you know, Celeste, "that Mrs. Wilson will be showcased at the tableau. Which means, of course, that your dressmaking skills will be showcased."

"It's exciting all right," Celeste said. She had been hearing for months about how Mrs. Wilson would be presented as an officer of her Mardi Gras society at a grand processional, or tableau, before the ball. It was a huge event, the penultimate pinnacle of Mrs. Wilson's social history as one who jockeyed for every movement upward she could garner. "I will be proud to have you model my work."

"Oh, but Celeste, sweetie, it's as much how you *wear* a dress as how it's made," Mrs. Wilson said. "More, even. Let's face it. Anybody and their sister can make a dress. Lord, I bet retards make them in factories all the time. I mean, the real flair is in the wearing of it, don't you think?"

"Yes. Of course." Celeste, practiced in the art of appearing unruffled by insensitivity, began unpinning and re-pinning the gold netting around the back of the dress.

She had tried to tell Mrs. Wilson that the netting would clash with the texture of velvet and had urged her to pick a grainy satin for the skirt of her gown, but Mrs. Wilson would have none of it. Mrs. Wilson had been looking for a specific effect, "a Marie Antoinette effect," she had said, "all swooped out on the sides, you know, but add a part hanging down the back. Almost a train, you know. A French queen for the Mardi Gras ball—*le bon temps*."

French like a New Orleans whore, Celeste had thought.

Mrs. Wilson had been coming to her dressmaking parlor for over twenty years, as had an entire parade of ladies and little girls carrying mounds of satin, Chantilly lace, dotted Swiss, *poi du sois*, crepe, velveteen—fabrics that cocooned their social stations in life like spun silk. She threaded embroidery into fine linen christening gowns, stitched the smocking across toddlers' dresses, sewed red and black velvet cuffs onto tartan plaid Christmas dresses, secured pastel netting over bridesmaids' skirts, and attached mother of pearl beads and Irish lace onto wedding gowns. She ran her tape measure around the busts, waists and hips of the women, down the lengths of their backs, an intimacy ripe with irony. She aided well-dressed ladies in elaborate deceptions, drawing and cutting patterns for designer copies—which was the most lucrative part of the business—and she deposited the women's folded bills and personal checks into her own burgeoning bank account. The stock market investments she made doubled, tripled, then quadrupled the fees provided by the ladies who commanded her services.

In recent years she had begun to look forward to a very comfortable early retirement. Now, in the midst of her forties, she was finally winding down, putting the last of her children through college, coming upon her own time in life. And she had taken more abuse than she would have ever predicted when she ran away from home at the age of seventeen, from wealthy parents in the Mississippi Black Belt, just to be with the man who loved her briefly, and very well, indeed, before he died.

A couple of her clients were not just from old, but *very* old, money—Old Mobile aristocrats who would never deign to boast as Mrs. Wilson did, but who held on to a slick, sterling silver barrier of aloofness, a much more subtle, polite kind of reminder that Celeste's purpose in life was to be at their beck and call, which often meant kneeling at their feet. Unlike the social unfoldings of Mrs. Wilson's Mystic Order of Mirthful Merry Makers, their Mardi Gras functions were written up in vast detail in the *Mobile Press Register*. Their King and Queen were treated like the blue-blood royalty they were born to be, their expensive crowns bought and paid for by money seeded by robber barons, then aged in timber, shipping, and double deals. Celeste hated them, save for one or two, with a fierce purity. She hated the low esteem in which she was held by them. And, having refused her own inheritance, having put it aside for her grandchildren, she hated the inherited currency her customers bestowed upon her after she worked on the hems of their garments, bowed there at their feet like a penitent parishioner seeking absolution.

But she hated Mrs. Wilson and her ilk a million times more, hated their hungry grasps at that higher station in life she had shunned, their shallow little battles, the meager stakes they raised above their means. Mrs. Clark Hogan Wilson epitomized it all, and Celeste had watched her for over two decades, coming up a notch or two here, down one notch there, her long, futile climb tearing at what little potential for a soul had ever rested in her heart in the first place.

Mrs. Clark Hogan Wilson talked about the local aristocrats—the Fillinghams, Dolans, McColloughs—as if they were more than passing acquaintances of hers. "Who will be the next Queen of Carnival?" she would ask. "Of course, we knew Maxine Dolan would have it this year, but next year there's going to be a huge battle between Lexus Dolan and that Mary McCollough. Their daddies are likely to come to blows. Isn't it delicious?" Celeste thought this talk of hers analogous to those pathetic women who discussed TV soap opera characters as they would friends or family members, filling their empty lives with the escapades and tribulations of the fictional characters portrayed by third rate stars.

Mr. Clark Hogan Wilson was a merchant who had made it to the top of the floor covering market in town, complete with television commercials on the local stations—"Let Hogie make your home homey," the jingle went—bringing in plenty of money, though never enough, in Mrs. Wilson's eyes, to erase his lack of a college education. As she aged, she shaded the truth about her husband by degree, until he became "an honorary Kappa Sigma at the University," and "an honorary member of the Wolf Landing Hunting Club," and "an influential player in city politics."

No one seemed willing to call her on her lies. Celeste, as always, chose to keep her stoic, perfected silence and her fruitful livelihood, for the sake of her children. Sometimes, though, she felt as if she were treading silent black waters, gasping for air, grappling for a lifeboat captained by Mrs. Wilson, whose history was the antithesis of her own principled past, an impostor of a captain who all the while pushed down on her, shoving her head under the waves, beating her back from the vessel with an oar.

"It will be nothing short of magnificent, Celeste," Mrs. Dixon was saying.

"What is that?" Celeste silently cursed the stiff netting.

"The tableau, of course. The tableau." Mrs. Dixon squirmed and giggled like an antsy kindergartner. "I know it's supposed to be very top secret and all, Francie. And I know it's going to be my first time as a guest at the Mystic Merry Makers' Ball, but can't I please tell Celeste just a little? Just a little about the tableau?"

Celeste pulled another pin from the shiny red satin wrist cushion.

Mrs. Wilson sighed. "Oh, all right. But Celeste had better not go blabbing our secrets to just anybody, because not just anybody gets to come to our ball."

"Celeste won't tell, will you, Celeste?"

"No," the seamstress said.

"All right, then." She set her handbag on the floor and sat up very straight. "First of all, there will be the most elaborate costumes you can imagine. All two hundred and forty members will be in the processional. Their husbands will be seated along the edges of the arena, wearing dignified tuxedos, of course. And the members will wear these gorgeous costumes. But naturally you know they are gorgeous, because you made lots of them yourself."

"Yes, I did," said the seamstress.

"Anyway, the theme this year is 'Let the Good Times Roll All Around the World,' so each group of ten or twelve ladies will be dressed in costumes native to a particular country. And they'll do a dance to some taped music—related to that country, you know.

And this will go on and on and on. Until the big moment."

Celeste fingered a sequin that had snagged loose from the bodice. "I'll have to fix this," she murmured.

"The big moment is when they introduce the five officers, one by one. And these spotlights follow them down from the stage and across the arena. And they do a Mardi Gras dance to some New Orleans jazz and the president introduces the queen and the queen commands the ball to begin and oh, I am so excited!"

"My goodness, Camilla, get a Xanax out of my purse and calm yourself," Mrs. Wilson said. "But I admit it will be a thrill to be followed across an arena by spotlights while hundreds of people seated in the audience watch. Kind of like being Miss America. And to think it might have been that Jewess Mitzi Stanton instead of me, if not for that tacky Hawaiian luau she threw. Goodness, I'm tired of standing on this step-stool."

"You can get dressed now," Celeste said. "I see what needs to be done."

Mrs. Dixon babbled on and on about the tableau while Mrs. Wilson changed clothes. "I mean, I've been to balls before, and they were nice. But this is the Mystic Order of Mirthful Merry Makers. They are known to have the best ball, besides the top two societies, of course. And you have to practically marry into those, you know."

Celeste almost said, "Yes, I know about marrying into even more money, because that is what my father expected, only I chose not to take my father's fortune and double it by merging assets with another family. I did not prostitute myself to a man I did not love." She often wanted to spit the truth at them, tell them what a sham it all was, their desperate bid for upward mobility. "When you marry for money, you earn every penny," her husband used to say, and Celeste knew that these women could have only reached their desired level by marrying into it, and they had certainly not done that. Too, marrying up would have been a long shot, at best, for women like them, shallow and unbeautiful as they were. No, the heart pine core of aristocracy they lusted after was a closed society, and they would never be allowed into the club. Not that club, the one in which she had been reared. Never that ultimate club.

Mrs. Dixon caught Celeste's gaze, pointed at a scrap of the

gold netting on the floor, and mouthed the words, enough of a whisper that Celeste could hear her. "That just does not go," she whispered, shaking her head, wide-eyed.

Celeste shrugged.

"Remember to bring your shoes to your next fitting," Celeste said again, when Mrs. Wilson emerged from the hallway that served as a makeshift dressing room.

"Yes, I know. I don't have to be told a thing forty times," Mrs. Wilson huffed, rolling her eyes at her friend.

"Oh, Celeste," Mrs. Dixon said. "My cousin Martha is coming down from Brannon to visit this weekend. I'll tell her hello for you."

"Yes. Do that," the seamstress said.

"And I warn you, Miss Mysterious. My cousin Martha will give me the scoop on you and yours. So if you have some big old juicy secrets, well—look out."

"I certainly will," the seamstress said. "Goodness."

"I know what, Francie. You must do the dance," Mrs. Dixon said. "Before we go, you must do the dance for Celeste."

"Yes, our little Cinderella. Our poor little Cinderella who needs a fairy godmother to transform her for the ball," Mrs. Wilson said.

Celeste gathered the cast off gown into her arms, gold netting stiff and scratchy. "What sort of dance?"

"The Mardi Gras dance. You know the one. Like this." Mrs. Wilson began to strut, the familiar Mardi Gras strut so common on the streets of New Orleans and Mobile. "Da-da-*da*," she sang, dipping and swaying. "Da-da-*dadada*. Da-da-*da*. Da-da-*dadada*. And here comes the good part." She did a half turn and broke into a backward strut while Mrs. Dixon joined her in the song. And they both danced their way out the front door, laughing a rowdy chorus of anticipation while the seamstress pressed the crisp gold netting to her cheek and contemplated their reverie.

When Mrs. Wilson returned the following week for her final fitting, gold shoes in hand, she was sans her usual appendage, the fawning Mrs. Dixon. She was also oddly quiet, the sulk lines in her forehead grooved in a fixed petulance as she stood on the small platform. Celeste re-pinned the hem and double-checked each seam, the zipper, the hook and eye, the malignant gold netting all webbed out like a cancer around the skirt. The room was a jumble of sparkling gold, yellow, green, purple—fluffs of flounces, bolts of beaded and brocade fabrics for the Carnival season. Last minute gowns lay about in various stages of glitter, some gaudily playful with festive flashes of rhinestones, others like garish Las Vegas neon, ready to play out to a night all boozy and sour with stomach-turning dances and sloppy, slathered-on kisses from strangers.

"You don't wear your gown on the float, do you?" Celeste asked. "It could be a problem getting—"

"Well of course not," Mrs. Wilson snapped, breaking her silence in two. "Don't you know anything? We have to wear masks and costumes that go with the theme of the float. My God. Why would you even *have* a float if you weren't going to have costumes? Just why?"

Celeste tugged at the sequined shoulder strap. Mrs. Wilson's flaccid skin pooched around it; more flesh spilled in a bratwurst-like bulge over the top of the scoop-necked back. "This seems fine," the seamstress said.

"I'll tell you what *seems*," Mrs. Wilson snapped again. "It *seems* to me that you often ignore what I say. It seems to me that you often behave rudely. Like now. You do not show one bit of interest in the workings of the float."

"I never cared much for Mardi Gras parades. I only went when my children were small." Celeste made gentle rearrangements in the gold netting that swept around the sides of the velvet skirt.

"And I admit I don't care much for the parades, either, so don't think you're anything special," Mrs. Wilson said. Her voice had an angry, tense tone that Celeste had not heard before. "I don't want to be gobbed up in those hordes of people on the sidewalk, that's for sure. The unwashed masses." She shuddered. "I'm telling you, you get a birds' eye view of the dregs of Mobile from high up on a float."

Celeste uttered her favorite of her standard remarks. "Goodness."

"You can't tell me you wouldn't like to be a float rider. You can't tell me you wouldn't like folks to be yelling to you for beads or moon pies. It's like being a queen. It's like being Cleopatra coming down the Nile on a gilded barge. I don't understand anybody that wouldn't like that."

Celeste moved to the other side of Mrs. Wilson's skirt, to the other pouf of gold.

"No, I don't understand it one little bit," Mrs. Wilson went on. "Oh, I'm sure plenty of folks would *say* they didn't want to be a float rider, but those are the ones that are so jealous they wouldn't ever admit how much they deep down want to take your place. But I can't for the life of me understand somebody that gets to be a float rider and then walks away from it like it's nothing. Like it's not worth a damn thing. Do you understand somebody like that?"

"Well, I suppose it's—"

"Somebody like that is just mean or crazy or stupid is what I think. Somebody like that maybe has brain cancer or some kind of schizophrenia to walk away from what counts."

Celeste knelt at Mrs. Wilson's back, checking the hem of the faux train, seeing how it lined up with the glittering three-inch heels she wore.

"It's a disgrace is what." Mrs. Wilson huffed and blew like a spooked pony. "It makes me want to spit to high heaven."

Celeste stood. "I'll send this over to Lawson's Dry Cleaning to have it pressed for you as soon as I get it hemmed. You can pick it up there on Thursday."

"You do that," Mrs. Wilson said in a voice thick with sarcasm. She stepped down, wobbling on her heels. Celeste caught her elbow, but the other woman jerked it away and stomped off to the hallway dressing room.

"I guess you see that Camilla Dixon, my little pilot fish, is no longer at my side," Mrs. Wilson, still boiling, shouted from the hallway. "She's like to have a breakdown, too, because I have officially uninvited her to the Merry Makers' Ball. As an officer I am allowed to do that. You see?"

"Oh?"

"Some people just don't know when to shut up. Some people say more than anybody wants to know, that's all."

"Yes. They do," the seamstress said.

"But not you. No. Never you. You don't do a damn thing to let on what cards you've been dealt, do you? You keep your trump hand right up against your chest, don't you?"

Celeste smiled. "I don't play cards."

Mrs. Wilson burst through the door, flushed and trembling. She flung the dress across the room. "See that you get this finished right away," she commanded.

"Of course," the seamstress said.

Mrs. Wilson snatched several bills from her purse. "I have your money. And, oh—here's something else." She dug down into her handbag, coming out with a handful of throws. "Since you won't be at the parade," she said, and threw beads, bills, doubloons, and a lone moon pie across the room, the dinging and clattering of the cheap trinkets like a percussive curse against the hardwood floor.

Celeste watched her priss her chubby frame through the front door, where she turned and scowled her best, deepest-wrinkled sneer at the seamstress. "Camilla was right about one thing, though."

"Really?"

"Yes. Really. She was right about how you ought to experience at least one of my parties. Maybe you could serve *hors d'oeuvres* for me sometime, or pop out of a cake or something equally cheap, like what you have chosen in life."

"Oh, I don't know," Celeste said. "I'm really only good at sewing. That, I am quite good at. But you might consider asking my son, Hollis. He does a little private bartending to help with college expenses."

"Is that so? Well, I'm sure I am honored that you chose to reveal something about your personal life to little old me. A son. And in college, no less."

"Just finishing medical school," Celeste said. "But he won't be available much longer. He'll be doing his internship. And he's engaged, too. A very nice girl, very down to earth. Mary McCollough."

For a split second it seemed to Celeste that Mrs. Wilson's sneer would be wiped away by utter shock, but it held steady, set there in the grooves of her face, her eyes ripe with pure hatred.

"You go to your choosing and rot like a trashy beggar in hell," Mrs. Wilson said, slamming the door hard enough to rattle windowpanes in the adjoining room.

Celeste retrieved the throws and the cash, then picked up the mangled purple velvet with its clashing Marie Antoinette gold netting. She walked over to her time-worn Singer sewing machine, spread the skirt back and out, and then set to work on the hem, the stabbing and clicketing of the piston-borne needle sealing her resolve.

The Mardi Gras season came to a drunken climax on Fat Tuesday and faded into the confessions of a hungover Ash Wednesday, and the ladies who came into Celeste's place of business were abuzz with the tales of intrigue, subterfuge, strife, and backbiting that so often accompanies large-scale social gatherings.

But by far the most buzzed about tale was that of the bizarre and shocking occurrences at the Mystic Order of Mirthful Merry Makers' events. All along the parade route, it was told, Mrs. Clark Hogan Wilson would go missing for an inordinate while,only to be found in the Port-o-Potty hidden in the bowels of the float, miserably shoveling moon pie after moon pie into her jowly little face, eyes glazed over in a sugary chocolate-induced haze. She would be brought up to her place high at the top of the float, a facsimile of a pink Matterhorn with purple clouds towering above the crush of the crowd, above the minions who were corralled back like sheep by grilled metal barricades. She would throw a few handfuls from the large box hidden behind a cliff in the Matterhorn, then, when no one was noticing, would make her way again to the Port-o-Potty, another stash of chocolate moon pies hidden deep in her bra and in the folds of her emerald green satin Swiss Alps costume.

Mrs. Wilson's mood picked up later, most agreed, as the members of the Mystic Order of Mirthful Merry Makers retired to the Civic Center to prepare for their tableau. Everyone agreed it was a beautiful tableau this year, maybe even better than any society in town. The China Dolls, Flamenco Dancers, Hula Girls, Belly Dancers—group after group, they waltzed, twirled and waddled their way across the arena to the applause of the crowd, the ceremonial flash and swoop of spotlights, the twinkling of sequins on satin.

Then the arena fell silent as the officers, in various states of elegance and pre-eminence, took the stage. Mrs. Wilson was announced first, illuminated by three white lights that tossed the glitter of her sequined bodice out to the audience as she began her walk down the stairs to the Mardi Gras song. The three spotlights brushed her round frame, the deep purple velvet skirt netted over by gold. When she reached the arena floor, she broke into the traditional strut while the onlookers clapped hands to the rhythm.

And it was told all over town what happened when she turned to execute her signature flair, to strut her backward strut. It seemed, they said, to happen in slow motion, that the heel of one gold shoe caught in the netting, and, in that instant, all that followed became inevitable. Her arms flailed, the crowd sucked in a collective gale of a gasp, the other foot stepped back, even farther into the netting, pulling the first shoe completely off, and pulling her the rest of the way down. She tumbled to her ample buttocks with a padded thud, sitting in the middle of the arena floor, legs outspread, all dignity seared away. Even worse, the jolting force of her landing, it seemed, had liberated one lone moon pie from the brassiere prison where it had resided since her chocolate binge on the Merry Makers' float. The chocolate covered disc of cake and marshmallow hit the floor beside her, cellophane glinting as it spun in the Miss America spotlight. And it did a twirling little dance of its own before coming to a rest on the waxed floor of the arena next to her cast off shoe.

From the hushed audience came a twitter or two, but these were hurriedly shushed by others, who then twittered a bit themselves. A long forever of stunned silence passed before a couple of the tuxedoed men—not her husband, who was frozen with embarrassed horror—leapt to their feet to help her up. One of them gallantly and discretely pocketed the moon pie in an effort to restore a fraction of dignity to the occasion. Then, like an awkward Prince Charming, he bent down to hold the sparkly gold shoe as she wiggled and worked her plump foot into it.

Of course, the music swelled again, and the processional went on. The other officers were introduced, and the president introduced the queen, and the queen commanded that the ball begin. And, after crying on the shoulders of her most bosom of friends, Mrs. Clark Hogan Wilson danced all evening with a smile fixed to her face, fixed like the grin of a stalked and trophied animal from a taxidermy establishment, attempting to make light of the ruination of her vertical advancement.

Efforts to put a gag order into effect for the members of the Mystic Order of Mirthful Merry Makers were futile, and the events of that evening were carried from function to function by wagging tongues, received with doubled-over laughter, and passed on. The story was unstoppable, and it grew exponentially, on its inevitable course of becoming a Mardi Gras Legend. The moon pie, too, became an icon, was auctioned off at charity events, passed from Mardi Gras society to Mardi Gras society and beyond, along with the tale of Mrs. Clark Hogan Wilson.

And the tale was told again and again, at bridge clubs and teas, in nail salons, beauty parlors, and shops. It was told at the country clubs of the nearly elite and at the exclusive clubs of the most elite. And it was told in the fitting room of the seamstress, Celeste, who knelt at the feet of the ladies, working the fine fabrics of their choosing. It was told over and over, while the seamstress, she with the most vindicated of hearts, turned bland bolts of material into crisp summer blouses edged in navy blue piping and full, cinch-waisted skirts swirling the colors of stained glass windows between her practiced and nimble fingers.

The Fall of the Nixon Administration

In light of my current situation with the law, I suppose it's a good thing I did not shoot Will Luckie in the back of the head when I had the chance. After all, if folks are going to get all tore up over the demise of a few pullets, then there surely would have been a mighty hue and cry over Will's demise—even though he is no better than any of the yard fowl I exploded with my dead daddy's—"D.D." for short in our family—Remington Model 1100 12 gauge automatic. And I refuse to say otherwise, even if they put hot lights in my face, withhold food and water, interrogate me for days on end, or attempt to beat any endearing words out of me. Will Luckie has single-handedly brought down the Calhouns and I will never forgive him.

You need to know that Will Luckie is a descendant of the mouth breathers who live out the Pipeline Road, where they pass their beer-ridden days hauling pulpwood, screwing one another's wives, and having an occasional trailer burning to collect enough insurance money to buy more beer and pulpwood trucks. He is through and through Florida Panhandle white trash—pure carrion—and ever since he entered our once picture-perfect lives, I have been subjected to his low-class ways.

First off, he keeps a pouch of Beechnut in the front pocket of his double knit shorts, which makes for a rather unnerving bulge that is, at best, in bad taste, and, at worst, just plain lewd. And he knows it. To be thoroughly honest, he rarely, if ever, wears underwear. I can safely say this because of the revealing nature of sand-colored double knit; it just does not afford the barrier as does, say, denim, or heavy cotton. And when the heightened level of sexual arousal that has settled upon my mother's abode is thrown into the mix—well, let me just say that I am quite certain—and I apologize for being so graphic—but it is more than obvious that the smarmy little gigolo is not even circumcised.

Plus, he spits. He spits that stinking concoction between his index and third finger, pulling his lips taut and skeeting that mess out in high, arching streaks of amber. His presence, ergo his spittle, here at Mimi's house, which has always been *the* showplace home in Pollard, has cheapened the entire property right along with the Calhoun name. At present there are tobacco juice stains dotted across Mother's patios, in puddles next to the ornamental urns, down the stone walkway that once wound so pleasantly among the pines, and all around the swimming pool where he passes the days sunning and sipping fruity drinks of gin bearing paper umbrellas. Lord knows, at this precise second three of mother's Waterford Crystal tumblers hold a few ounces of that nauseating looking, tobacco-infused saliva. I have even regularly found one of Grandma Lucie's sterling silver goblets perched on the toilet tank, floating those little black flecks across a phlegm-glazed surface of bubbly brown spit. I have told Will Luckie repeatedly how repugnant it looks. He laughs every time. "Tell it to Bob Haldeman," he says, laughing.

My God, how he laughs! He laughed when I told him to wear a shirt to Mother's surprise birthday luncheon last month. Knowing that the leading citizens of Pollard would be there, taking mental notes on the progress of Mother's debauched incapacitation. He laughed and said that if he was going to stand around the pool nibbling cocktail weenies with a bunch of tight-assed holy rollers, he had to be prepared to bail at any second. Thus, the aforementioned double knit shorts. And the chest hair with those hideous gold chains garlanded into it like some kind of pornographic Christmas tree. And yes, he did at one point do a cannonball into the water, which soaked the fondue table and Mayor Burgess's wife Kathryn's silk skirt. And when Will Luckie emerged from the water it was painfully obvious that the famous nude shorts he wore were also soaked, displaying yet another level of phallic information we did not require; the energy that went into avoiding eye contact with his vile, blue-veined interloper would be enough to fuel all the paper mills in this county. I have never been more mortified. That is how much he cares about making the right impression with influential people. Plus, he even threatened to invite John and Martha Mitchell to the party to strew feathers hither and yon. Instead, he rounded up Charles Colson, a Buff Orpington and his favorite, and, as an encore, proceeded to introduce him to the guests, all the while stroking him and making absurd little kissy noises at him.

The thing that absolutely stuns me is that people—even well-bred ones—seem to like him, up to a point, contrary to all personal moral codes, as they surely must object to his gene pool and his flimflamming of my mother. Maybe it is because he drags out that cheap guitar and sings country songs with a disturbingly rich voice or tells those "humorous anecdotes" that always eventually descend into the blue depths of hardcore porn. Maybe it is that subtle layer of pansexuality that seems to intrigue both genders in spite of themselves. Maybe it is the Newman-blue eyes, the dimply Kirk Douglas smile, or the George Hamilton tan-lacquered physique, enhanced by his two decades in the Marine Corps. No matter. I consider him the idiot savant of a Svengali, who tapped into Mother's sense of herself as a poet. Mother should have lived the life of an artistic expatriate rather than "atrophying" here in Pollard. She never did appreciate her status.

Status. The state of us. There is the crux of it, as far as I am concerned. Mother has called me shallow, but civic responsibility should never, in my opinion, be taken for granted. You cannot fully appreciate this whole fiasco unless you understand that the Calhouns are the single most prominent of the three most prominent families in Pollard, which is prominent in itself as the county seat. "We occupy the penultimate position of prominence," Mother used to like to say, given her penchant for alliteration. Because of this, and out of a sheer sense of civic duty, I am President of the Ladies' Club, parliamentarian of the DAR, Brownie scout troop leader at the Methodist Church, Sunday School class coordinator at the Baptist Church, and I would have beat out Bitsy Burgess

Swafford, the mayor's evil daughter, as president of the Daughters of the Confederacy, if not for the shame of Will Luckie. As it is, I feel that my genetic destiny as a community leader has slipped. If I had chosen to do nothing, it could have taken years to rebuild the family name; so I did something about it, albeit apparently too much to ever hope to repair the Calhoun name now. And Mother? Mother simply fails to care one whit about the shambled legacy she has foisted upon me.

You see, my DD's DD was a circuit judge who survived The Crash and three bouts of cancer before he died of age; naturally, he knew everybody and all their legal business. My DD was a banker with the foresight to buy all the timber land and mineral rights he could get his hands on so naturally he knew everybody's financial business. He was a philanderer and died of gallstones. My husband, Winston Dozier (though try as I might, I can only contextualize myself as a Calhoun) is a physician—the only one in town besides Dr. Dave, who is ancient—and Winston knows everybody's personal business so it does not matter that he is a tad prissy for a man. And my mother is from an extremely well regarded political family in Birmingham, Alabama. Did you know that right this second her brother is some Big Ike in the Nixon administration? Hell, she and Daddy went to the first inauguration—and the main ball, not any of the little rinky-dink ones. And she acts like it is no big deal that the Nixon administration is falling into a mangled heap, running around like a bunch of decapitated biddies. So you see, she could know everybody's political business if she had the inclination. On top of that, it is said that she is the wealthiest woman in three counties, thanks to her DD and my DD. And after just shy of a year of mourning my daddy, what does she do? She takes herself a boyfriend twenty-two years and seven months her junior—making him four full months younger than me—and sets all the town's tongues to wagging about my own family's familial business.

Are you beginning to fathom why Will Luckie might be so intrigued with my withering up old mama? And why I have so much to lose?

Of course, I have attempted to be fair where Will Luckie is concerned. It simply would not be Christ-like to do otherwise. I am the first to concede that Mother is not, well, "ordinary" is the adjective that comes to mind. She is a bit of an eccentric, as so many of the wealthy are, and she has always been fond of drama. She is not above pressing a palm to her chest or the back of a hand to her forehead and uttering plaintive little bleats of suffering peppered with curses. Mother can swear with the fluency of a wounded sailor. Naturally, her dramas and her imminent death are all in her head; Dr. Dave has been giving her sugar pills for years. And me? Well, I am the devoted daughter, childless, without siblings, with only a limp-wristed Baptist husband to help with my mother and her shiftless little slut of a boyfriend. Now don't get me wrong, I heartily embrace my daughterly duties. Heaven knows, I have never failed to be at her side when she was mid-crisis, even throughout the hypochondriacal frenzy of her golden years, living with my husband in the shadow of Mother's big white-columned three-story. Many are the times I have delivered satin bed jackets and Merle Norman cosmetics to her hospital rooms, spoon fed her while that popping jaw of hers nearly sent me over the precipice and into a ranting, maniacal conniption fit, and taken all the verbal abuse I should have to stomach in five lifetimes.

"Cece, I cannot bear the thought of dying without seeing you living your life," she says. "Run off to Nepal, for God's sake! Go to a goddamn nude beach in Europe. Have an affair in Lisbon and breakfast in Madrid. Do not fester and stagnate as I once did." Or: "Cecelia LaRue, you have no hunger for life. Where is the passion you should have inherited from me? Jumping Jesus, if you would just come alive you would begin to claw at this provincial little coffin of a town." Which is just a pure and solid lie. She was perfectly content with her life BWL (Before Will Luckie).

"She overshadows you," my DD used to say. "You've got to learn to talk louder, act meaner, and cuss dirtier than she does." Easy for him to say, with his bourbons and baseball. With his hunting camp whores and wooded weekends. But it simply is not in my nature to be overbearing like Mother. On the contrary, I feel that I should project an image of calm competence and ladylike strength, what with my position and all. Heaven knows, I have even been called a saint by some who have observed my devotion to Mother.

Our maid Lindia only calls me a fool. She has even gone so

far as to tell me she thinks I should get a new husband. "One that don't swish," she says. "Leave Pollard, and let the chips fall." Lindia even thinks Mother should be allowed to have her way with this—"character" of hers. "She deserves him," Lindia says. "She went long years not getting none from your running around daddy. Well, she's damn sure getting plenty now."

But I cannot let it go. Not when the whole town is watching and talking and looking at me with the false pity of peons who just eat up a good, high-society scandal with the same sticky spoon. Not when Mother and Will Luckie go on trips to India and Morocco, come back loaded down with expensive trinkets, ivory, rich fur pillows, hand- woven rugs—my God, her home decor has become a bohemian ode to the Kama Sutra. And of course you know who is paying for these trips and trinkets: yours truly. I am not only paying with my birthright, I am paying with my once impeccable reputation. Just listen at a few of the other things that piece of filth has done to cause an avalanche of shame to come cascading down on the Calhoun family:

First of all, he moved in with her after just two movie dates and one dinner date to Rosie O'Grady's in Pensacola. Swept her right off her chubby little size five feet (mine are size nine; she refers to them as "Jesus Christ walk on water skis"). I believe the off-color line he wooed her with was, "Baby, you sure do make my rat crawl," or something equally disturbing. At least, that's how she tells it, delighting at the gag reflex-inducing reaction she gets from me and anyone else with common decency. No marriage has ever been discussed (as if I could allow that!)—just a craven union of depraved lust and musked-up sin, which in and of itself is all the town ever needed to justify looking down on me.

Second of all, he buys lubricating jelly and female hygiene spray at Mr. Cleo Williams' pharmacy, and I don't have to tell you the lurid tales that swarm around Billy's Barber Shop and the House of Hair in the wake of that. Don't even ask me about the hand-held muscle massager.

Thirdly, I think I already mentioned he laughs at me and runs me down to my face and behind my back. He calls me a "social-climbing flippy-tailed prissite," as if I have to do any climbing. It is just that I do care what certain people think. It's my nature.

Yet he says the crudest things to me, obviously intended to wound and provoke, but I usually mange to hold it in, just as I have always done with Mother. "You need to loosen up, girl," he will say. "You got the biggest bug up your butt I ever seen. Must be one of them dung beetles. You need a dose of Uncle Luckie's Root Treatment." Or he leans in close and whispers, "So who's cutting your stove wood? Cause I know your old man ain't got the ax for it."

Winston has even witnessed him toying with me, insulting me, yet my own husband refuses to take up for me. All he will do is bring me samples of knockout pills to settle my nerves then turn around and give Will Luckie all the free medical attention he needs, and then some. Knowing that "Uncle Luckie" doesn't think Winston has any testosterone, all the time asking why Winston and me don't have any babies after six years of marriage. Then, when I try to tell him something like I guess Jesus isn't ready, he says, right in front of Winston, "More like Winnie ain't ready, and he won't be ready unless you get yourself a dildo. Maybe that would turn him on." Then he laughs while Winston blushes. Of course.

"Bet I could take care of Winnie's retreads if he made a little pit stop on my turn." The gall. My mother's boyfriend flirting with my husband! "Hey, Doc," he says. "My dick stays harder than Chinese arithmetic. I need to come in and get it de-pressurized, alright? Just drain off a little fluid."

I swear I am not exaggerating. He continues his slimy talk and his questioning of Winston's virility just because he knows crude behavior is one of my Achilles' heels and my husband's effete demeanor is the other. I already told you Winston is a touch feminine, but that is just the way of some folks with superior breeding. Plus, I always used to say that there's more to a successful marriage than wallowing around in bed linens. But don't try telling that to Mimi or Will Luckie. Their sordid little soiree goes on in front of all of Pollard. Here's what I mean:

In recent years Mother has taken to routinely calling the police department, fire department, or ambulance company when she needs little errands done. Once, at the conclusion of one of her extended hospitalization-slash-vacations, she even phoned up Cheatham Jackson at the colored funeral parlor to drive her the four blocks home, just because the hospital ambulance was out on a call and she simply *had* to get home right that very minute to set up for *mah jongg*. Yet this town's three bored cops—plus assorted paramedics and firemen—seem to get a kick out of it, driving up to the big house, sirens blaring and lights ablaze, to see what the eccentric socialite wants this time. This behavior never used to bother me too much BWL, as it was quite harmless then. Lord knows, I used to sometimes be there to enjoy the company, when Mother would wave the back of her hand at Grady Fortner, a big fat semi-winded paramedic. "No, darling," she would chirp from her multi-pillowed perch beneath the yellow dotted Swiss canopy. "I'm just fine. Really. All I need you to do is run to the kitchen and pour a little Tab over ice."

And he would.

"Run to the liquor store for me, sweetie pie, and pick me up a fifth of Crown. I'm all out and I'm parched as a goddamn nun's drawers."

After a two a.m. call, the honeyed command might go something like, "Be a sugar-doll, won't you, and run downstairs to the garage. I woke up with this feeling of dread that I forgot to extinguish the lights on my automobile. Oh—and if it's necessary, be my precious and check the battery."

But after the arrival of Will Luckie the visitors became more like salivating voyeurs at a peep show in a Bourbon Street sex salon. Lord, they can't get to Mother's fast enough to gather fodder for the next tale they will share at the barber shop, and she never lets them down. Just a few weeks ago, when Mother's hairdresser accidentally fried the hair he was supposed to be touching up with henna highlights, it turned into yet another show for the P.C.P.D.

When I laid eyes on Mother, all done up to perfection except for the frizzled tufts of hair zigging and zagging from her scalp, I briefly hoped it would be the death knell for Will Luckie, scare him off, maybe. After all, she looked like Bozo the Clown with a singed Afro. And mother's looks, which I did not inherit, by the way (I only inherited my place in the pecking order of Pollard), are known to be strikingly beautiful, even at her age and poundage. She has flawless skin, too smooth for wrinkles to appear harsh, and the greenest eyes this side of Vivien Leigh. I, of course, had acne and kept several Pensacola dermatologists in business throughout high school, and I have these washed-out brown eyes. Where Mother is petite, albeit a hair chubby by now, I am a ski-footed Amazon with a thick waist and saddlebag hips. But I have nice hair, a dazzling smile, and a moral character, which is really all that counts.

Anyway, the evening of Mimi's hair frying incident, I sat in the dark with her in the study, waiting for her Man. A strobing of firelight hit her face, playing upon the burned out barbs of frizzed hair. She held a cigarette in her left hand, a scotch rocks in her right, smoking and sipping in the slow silence. Her pearl-handled Derringer lay in her lap.

When the doorknob rattled to his touch, Mother simply sat, smoked, sipped, inhaled. When the slat of light from the porch fell across the room she exhaled.

He flipped on the study light, jumped, and uttered, "Sheee-it."

Mother drew on her Virginia Slim, blew a cool plume of smoke. "Will, darling." Pause. "This is the new me." Pause. "Like it?" Such timing would be a thing of beauty if not for the circumstances.

That man regrouped quicker than any man I have ever encountered. "Mmmm, baby," he said, all the while unsnapping that hideous pink cowboy shirt with the embroidered yellow lassoes he is so fond of. "That is hot. You kind of look like a soul sister."

"Good," Mother said. "Because if you didn't like it I was reconciled to the idea of putting a bullet into my feeble brain." She picked up the pistol with a dainty little flourish. "Here, sexy. Do something with this instrument of death."

He took the gun, steady slurping at her neck while my lunch wanted to be upchucked. Of course, I might as well have been invisible, and he kept on lapping at her like a horny mutt, talking about how he always wanted a taste of dark meat.

"Ooooh, darling," Mimi squealed. "You know that makes me want to give in to wild abandon. It's absolutely criminal!"

He grunted. He still had not acknowledged me, you will note, intent as he was upon whipping my elderly mother into a hedonistic frenzy. Well, she went into a frenzy all right, and she shared it with the town of Pollard. While that skanky man licked her neck like it was the last lollipop on the planet, she called the police. As was the routine, an officer—this night it was Paul Baggett—let himself in with the spare key Mother had given the department to keep in their one and only squad car. Baggett just stood there, smirking; I was overcome by a paralysis of shame.

Mother stood and swept an accusing arm at Will Luckie, who was mixing himself a fruity gin drink at the bar. "Officer," she panted, "arrest this man!"

Will laughed. I felt defeated.

"Arrest this man on the grounds that he's too goddamned sexy!"

Paul Baggett, too, began to chuckle, licking his chops, I am certain, at the prospect of playing barbershop troubadour the next day.

"Oh, you think I am funning with you?" Ice cubes clinked reiteration in mother's favorite scotch glass. "Well, if you don't arrest this man immediately, I am going to have to tear off my clothes and make love to him with the ardent fervor of a sixteen year-old. And God help your conscience if I have a stroke from it."

Paul Baggett ended up having a beer with them. I went home to Winston.

Sometimes it occurs to me that my daddy died of gallstones and Will Luckie is full of gall. My daddy smoked expensive Cuban cigars and Will Luckie spits. They are day and night. My daddy was a gentleman, even if he wasn't faithful and got drunk a lot. He took care of us. And you know, my DD always told me I would never have to work, that the money would take me into old age, a plush casket, and a choice plot overlooking the Escambia River, with plenty left over for a dozen children. Of course, here I am, childless, because Winston has such difficulty with The Act that we've taken to separate bedrooms over the years, making blundering attempts only when he's had enough merlot, which is difficult for a teetotaler. And Daddy certainly never figured on mother having a geriatric sex-fest with a redneck cowboy swinger who is as low-down as gulley dirt, talks to chickens, and has his eye and his fist on my inheritance.

Oh, Lord, the chickens. I *must* tell you about the chickens. They were the deserving objects of my rage after Will placed the absolute last straw across my load-weary back. He brought three hens and a rooster when he moved in with Mother last fall, then had the nerve to convert the gardener's shed—which sits near my own yard—into a chicken coop. It sends that fecal chicken yard odor across both our back lawns, not to mention the pre-dawn rooster wails and nonstop clucking and flapping. The half-assed fence he put up routinely fails to contain them at all times, so they end up wandering over to the pool and even into Mother's kitchen just last month. Of course you know what Will Luckie did, and Mother and Lindia, for that matter. They laughed. Here you have a yard hen, filthy, full of parasites and histoplasmosis, meandering about the place where food is prepared, and those fools thought it was just about the most humorous occurrence of the decade. I spent the evening Cloroxing Mother's kitchen floor, an already festering incubus of resentment building toward those damned birds, that multiply worse than rabbits.

You see, he has kept on adding more of the feathered beasts throughout the months of his cohabitation with Mother. A few more pullets, another rooster, a couple of Dominekkers, all slick-feathered in rust and green, and then the guineas that got into my winter garden and landed us all in court (the judge, of course, who was utterly taken in, would allow me to sue neither Will nor the guineas). He even bought Mother a peacock, which she adores because it is so flamboyant, like her. It is even named for her—Maureen. Will Luckie named it, of course. He said he could justify using her name for the male bird because it fit in with the whole Watergate setting of the chicken yard. Oh, did I forget to mention that he put a sign on the chicken coop that said "Watergate Hotel" and named each chicken after that whole Nixon bunch? And with no regard whatsoever to gender. Well that is precisely what the no-count fool did. It started out as a cynical joke, as Will Luckie makes no secret of the fact that he believes he fought in a great big con job (i.e., Vietnam) and spends a great deal of time belittling Republican politicians (of course, my DD is turning in the grave in a whirlwind of cremated ashes at the prospect of Mother copulating with anything resembling a Democrat). But the chicken project took on a deeper meaning for him when he began keeping a daily log, entitled "The Chicken Sheet," in which he records each bird's name, egg production, idiosyncrasies and infirmities. The shell-shocked buffoon began to see the ornithological specimens in a new light; they took on the personality traits characteristic of *homo sapiens* in his deranged mind.

"Martha Mitchell looks peaked today," he writes in the log, or "G. Gordon has been spurring Haldeman all afternoon. Haldeman won't even look him in the eye," or "Erlichman is starting to realize he don't carry no weight in this chicken yard—he has been trying to show out but everybody else ignores him," or "McGruder—three eggs but not a lot of enthusiasm—maybe constipated?" and on and on. It is the only thing near a job I ever witnessed him doing, so you can see right there how useless and sorry that man is. And I am here to tell you he takes that job seriously. J. Dean, Erlichman, J. Mitchell, Seccord, E.H. Hunt—these are their names. There is even an Egil Krogh, which he spells E-a-g-l-e C-r-o-w. And the fastidious detail that goes into the recording of the daily lives of the yard fowl is quite disturbing. He acts as if they've evolved beyond pet-dom, as if they are his bosom buddies, chatting with them as he inventories the nests, caressing that nasty, slimy-looking plumage. Chuck Colson grew so tame from the attention that he let Will Luckie loop a chain dangling a diminutive gold crucifix about his gullet, which he wore for the past month. But it gets even more insane. Just a few days ago, Staff Sergeant Luckie added a bit of green cloth to the chain. He then pinned to the cloth some kind of ridiculous war medal he supposedly earned, making that absurd chicken look like the military dictator of the Watergate Hen House. I swear, I sometimes think that his tours of duty in the jungles of Southeast Asia effectively booby-trapped his little birdbrain.

When a raccoon got into the shed last month and assassinated Tricky-D, that inbred idiot actually got teary-eyed and planned a funeral for the mangled carcass. Then insisted that the family attend. He strummed his guitar and sang "Amazing Grace," all weepy-like. I had not known until that incident just how attached to the poultry he had become. This display of emotion was far and away different from his randy romancing of my aged mother. And this realization of mine undoubtedly saved Will Luckie's life this morning. Let me tell you how it all unfolded:

Winston said he had to stay at the hospital to deliver a baby, so

I took a knockout pill and went on to bed, hoping to numb myself with sleep. Sometime before midnight, however, I was awakened by the horrific screams of one who was surely being murdered very, very slowly. When finally, through a fog of cabernet and valium, it dawned upon me that the peacock, Maureen, was the source of the utterances, I was quite relieved, yet could not go back to sleep with those howls punctuating the night. I made my way down to the kitchen and out the back door, which had been left standing wide open. Of course, I assumed that Winston had come in and was reassured by his Cadillac parked in the driveway. But something felt odd; the night seemed a trifle off center, and the scuffling sound coming from around the chicken coop, accompanied by an occasional peacock shriek, drew me to take a silent stroll that would be the terrible undoing of all to which I have grown accustomed.

This is so very difficult, putting into words what I saw there in the moonlight that glowed through the gauze of leaves above. Those garlands of gold (some purchased by my own mother), the ones that were always nestled in the chest curls of Will Luckie, caught the cast of the full moon. He leaned against the outer wall of the old gardener's shed, his breathing filled every few moments with a purring moan, fingers playing across that military-hardened stomach of his. He was caught up in the most intense display of sexual pleasure I have ever witnessed, and I have to confess that some of that pleasure spilled into my own psyche. I felt a mesmerized longing, a huge gulp of desire such as I have never known, until it dawned on me that my own husband was the source of Will Luckie's pleasure.

I have told you about our conjugal difficulties, so it was outside of my frame of reference to see Winston, kneeling there, so caught up in such a perverted act, so absorbed by what he was doing, so oblivious to his surroundings, emitting muffled groans quite unlike the twitters of counterfeit passion he has offered me over the years. I could not move until the lunar light revealed Will Luckie's gaze upon me. And he—you will not begin to believe this, I know—he actually grinned, raised his right hand, extended his index finger, and crooked it at me three times. Can you imagine? Here he is being carnally devoured by my husband, and he has the egomaniacal nerve to invite me to the party! Have you ever in all your life?

The strangest part of this perverse scenario, and I can barely admit it to myself, is that I came within a hair's breadth of walking over, surrendering to God knows what. It was hypnotic, and the stirrings within me were so white hot and demanding. All I knew was a feverish desperation for some implied promise of satisfaction, something I know very little of, unfortunately; but, just as I started forward, Will Luckie let out a gasping moan that sent me headlong toward the sensuous safety of my own bedroom.

Needless to say, I did not sleep at all that night. My bewildered arousal and shock gave way to a mulling inventory of the scores of wrongs done unto me until, as dawn broke, I found myself in the throes of a righteous rage that wanted only to be visited upon Will Luckie. That is when I made my way to Mother's garage and loaded my DD's shotgun.

I paused at the door to the study, where Mother's man-whore had apparently passed out, and contemplated his murder. There is no doubt that I will roast in hellfire for all eternity behind the homicidal inklings that rustled about my brain, but at this point I fail to give a shit. You see, when earthly anguish (as in the form of one's lunatic mother, her sexually ambiguous leech of a boyfriend, and my cheating impostor of a husband) becomes infused within the pores of one's flesh so that Lucifer's den looks to be a relief, then the time to act has arrived. And so I acted. And I did Will Luckie one better.

I acted upon those goddamned yard birds of his. Chuck Colson met me at the gate, having been taught to hold high expectations of those humans who serve him. I laid the stock on my hip, got my palm beneath the barrel, and fired, silently thanking my DD for teaching me to shoot. It struck me that a shotgun went a long way toward decimating coop fowl, effectively blowing them to smithereens, as it were. You have never seen such a tornado of feathers in your life, a maelstrom of beaks, guts, gristle and feet. A few wings in the throes of dancing nerves, jitterbugging against dirt-grained blood in the chicken yard, slinging dots of bright red against the shed. I managed to annihilate Erlichman, Seccord, Krogh, and Liddy before folks came running. I accidentally fired into the bay window in Mother's kitchen trying to hit Martha Mitchell, who had flapped over to the patio thinking I would not notice her there, trying to blend in with the potted white begonias, and the sound of breaking glass tinkled like wind chimes into the hurricane of squawks, screeches and stacattoing wings on Mother's dewey green lawn. I got John Dean and Haldeman, vaguely aware of Will Luckie's stream of curses, his moan of anguish as he raked through meaty feathers for his Bronze Star and crucifix, a moan quite distinct from the orgasmic howl of the previous midnight. My mother's profane shrieks of hysteria against the tableau of sounds grated against my very last nerve and I admit to a flash of a desire to turn the gun on her. That was when Angus Stevens from across the street wrestled my DD's gun away from me. Of course the P.C.P.D. was absolutely thrilled to wheel up to a real emergency—a bona fide chicken massacre—at Miss Maureen's.

Mother was in her vicious-tongued mode. "CeCe, you have lost every bit of your goddamn mind!" she screamed, as down snowflaked upon the wig she still wore behind the hair burning. "Is this what you foresaw when you gave your heart to Jesus? Murdering sweet creatures that give us our morning nourishment?"

"Oh, the humanity!" Officer Baggett murmured.

"If you had only lived life a little, you would not be capable of such cold, lunatic rage!" Mother went on. "And didn't I always try to get you to live a goddamn life? Didn't I?" She quieted a moment and actually took a deep breath. "If you could only learn to live and laugh. Laugh at yourself. Laugh at this absurd life! Then you could never be so vicious as to murder poor Will's friends. You have no idea what you have done to him. Goddamn, I need a Bloody-fucking-Mary."

Of course, I did not argue with her, not in front of the police and the neighbors. It would only encourage her to provide more raw drama for the townspeople to view. And I certainly did not tell her about Winston and Will Luckie. I can never do that! Lord, what would folks think of me then? I do not believe there has ever been a homosexual incident in Pollard, and I am not about to go down as a witness to the first homosexual incident on record.

As I climbed into the police car—Baggett insisted that I sit up front with him—I spied Will Luckie by the pool. He had that little net he uses to clean leaves and bugs out of the chlorined water, but on this landmark morning he was dipping at some of the feathers, still drifting on currents of air like ashes from a barrel burning, or a cremation, that had landed in the pool. His shoulders were hunched over, shaking. It was obvious that he was sobbing as he dipped the remnants of the Watergate conspirators out of the cold liquid. I was able to take a little satisfaction in that. Hell, he is probably having a huge funeral for them as we speak. I wouldn't be surprised if he purchased marble slabs and headstones with more of my inheritance money—created a memorial garden for the Watergate gang, with an air-conditioned vault for Chuck's remains, of course.

So here I am. Mother is not pressing charges, of course, but James Caffey, her attorney, says that the state might have to, because firing into a residence is a felony. I imagine that Mr. Caffey is working on bailing me out right this minute.

I suppose jail is quite reprehensible in a bigger town than Pollard, but here it is quite homey. Baggett, Trent Givens, and Rita, that sweet little dispatcher who does the wake-up call service, brought me lunch from the Jitney Jungle, let me use the phone to cancel the Ladies' Club meeting this evening, and they even rolled a TV into my cell so I could watch the Watergate hearings. That John Dean is testifying. He is kind of a squirrelly little man, but have you seen his wife? Maureen? She is gorgeous, not a blonde hair out of place. Perfect skin. Big eyes and big earbobs. She has style. Even a stylish nickname—"Mo." I almost feel bad about shooting her husband.

I must insist upon one thing. You cannot tell a soul about Winston's indiscretion. Surely I can trust you folks. Surely I have nothing to worry about where you all are concerned. Hell, we don't even know any of the same people I'll bet. I mean you two are from Pensacola, right? And you are in for assault? No, I am certain we could not know the same people. Moreover, we understand our status, one to the other. Status is *tres* important, a thing worth fighting for, a thing worth preserving. You know, after lo these many months of Will Luckie's ill-mannered, low-life ways, it is a relief to have this sense of clarity about the state of us, don't you think?

from *The Fall of the Nixon Administration* / Novel

Chapter 2
Mimi

I have often wondered over the years if Cecelia LaRue Calhoun were not fathered by some stranger who drugged me unconscious then had his way with my pliant flesh—flesh that momentarily encased a rare, ripened ovary, as CeCe was the product of my only pregnancy. This stranger could have been anyone--a rapaciously randy Fuller Brush salesman, for example, or an errant milkman who harbored milky lust among the clattering bottles. Perhaps a love struck elevator man had me between floors or carried me down to the underground world abandoned by the Phantom of the Opera. Maybe it was the Maytag repairman, who hypnotized me with the rhythm of the wash cycle before he gave me a spin, spilling his seed into my delicates. He could have been any of the men who have fringed my life with their necessary presence, men with whom I would never have willingly carried on, but who might have harbored some kind of furtive desire for me. I don't mean to sound conceited, but it is the only way I can explain Cece's being born of my body, in the same bed where my own mother birthed me. We bear no physical resemblance to one another, neither height, breadth nor hue, and I feel like a munchkin standing beside her. Furthermore, she does not physically resemble my departed husband, Wickham, certainly does not have his quiet recklessness. And, although Wickham was a trifle overly concerned with the impression we made as a family, CeCe's prudish temperament goes to another level and is an utter mystery, which is why I often speculate upon her parentage, in a hypothetical way. The result of our tenure together has become a cacophonous back and forth between two who have chosen, with a deafening resonance, completely different paths in life and are determined to grab the other by the arm and drag her, kicking and screaming, down that chosen path. It is beyond absurd. Oh, I love her, of course. She is my child, after all—mine and some mystery man's. But it should be apparent to any fool that we are poised on opposite ends of the artistic and emotional spectrum, and ne'er the twain shall meet, I suppose.

I am a poet. CeCe is a priss-pot. The Poet and the Priss-Pot. It sounds like the title of something, and I do appreciate the alliterative nature of our roles in this life, the complementary angles we share, biologically, but God help us if we try to understand one another. That child is living the life I have finally, with an uncharacteristic clarity of mind, decided to wrest free of. I am speaking, of course, of the muted gray, small town decadence of rural redundance, banal chitchat, and social ass kissing. The lame land of the lumpen proletariat. After decades of carrying an unconventional core of creative ecstasy in my bosom, muzzled and harnessed by the life I chose at the weakest of moments, I am finally freeing my pent up spirit to taste all the pleasures of the flesh in my waning years. And it was Will Luckie who tapped into that gusher of a wellspring.

You see, just as my daughter bears no resemblance to me, Will bears no resemblance whatsoever to my late husband, Wickham Calhoun, who passed away in June of '72, on the heels of the Watergate burglary. Not that the break-in at any way caused my husband's demise, although I do see a certain symbolism at work, looking back on it. I mean, those little gall stones that eventually were his undoing masqueraded for the longest time as gas, ulcers, and general malaise, so there you are. His gall bladder was burglarized, I like to think, by those galling stones that caused his liver and pancreas to go into full revolt against his health.

Anyway, Wickham was wealthy, refined, disloyal, avaricious,

subtly controlling. He cyclically tolerated and tormented me, in his own quiet way, growing more and more ashamed of my antics over the years. Will, on the other hand, delights in my flashes of insanity, is pure and kind-hearted, with an accepting devotion—not to be confused with sexual fidelity—and a rare generosity born of poverty. He is an innocent in so many ways. He is lustful, yes. He is bawdy. He is even quite raw, knows no inhibition. He is the essence of *id*. He is like unto a mythological wood creature who unabashedly feeds his desires. But vulnerable in so very many secret ways. A true diamond in the rough.

I do not call what Will and I have love. Certainly not romantic love, true love, the idealized love of the poets and of youth. I am not some silly old pre-menopausal woman grasping at someone to marry, make me whole, give my life meaning, be my knight with the armor and all. That would be truly naïve and pathetic. All I am doing is eating the proverbial peach, living in the moment, exercising a lust for life, and joining in the sexual revolution, which was tailor made for me, what with my repressed bohemian spirit and all. Not to mention the big o.

I had always known I had incomplete physical love with Wickham. Yes, it was tolerable with him in bed, in the beginning, but it was never anywhere near fulfilling. If I had not been such a wanton woman before our marriage, perhaps I would have been content with the kind of one-two-three loving my husband gave me, but, unfortunately, I knew better. I knew because, unbeknownst to Wickham, I was not a virgin when we married, and my only other experience with love was so complete that I suppose no one who followed would have passed muster.

When I was a girl, the soldiers were going off to Europe to chase the Nazis back into the maw of Hades, and short-lived love affairs were the affairs *du jour*. So it was that, in Memphis Tennessee, over a period of nine days in August of 1942, I had my own affair *du jour,* which became the *piece de resistance*. I met a pilot whose name I cannot utter without crying, a handsome young idealist minted in California-golden hair and skin, who made love to me at the Peabody Hotel for the entire nine days before he was to report down to Pensacola to get his orders. It was nothing short of magical, my handsome pilot, the Scott to my Zelda. His lips traveled the entire terrain of my flesh and the muscles deep inside me swallowed themselves in shudders of profound ecstasy. I am not ashamed to say that I cried out, breathless shrieks of delicious satisfaction. It was in the throes of this fevered, pink, and dampened desire that I wrote poems to our love, to divine desire, and to his duty. Over the following months, letters dense with passion flew back and forth across the Atlantic between us. And, later still, more poems to his death over France, lines that pulled me down into the heart of darkness and loss of will. I was so tightly bound up in that true, true love that I even contemplated suicide, thinking to join him on the other side. Of course I lacked the nerve, so, true to the coward I was, I quickly married Wickham, he who offered emotional insulation and financial security, he who pleased my mother and father's ambition for me. It was the one thing that did me in as an artist, casting myself in a role that only caused frustration and fits of nervous exhaustion over the years.

I tried, and valiantly I believe, to be the wife I was expected to be. I joined his Methodist church, organized rummage sales and cakewalks for dried up little old ladies. I charmed my husband's cronies and the wives of the cronies, walking a delicate line between flirtation and camaraderie. I did volunteer work, offering myself up as a Pink Lady at the hospital, cheerfully bestowing *The Reader's Digest* and *The Pensacola News Journal* upon my bedridden charges, thinking it ironic that I, a Scarlet Woman, should presume to pose as a Pink Lady. I gradually joined the clubs, commiserated with other ladies about the tragedy of fallen cakes, dry rump roasts, and poor help. Pre-Lindia, I went through the requisite number of maids, and then some, directing them to serve from the left, directing them to commence cutting the crusts off bread for dainty little cream cheese sandwiches, directing them to make certain the celery is well strung, directing them to polish my DM's extensive collection of silver for teas and such—events that were written up every week in *The Pollard Gazette*.

But, alas, I was always a few beats out of step. In the Piggly Wiggly, I was always pushing my cart against traffic, a disoriented goldfish swimming upstream against the minnows. I did not care if my whites weren't white, if my husband had ring around the collar, if my floors did not shine and sparkle and mirror my reflection. I did not want to be rescued by the Jolly Green Giant or Mr. Clean. Still, I blundered my way through the grocery shopping and compared notes about purchased products with the other hausfraus at the next Bridge Club meeting. And I would always, invariably, do something that Wickham found distasteful, whether it was taking CeCe skinny dipping in the pool with me, or dancing a whimsical, seductive tango with Mayor Burgess, or siding with those two or three Pollard souls who favored desegregation, and a stifled resentment grew inside me. How dare he find me, the cosmopolitan free spirit who could be the toast of New York or Paris, distasteful?

I tried to be a good mother to Cecelia, but I was miscast in that role as well. I wanted to be dancing barefoot on the beach at Rio de Janeiro or reading my poems in some smoky coffeehouse in Greenwich Village. I wanted to retrace Hemingway's footfalls and scrawl heady lines at some Parisian *café*, relive my affair *du jour*. Instead, I was schlepping baby food, sterilizing glass bottles, and rinsing green shit out of diapers dipped downward into the toilet, before pitching them into pails of ammonia. I was locked into a desperate mind set, a bid to prove my fitness as a mother, heed all the Dr. Spock-isms, keep my little doll dressed in bows and embroidery to show off at the park at the biweekly gathering of breeders. And my doll, my little play pretty, grew into an individual, a person, a real, human child who frightened me with her dependence upon me, who looked up at me at times like a stranger. I knew I was no glowing and serene Madonna, that I would not do well this job of motherhood, and, sure enough, CeCe seemed to be always sizing me up, measuring me against the other mothers in the neighborhood, quizzing me, trying to trip me up.

"Who invented the hot dog?" she asked when she was five.

"Phineas T. Hot Dog," I replied matter-of-factly. And she believed me.

"Who invented the hamburger?"

"Baron Strom von Burgermeister of Hamburg, Germany."

"What is that rubber bag for?" she asked at six, of my douche regalia.

"It's strawberry washer," I said. "You just fill it with water and spray down the fruit." Which, I suppose, is true in its way.

"What does daddy do at the bank?"

"Oh, he has such fun! He sits on a huge pile of Oriental pillows inside a giant, elegant safe and counts his money."

"Where does the bank get the money?"

"Well, darling, they steal it. But only a little at a time, you see, so no one will notice. For example, they stole ninety-seven cents from me last month, which doesn't seem like much, I know. But when you multiply that by the hundreds and hundreds of customers, well, there you are."

"Why do we go trick or treating on Halloween?"

"Don't tell a soul, but it's a dark chocolate conspiracy by Mr. Brach and Mr. Hershey to make money by bribing little devils not to roll our yards with Scott Tissue or light paper bags of dog feces afire on our front porches."

"Why don't you put your hair in pink rollers and watch *The Secret Storm* like Janet's mother?"

"Because, Sugar, hair rolling is for hairdressers and my life in and of itself is a magnificent soap opera that I am living out just to see what will happen next."

"But why aren't you like the other mothers?"

Here I would give her one small dose of truth. "Because, Precious, the war did things to me."

Chapter 6
Lindia

I didn't vote for none of Richard Nixon. And ain't I glad, now he's bound to be run out of office? Wouldn't that be a sight, if I had done voted for Richard Nixon, after all me and The Right Reverend Johnson went through—all the meetings, the organizing, the planning, the meanness we had to put up with. One night, real late, they even put a cross in our yard and set it afire. It was November of '51, and I can still remember smelling the gasoline and feeling the heat off that flaming cross all the way inside that cold little shotgun house where we lived near Panther Burn, Mississippi. I looked out the window and it was like a Christmas scene, the cotton fields across the highway all white like the snow I ain't never seen but in pictures, just pure white fields that must be something like real snow, behind that fiery cross in my front yard where I had combed the dirt into pretty swirls with a rake. I almost expected the cotton fields to go to melting, up against all that heat. Then, in a week or so, the cotton was picked and the fields were scrubby and ugly again, and there were little bits of cotton all along the roadside. But we left that nubby, black, stick and pieces of burnt-up cross in the yard just so they'd know we could pass it, day after day, and not be tormented by it.

It was still there on the day I moved away, just after Henry died. I carried his body back to Warm Springs and told him goodbye there. I gave all his papers and plans and letters to his brother Rodney. See, Henry aimed to work on changing the laws, for voting and all, and he had begun to make a mark when he died. That burning cross came behind him asking the town council for more money for the colored school. I figured Panther Burn didn't want to give off no money to the colored school, and I reckon they made their point. But Henry said it was more likely a reaction to all that Willie McGee mess earlier in the year, after more than one trial that brought communist Yankees down to Laurel to try to defend a colored man who beat and raped a white woman, or so they said. That Willie McGee was executed in May, and it was even put out on the radio, the broadcasting of the execution, which Henry said was barbaric and wrong. The white folks were in a state, to be sure, and Henry and me caught some of the brunt.

Anyway and in spite of, Henry kept on and on and on till he couldn't go no more. Finally, he up and died of a heart attack on a spring day, all of a sudden like. That's how fast a woman's life can change. When a man comes in or a man goes out. That's when a woman's life gets changed up. I ain't one for change, though. It's hard for me. Henry even called me a "creature of habit." Like I told you, I started keeping this diary and writing letters to Henry on the day he died. It's how I honor our time together.

Another way I honor my deceased is in my civic duties. Like I said, I voted for George McGovern, just like I knew Henry would have. I always vote like Henry would have if he had ever got the vote. It's kind of like a gift on top of honoring his memory. But Will Luckie says I ought to let go of the past, says a new man would breathe life back into me. He says I'm wasting away and that I have a dry puff. "You'll have a bumper sticker on your car," he laughed, "that reads 'Dry puff behind the wheel'."

Of course I couldn't be mad at him, even though it was more of his nasty talk. He said it with care, like he really wanted to see me have a better life in relationships. Another thing he said is that it was wrong to vote the way a dead man would vote, for that reason alone. "You ought to vote for your own personal convictions," he said. "Sure, you'd likely come to the same decision on a candidate, but it would be your independent choice. Ain't you heard of women's lib?"

Well I know some about the woman libbers. I know they're a bunch of rich white women that feel bound up in girdles and brassieres. And I understand the symbolism. I ain't ignorant. I just don't know what them woman libbers have to do with me, besides the fact that I work for one in Miss Maureen. She says she's a "free spirit," and wishes she was an original suffragette but was born too late. "But now there is liberation everywhere," she'll say. "And I am not about to miss this fresh wave of freedom! Thank you, Betty Friedan."

"Who's that?" I asked her one time. And she not only told me, she ran and got this book for me to take home. *The Feminine Mystique*.

"More like The Feminine Mistake," Miss CeCe said, all snotty like.

"It was a breath of fresh air," her mama said. "And now there are so many more air-fresh female voices in the world—Kate Millett, for example. And, oh—*Fear of Flying*!"

"That is nothing but pornography, encouraging women to have random sex with whomever."

"My Lord, it's a *novel*. And that is *not* the gist."

"I am aware. That it is fiction."

"Have you read it?"

"Of course not. I don't read pornography."

"You might learn a thing or two."

"Mother, I am not having this salacious conversation with you! It gives me the dry heaves."

"Them heaves ain't the only things that's dry," Will might throw in. And I can't help it. It makes me giggle inside.

Yep, that CeCe is another story. She'll get on her soap box derby about how America is going to hell in a handbasket on account of loose morals and the youth. "Our country was great once upon a time," she'll say, "but I don't see how we'll ever make America great again, what with all of the free love and the drugs and the vulgarity of the hippies and what not. There's even race mixing going on. No offense, Lindia, but it goes against my Christian sensibility to think of the mongrelization of any race—even the black race. I mean, the Tower of Babel told that tale, didn't it?"

I didn't bother to say how some plantation owner or overseer or random white rapist or another had done a little bit here and there to lighten up my own skin. There was no point. Some folks are thinking listeners and some folks never will be.

She'll blabber on and on and on about the woman libbers and what all they be up to. "They want birth control pills handed out to adolescents just like lollipops, even though abortion is running rampant ever since that despicable decision last year. Do you know there's even talk of an abortion clinic in Gainesville? Just right down the road? In a college town!"

"Well, they certainly don't need those clinics in retirement communities," Miss Maureen will say.

"And do you know they put those teeny-tiny fetuses out with the trash? I saw pictures of it. Their teeny-tiny feet and teeny-tiny hands!"

"Have you ever heard of a teeny-tiny hemorrhage? No? Oh, that's right—a hemorrhage is a big thing—and that's how your third cousin Gloria from Atlanta died. Just hours after she had one of those back alley things."

"But you told me Cousin Gloria died of pneumonia!"

"Well now you know the harsh truth. And I hope you won't be casting any stones, Miss Christian Methodist."

But nothing will shut that child up when she gets tuned up. "Lord help us if they get the ERA through and Uncle Sam starts drafting young ladies into combat," she has said many times. "There will be all kinds of fraternizing, you just know there will. And probably the military will offer its own abortions to the young ladies. Imagine!"

"The draft ain't used anymore," Will Luckie might answer. "And as long as there's unwanted pregnancies and coat hangers in the world there's going to be abortions."

"Well, the bottom line is, they hate men is what," she'll say. "And they're mannish, like that Billie Jean King."

"Athletic is more accurate," Miss Maureen will come back, "and a little exercise wouldn't do your frame any harm."

"Well, if that's not the pot calling the kettle then I don't know what!"

"Oh, CeCe, the point is that we could all use a little exercise, and it doesn't make us mannish."

"And they are just plain rude and shrill and too demanding. I could never be like that. If they were at all attractive or demure and ladylike, they'd simply use their feminine wiles to get their way. Everybody knows how easy it is to twirl a man around your little finger."

Although I ain't never seen *her* do that—use "feminine wiles." She just yaps out orders to that pansy husband of hers—and to anyone else, including me. And whatever you think you know, she knows more. She'll go to hollering things about how the country's done turned away from Jesus and about how socialists and communists have taken over where democrats used to be. And you *know* Will is going to poke at her and poke at her until she stomps out the house and across the yard to that prissy husband. And I'll just be shaking my head at the furor that can be flung up behind politics these days.

Here's a thing: Will Luckie voted for George McGovern, just like I did. He's the only white man—the only white person in Pollard, aside from Miss Maureen, I bet—to vote against Nixon. We talked about it in the kitchen one day. It all went back to his time in the war.

"If I hadn't seen what it was like over yonder, I probably wouldn't vote for no damn body." He was leaning against the counter, holding a stem of Miss Maureen's crystal for a spit cup.

"Over in them jungles?" I had seen that scar where some jagged metal had hit him in the thigh. It was a nasty looking thing.

"Damn straight."

"Did you lean on the Lord?" I'd heard Henry say there wasn't no atheists in foxholes, but Will shot that down.

"I leaned on my *brothers*. Jar heads. Never thought much of those who yell for the Lord in a pinch and forget about what all he said the rest of the time."

I had to bend. "That's what my Henry always said. Trusting in the words of Jesus is as far as you need to go."

"That's the damn truth."

"But Miss Maureen says religion is the opium of the people."

He sighed. "Folks quote that quote out of context all the time. And that damn woman is all the time bragging up context. I'm going to have to have a talk with her." He chuckled. "A 'come to Jesus'."

"Sir?"

"Stop with the 'sir'. It's just that I made it my business to read up on communism. Karl Marx. The goddamn history of Viet Nam. Before I even joined up. Hell, I was in high school."

"You don't strike me as one to be so serious in school," I said, before I could check myself.

This time he laughed real big. "I wasn't. But I *was* curious about things I wanted or needed to know. I've never been a great student, but I ain't stupid. Know what I mean?"

"I sure do." And I did. Like I said, I ain't ignorant.

"Here's the whole quote. I thought it was so pretty I memorized it. Ready?"

"Yes, sir."

He gave me a squinty-eyed angry look.

"Yes, Mr. Will."

"Here it is: 'Religion is the sigh of the oppressed creature, the heart of a heartless world, and the soul of soulless conditions. It is the opium of the people'."

"That *is* right pretty. It gets us through."

"If that's your inclination."

"Why you went into the marines to begin with?"

"Adventure. Belonging. Seeing the world. All the things that son of a bitch recruiter at the bowling alley in Pensacola talked about to me and Greg."

"Greg?"

"My high school buddy. Old Greg. A k a 'GooGoo.' We were desperate to get the hell away from Pollard just as soon as them diplomas were handed off, and that damn recruiter made it sound like paradise, the USMC."

"Y'all was just babies."

"Yep. Playing pinball and picking our snot noses at the bowling alley. Fresh out of high school. PFC Jacobson swooped down on us like a vulture, talking about how we could go in as buddies and glide all the way through. Made Vietnam sound like a little mud hole where you had a lot of down time." He spit in that pretty crystal.

"Doesn't seem right to go after babies."

"No shit. Thing is, I knew the history, about all the war over yonder. Soldiering is in their damn blood. But at the same time Greg and me felt fierce about fighting the commies, you know?"

"Godless folks."

"It's not the godlessness we was fighting. It was the ideology."

I gave him a look, but he just kept on going.

"Khe Sanh is all it took to really put it into perspective," and his voice kind of trailed off while his eyes looked out into some other way of knowing. It's hard to describe.

"Miss Maureen said, too, that war changes folks," is what I offered.

He startled, then, "Yeah, that's a fact. You see that kind of shit—war shit—and you're going to either do one of two things: live your life like a fart in a whirlwind or live it like a fart that's thick enough to track a chicken in. You know?"

He did like that sometimes—talked real serious and deep one minute, then went over to crude and rude town the next. He would talk all proper grammar for a little minute and then go to redneckin' it up the next. I don't know why that surprised me because I do the same thing. I speak one way at work and another with Brenda and them. And there was my truly official "Mrs. Rev. Johnson" way to speak, which was soft, refined and mostly unused since my husband's funeral. Mr. Will was looking at me real hard, behind the "living life like a fart" thing, and I believed he wanted me to understand, so I nodded. "You were robbed," I said.

"Hell, yeah. Robbed, duped, fucked over forty different ways." He spat in the glass. "Motherfuckers."

"Henry always said it takes hard times to get folks to take action."

"Well nobody has to kick me in the head. Wasn't no way I was going to vote for that slimy motherfucker. And come, bleed, or blister, something's got to give. His ass needs to go and go fast."

"It's a shame, alright."

"It's way past a shame. It's against the law. His ass belongs in a cell."

I think that was the day I finally decided Mr. Will was all right.

All the Way to Memphis

"The truth does not change according to our ability to stomach it."
~Flannery O'Connor

Clista Juniper was a meticulous woman, from her immaculate housekeeping to her perfectly enunciated sentences; from the way she comported herself with pitch-perfect professionalism to the way she presided over the Hinds County High library. The school was situated between the county seat of Jackson, Mississippi, and Raymond, which was known as "the other county seat," a fact that amused her with its ironical aberration, its lack of order. It even extended to her daily wardrobe, which consisted of tailored suits in every shade of beige so that the coral lips and nails, with matching pumps, her trademark, would stand out all the more, her platinum-dyed hair double-French twisted in a tight, inwardly curling labial sheen, a la Tippi Hedren. Indeed, her colleagues—for she had no real intimates—often teased her about her early sixties look, whereupon Clista might express her practiced, breathy giggle and respond, "It is me, the look. Always has been."

"Right down to the girdle?" a teacher might ask.

"Absolutely."

"With the clips and all?" another might chime in.

"Certainly."

"They still make those?"

"I have always believed in stocking up."

"What's a girdle?" a neophyte, a young woman poorly read who took no note of puns, might ask.

So Clista, though she was senior staff at sixty-something, would leave it to another woman, a fifty-something, to explain, getting back to her shelves and her silence and her computerized Dewey Decimal System (although she maintained a card catalogue as well), shushing students with a coral pucker against her coral-nailed index finger.

The automobile she was driving on this day, her champagne-colored Cadillac, was as meticulously kept as she, although, on this particular day, she was thinking of taking up a former bad habit and filling the car's ash tray with coral-printed filters on the butts of fags she had smoked. She was on edge, shaky, the twists of her coif slightly wispy, like the frayed nerves she so tightly held inside the emotions she rarely let loose. She had let loose this morning, though, before doing her usual ablutions and her make-up to step into the Cadillac and drive not to the high school, where she would be expected after the weekend, but north, to some indeterminate place-- she knew not where.

When she saw the figure in the distance, on the side of the highway, she knew immediately what she would do. And, even though Clista was nothing like the sort to pick up a hitchhiker, she would certainly make an exception on this day, as she put her life, her profession, her town behind her, making a sure-to-be futile attempt to run away. This was a day of making all kinds of breaks, the shattering of facades, the clattering of realities, a day to step out of character and try to locate her self, if there ever was such a thing. It made a crazy kind of ironic sense to pick up a hitcher, who, as she drew closer, looked more and more like a teenage girl, finally becoming one, sturdy but slight of frame, like a gymnast. Certainly not threatening, like the haggard and tattooed serial killer stereotype that had forever lived in her wagons-circled mind. She pulled to the shoulder of the road and watched in the rearview mirror as the girl gathered up her things and bounded toward the waiting vehicle, then, catching her own eyes in the reflecting oval of silvered glass, saw a shadow of the emotion and primal fear that had captured Clista in the pre-dawn hours this morning, when she shot and killed her husband of forty-something years.

It was only an oddity to her now that she had done such a thing; it seemed distant and sketchily surreal. Strange how rapidly those tautly-bound emotions came undone, ramping into the kind of sight-blotted rage that would allow a person to do murder, settling afterwards into a numbness of spirit and mind that allowed her to believe in the possibility of, simply, running away—to almost believe it never happened in the first place. The numbness vibrated in an ear-humming buzz, as if her entire skull were swaddled in layer upon layer of cotton sheeting or felt, but there were fuzzy sounds of car doors and heavy canvas bags thudding into the leather seats. Then a voice, a face, something like words.

"What?" Clista managed.

"It's just that you've saved my life, that's all. If I had to be in this nothing place just one more day, just one more day, I would go nut case. See, my family is an insane asylum. My dope fiend mother especially. And so I just now packed up my shit, marched my butt down that dirt lane, and sat myself on the side of the highway. And here you come right off the bat. Shit, what's your name?"

It was a jarring question, and inside of Clista's hesitation, her guest continued.

"I'm Savannah. But I don't think I'll keep that name. Doesn't sound bluesy enough. Sa-van-nah. It's a city in Georgia. Which is known for peaches. But what about Georgia? For a name, I mean.

Clista was still thinking about her own name.

"Do you have any chips or something?" The girl had not taken a breath. "I'm always hungry. I'm definitely set on a different speed than most other people. Are you going to put it in drive?"

Again the out-of-left-field questions caught Clista off guard. "I—yes," she said, pulling back onto the pavement. Ever prepared for emergencies, she gestured at the glove box, where Savannah found a pack of cheese crackers.

The girl tore into the package with her teeth, orange crumbs scattering, then, "I love states for names—Bama, Carolina. Cities, not so much. Missouri is nice. What's yours?"

"My—"

"Name."

"It's Clista," she said, thinking, and I murdered my husband this morning, because he did the unimaginable and betrayed our decades of sameness and safety and "understoods," and "inasmuches" and such immaculate respectability as most couples never achieve. He took all that was invested in our public presentation as a couple and crumbled every iota of trust into talcum powder and the fairy dust that magically transformed me into a cold, cold killer.

"—so of course you know that," Savannah was saying.

"Know what?"

"What I was saying. Are you alright? I was saying how your name sounds something like a female part, but I guess you caught a lot of teasing at a certain age, so of course you know that. Junior high is hell for everybody." She sucked in a breath. "I'm sorry if I offended you. Sometimes I go over the top. My mind goes faster than I can talk and I try to keep up and so words get blurted out before I know it. You know?"

Clista was not accustomed to such talk, talk of female parts with sexual references, cursing, and just plain chattiness of a distasteful bent, as she had no good best girlfriend, having kept the world at a polite, respectable distance. This girl, however, felt unthreatening in spite of her verbiage. "How old are you?" the driver attempted to divert.

"Twenty-six," was the reply. "I know, I know. I look sixteen. I get it all the time. It's because I'm so small-boned. And flat chested. I've thought about store-bought tits, implants, but I just don't believe in doing that shit to your body." She sighed with a flourish. It's a blessing and a curse, being my size. I mean, when I tell people I'm a blues singer, they laugh. 'Ain't no big, bluesy voice gonna come out of that little thing.' Plus I'm white, obviously. 'Little bitty white chicks can't sing the blues.' Folks just don't take me seriously. When you've lived through the low down dirty shit I've lived through, you can damn sure feel the hurt. Like, what do you do when it takes your crack head mother two years to get rid of a man who's pushing his hands in your panties and you're nine years old? Two years!"

"Oh, my!" Clista drew away from her, an instinct, and was immediately embarrassed.

"Well, it wasn't my fault, you know."

"Of course not. Absolutely not. I'm so sorry. I'm just not accustomed—"

"My point is, that's just one of the crappy things I've experienced. And it wasn't even the worst. But I keep it upbeat, you know? Keep it in the sunlight. Positive thoughts. Let it out in the lyrics. So do you believe I can sing?"

"I would imagine so," Clista said, thinking instead that betrayal felt like the big, silver blade of a very sharp knife slicing cleanly through the jugular. He betrayed me and I was unleashed in an unthinkable way, into utter insanity. I was not responsible, nor do I regret. The lioness kills to protect her vulnerable offspring, after all. Is there an analogy to be had? Does it even matter?

"—and my boyfriend—he's a tattoo artist—he did all of mine, see?" She turned her leg to reveal the serpent-like lizard inked around her calf, winding toward its own tail; turned a shoulder bearing a crucifix, Jesus and his blood upon an elaborately detailed cross, the eyes of the holy martyr cast up in surrender to the Father. "His name—my boyfriend's—is Dakota. A state, right? It fits with my world view. He is amazingly talented. I mean, isn't this gorgeous?" She pulled down the front of her t-shirt to reveal, just above her heart, a small but beautifully intricate insect of some kind—something like one might find in a fly fisherman's tackle box. "I have others, but they are in hard to find places, if you know what I mean."

Clista's husband was a fly fisherman with a vast, three-tiered tackle box loaded with treasured lures, some even from his navy days, the days of their courtship. He took regular and frequent fishing trips to Colorado at solitary resorts, to the Rocky Mountain streams where he danced his line in the rhythmic ballet of a cast. She did not accompany him as she had no interest in his hobbies other than as fodder for those sometimes necessary social conversations:

"Paul loves his lures as much as he loves me," she might joke, "but at least he finds me more alluring." Not that she alluded to any sort of physical sensuality between the two of them. Clista had always found that particular expression of human instinct to be distasteful at best, more of the time disgusting. There were un-artful fumblings early in their union, a marriage that followed a courteous courtship, but they soon settled into a life of platonic rhythms, ebbing away into separate workdays, flowing back into their isolated split-level home in the evenings. And no later than ten p.m. they would be tucked into twin beds connected by a night stand bearing an antique Princess telephone, pink, with a nine millimeter loaded and at the ready in its French Provincial drawer.

"—so why don't you just take a look," Savannah had opened a cell phone and was scrolling through some photographs. "Here you go," and she turned the screen to Clista.

"Oh!" It came almost as a shriek paired with another recoiling of her whole body. The wheels left the blacktop for a few seconds.

"Holy Christ—what was that?" Savannah looked at her as if she had two heads and then studied the screen of her phone, a close-up of her pubic area and the peace lily engraved above the curls. Her face fell. "Oh. I thought you wanted to see my other tattoos. Sorry."

"No, it's alright. I—I'm just not accustomed to such images."

"No shit. Well, I didn't mean to scare you. I mean, it's just skin, basically. I've never seen what the big deal is. Skin is skin. It holds in our organs. Sex is something else, but it really amounts to just rubbing. But you're the driver so I sure as hell won't fuck with you. But you have to know up front that I was born without a filter."

"Filter?"

"You know, I tend to blurt out whatever's in my head. I'm ADHD, so it kind of goes with the territory. I'll try to watch my mouth, though. I mean, you could easily just dump me on the side of the road again. And there I'd be with my thumb out. Again."

"I won't do that." Then, for no real reason she could fathom, she added, "I'm going all the way to Memphis."

"For real? Holy shit, that's awesome. How lucky is it you picked me up? And don't worry—no more tattoo pictures," and she laughed a trilling, lively laugh.

Paul had a tattoo, from the time he served in the navy during the Vietnam Conflict. It was of two intertwining snakes encircling a cross, the word "Bound" crowning the top of the cross like a bent halo. He said it represented his love of country, how bound up in it he was. And he believed in what he was doing in fighting the Red Menace off the shores of Southeast Asia, even if he never had to dodge any bullets.

"Your husband?"

"What?" Clista had not realized she had spoken.

"The serpents. So symbolic. I mean, my Uncle Jessie actually fought over there—lost a leg and an eye. He has a cool glass eye he always entertained us with—my cousins and me—when we were kids. He'd take it out and toss it up in the air and catch it in his mouth like popcorn."

Clista shuddered.

"I know, pretty gross. But not if you're a little kid and not really at all if you think. I mean, look what he's been through. He deserves to do whatever the hell he wants, huh? He doesn't have a fake leg anymore. He used to. And he could make it do fart noises, another thing little kids love."

"Goodness!" Paul was not allowed—had not been allowed—to fart in her presence. Clista insisted that he step into the bathroom or outside if that urge was upon him. On those occasions when it happened serendipitously, he apologized with abject humiliation to her stony disdain.

Black earth was turned in the fields bordering Highway 61. It was planting time and within months the black dirt would turn to snow, and cotton puffs would litter the roadside after picking was done. Picking. To pick off. She had killed him, shot him in the head right there in his study, where she had found him before dawn, crept up to the door, borne witness to the sounds of lecherous, staccato-rhythmed motions and gritty, profane talk. He was preoccupied enough not to notice the slight click as she eased the door open, just a crack, just enough that she could see the man facing him on the computer screen, knew immediately who he was—the man in the photographs holding stringers heavy-laden with fish—the best friend from the navy, Spencer Kraus, also married. She fetched the gun and returned to wait it out. He did not notice, even when the screen had gone dark and he had lain his head down on his arms, exhausted, as she padded across the carpet's soft pile in one dreamlike motion, squeezed two bullets into his skull, turned and left just that quickly, with the stealth of a jungle cat.

"So tell me more." Savannah's words, again jarring.

"What do you mean?"

"You just said you were a cat."

"What?"

"Yeah, a jungle cat. And I'm thinking, what the hell?"

"I'm sorry," Clista stammered. "I'm just upset." She had to watch her words, slipping out unintended and quick, like minnows darting across currents.

"Well, then tell it, sister. What did the son of a bitch do?" She pulled out a pack of American Spirit cigarettes. "Okay if I smoke?"

"Yes." Her surrender felt like the beginning of some kind of relief. "But only if you light one for me."

***

The sound of clattering dishes and running water came from a kitchen in the back of the diner. Savannah was putting heart and soul into devouring her sandwich, dousing it mid-chew and frequently with Dr. Pepper. "Thank you so much for buying," she gulped. "My money situation is pretty busy, but that'll change when I hook up with Dakota."

Clista had attempted to force down a salad, but nausea made that impossible so she nibbled a couple of Saltines. She had bought her very own pack of cigarettes, Virginia Slim menthols, the brand of her younger years. You've come a long way, Baby, the old advertising jingle rattled around in her head. She exhaled a mushroom cloud of smoke. "I can't think, can't know what to do."

"Sure you can." Savannah leaned across the table, speaking in a hushed but animated tone. "You can absolutely know what to do. You just have to connect all the dots. That's what My Uncle Jessie used to say, anyway. But he was pretty PTSD. You're probably kind of PTSD about now, too."

"The dots are scattered, all across the floor," and she thought of throwing jacks as a child, the scattering stars, the ball bouncing. "That's the way the ball bounces," she murmured, smiling.

"Okay, okay, you're not going all mental on me, right?"

"No. I've already been mental. Can I go sane on you?"

"That would be good, but dude, your life is going to go end over end either way. I mean, you've got to either get a new identity and disappear—and that's really hard—or go back and come clean—and that's really hard, too. Man!" and her eyes widened at the enormity of it all.

"Are my eyes still red and puffy?"

"Yeah, but that's good. I think it keeps the waitress from coming over too often."

Clista took out her compact and applied a fresh coat of coral to her lips. I am a coral snake. She blotted with a napkin pulled from the stainless steel holder.

They were in a desolate part of the state where the crook of the Mississippi separated Arkansas, Tennessee and Mississippi, at Buck's Diner, where time had stopped decades earlier, an eatery with worn red plastic seats, dull chrome, and a hanging musk of aged bacon grease. It was just past the lunch hour, so the two women had the place to themselves while a sour-faced teenager bussed a few tables. A grizzled looking cook sat at a booth near the kitchen door, smoking, chatting in a low, gravelly voice with the one waitress, who sauntered over to the travelers once in a while, called them "honey" and "sugar" and "baby" as she offered more tea.

"Man, you're in some serious shit. I've known all kinds of people slogging through all kinds of shit. Hell, my own mother only had me because she couldn't afford another abortion. She was a drug addict. Cocaine. Sometimes she did men to get money for it. Now she's killing herself with meth. I was trying to help her get straight, but that stuff is insane. In-fucking-sane. You really saved my life by picking me up."

A hopeful little ripple went through Clista. "Do you think maybe that cancels out the other?"

"Maybe so," Savannah grinned. "Maybe the karma is right now. Maybe that's a reason to keep running. Or to go back."

"I can't believe I actually told you everything. It's not like me at all."

"But it is me. Seriously. It's something about me," Savannah said. "People tell me stuff all the time. Strangers. I mean, I'll be in the check-out line and somebody will just unload their whole entire bizarre life story. It happens all the freaking time."

But I don't confide in anyone, Clista thought, still marveling at how Savannah had coaxed the darkness out of her.

"What did the son of a bitch do?" she had asked.

"How do you know it's about a man?"

"Always is. Your husband?"

"Yes."

"So come on with it."

"No."

"Come on. Tell it."

"I can't."

"Just say the words."

And Clista's fingers had tightened on the steering wheel of the smoke-filled champagne-colored Cadillac. "My husband betrayed me."

"You know it."

"He lied and cheated and did it from the start."

"Uh-huh."

"And it's worse than that."

"How?"

"My husband betrayed me."

"Tell."

"With a man."

"Holy Christ."

"A double life."

"You're right. That is worse. Way fucking worse."

"I was faithful to that man forever and he was faithful to his man forever and I caught him in a despicable act and I killed him."

"Killed?"

"Shot."

"The fuck you say!" And Savannah had turned her body fully facing her in the car. "You are so not the type!"

"Apparently I am." And she had pulled onto the shoulder of the road, rested her head on the steering wheel and howled like a wounded animal as Savannah, effervescence disarmed by the rawness of it all, tried impotently to console her.

***

The waitress sauntered over. "Here, Sweetie, let me get this out of your way," and began collecting plates and utensils, blood red fingernails clicking against heavy white glass.

Savannah picked up the last of her BLT and pushed the plate. "Are you still taking me to Memphis?" she asked as the waitress sauntered away.

"Of course."

"You're not, like, dangerous or anything, right?" It was almost a whisper.

"I have no weapons or designs upon your possessions."

"I know that. It just felt like a question I had to ask, you know? I mean, how dumb would I feel if something really happened—and I know it isn't—but something happened and I never even asked the question in the first place. Man, would I feel dumb."

"Certainly."

"Plus, I just got to get to Memphis."

What will you do when you get to there? Where will you live?"

"With Dakota, of course. He'll come pick me up wherever you and I land. He has a place off Beale Street, right in the thick of things. Man, I can't wait to go out to some of those clubs. Not the touristy ones on the main drag. The real ones. The ones you have to just happen into. But the first thing I'm going to do—and I know this is stupid and touristy and all—but I'm going to get me some barbecue."

"Can I join you?"

"Sure. Are you like, buying?"

"Of course. It'll be my last supper."

"Holy shit. You're not going all suicidal or anything, are you? Because that's even more messed up than what's gone down. Seriously."

"You're right. Besides, I don't know. Could I actually go home to that—mess, and put the gun to my own head? I just don't see it."

"Well, you know they say it's a permanent solution to a temporary problem, right?"

"It would certainly be a problem for both my permanent and my temple," Clista said, but her puny, half-hearted attempt at punning fell on deaf ears.

***

Memphis was a presence she could feel well before hitting the outskirts. It was in the whispery thrum of potential stories in song—a spiritual imprint that webbed out and out to the rising hills and farms, cascading down the Mississippi River to rich Delta dirt.

Savannah must have felt it, too. She threw her head back and let fly several bars of melodic anguish, big and rich, at odds with the tiny vessel making the music. "You might think you're living large, baby, but you'll be dying when you get home. You might think you're hitting the mark, baby, but you'll just be trying when you get home." She turned to Clista. "What do you think? It's something I've been working on."

"You're very talented. I don't know a lot about the blues, but you have a unique sound."

"Unique good or unique I-can't-think-of-anything-good-to-say-so-I'll-say-unique?"

"Definitely good. Raspy good."

Savannah beamed. "Thank you. And you're wrong about the other."

"What other?"

"The blues. You know a hell of a lot about the blues."

"I do? Well, yes, now."

"No, always. Can you talk about your life? Yourself? I mean, okay, you spent a very long marriage being some guy's beard, but that doesn't happen in a vacuum, you know?"

"A beard?"

"You know the wife of a gay man who lives in a really deep closet."

"There's actually slang for it?"

"Sure. You don't know a lot about sex, do you?"

"I know it's messy."

"Okay, see, this is what I mean. You don't like sex. That's how you and your husband connected, on a really basic level. So if you think about it, it was not a bad arrangement. You each got what you needed. You just couldn't handle knowing it, right?"

"I'm not sure. What I've done is so much worse than knowing anything."

"Who really knows anything?"

"What do you mean?"

"Well, my boyfriend Dakota, right? He believes that there is nothing but thought and that we've thought all this up. Like, you thought me up on the side of the road and poof, there I was. You thought up a husband who used you as his beard so you killed him."

"This is all a lot of pseudo-philosophical malarkey."

"Oh my god, you said 'malarkey.' You are so not the type to kill a person. But anyway, here's the thing."

"I suppose I could just think him back alive, correct?"

"Well?"

"You must be crazy."

"Yeah, I am, but so is everybody—including you."

Clista's muscle memory sprang into a mode of defense that immediately fizzled. Crazy? With such a buffed and polished image? With a picture perfect life? With the dead husband laid out across his computer desk? "Maybe I can think him back alive?"

"Damn right. It's got to be worth a freaking try."

They ate just outside the city limits at Uncle Stumpy's Bodacious Barbecue Bin, thick brown sauce crawling across their fingers, down their chins, sticky napkins piled on the tabletop. Clista found herself laughing at the mess of it all. "This is real barbecue. I've never had the real thing," and she sucked on her fingers just like Savannah did. And when Savannah flipped open her cell phone to call boyfriend Dakota to come and pick her up, Clista studied the way the young woman cocked her head, trilled her voice up and down, like a delightful little bird, as she spoke. Twenty-six, yet so much like a young girl—enthusiastic, forward looking, hopeful, on the verge of a dream.

They embraced in the parking lot. "I never knew," Clista said. "How could I not know?"

"But didn't you, really? Come on, didn't you? Way down deep? In your guts?

Clista opened her purse and withdrew the compact and tube of coral lipstick. "I guess that's a thing to consider." She reapplied her signature color, pulled out a Kleenex and blotted a kiss onto it. She folded the Kleenex and handed it to Savannah. "If you're ever really low, give yourself a kiss from me."

"Oh, I've already been plenty low. I'm aiming for up now. But, just in case, thanks."

"You'll be okay here?" Clista glanced around the parking lot. It was not the best neighborhood, judging by the buildings in various stages of disrepair, and day had fallen into dusk.

"Oh, hell yeah. Dakota won't be too long."

"But it's getting dark and you're unfamiliar with the area." There was a pharmacy across the street that was well-lit. "You should go to the bench by that drug store."

Savannah giggled. "Are you kidding? Nothing's going to happen to me. You should know this about me by now. No point in letting worry rule your world, huh?"

"I guess."

"So have you decided what you're going to do?"

"Yes, I have."

"And it feels right?"

"Yes."

"Good."

The champagne colored Cadillac was warm from the sunlight trapped inside just a short time ago—invisible but there, the traces of a star. Clista rolled down the windows and waved as she waited to pull out of the parking lot. She looked back for a few seconds longer to see Savannah arrange her possessions and plop down on her duffel bag next to the front of the rib joint, a snapshot of a reality Clista had enjoyed for a day. She wasn't sure if the woman—no, the girl—was a chance that fell out of the sky or a providential event sent by some spiritual presence in an effort to set things right. Maybe the girl really would fade from existence once Clista turned away, so she hesitated for a moment, not wanting that vibrancy to dissipate, like the rays of the sun were.

"Just go!" Savannah shouted, waving her off, laughing.

Clista giggled, a genuine sound, pressed the gas, and pulled away. She started to roll up the windows, but caught herself, even told herself "No," right out loud. Then, at a glimpse of her eyes in the rear-view mirror, she even whispered, "You crazy fucker."

And she left the windows down into the evening, rolling south through the farm country, past the scrubby towns and lives of folks left behind. The push of air blew a rhythm of comfort into her soul, disengaging strands of platinum blonde that whipped about her face, growing into a small hurricane of color-treated hair spiraling around the eye of coral lips. She would drive well into the night, until she made it all the way home, consuming every millisecond with the fierce energy of thinking, thinking hard, thinking him back alive.

Looking for John David Vines

Christy Logan looked across and around the dim interior of the Palomino Lounge outside Columbus, Mississippi, as she and her best friend Malia took up residence at a round table off to the side. The crowd was sparse, as it was not yet mid-afternoon. The pool balls clicked against each other, cue heels thudded against the concrete floor and punctuated muted country classics. She inventoried the scattered knots of faces. No JD. But she had sensed he would not be here. Still, she searched through the scattered wisps of smoke and hazy light from Christmas strings stapled to the ceiling, trying not to let her disappointment show. She waved at Miller Sams, the bartender. "Send us two Bud Lights," she half-hollered. She had dated Miller five years earlier and liked to believe he was still not over her, liked to believe that none of them ever really got over her, intoxicating as her effect upon men was known to be.

Malia fidgeted and squirmed her broadening ass into a chair with a curved back. She had crossed into the territory of her thirties with a surrendering nod to her thunderous thighs and fat-dimpled behind that Christy could not fathom. Malia was married, though, and happily, or so it seemed. Sometimes her husband, Dewey, joined them at the clubs, but mostly he stayed in front of the TV rigging his rods and reels when he wasn't working at the car lot. And he never seemed to mind that his wife went out with Christy to the bars. Most married men would raise a fuss about that. Maybe he figured no one would find his wife attractive enough to hit on, especially with Christy around; or maybe he really did trust her to keep her vows. Christy herself was twenty-nine, just beginning to steel her ego against the foray into the next decade of her life, suddenly a-panic that she was singular as opposed to plural, an "I" rather than an "us." In that regard, she secretly envied her friend.

Malia lit a cigarette, a Capri menthol 120, and held it between her nails, sculpted and red, like patent leather under the pointed bits of light. She exhaled a rushing cloud of smoke. "Well," she said, smirking, "I had to shave Dewey's butt last night."

"Did not!" Christy drew her nose into a deep crinkle of disgust.

"Oh, honey, yeah," Malia said. "And I'm here to tell you that is one hairy man."

"God!"

"Took a pile of hair off that man's ass this high." She held her palm four inches above the table top. "I'm 'on start calling him Sasquatch."

"Gag me one time, why don't you," Christy said, maintaining the nose crinkle.

"Well, shit, it was the only way I could get at those carbuncles. He's got three of the damn things scattered all over his butt. Has to sit on a ring of foam rubber like he's got hemorrhoids or something."

"That's what you get for marrying a man ten years older than you."

"It ain't no big deal."

"God, I couldn't be married—all the time having to do gross shit like that," Christy said, reappraising her rush at the altar. But JD wouldn't have carbuncles. JD was too handsome and polished to need his butt shaved, ever.

"Aaah." Malia flipped the back of her hand and shrugged as Vicky the waitress set two beers down on the table.

"How y'all doing?" Vicky said.

"Just barely," Malia said.

Christy leaned forward, waiting to seize an opportunity to ask about JD.

"Where's that crazy husband of yours?"

"Hell," Malia said and drew on her skinny little cigarette. "He's laid up at the house, legs all swole up with the gout."

"I thought it was the carbuncles had him down."

"Honey, no. On top of the carbuncles, he's flat laid out on the bed with his shit swole up."

"Gross."

"Hell, that man is a train wreck. Just a pile of writhing misery."

"And I see you ain't at home a-holding his hand," Vicky said.

"Are you serious? Cause you know I don't give up my nights out. But I told him he could just as easy set his ass on that foam rubber ring and prop his legs up in a bar as he could at home. Sometimes he just likes to be miserable. But, hey, that don't mean I got to be."

"Ain't you even going to cook him no dinner?" Vicky asked.

Christy peeled at the Bud Light label, growing antsy and impatient with the conversation.

"Shit, I asked him what did he want and I'd go to the store and get it. I would've cooked him a pile of chicken or a steak, anything. But he was being all pitiful and puny, trying to get me to feel sorry for him, said he didn't want nothing but some Popsicles. Ain't that fucked up? So I went to the Food Tiger, got four goddamn boxes of fucking Popsicles, shoved them in the freezer, and went on my merry little way. Ain't that just some flat-out fucked up shit?"

"But if he's got the gout, how—"

"Hey Vicky," Christy interjected. "You seen JD this afternoon?"

Vicky's left eyebrow twitched upward. "Careful, honey."

"Come on. Has he been by here?"

"No, he ain't. Sorry. Or, hell, maybe I ain't sorry. You ought to give that man a wide way to go."

"Did I ask your opinion?"

"Okay, okay. Just remember who said it." She carried the round wooden tray back over to the bar.

"See? Somebody else agrees with me. John David Vines is a womanizing son of a bitch and ain't even about to leave his wife."

"Shut up! Don't nobody know what's between us. Nobody. We got a deep history together." Christy tossed out the quintessential bitch gaze that had been one of her staples throughout the last half of her twenties. It was a look that had sent more than one man into a blundering marathon of ass-kissing apologies and more than one woman into a fetal, tear-infested restroom retreat. And it had its desired effect upon Malia Dobbins.

"So are we going to stay here?" Malia asked.

"Long enough for this beer. Then we'll try some other bars."

"And he said for sure he'd meet you?"

"I told you already what he said. He said he'd do his best to get out this afternoon, that he'd borrow a car so his wife couldn't find him, that he'd run by the usual places. He said we'd talk about things."

"Things?"

"Yeah, things. Important things." Christy took a long swallow of beer. Her first romance with John David Vines was when she was nineteen, working as a teller at the First National Bank during the day, spending weekends at the bars, dancing to honky-tonk rock bands, learning how to use the power she was discovering she had over men. She had always been noticed for her looks, the black-haired, green-eyed, bold-breasted looks of a bar-girl queen. She was drafted to hand out the trophy every Sunday at the Dirt Track Races, and at the Flat Track Race every Thursday night. She ran for Watermelon Queen and won in a landslide. When she walked into a bar, men hollered her name, bought her drinks, and talked louder than usual; women either maneuvered into her small circle of girlfriends or watched her from across the bar, downing drinks and jealousy, but hoping to capture some of the magic.

John David Vines was one of the first to get deep into her panties. He had magic of his own. He was four years older, a boy she had watched on the football field when she was a freshman in high school, not yet pushed out at the breasts and hips. JD was golden and blonde with an edgy attitude that drew the attention of the kind of females who liked to taste danger. He never noticed Christy in high school, but when he came back to town after a stint in the Army he could not overlook the hottest girl in any club, and he courted her, ran his tongue along her neck and pulled her red underwear aside to touch her with the kind of knowledge the other boys did not begin to have.

She was not a slut, though, did not honor just anyone with that regal warmth between her bronzed thighs. She had lost her virginity to a blundering, pencil-dicked baseball player back in the eleventh grade and decided not to hand it out to anyone who did not show a plethora of potential. Which made her all the more desirable, since those few males who had that honor bestowed upon them could pass in the knowledge that she had knighted them in recognition of their sexual prowess. And everybody else knew it, too. Other women were intrigued when they heard who was Christy Logan's latest all the way man; consequently, for that chosen man even more pussy became available, increasing exponentially with each score thereafter. It was the strongest reference one could hope for.

She managed to keep herself from giving in to JD for a long time, though, in spite of his practiced fingers. She only let him put it in part way, at first, keeping him fevered and amped up on hormones. She had him where she loved to get men, on the teetering edge of potential ecstasy, where they filled her head with lush words, Mississippi sonnets of desire, and odes to her heart-pumping presence. She feasted on the rush of it all until it played out, most times growing tired of it after a while, moving on to the next man without ever letting the current one put it all the way in. But JD had a way with his touch and it was only a matter of time before her long, tanned legs were slung around his back, thighs sliding in a slick rhythm that snatched all sense of control away from her, leaving her the one wanting more, her sexual compass in pieces on the floor. It was too, too, frightening, and she quickly broke it off, breaking his heart, scoffing at his pleas to get married and have his babies, moving on to the next rush of power.

Christy rode the wild-child, hot-chick reputation for several years without slipping into slut-dom, but the latter part of her twenties found her reflection in the fluorescent-lit bathroom mirrors more hardened and drawn with precursor wrinkles. She married briefly, at twenty-seven, to an older man who had a little money and premature ejaculations that left her irritated by his ineptitude, left her spitting disgusted words at him until she realized he wasn't worth what little wealth he had. But she was married long enough to have a baby, a little boy who reminded her too much of his wimp of a daddy, a little boy who was now being raised by her mother. The thing that had grown in her left scarred stretch marks on her stomach and thighs, gave her breasts too much of a sag to tolerate. She got herself some implants, "store bought titties," Malia called them, and stepped inch by inch toward a metamorphosis into that which she had resisted up until now, up until she took up with a married man and ex-love named John David Vines. She knew, deep in the back of her head, that she was just before turning into a bar skank.

***

The crowd at the 45 Club was ushering in the after five spirit, thick with conversation and laughter. Christy and Malia had executed passes through the Three Pigs, Peggy's, and The S Curve, feeling the growing swell of happy hour with each stop, giggling more easily with the friends and acquaintances they encountered.

"Y'all know Godzilla Dobbins, don't you?" Malia asked a group clustered by the bar at the S Curve. "She's my monster-in-law, Dewey's mama. She hates my guts but she's the one got us together in the first place."

Oakley Starnes, Tim Hilyer and Tedder Bumpus, all friends of Dewey's, chuckled at the reference.

"That old woman is mean enough to scare the buggers out of a bugger-bear," Tim said.

"No shit," Malia said. "Still and all, she brung us together. It was back when Dewey was dating this Pentecostal churchwoman, you know, Babs Elmore. She was one of them Walking Elmores that used to walk up and down the highway of a day, walk to town, walk to the next county. Anyway, she took up with a Pentecostal Church, then she took up with Dewey, then she broke his heart. And you know what Dewey's mama said?"

"Naw."

"Tell it, then."

"Godzilla said, 'Boy you need to quit mopin' and moanin' around the house, laying all over the sofa eating up the cushions with your butt crack.' She said, 'Son, forget about that church woman and go on out to a bar somewhere and find you a nice woman that'll make you happy.' Ain't that some shit?"

Christy let laughter and smoke billow up around her thoughts about JD.

"Old Dewey's stove up, huh?" Tedder asked.

"God, yes. Got the gout and the butt carbuncles, and—I forgot to tell you this, Christy—he's got some seed ticks in his head that's been living there since he went hunting in the woods last Tuesday evening and won't let me pull them out."

"How do you keep from puking at all the shit you have to do for that man?" Christy said.

"It ain't nothing, really. But I admit I like to fell out and fainted when he showed me them seed ticks and said we was going to have to let them suck on his scalp a while till they get big enough to grab a-holt of."

"I pulled one the size of a big raisin off my wife's head not long ago," Tim said.

"Gag a maggot," Christy said. "Look here."

"No, you look here, Tedder said. "Come on and dance with me, Christy."

"I ain't in a dancing mood," Tedder was also a high school friend who had always harbored a crush on her, as did many of the other boys she grew up with.

He leaned close to her ear. "One day," he said. "One day you going to let me touch it, ain't you?"

She punched him hard in the arm. "Have any of y'all seen JD?" she asked.

Oakley cleared his throat. Tim looked down at the floor.

"I know y'all have."

"Naw, we ain't. Really," Tim said. "Go on and dance with Tedder. Give him a thrill."

"I said I ain't in a dancing mood."

"Remember the time old Dewey put that bull catfish in the wading pool?" Oakley said.

"Oh, hell, now that was some fuuucked uuuup shit," Malia drew the words out long. "He was so fucking proud of that big-ass fish that he blowed up this blue plastic wading pool we keep in the shed for our little nephew. Then he called up Bobby Pollins because Bobby had told him he wasn't no kind of fisherman. He just had to show the damn thing to Bobby, you know, so he could make like he had a dick after all."

Christy pushed her thumbnail against the label on the beer bottle, under the gummy-wet side of it, against the cold moisture.

"But Bobby didn't come over till the next morning and that fish stayed in that little blowed up pool all night, and it was February, you know, and the temperature dropped."

The men laughed, threw their heads back, then bent forward in a rhythm of humor.

"So Dewey got all puffed up, so proud of this big fat dick hanging between his legs, and walked Bobby round back to look at the fish. But the water had done froze and that fish was laid over on its side, just wall-eyed dead. And I guess poor old Dewey's pecker shriveled up like a old pea hull or something, but all he said was, 'I reckon I need to go on and skin that one, don't I?' Poor thing."

The laughter wrapped them all, until Christy punched through it, tearing at the label on her beer bottle. "Where the hell did y'all see JD? Huh?"

"To hell with JD," Tim said, grabbing Christy's forearm and pulling her over to the small dance floor near a jukebox that fuzzed out a Randy Travis song.

"Why you want to be grabbing me like that?"

"Cause you make me lose control, baby," he said, laughing.

"Why do y'all change the subject whenever I mention JD?"

He pulled her in to his body and they moved to the slow country rhythm. He leaned his lips close to her ear, sending tickles of air down the flesh of her neck. "I get jealous when I'm trying to impress a woman and all she does is go on about some other man."

"You are full of shit."

He straightened up to look her hard and steady in the eyes, a look ripe with interest, coaxing her intrigue. "Am I?" And he pulled her in again, arms encircling her, tightening, every subtle ripple of muscle against muscle telling her the tide was turning, honky-tonk currents were swirling past, threatening to carry her down under.

She wanted to throw a smart remark in his face, toss her hair back, do her bitch walk away from him, but she just as much wanted to finish the dance, nice as it felt to forget about JD, if only for a few minutes. So she let him push his knee between her thighs, breathe into her neck, stroke his palm down her back until it glanced the upper regions of her ass. But when the music ended, the panic set in as never before, so she lifted her eyes to meet his, squinted hard and mean. "You," she said again, this time with an index finger pressed to his chest, "are full of shit." She strode over to the table, gathered up her purse and Malia, and they headed out for the next bar.

***

The ladies' room at Martin's River House Club had four stalls and a bank of sinks backed by a big mirror. Flushing rushes of water, the clunk-clunk of the paper towel dispenser and gossip-toned conversation echoed against tiled walls.

"This is the nicest john of all the bars," Malia observed as she touched up her makeup. "Too bad the damn club sucks." She had been acting a shade different since they left the 45 Club, close-mouthed, but now she engaged in restroom girl talk.

"You told that right," came from Jennifer Gainus, who was bent over, head down, brushing her thick-curled hair. She straightened up fast, throwing her hair out in a puffy fluff of spiraling waves. "Only reason I come here is to see is anything going on, just in case there is, just to check it off the list and move on, you know?"

Christy contorted her lips into a tight 'o' and re-coated them with frosty bronze lipstick before blotting them with a square of toilet paper. "So have you seen JD?"

Malia rolled her eyes.

"Not lately. I seen him last night at the Playmore." Jennifer crimped and pulled at her hair, bringing it farther out from her head.

"Damn, girl, if you hair gets any bigger you're going to have to steal the Sasquatch title off of Dewey."

Jennifer laughed, then let her voice get fierce and low with the promise of a newsy tidbit. "I have to tell y'all, though, what I heard about Tim Hilyer."

Christy's level of interest doubled. "Yeah? We was just with him."

"Well, he's on the make, wife or no wife, so be careful. My sister-in-law seen him out back of the Playmore last night, back behind the dumpster, getting himself a blow job from damn Screwsie Dawson."

"Goddamn," Christy breathed. "He ain't just on the make. He's sunk way the hell down."

"No shit," Malia said. "What I hear is guys go back for more of them Dawson blow jobs cause if she really likes you she takes out her upper plate."

The three of them let squealing laughter echo up the tiled walls. Then Jennifer dug through her purse for a compact. "You better watch JD's wife don't get wind of the two of you, though, Christy."

"Shit. She'll know before long, and she ought to know by now. I been leaving clues behind lately."

"You are crazy, girl."

"Seriously," Christy said.

"What in the holy hell you been leaving?" Malia asked.

"Oh, just little things. A earring here, a Kleenex with my lip color on it there, but she's so dumb she ain't figured it out yet."

"Hell, if you want her to know, just call the bitch up," Jennifer said.

"That'd just make JD mad. No, the clues I'm leaving could be, like, accidental, you know? He couldn't get mad about that."

"So she ain't picked up on any of them clues, huh?"

"Hell no. That must be one dumb as dirt woman. Shit, I'd leave one of my thongs in the car but she'd probably just pick it up, take it for a Scrunchy, and put her damn hair up with it."

A fresh wave of giggles bounced from the lavatory walls, as the three women shared more bits of gossip. Malia did an impersonation of Dewey trying to see his butt in the mirror and the giggles were magnified in volume. The three of them chatted, primped, and preened, making ready to move on to the next club, hoping for another drama or two, perhaps even their own.

***

The parking lot at the Playmore Lounge was almost full when they turned in around seven-thirty. A Dangerous Thing, one of the local dance bands, would be playing tonight, but not until nine, and would go until one or two. JD always showed up at the Playmore at some point of an evening, just like everybody who frequented bars on the back side of town. At once it occurred to Christy that JD had never offered to meet her at the Ramada Lounge or the Montclair, or any of the bars where a more upscale, professional crowd gathered. She had frequented those bars fairly regularly before JD, but they only met at the rough-around-the-edges places where he would not be seen by his wife's friends.

Christy glanced over at Malia, who had gone quiet once again—for her, an aberration. A few clusters of folks were scattered about the parking lot. A young couple made out against the passenger's side of a Toyota. Jukeboxed music rode the neon glow lighting their car's interior in a haze of red. "I don't want to get out here yet. Let's just drive around some."

"Alright," Malia sighed. "But I'm a couple of beers into my buzz. Don't let me fuck up in front of a goddamn squad car."

"You're doing fine."

"For now, I guess. Where you want to go? To the bar at Sipsey?"

"Hell, no. You saw the Simms boys' pulpwood truck there and you know JD ain't going nowhere them Simmses are hanging out. Every time he runs into them he breaks a pool cue over somebody's head."

"No shit. Them Simmses ain't good for nothin' but the four F's: fuckin', fightin', and fixin' flats." She gave Christy a suspicious sideways glance. "So where you want to go?"

"Drive down the strip, okay?"

Malia looked at her then with a sudden expression that Christy had never experienced, so buffeted as she had always been by beauty and desirability. It was an expression of concern, even pity, and it took her breath with its quick intensity. "You don't want to do this, hon."

"Goddamn, don't look at me like that. I just want to see is his car at any of the restaurants on the strip."

"We ain't never gone chasing him down when he was with his family. That's over the line. That ain't right."

Christy slapped the dashboard with her right palm, hard. "I ain't chasing him down. Just go the hell to the strip and drive through the Wendy's and the McDonald's and whatever the hell other burger joints and restaurants you see."

"Okay, okay. But I ain't getting out and neither are you. If you want to make a scene, save it for the Playmore. Not in front of no damn young-uns."

"I ain't stupid."

Malia said nothing. She put the car in drive and turned out of the parking lot, onto the highway back to Columbus.

When Christy had first confronted her reflection in the mirror after the birth of the baby, she had collapsed in a sobbing heap on the hospital floor. It was too much. The dimpled flesh of her stomach was supposed to be flat and firm, a backdrop for the sexy emerald navel ring she wore. And her hipbones! They had fanned out, widening her lower body. Her whole skeletal and muscular ecology, it seemed, had been upset. Her breasts were swollen huge and hard with milk that seeped from her nipples, leaving round wet spots on her nightgown. Once emptied, those breasts spilled lower against her chest. It had taken almost a year and a good chunk of money to coax her body back into the kind of shape she could bear to show a man, and just in time for JD. JD told her she was beautiful, that his wife had let herself go after having their two children. JD kissed her stomach, told her stretch marks were a badge of honor, like the scar on his chest from being cut in a bar fight when he was stationed at Ft. Benning. He called her store-bought titties magnificent, reassured her that she was the most lovely, most luscious woman he had ever known or could ever hope to know. Where he had known just the right touches to her flesh in their early romance, he now knew just the right words to say to her flagging, aging ego.

***

His car was parked at the Mexican Kitchen, his favorite restaurant. Malia had ridden her around the vinyl-lined, play-grounded drive-thrus of every ticky-tacky fast food joint on the strip before it occurred to Christy that he might have picked a place he liked better. Malia pulled into the parking lot across the street from the restaurant that was roof-topped with a life-sized team of heavy plastic horses pulling a wagon. One of the horses had fallen over, its white plastic legs stuck sideward, like a carcass ripe with rigor mortis. The stucco building spilled light through two glass doors and a bank of windows on the upper level. Christy and Malia sat smoking Capri cigarettes, like partner cops on a stakeout.

After the second cigarette, Malia sighed. "This is boring. Let's go back to the bar and dance."

The bitch look came across Christy's face with authority.

"Well the plan was to have a good time. Dewey's probably having a better time than we are, him all laid up, even."

"That's his car. It can't be much longer."

"Only a lifetime."

"What kind of a friend says that? How come you want to say things like that to me?" Christy threw her cigarette through the open window, something in her emotional gut telling her she should not have asked.

Malia put both hands on the steering wheel, looked thoughtful for a moment, then turned her face to her friend. "Tedder told me, when you was off dancing with Hilyer, that JD's been avoiding you like crazy."

"You're lying." Christy felt cornered, hemmed in, desperate. "You don't know what's between us."

"Honey, JD ain't worth all this. Tedder said—"

"Tedder said shit. Tedder Bumpus is a dumb-ass redneck from Gordo who—"

She stopped, the parking lot's light hitting her arms as she leaned forward, palms on the dashboard.

JD strolled through the glass door of the Mexican Kitchen and out into the open night air. He was followed by two small boys, dark-haired little boys maybe six and seven years of age; running, rambunctious little boys who wrestled and horse-played their way across the pavement and into their daddy's car. JD leaned against the hood and lit a cigarette, his muscular frame bathed in fluorescence.

Christy reached for the door handle, but Malia leaned all the way across her taking her wrist. "I ain't letting you do that, honey," she said in a soft voice.

Christy was crying, had not realized it, but now she knew she was crying, watching JD lean against the hood of his car, smoking like a cocky, never-caught thief.

"Let's go." Malia reached for the keys.

"No," Christy said, still watching as a woman approached JD, a plump woman with dark hair, who Christy knew was his wife. And the plump woman took the cigarette from his lips and thumped it out onto the highway. JD laughed and grabbed the woman, twisting her arm playfully behind her back and the woman was laughing, too. Then one of the little boys stuck his head out the back seat window and JD let go of the plump woman and pretended a punch toward the boy, who ducked back inside the car. And before the woman walked around the car she looked up at JD and said something that made him throw his head back and laugh like Christy had never, ever seen him laugh. He was still laughing and shaking his head when the passenger's side door closed.

Malia had her arm around Christy through the whole of the scene in the parking lot, Christy's eyeliner and mascara smudged and smearing as she rubbed at hot tears. Then she stopped, abruptly, bitch-look overtaking vulnerability, overriding it as unacceptable, an effigy giving in to the first real gulp of a bitterness she had barely tasted up until now. "Get me the hell away from here," Christy said, "before I kill his ass."

***

The Playmore was rocking. A Dangerous Thing covered songs like "Strokin" and "Knock on Wood," classic songs that pulled folks onto the dance floor, but the band was taking a break by the time make-up was refreshed and emotions packed away. Christy and Malia found themselves reunited with Tedder, Oakley, and Tim, who had made their way there via Burt's Game Room, where they had seen Joey Taggart and Sonny Sams get into a vicious fist fight in the parking lot, a fight during which Sonny kicked Joey's butt for telling lies on Sonny's girlfriend.

"Good," Malia said. "I never did like Joey Taggart. He ain't nothing but one of them long, tall, raw-boned fellers with a headache for a face."

"Well, it's one messed up face right about now," Tim said. He turned to Christy. "You're mighty quiet, girl."

She gave him here practiced glare. "I was just thinking."

"About what?"

"About how stupid men are to fight over women, for women, about women."

"Shit. We'll do just about anything for pussy. And y'all know it."

"Ain't that the truth," Tedder said. "Hell, Lisa said that old man Christy was married to would get so beside hisself he'd water the furrow before he could even go to plowing."

Christy rolled her eyes. "Don't remind me."

"Hey, Malia, what about you? Will old Dewey jump through hoops for that good stuff?"

"He's a man, ain't he?"

Christy was glad to let her carry the conversation now, now that she had gotten her answer to the question of the evening. Malia went on, holding forth. "Dewey's so horny all I got to do is aim it in his direction and he's all over it. Or he'll say, 'Baby, why don't you put on them "fuck-me" pumps and crawl up in the covers with a tired old man.' Ain't that some shit?"

"He ain't real romantic, huh," Tedder said.

"Dewey Dixon? I'll tell you Dewey's idea of romance. He called me from work one afternoon a couple of weeks ago and said, 'Dust off that ol' puss, Baby, cause I'm coming home for a sardine sammich and then I'm fixing to lay some pipe up in there.' And that man didn't understand why I just went on to the Food Tiger, went on about my business, carried my mama her hormone prescription, didn't give him another thought. Had his bottom lip all run out by the time I got home."

Malia's audience laughed, swapped Stupid Romance Trick stories while Christy let it all become nothing more that air rushing at her ears, air becoming the angry sound of the ocean, as if she were ear-muffed by two big conch shells. She wished the band would start up again. She wanted to dance, to move, to feel as wild and beautiful as she had as a teenager. She wanted to lean her body into Tim Hilyer's and make him want her more than any wife could ever be wanted, and she let her eyes go to his. The group was still talking, laughing, mouths moving soundlessly in the smoky dimness, but Tim's eyes cut to hers more and more frequently, sending her a look she knew. She smiled him an answer, then slid her glance away.

At the bar, Wendel Mitchell was serving up beer after beer, filling trays for Gail, Jo-Jo, and Katrina, the three Saturday night waitresses. Colored lights danced around the Playmore's huge party room, and the clusters of faces were like photo images of the faces Christy had seen here last week. It never changed much. Most of the men at the bar had occupied the same barstools for years, and the predictability of their attitudes, of the music and fights and soap operas playing out from night to night kept fear at bay, for a little while. At the far end of the bar Susie Dawson stood between the legs of Karl Thornton, her palms rubbing his outer thighs. Karl's divorce was final and he was looking to get laid, Christy figured. And it wouldn't be difficult with Screwsie Dawson staking a claim there in the shadow of his crotch.

Somewhere through the padded silence Christy finally heard the electric buzz of a bass guitar, the rattle of drumsticks against a snare and a cymbal as the musicians took their places. There was a picking and tuning of strings, a random strike or two at the drums. Then, finally, a blending of rhythms into a tune and the gentle rock of singing guitars. A slow song, another old dance standard, "My Girl." She had danced with JD so many times to that very song and he could go to hell as far as she was concerned. A sting of tears tried to rise up to her closed eyes now, as she pressed against Tim's chest, her cheek against his shoulder, moving with him on the dance floor. She slid her arms up and around his neck, fingertips brushing the flesh of the back of his neck, and when he pushed his lips against her own neck the warmth of his kisses took her. She would be alright if only she could have another shot, another chance, and she would go on peeling the labels off beer bottles for however long it took. She squeezed the back of Tim's neck, pushed her hips forward, let her crotch rub a tempo against his thigh. She would try for as long as she had to, beginning with Tim Hillyer.

And she didn't care if her fingernails went to nubs from peeling back labels as long as she could have another shot at that which she kept cloaked in fragile power and musky promises, the kind of love she craved and hoarded and inevitably hurled away.

from *In a Temple of Trees* / Novel

August 1990
Three Breezes

On any given Sunday morning Cecil Durgin would take an hour-long drive through the game preserve, across Round Swirl Creek, and down the rutted logging roads crisscrossing McCormick's spread. The drive would be slow, contemplative, even soothing at times, walled behind sentinels of bark and foliage. Sometimes he would stop and watch the woods, all whitewashed in silent brightness, little slices of light splitting and splintering the maze of still life, searching for her. If it was raining like a son of a bitch or graveyard cold or suffocating with heat, Cecil would likely be in the woods if it was also a Sunday morning. This was the only place where he knew, deep down, he was meant to be.

On this Sunday he was visiting, one more time, with the familiar guilt which came, with more and more predictability, whenever he disappointed his wife. He was wondering, one more time, if he should just be done with marriage, let Earline find herself a man who could keep off of other women. Maybe he should teach himself Spanish, cloak himself with a whole new set of words, and go away to Mexico, let himself be absorbed by yet another culture, shed his present life like a snake slipping its skin. After all, the children were grown and gone, to bigger towns where time had moved a little closer to the next century. Three Breezes, Alabama, was, in more than a few ways, stuck in the past, stuck like Cecil's own conscience, full of untapped intentions and unspoken truths.

The pickup bounced over red clay washouts, jarring Cecil with the reality of his reliance upon Earline, his dependence upon her strength and her ability to wait him out, a wait going on for two decades now. She had given more than any man deserved, and if he was a real man he would leave her—or make it right. Petite and dimpled at the cheeks and elbows, Earline was a tender mix of innocence retained from youth with a deep, even wise, understanding of him. When they made love she held him cautiously, her warm brown skin like minted bronze against his. Yet when she looked up at him with almond-shaped eyes the color of buttered molasses, those eyes would sometimes take him with a startling passion; and that sudden glance blurred, for him, the deliberate lines he had set up in order to survive. It was in these moments that her eyes expressed what her body had been denied, what he sensed she wanted, though it was never discussed.

He caught his own eyes in the rearview mirror, eyes in their mid-forties. Goddamn, he was a grown man, way grown enough to use his brain when it came to his urge to rescue emotionally stranded, romantically shipwrecked females. But in the same moment, he knew it would go on and on as long as the woods remained mute, as long as he held on to what Earline considered dubious reasons for keeping his own silence.

Ironic, he thought, that a person with such a silent soul would have made a living with his voice, as a radio disc jockey with a Christian preacher for one alter ego and a verbally outrageous, money-tossing talent agent for another. Maybe it was the comfort of just having a voice, any voice, to fill in the quiet gaps he was forced to guard. Whatever the reasons, he was by now a fixture in Three Breezes, a prominent businessman who moonlighted as a cook for the McCormicks and others, just to keep a finger on their pulse. Just to know they were fully aware of his presence, a presence he knew, even if they did not, alternated between shadow and form.

The shadows were everywhere, it sometimes seemed to him. The unusual circumstances of his growing-up years, cloistered in the garage of his phantom parents, threw reaches of dimness into every other aspect of his dealings with folks in the vague, white world. He did not have the luxury of complete exclusion, as did other Negroes, instead walking a marginal tightrope along the borders of the Prices' lives. He addressed them as "Miss Sophie" and "Mr. Austin." He followed the required codes of society while he deciphered the hieroglyphics lying just beneath the surface. He learned to read Miss Sophie's every expression, to know when he was to remain on the periphery of a social encounter with pale interlopers or when he was to retreat to the confinement of the building that once housed Mr. Austin's black Studebaker. He also knew when he could immerse himself in the fantasy of family living in the Prices' home, most nights taking meals with them, developing an awkward bond with the man who did not want to be a father to him but tried to become a fraction of one, out of love for and loyalty to his wife.

The forays into social life on Pitch Hill, too, were shrouded in brown and gray fogs. Even though he had friends and a place laid out for him in the black community by Otis and Gladys, he could still hear the uncertainty in the voices of the outcast, feel the subtext of suspicion in their expressions. In spite of this, he was included, was invited to the birthday parties of the other children, and became popular as he grew older, popular as an athlete at the colored school, popular with the girls who glanced up at him, coy and with easy give in their open stances, popular with the boys who kidded him with genuine affection and called him "whitey" and "Mr. Clean" because of his upbringing.

Every once in a while he slept over with his friends, went into their homes, breathed in the familial atmospheres and puzzled over the way each little shack full of humans had a distinct scent hidden beneath the dinnertime smells of pot liquor and larded grits cakes. Most often he stayed with Tony Mack Franklin, whose mother made a point of giving Cecil a place of honor at the table, hugged him, and called him her adopted son. But in spite of the veneer of unconditional acceptance there was always a hazy feel of all that was unspoken between them, the questions unanswered, his alien spirit. And that disfigured darkness inevitably crept into his soul, and he had to look elsewhere for form.

He thought he had found a certain kind of form in his work at the station, hidden away while his voice stole its course through the atmosphere of Cole County, an aspect of feigned anonymity he appreciated. Still, he knew it was a role, a character he took on for protection. The Reverend Durgin could, after all, be good, could be purified by the blood of Jesus, could be forgiven. The vicarious love of the Lord, the love *for* the Lord he had picked up in Gladys's church, was well-intentioned enough, when he did not contrast it with the tradition of Judaism Miss Sophie had instilled. Whenever he did ponder it, he knew Miss Sophie's God to be more genuine, the giver of unconditional love; yet he needed a God who required redemption, no matter how superficial or out of reach. At the same time he envied Earline's relaxed comfort in the love of Jesus, the way her trust allowed her to fall back into the arms of Christ. He tried to replicate it through his radio program. But in his most weary, soul-honest moments he knew Cecil Durgin as preacher-man ministering to others was only another insincere patch of gray in his heart, a futile, clutching bid at cleansing his own fouled soul.

He thought he had found yet another kind of form, a tangible one, a belonging, in his political work. He had been intrigued by the Freedom Riders, the thundering changes exploding across the state in the early 1960s, thundering in places other than Cole County, itself an isolated fiefdom like so many other rural counties, ruled by the lords of the manor and the county sheriff.

He had even spoken out via the radio program he put on as a teenager, full of a sudden bravado fueled by the persistent, stoic folks he saw on the news each night, inspired by the whole notion of nonviolent noncooperation. He was surreptitiously prodded, egged on, by Miss Sophie, who also caught the fever and temporarily lost the level head which was otherwise so protective of him. Not yet out of high school, he broadcasted a talk on the inevitability of integration and the righteous work of the Student Nonviolent Coordinating Committee, and as a matter of course, he paid with another piece of his dignity. The white men who were such a presence in his life felt compelled to remind him of his ties to them, humiliated him in front of an audience of dove hunters, sent him into a dusty field clodded with plowed dirt to pick up the dead birds as if he were a trained dog. They humiliated him in a way that still brought him to angry tears if he let it replay in his head. So he did not think of it, just as he tried not to think of the one particular woman and the blood on his hands.

Other than the solitude of the forest, the only things he discovered over the years that gave him a place, the form and belonging he lacked, were his brief involvements with the women whom he saved from victimization of some kind, or from themselves. It had not been a horde of women, but one here, one there, sometimes spaced out so that four or five years passed between them. He did not see himself as a womanizer in the traditional sense, as some in the community did. In fact, he felt only disgust for men who used women, put them in the same category as the five particular men who abused Charity Collins and the one particular man who tortured her, making murderers of them all. He was not motivated by the soulless cravings fueling the white men, he told himself, continuing to justify his entanglements. And, indeed, the encounters did give him a rush of peace and a heady charge of passion, brief respite from the pain inhabiting him since the age of twelve. It was a little like the thrill of bringing Jesus to others, offering up radio show salvation. It had an addictive quality to it, he knew. And he knew he would always go back to it, to the chance of making it up to her, hoping in vain for resolution.

He parked his truck and let the motor idle while he squinted into the trees. Sometimes he caught a glimpse of her, a searing flash of skin and dark hair, and for that isolated instant he would be overcome with the brief peace of another second chance. This time he would put it right. This time he would come out from behind the holly bush piercing his face and neck. He would charge out of the shadows with his KA-BAR knife, the one he carried every day now, in a long leather sheath secured to his belt. He would cut the throats of the men who hurt her, watch their blood puddle across the lawn at DoeRun, and not give a damn if they strung him up or sent him to prison. And he would have at once spared Earline her pain and obliterated his own, having done what his conscience intended before it was cowed and hemmed in by fear.

He pulled back the coverings of tree limbs with his imagination, sifted layers of leaves through his field of vision, tried to conjure her up from the mists mingling with her spirit. He put his full concentration on a bank of vines, hoping to wish her from beneath the tangled, rooted stems and into his arms. He thought he heard a faint, muffled giggle, a sound padded by damp earth and cool, green cover. It had to be her. He watched for a long while, every nerve ending in his body vibrating with determined expectations. He waited as the humming anticipation faded to a whisper and fell silent. It was only then he could complete his ritual of solitary searching, giving up his latest attempt to will her out, to coax her back to life and finally force his relinquished redemption.

***

Wade Connors fumbled under the seat of his patrol car and brought out a copy of *A Brief History of Time,* thinking to read while he waited for Cecil to get there. He was on a physics kick lately; for months he had only read titles related to the paradoxical theories that, surprisingly, gave him a sense of order and calm in the chaos of the universe, and he liked to think on it. Last fall he was on a self-help kick, immersing himself in pop psychology until he had trotted out and examined every dysfunctional emotional demon he could unearth from the repertoire of his own damaged psyche. Before self-help it was Zen everything, from Motorcycle Maintenance to Suzuki. Before that it was a Stephen King–Edgar Alan Poe–athon. And before that *To Kill a Mockingbird,* four times in a row. Sometimes he got stuck on a particular writer, sometimes a genre, as with the true crime binge he went on one summer, in between Victorian erotica and short stories set during the Civil War. This was the way he went at reading—consuming books by random categories, getting down inside an author or a subject until he had answered his questions or had more questions than ever in his quest for the ultimate answer. That, he decided, was becoming pretty futile, but this quantum physics shit was right on the mark, and he felt as close to the answer as he had ever felt in his life.

Too, he was reaching for the book to help him keep from stewing over the upcoming election. The reform which would raise taxes on property would be pushed through the next spring, and already the panic was underway, paper mills and the big landowners supplying them determined to stack the legislature with opponents of any change whatsoever. And if they succeeded, and if folks went to voting a straight ticket like the dumb asses they were, well, Wade's job could disintegrate like Scott tissue in a toilet bowl. He needed Cecil's help in a big way.

He was parked in the gravel yard at WDAB, a squat brick building perched on a hill just south of the Three Breezes city limits sign. It felt more remote than it actually was, surrounded by dense pine and oak shielding it from view of the passing cars on Highway 33. They could see the transmitter, though. That big-ass stick, boasted to be "the biggest stick in the state," sent little old Cole County way the hell out across the airwaves, all over Mississippi and Alabama. It was erected there in the 1930s by a hard-shell Baptist preacher from Columbus, Mississippi, who had big dreams of becoming a famous radio evangelist. It had to be sold, though, when it eventually came out how the preacher fleeced his flock and romanced a rich old widow woman to get the money to put it there in the first place. Austin Price came in, bought the station, and enhanced the stick in increments. Cole County was just a dark little tucked-away crevice in the South, but for that big old stick. Sheriff Connors thought it ironically fitting that the station had passed from a '30s holy roller to a '40s atheist and then to a '60s Negro preacher who could be considered half Jewish. Maybe it was an example of chaos theory in action.

Wade considered Cecil the man a paradox: black-white, Christian-Jew, whore hopper–family man, master of the spoken word over the radio, and man of few words in person. Most of all, he saw Cecil as outwardly serene but sensed a molten core which was anything but, a perception he couldn't explain. Even Cecil the deejay was a multiple personality, alternating between the Sultan of Salvation, who peddled gospel music and commonsense scripture, and the Moonpie Man, who purred over jazz and blues. Maybe the mix of enigmatic contradictions had something to do with the odd circumstances of Cecil's journey through life. In any case, Wade, several years his junior, had always looked up to him. That in itself was odd, given the times. Odd that his choice of a hero to worship was one who was outside the bounds of his own race. But in Wade's estimation Cecil forever seemed to have it all when it came to cool.

In Cole County Cecil's voice wafted over the airwaves of

WDAB, "a little dab'll do ya," the station just outside the county seat of Three Breezes. Weekday mornings, which were hired out to a white deejay, were devoted to agricultural news and items of local interest along with country music and easy listening. On weekday afternoons, beginning at 1:00 p.m., folks tuned in to Cecil for a variety of chitchat, Top 40, R&B, jazz, blues, a little country—a patchwork of sounds, something for everyone, and his show went late into the night—heavier on rock and roll, R&B, and blues—on Fridays and Saturdays. But Wednesday evenings and Sundays—a.m.'s, afternoons, and evenings—were set aside for the gospel groups Cecil promoted, along with his common sense preaching, community notes, and spiritual advice for whoever called in.

His rich, velveteen voice, thick with the African American dialect of Mississippi state-line mud, drew in listeners of all classes and races; many praising God right along with him; others hungry for a slice of rural culture straight out of the early days of radio, jarringly anachronistic in the years building to a new millennium. No mass-produced tapes of hyperactive, egocentric disc jockeys had ever been broadcast over the airwaves of WDAB. Cecil was among the few remaining of a dying breed, the sure enough live, no-rehearsals-allowed, hometown deejay, who still preferred old vinyl to the cassettes he played as well, and who took it as it came.

Yet his was not considered a throwback to the radio shows of the '40s, as he had done his broadcasting since he was a teenager in the early 1960s, creating his own individual stamp on the genre; his longevity only legitimized the flavor of his style. Too, Cecil learned the business well under his tutelage with Austin Price. It was Old Man Price who set up Cecil's initial foray into the business on-air, a biweekly rock session which began when he was only sixteen and soon spilled over into the weekends. The sounds of Little Eva, Chubby Checker, and the Dynatones crackled across the hills of Cole County with a vibrant innocence, gathering in mostly colored fans who were not previously well acquainted with the station. This boosted Austin Price's advertising market, which surged as Cecil was discovered by even more area teenagers. Within a few years the show had become a Motown-laden soulfest and Cecil was a solid hit with even the white kids in the county, just getting their first taste of Sam Cook, Martha Reeves, Wilson Pickett, and Otis Redding.

When Wade was in high school, he was aware of scandalized whispers about white girls going out to the station to hang out with Cecil, but Wade thought nothing would be more cool than to kick back with a real disc jockey and listen to good music all evening. The less-than-appealing parts of Cecil's job included, of course, his duties as Old Man Price's chauffeur and general gopher, but he managed to carry even those duties out with an aura of suave calm Wade envied. Over time, Cecil learned the business inside out, from bookkeeping to advertising, with no formal schooling necessary. By 1982 the station was his, having been willed it by Austin Price.

His religious talks were earnest and homespun, his blues promos earthy and charged with sexual innuendo. He walked the line between salvation and sin with a rare and innate agility, imbuing his work with an informal honesty which allowed him to conduct his life as needed, no rush, no agenda. If a friend dropped by the station, he would either step outside and let the airwaves go silent or have a willing partner for a boisterous on-air chat. If need be, he would leave to preach a funeral or emcee at a blues club or honky-tonk. Thus, the radio programs he anymore personally conducted were, on occasion, hit and miss; yet folks knew, in spite of the silence, he would always be back. That was the essence of what Wade admired about Cecil. Cecil was solid. He might have a wounded spirit, or a secret wellspring of rage, but the fact that he was so unflinchingly solid demanded a level of trust from others Wade had found to be rare indeed.

Wade had just settled back with his book when Cecil's pickup wheeled into the parking lot, a few minutes late, as usual. And, as was usual when he met with Cecil to talk political favors, Wade had to fight back the feeling that he was intruding, with his petty little world, on a true man of God, albeit a bawdy one. Cecil seemed to have the spiritual strength of an Apostolic Army, but he definitely had the moral flaws of a lost Lamb under siege, and Wade knew he was going to have to try to confront one moral flaw named Kim Davis, along with the politics.

"So it's going to be a mean one, huh?" Cecil asked.

"Meaner than any I've ever been in. Seems the big dicks in Monkey Town been counting noses like crazy. They done all the polling they need to tell them Cole County'll probably be the key to the swing vote when that tax bill comes up."

Cecil shook his head. "So they ordering up one legislator, right?"

"Absolutely."

"Well, that shouldn't be too hard to pay for."

Wade laughed. "No shit. I just don't want the guy they pay for to carry off my votes, you know?"

"I hear you."

Wade cleared his throat.

"What you need? The usual?"

Wade shifted against the fender. It was just like Cecil to get straight to the point. "Well, yeah, the usual, but you need to know they'll be on your ass, too."

"Ain't nothing new."

"Well, it's fixing to be. I hear the big mucks around here are already plotting your character assassination. They don't mean to pay taxes on all the trees this side of Tuscaloosa."

Cecil gave a gentle chuckle. "I'm scared shitless, man."

Wade reached into the open window of his car for the mangled cigar he kept close by for an occasional gnaw, having given up smoking back during the self-help phase. He was never sure how much to say, how much he was supposed to know about Cecil's personal life. "Look," he said. "I ain't saying you should be scared, but you better take this one seriously. Folks get downright crazy-mean when it comes to big money. If you got any secrets, like maybe some sugar off to the side, they bound to find it."

Cecil narrowed his eyes. "Come on, man. Them mucks you talking about. It's just Old Man Davis, Roscoe Bartley, and them, right?"

"Basically."

"They won't touch me."

Wade zipped a streak of tobacco-infested spit across the gravel. "Ain't nobody can't be touched. Everybody has something to hide."

"That ain't what I said. Ain't what I meant," Cecil said. "It ain't that they can't touch me. They won't."

"Well, ain't you confident."

"Just a little," Cecil laughed.

Wade was not too surprised by Cecil's lack of concern. Even though folks did get crazy-mean when big money was at stake, Cecil, whose reputation for getting out the black vote was so legendary he was routinely visited by politicians of all stripes right up to the state level and sometimes beyond, kept his own power very low key. And, unlike most citizens of Cole County, black and white, he was not intimidated by McCormicks and Bartleys and others who had been entrenched in absolute power for generations.

"All right, then," Wade said. "Thought you ought to know they mean to dismantle you this time. But, if you ain't worried, at least be on your guard, okay?"

"Yeah."

The sheriff got into the patrol car, turned the engine over, then leaned out the open window. "Oh, and Cecil?"

"Yeah?"

"You'll be singing my praises, won't you?"

"You and Jesus, man. All the time."

"Thanks."

Wade wound the car through the pines and back to the highway, trying to think of another way to avoid the office. His deputy, Ray Jones, was keeping an eye on their only prisoner, one of the no-'count Pierce boys from deep in the woods. Ray, also known as "Booty" in honor of his obsession with women back in the high school days, wanted his boss back in time for him to go to church this morning. They had already agreed to do a Sunday afternoon in the office catching up on paperwork, so Wade had a couple of hours to kill. He thought about stopping in on Tammy Sims, but knew she would be out snake hunting today. If it was not a Sunday he could go hang out at the Co-op for a while, listen to the farmers who brought in gossip to trade for Treflan and fertilizer, empty seed barrels rolling across the beds of dented pickups. Hell, maybe he would just ride around a while and listen to the radio. He turned the radio on to Cecil's deep-voiced Sultan of Salvation.

"Here goes a sound that'll get right down in your spirit and get your limbs to jumping," the Sultan said. "Yes, Lord, make you move. Sling them arms, jostle them legs, and play them shoulders.

The Lord loves it when you let your shoulders play. So here comes the Blind Boys of Alabama to get your blood going and your shoulders to playing."

Wade grinned. He spat a line of cigar juice through the car window and turned up the volume, sending a jubilant rhythm out into the oppressive, high-noon heat of a Sunday in August.

Appomattox

She couldn't decide what time of day it was, but it felt like midmorning. She had to go by body clock since her fingertips had earlier discovered, upon finding and opening the room's only window, that it was covered with a sheet of plywood, the door closed and locked on the outside. The room was humid with the damp odor of sock sweat suspended in the dark like paper mill smog. There was a lamp, though, and she fumbled to switch it on. The honky-tonk rock of Lynyrd Skynyrd backdropped the clutter everywhere: several rods and reels leaning in a corner, an assortment of pornographic magazines sprawling a montage of tits on the floor next to the bed, two tackle boxes, a chest of drawers spilling jeans and T-shirts, a couple of mounds of what had to be dirty clothes, which explained the smell. Kim "Honey Drop" Davis sat up, too fast, on the edge of the bed. She put her head down, dizzied by a spinning grogginess making her queasy all over again. Pills. They had given her pills, she remembered. In between all the yelling and cussing, they had agreed that she needed to be unconscious for a while. Two white boys at least a decade older than she was, one a mook-ass halfwit and the other a cold-eyed vessel for all the demons of Dixie.

She could hear snatches of the argument before she passed out, and she willed some pieces of it to replay through in her head. "Where the hell did you ever get the idea you was supposed to shoot his ass?" and "You ain't got no verbal skills. Hell, you got a terminal case of infantile literalism. Don't you fucking know that words have more than one meaning?" and "This ain't like the good old days, shit for brains, when just any old nigger could be offed."

And what in the hell, she wondered, was she doing here? She couldn't make sense of any of it.

The mean one was still yelling and cussing in spurts, going on twenty-four hours later. She could hear him once in a while, above the rock music thumping through the trailer. Yes, it was a trailer, she remembered, where the scrawny, ponytailed one called Ronnie brought her. A trailer where the other one called Claud made her swallow some pills that knocked her on her ass.

Claud was the one who brought her up short with unfamiliar fear, but it was Ronnie who picked her up in the first place. He slung gravel when he wheeled into the parking lot at WDAB yesterday afternoon, just a while after Cecil left, ran off to some hunting camp to see some slut, probably. She was not about to follow Cecil's instructions and get a new tape started on its way to whatever rural radios were receiving WDAB's transmission that day. He slammed through the door and hollered at her. "Where is he? Where the fuck is Cecil Durgin?"

"Who wants to know?"

It was then that he pulled the nine-millimeter out of the back of his jeans. That fast and for no apparent reason. But he struck her as more nervous than anything else. "You just better cooperate with me 'cause I ain't nobody you'd like to have to deal with, okay? I'm a mean motherfucker, okay? Now where is he?"

She thought of the Smith & Wesson in her own purse, the sequined emerald green bag cradled beneath her right arm. She also knew not to go for it, not now, not with that big barrel of steel pointed in her vicinity by a very skinny, very ugly, very jumpy Saltine. "Look, Sweet," she said. "Calm down. He'll be here any minute I bet."

"You a goddamn lie. I bet you know right exactly where he's at."

"Even if I did, you think I'd put a crazy white man toting a gun onto him?" As soon as it came out of her mouth she wished she could take it back. She heard one of Cecil's sayings in her head: *You done let your alligator mouth overload your mockingbird ass again, Honey-gal.*

"Shit! Why does everything get fucked up when I do it? Huh?" He threw his fist against the wall, sending a framed picture smacking into the floor just as his expression morphed into one of recognition. "Wait a goddamn minute," he said. "I got a gun so fuck you, okay?"

"And I want to know why you come up in here with a gun."

"Can't you just do like you're supposed to? Huh? Shit. Don't nobody do right by me." He grabbed her arm. "Come on."

"What for?"

"You're fixing to go with me."

She wrenched free. "I ain't going nowhere with your crazy ass. You might as well just shoot me now."

"Well—Well, you think I won't? Huh? You think I won't blow your face off? Huh?"

Her mouth took her across the line again, too far. "No, Baby. I think you'd fuck that up, too."

"Goddammit! You ain't the goddamn boss of this here!" He got another grip on her arm and tightened it as she tried to clamp the same arm down harder on the purse. "I come all the way across the county to round that nigger up and goddamn if he ain't here. Don't nothing go right for me. Nothing. Fuck!" He jerked on her with more wiry force than she imagined he could have, sending the green spangled purse skidding across the floor.

"Who the fuck do you think you are?" she yelled, drawing back her leg to aim it dead into his left shin, eliciting from him a kicked-dog yelp. He did not, however, let go of her arm.

"You can't do that!" he said, lifting his wounded limb, hopping sideways. "You've done hurt my leg, now."

"You can't come up in here waving a gun at me and expect me to kiss your narrow ass. I don't do no kind of ass kissing." And she drew back, kicked him again, harder.

"Ow!" He hop-danced her against the wall, their feet sending pieces of the broken coffee cup tinkling across the floor. "Fuck! Them is some pointy-assed shoes."

"Leave me the fuck alone!" She squirmed against his hold, but he had too much of his meager weight pressing her into the wall, left forearm against her chest.

"You're going to get your ass still," he said, " 'cause I got my Pitbull with me," and the deep, hollow clack of the hammer being thumbed back gave her pause.

Her beaded pocketbook was long gone, she was pinned against the wall by someone who could crush her windpipe if his arm slid any higher, and she was in the dark about who and why and all the etceteras that went along with it. She had to use her head. "You're mashing me," she said.

"Well, you made me do it, acting like a crazy fool."

He was flat sure disgusting, with that mangled ponytail raked in greasy brown rows back from his forehead, where a raised vein pulsed a blue line across his flesh. He was close enough for her to see a scattering of tiny skin tags along his left eyelid, rubbery little bits of flesh mixed in amongst thin eyelashes. He leaned even closer to her face; his expression was more fearful than menacing.

"I'm going to catch hell because of this." He pressed the barrel of the pistol under her chin. "You've done fucked it all up and you're coming with me. I ain't about to show back up at the trailer with nothing."

The steel was cold, the blue vein throbbed, and he was too tense and haphazard for her to chance any resistance. Not now. She was right fond of her face, so she decided to wait until her head was not in danger of being exploded before she acted. She would think of something, she knew. He didn't seem too bright. She nodded yes.

"You ain't going to be a pain in the butt, right?"

She nodded again. She couldn't think what this man might want with Cecil, but, angry as she was when she first arrived at the station, she was now overcome by a need to protect her man, or her ex-man, or whatever Cecil was to her now, with a little curiosity thrown into the mix. What could this boney-assed redneck have to do with Cecil Durgin?

He lowered the gun and pushed her toward the door.

"Hey," she said. "Would you be a Sweet and grab my purse for me? I don't go nowhere without it."

"Aw, to hell with the purse," he said.

"If you say so, baby, but if some laws come up in here, find my car out yonder, my pocketbook on the floor, and no me, well, you know they're going to think foul play right off."

He narrowed his eyes in pained contemplation. "Shit," he said. "You stand right there, by the door." He kept the pistol trained on her. "Don't do nothing with your feet. If you kick me when I come back over there I'm going to shoot you for real, okay?" He backed over to the purse, scooped it up, and put it under his own arm. Then he led her out to a dented-up blue pickup patchworked with Bondo, "Get in." He pitched her handbag into the bed of the truck.

"Why'd you do that?"

"'Cause if you're like the women I know you got some of that Mace shit in that bag. I ain't stupid, you know."

"You going to tell me what this is all about?" she asked as they pulled out onto the highway. She studied the serpent tattoo coiled around and around his right forearm, the fingernails on that hand acting as vessels for black grit.

"Can't."

"But you would if you could?"

"Yeah." Out of nowhere he decided to pound on the steering wheel, five times, punctuating each hit with a "Fuck!"

Honey had run several scenarios through her head, plans for the upper hand, and the only sensible one was to keep him talking. Her own weapon, after all, was out of reach. Besides, she had only shot the thing a few times, certainly never at a real, live person. She only planned to use it to threaten Cecil into releasing her from their contract, and that had damn sure turned into one big joke. Best to rely on her charm for the time being.

"Claud is going to be pissed," he said. "Peee-oh'd," and he looked as if he might cry.

"Who's Claud?"

"My big brother. Mean motherfucker, too. Way meaner than me."

"You think he might kick your butt?"

"He's done kicked it all my life. Thinks he's the only one knows how to do anything right."

Honey sighed. "Don't I know, Baby. I got a big sister my own self. Marietta. Been telling lies on me since we was on all fours. Kept me up in some trouble when we was growing up. But I'm fixing to bust out. She's going to be sorry as hell."

"What you going to do?"

"Not much. Just make me a name as a singer. Win me a Grammy or two. Ain't nothing to hold me here."

Ronnie opened a pack of Kools and offered her one.

"No, thank you, Sweet. Bad for my voice. So what's your name?"

"Ronnie."

"I'm Kim. That's my real name. Just Kim. Not even Kimberly. One damn syllable. So I sing under 'Honey Davis.' Except Cecil's done got to billing me as 'Miss Honey Drop.' But who am I kidding? I ain't nothing but a fucking 'Kim.' A one-syllable individual."

"Least it's easy to spell."

"Yeah. But I'm still a one-syllable individual trying to live a twelve-syllable life." She tugged at her skirt. "You like music? What you listen to?"

"Rock. Country. Not no nigger music." The unlit Kool bobbed as he spoke.

She resisted the urge to explain the history of rock. "Sweetie, you got to like a little blues or jazz."

"Jazz? Jazz is pure fag music."

"You ain't right."

"Hell, I seen this jazz singing man on the TV. Had on these shiny shoes like a woman. Hell, he flamed so much you could set his hair on fire and nobody would notice."

"Well you ought to listen to a little more before you make up your mind, Sweet."

"No way. Who the fuck listens to jazz? Can't nobody understand it. Hell, you can't dance to that shit."

"All right. Blues, then." Honey leaned her head back, closed her eyes and sang a few bars of "Got Took by a Thief Called Love" with all the sexual energy of a live club performance. Then she cut her eyes at him. "What you think? I wrote it myself."

"Damn if you don't have a nice voice. It's still nigger music, though."

"Well, Sweet, what else I'm going to sing?"

"No shit. Hey, you know what?" he said, flipping open a metal Zippo, sending lighter-fluid fumes across the cab of the truck, "I sure hope Claud don't make me hurt you. You ain't so bad." He snapped the lighter shut, and she caught a flash of a cartoonish Robert E. Lee waving a Confederate flag etched on the stainless steel.

"I don't see why Claud would want you to hurt me," she said.

"'Cause you know too much."

"Wait just a second, Ronnie. Let's think about that a minute. I don't know shit."

"Well," he said, "you know I come hunting Cecil with a gun. If something was to happen to him, you'd put the law on me, wouldn't you? You a damn lie if you say you wouldn't."

"All right, yes. But you could have avoided that whole problem if you'd have just come in the station and asked, real nice, where's Cecil, then come back later if I didn't know. There's something to be said for manners."

"Aw, to hell with manners. Besides, I was nervous," he said. "I was real nervous. I didn't know you was going to be up in there."

"So what you wanting with Cecil?"

"I was trying to help—no, hell no, I ain't telling you nothing."

"I figure I got a right. You've done carried me off. I figure I ought to be let in on it, you know? Fair is fair."

He ignored her, so she tried another approach. "You know, Ronnie, you could always carry me back." She gave him her most luscious smile. She could work this guy, she knew. Easy. She just needed a little time.

"Shit, I would. I really would. But I reckon I better run it by Claud first, now that I've done fucked everything up."

"Come on, Ronnie. I'm just a shit load of trouble. Everybody says so."

"Forget it."

"Hey, I bet you could use some money. I got eight hundred dollars in the bank. Swing by the Farmers' Bank and let me get it for you, okay?"

"Ain't going to happen."

She sank back in the seat. "So where are we going?"

"Mine and Claud's trailer. 'Bout thirty miles."

She had decided that was good. Thirty miles was a nice long piece. You could sure enough jerk a guy around in the time it took to drive that far. "Is it just you and Claud?"

"Yeah. He run off his last girlfriend two months ago. Serena. She was a old bucktoothed thing. Hell, she could eat a apple through a knothole. And mean? Talk about a bitch."

"Y'all didn't get on, huh? You and Serena." Three Breezes was way behind them, Mississippi straight ahead, so Honey settled in to the conversation.

"Hell, no. That bitch was always doing shit just to piss me off."

"Like?"

"Well, like—" He screwed up his face for a few seconds, deep in thought, then blurted, "Like putting the stick butter in the refrigerator. I like the butter to be warm, okay? You know, room temperature. So it's easy to slap on the toast, don't take so long to melt, okay? But hell no, she said it'd go rancid and we'd all die. It wasn't even none of her butter, neither. She liked tub butter. She had her butter soft already. Ain't that a bitch? Didn't even use no stick butter. Which do you like? Tub or stick?"

"Well, hell, Ronnie, anybody with half a brain likes stick better," she said. "But what happened to make your brother run her off?"

"Claud said she was a sye-co-fant."

"A what? A psycho?"

"A sye-co-*fant*. He's all the time using big-ass words. Claims I ain't got no verbal skills. Calls me some kind of a infant literal about it. He said a sye-co-fant is one to follow behind waiting for the crumbs to drop. He said Serena was only good for throwing crumbs to. And he was right. She was all the time playing up to him. He don't like women that's all the time kissing his ass. Done told you he's a mean motherfucker."

"What about you?" She turned her body toward him, throwing her arm across the back of the seat, wishing she had dressed a little more provocatively today. A nice view of cleavage would come in handy about now. Well, at least she had her legs to work with, a short skirt. "What kind of woman do you like? An ass kisser or a bitch?"

"I ain't picky like that. I just want one with a warm pussy."

"Come on, Ronnie, cute guy like you can be picky as he wants to be."

"Yeah?"

"Sure, Sweet. You ain't trying to tell me you don't have a lot of luck with women, 'cause I ain't believing that shit. There is some flat out dumb-ass white girls running 'round here if they don't have nothing to do with you." She slipped off her green patent leather heels and turned all the way sideways, leaning her back against the door, drawing her left knee up, foot on the car seat. Give him part of the view, she thought, smugly satisfied when he looked. He was a total amateur. This would be too easy. "Yeah," she went on, "me, I got men after me like bloodhounds, but I'm jonesing for one that won't leave his wife. Ain't that some shit?"

"I went out with a married woman one time. Her husband throwed brick acid all up in my bass boat. That was all she wrote."

"Was it worth it?"

"Hell no. You kidding? Ain't no kind of pussy worth a bass boat."

"I don't know, Sweet. I've had men act all kinds of crazy just to get a half a look at mine. It's right pitiful to have a big old strong man crying and begging for it."

"Ain't done it."

"Oh, yeah, Baby. All the time. Just last week I had a white insurance salesman offer me three hundred dollars just to get a look at my tits. I ain't lying."

"Did you?" His voice had the eager tone she was coaxing.

"Oh, I've done shit like that before. I mean, cash is always nice. But I was going with Cecil when this happened so, no, I didn't. Of course, looks like Cecil and me are over and I ain't long for this part of the world. So, you got three hundred dollars? You got three hundred dollars I'll show you some kick-ass tits." She laughed her hoarse, seductive laugh.

"Can't be that good." He squinted his eyes at her chest.

"Must be, 'cause I get that shit all the damn time. But what about you? Cute guy like you bound to have a woman. You been bullshitting me about that, right?"

"I do all right. Well, sometimes. Not as good as Claud, though. Hell, women get all over him. He gets more ass than a toilet seat. He's got this what you call magnetic type of a personality, which I ain't."

"That ain't so, Baby. That just ain't so. You got a real sweet personality, just the kind decent women like."

"Yeah?"

"Hell yeah, Sweet. And I know what I'm talking about 'cause

I know what women want. I'm the Love Guru. Folks talk to me all the time about their love lives. You ever been in love?"

"Well, just once. Sarah Pugh. Except she said she wouldn't give me none unless I married her. So I did. I went and married her ass, brung her out to the trailer to live with Claud and me. But hell, she didn't appreciate nothing. Sat on her fat ass all the live-long day and looked at the TV. Then she started going out to the clubs of a weekend. Wouldn't clean up or nothing."

"But she gave you plenty, huh?"

"Plenty of nothing after about six weeks of being married. Got to where she didn't never want to."

"That's cold."

"No shit. I was so horny back then that—I had a beard and a mustache back when we was married, and I'd get so horny I'd wake myself up in the dead of the night with my finger in my mouth. Had to shave the shit off where I could get some sleep."

"Ooh, Child, what happened to her?"

"What happened was I throwed her out for fucking Claud."

"No!"

"Yeah. That bitch was a damn lie. She weren't worth the pussy she was mounted to."

"But weren't you mad at Claud?"

"Naw. She was a whore. She done it with half the county. I guess she had done saved it up for so long she thought she better get all she could, once I broke it in. And she's still giving that stuff away. Done skin't every pole in a hundred square miles."

"No!"

"Yeah, that thing is about as blowed out as a throwed retread on a eighteen-wheeler. Probably be like fucking a dried-up mud hole."

"Well, she was crazy to give up a cute husband with a nice personality—"

"Ain't magnetic, though."

"Magnetic ain't so good."

"Claud says it is. He's got a magnetic personality."

"No. Look here. You ever held a magnet over a bunch of nails?"

"Yeah. So what?"

"So what is this. It picked up a bunch of nails, right?"

"Supposed to."

"Picked up the shiny new ones and some of the old, rusty, bent-up ones, too."

He turned to her with a blank expression. This guy was dumber than she thought.

"What I mean is, you got a magnetic personality, you're going to draw some shitty women your way, right up in amongst the good ones," she said. "But the good ones, the decent ones, will just naturally come to a man like you, and come of their own free will. No magnet necessary."

"I lost that old magnet anyway," he said.

"You got any other family?"

"Well, I got a mamma and a sister somewhere."

"Somewhere? You don't know where your own sister is?"

"Naw, it's been since she was a baby. She's all growed up and haired over by now. See, they took off when I was five. Daddy wouldn't let Mamma have me and Claud. Said boys belonged with their daddy and she was a whore, besides."

"Your sister?"

"No, my mamma."

"Seems like you folks is crawling with whores."

Ronnie laughed. "No shit. It's hard to find a decent woman that ain't butt-ugly and knows how to take care of a man."

"Well, this woman right here knows just how."

"Shit."

"You tell me I ain't right, then. It's like this. A man wants two things. A mamma and a whore. The problem is most women want to be their man's friend, don't want to be a mamma when he's low and needs to be puffed up. Or else they take care of him like a mamma and don't want to be a whore in the bedroom. Every man wants a whore in the bedroom, right?"

"Why would you get a whore if you got a wife?"

"No, Baby, your wife's going to do for you anything a whore would do. See?"

"I reckon."

"Look here. If Sarah had give you a good blow whenever you wanted her to she'd have lasted longer as a wife, right?"

"Hell, yeah. But she never done that. She thought it was against Christ. Told me I was eat up with sin." He turned down a narrow dirt road. "Bent Spike Road," the sign said. This trailer of his was going to be isolated. She was feeling more and more pushed into a corner.

"Shit, Baby, anybody gets a blow job from me thinks it's the Second *Coming* of Christ." Miss Honey Drop did not like the idea of going very far down this rutted road. Maybe it was time to turn things around. "You like a good blow job, Baby?" She let her foot slide down and over, pressing it against Ronnie's thigh, then lifted her right foot to the seat to give him the whole view. He looked.

"Who don't?" He squirmed in the driver's seat.

"Nobody that's had one of mine. But I don't give them out to just anybody." She pressed her toes harder into his thigh. The paved road had disappeared. She moved her right knee from side to side, successfully mesmerizing him.

By now his driving was suffering because he was focusing more on her emerald green nylon panties edged in black lace. "What you doing?" His voice had that generic male tone of arousal, telling her she was definitely getting somewhere.

"Oh, I'm just doing what comes natural to me when I meet a good-looking guy I like." She kept the knee moving, opening and closing her thighs.

"Yeah?"

"So, what you think?" Honey slid her foot over to his crotch to gauge her effect. Damn, I'm good, she thought, when her toes found solidity beneath the denim. "You want the best blow job in the Southeast?"

"Hell, yeah," he breathed.

"You better be sure. They say it's so good won't nothing ever feel right again. You sure you want yourself a Second Coming of Christ blow job?"

"Damn right."

"Pull over, then." She sat up to move next to him, marveling at how weak men were, as a rule.

He slammed on the brakes and skidded the truck across gravel, then unzipped his jeans in a rush.

"Slow down, Baby," she said. "Take it easy. Miss Honey Drop's blow jobs got to be savored." She rubbed her hand over his penis and glanced down. It looked like a stunted mushroom with a slitted little eye in the middle. Damn, she was a desperate bitch to be bargaining a blow job with this racist, no-dick idiot. She wondered if she would be able to get through it without gagging.

He moaned. "What you waiting for?"

"I told you I don't give these out to just anybody." She steady rubbed his penis, eliciting more moans and sharp breaths. "This makes us a connection. Two people who will treat each other right. You agree?"

"Anything you say. I can't stand this. You got to get started else I'm going to squirt."

"Mmmm. Just so we understand. I want to do it just like you want it, with a little of my trademark technique thrown in. I had a engineer out of Vicksburg tell me I ought to get a patent. How you like it, Sweet?"

"I like it now."

She leaned down and gave it a little nudge with her tongue, then straightened up. "Say please."

"Please. Goddamn, please."

"And you're going to turn round and take me back to the station after, right?" She rubbed a little faster.

"Right. Yeah. Damn right. Shit! I mean—what the fuck?"

"Fair is fair, Baby. You get, I get, right?" She drew her hand back.

"What the hell? Why you want to stop? Come on, now. Get at it."

"Well, Baby, I do want to. I really do. But I can't give without getting back, you know?"

"You'll get back. I'll tote you back to town as soon as you take care of this here."

She studied his expression, seeing the look she knew better than any other. The lying look of a one-track man. "You know what, Sweet? I think you ain't about to hold up your end of this deal."

"Fuck!" he beat the steering wheel with his fist. "You been fucking with me the whole fucking time!"

"Ronnie, come on. You don't need to take me out to your place.

I ain't no good to y'all."

"Shit! You been fucking the hell with me. Well, you done done it now. You done got my goober hard. You done got it all fucked up." He took his penis between thumb and middle finger, as if to offer proof. "What I'm going to do with this? Huh? What I'm going to do with this now? When my pecker gets done thisaway it don't go down by itself. Ain't no way. What I'm going to do with this?"

Honey sighed. It was clear he was single-minded about getting Claud's stamp of approval on the whole deal. "I don't know, Sweet. Maybe you could stick it up your brother's ass."

Ronnie flailed at the steering wheel, sputtering expletives. "I ought to make you go on and do it," he said. "I got the gun, you know."

"I ain't about to suck your old knobby dick for nothing," she said.

"You a damn lie! The thing ain't knobby!" The blue vein on his forehead welted up across his forehead. He opened the door and stood next to the truck, again indicating his sawed-off midget of a member. "You can't look at my pecker and say it's knobby."

"Sure I can," she said. "It looks like the back end of a turnip root."

"It ain't done it!" He was red-faced, livid, a greasy-haired, ponytailed Rumpelstiltskin, on the verge of stomping his foot and splitting the earth open, with his solid little button of a penis nodding in agreement.

"Believe me, Sweet, I've seen all shapes and sizes, and you a low-built motherfucker. That there is a knob."

"Shut the fuck up!"

"A damn nubby knob."

"Ain't!"

"Is, too. It ain't no more than a nubbin."

"A nubbin?" He took it again between thumb and cussing finger, seemed to be contemplating her critique. "Well, whatever it is, it's damn sure got to be drained."

"Well I sure as hell ain't going to be the one to pull the plug."

"Shut up and hand me that jug of motor oil in the floorboard."

She picked up a plastic bottle of Pennzoil. This was a good

sign. When he got his head under the hood to put oil in the engine, she could get her purse, her gun, and get the hell out of there. She was formulating the plot in her head, how she would drive right over him if she had to, when it came to her what he was doing. He had oozed some of the oil into his palm and set about masturbating.

"Good God almighty," she said. "I've seen a lot of sick shit in my life, but I ain't never seen nobody beat off with Pennzoil."

"Does right tolerable," he panted. "And I like the smell."

"Well, shit, go off in the bushes or something. I don't want to watch you go to flinging that mess at me. Are you crazy?"

"Shut up," he said, blowing and sweating in the summer heat.

"Go on away from me with that shit!"

"Shut up, else I'm going to aim it right at you," he panted.

"I ain't believing this shit," she muttered. "No-dick redneck motherfucker going to beat off with goddamn thirty-weight. This here is some sick motherfucking shit." She turned the rearview mirror so she could check her makeup, her hair, then picked up a magazine rolled up on the dashboard. A whole magazine about fishing and chasing down deer, but she would be damned if she was going to acknowledge what he was doing. She started flipping pages, summertime cicadas vibrating, punctuated by the slapping sound of Ronnie giving himself a lube job.

Writing the Mud Life
Essay (post-2016 election)

"Flannery O'Connor, attacked by her critics for her 'dark' and 'pessimistic' vision of life, observed that no writer is a pessimist; the very act of writing is an act of hope. And so it is."

Joyce Carol Oates
from the Introduction to *Writers at Work*

Bitterness, elation, rage, hypocrisy, grief—the atmosphere these days is electric with a spectrum of post-election emotions. Autopsy in progress, there has been a constant dissection of the time-honored slinging of political mud (Mud? More like excrement this past cycle). The Ruskies' lobbing of cyber-mud and fake mud is in post-election analysis that loops into infinity and beyond on the old fashioned boob tube; it seems that Boris and Natasha have pulled another fast one on Moose and Squirrel. The Facebook is thrumming with insults, rantings, and "un-friendings." Families are falling out, and the good old U S of A seems snagged in a Bizarro, alternate universe—with "alternate facts" (once upon a time known as "lies") of its own.

Oddly enough, an aspect or two of my own personal life seems to parallel the larger carnival in progress. While the electoral college has been conned by the basest of propaganda and most hyperbolic of guarantees, election year took me on a smaller-scale emotional ride, with a conniving, thieving business associate leaving me a shell-shocked, wound-licking survivor of the kind of ego-flattering promises and lies that always, *always* translate into utter self-deception. The irony is both heartbreaking and delicious—both decimating and emboldening—because I am a writer. Writers can salvage just about anything, rise like a Phoenix from the PTSD ashes of an emotional arsonist's deranged flame, armed with more and better words to weave, to wander through that wreckage with a strong sense of purpose: self-awareness, insight, and hope. It's way cheaper than a therapist. And I hope the country can make a similar journey back to a mentally and politically healthy state; the alternative is unthinkable.

Readers and reviewers often ask me if I'm an angry person, if I feel aggrieved, resentful, if I've been basted in childhood traumas, if I'm eternally simmering with a well-earned fury. Why else would I write about such harsh comeuppance for shallow social climbers, heartbreaking clarity for honky-tonk chicks chasing down this month's married man, disappearance or even murder for child abusers, or disemboweling retribution for Klansmen who were the architects of searing lynchings. "Is that why you heap such revenge on those beyond-the-margins characters? Are you working through some anger issues?"

My first instinct is to say, "Um . . . no." No personal grudges here (with the exception of a cheating former spouse and the above-mentioned conniving, thieving business associate, who have been or soon will be dispatched, absolutely). No battered inner child screaming out in primal agony. No past abuse, past lives, or a life past hope. Just the garden variety dysfunctions that saturate families in general. I'm actually an unbearably sunny optimist, devotee of the glass half full, a downright, goddamned Pollyanna, if you want to know the truth (of course, I'm also fond of saying that you really, *really* don't want to piss off a writer.)

Or maybe I'm just being polite. After all, I *am* Southern, and as such, would rather be dead—or worse, a pariah—than impolite. *Of course* that hair style/outfit/décor/child's behavior/recipe/idea is *wonderful*. To say otherwise might—gasp—hurt some feelings. Can't have that, can we? What phonies we are, with our cheap validation, endlessly insisting, "Oh, no, after *you*," a la "Chip 'n Dale," babbling little chipmunks of Southern charm, "nattering nabobs" navigating this superficial comedy of manners we call Life. In that respect, I truly do have some deep grudges when it comes to society in general, the institutions we claim to value, the ways we mistreat the people we do not want to look at.

There is a bigger lie here, a lie that Southern writers in particular have been wrestling with for generations. After all, if we lie so easily in our personal lives, with our quaint conventions and our saccharine, Christ-wounding "Bless your heart"s (if you are a Southerner who ever, *ever*, uttered that evil bleat, you have, indeed, devastated our Lord) perhaps that is symptomatic of something more insidious, more deeply embedded—a more elemental kind of Lie. If I'm really most sincerely honest, maybe I should address *that* deep dark something-or-other. But to do so is to attempt to address a gritty, despicable truth, and, as we all know, to quote a classic Jack Nicholson character, "You [Southerners] can't handle the truth."

By "truth," I mean the historical truth, the soaked-in, subliminal semen that keeps the seeds of racism and misogyny just a-bubblin' away in that big ol' pot of collard greens on the stove over yonder. The election of the Carnival Barker in Chief has me pondering this more and more. It is against the rules, engraved in stone, damn it: you simply do not take a sharp stick and poke at the "R" monster in a cavalier manner; you don't conjure up the demons of Dixie and the beyond-the-Mason-Dixon devotees of the Gospel of Whitey and then whistle a happy tune past the cemetery expecting that all the bad juju will—poof—evaporate, post mortem. *This simply is not done,* and yet . . .

When my high school English teacher, Mrs. Florence Fouts, wrote nice things on my compositions and urged me to pursue this thing called writing, it was flattering—heady, even. It was 1970 and words seemed to be more powerful than ever. 1968 had happened. One could not *not* look. In the midst of the upheaval, I was inspired by a *Scholastic Tab* paperback compilation of high school newspaper editorials from all over the country. I discovered a world of social issues outside the realm of the Apartheid South I knew well, hoped to see change, and fast. I read about Stonewall and gay rights and all manner of commie pink-o propaganda while my upper middle class parents had no clue what was infiltrating my elastic and malleable adolescent brain. And, lo and behold, it "took". I remember writing an anti-Confederate flag editorial for the school paper, catching only a little grief from white students, making inroads toward friendships (though not lasting friendships) with black students. And, lo, these words were spoken unto me: "I never thought of it that way." Holy crap! My writing could influence others! That was a rush that would only become more addictive.

My love of words was powerful strong, and I continued to play with them as I navigated my maze to maturity, through the poetic angst of teen tears to the heavy-handed academia of term-paper pronouncements. And when my American Short Story professor gave us a choice, for our final exam, between analyzing a classic short story or writing one of our own, I jumped at the second offering, after which said professor steered me over to the Creative Writing Department.

With the encouragement of the creative writing instructor (who pretty much *was* the Creative Writing Department), all (twelve) of us students submitted here and there. And the first short story I had accepted by a New York literary magazine was a tale of integration seen through the eyes of a poor white junior high school girl, Rota, navigating a maze of both race (through the school's sole black student—Mary Alicia, the barrier breaker) and class (in Mary Alicia, Rota discovers her own superiority, and it soils her spirit). The title: "The Day the Niggers Came." The dialogue: dialect. I maintain that the title, in which I made shameless use of that incendiary "n" word, is the reason the story made its way to the top of the slush pile. It was the 1970s, and Southern Gothic was all the rage, the "n" word a fixture. However, when the story was re-issued, post 2000, I changed the title to "Mixon, Fla., 1962," for the obvious reason, and purged it of dialect, for the obvious reason. Times are much different in this, the Twenty-first Century. But the underlying attitudes, the subtleties steamed into our pores along with the southern humidity, are still very much with us. And those who deny it the most are the most complicit perpetrators, gummed up as they are in the cogs and gears of their own willful ignorance and stubborn lack of self-analysis.

Because so much has been yammered about the much needed "conversation" surrounding race and history and truth, and with so little follow-up (as in, actually conversing), the Big Lie of "post-racial America" seems bigger than ever. How else does one explain the shameless audacity with which racist, supremacist, Klans-ist elements were "whistled up" for the 2016 election? And those who pretend that the knuckle-dragging, mouth-breathing contingent was a mirage are enablers of the most pernicious ilk. That seemingly normal, everyday folks would align themselves with the kind of forces that fed the Third Reich certainly explains our tendency to repeat history. There is clearly a segment of the populace that is easily manipulated via emotional appeal, essentially via fear, the go-to emotion for authoritarians. As for the others, the cynical opportunists whose souls were sold, are being sold every day, for influence and money—may you all spin eternally on a scorching spit at Dante's Hot Destination Spot.

It is essential that journalists point to the Emperor and insist that he is naked, even though he is strutting and crowing without the slightest whisper of a blush of embarrassment. After all, his advisors have poured golden showers of praise over his finely appointed duds, primped and perfumed him, sculpted his fluff of a coif, and stroked his outsized, outsourced ego. And his poor, duped, denial-ridden subjects are cheering and adoring him, trying like crazy to keep all eyes averted. They don't dare look too closely; it's as if there is a gut-level understanding of their irresponsible lack of good judgement. If you watch them very carefully, you can see a hint that they are afraid to truly see. It is a shadow of honesty, but it is there, in the glance askance at that testicle spectacle, where resides another dimension to their fear. By god, some of them *do* know he's in the buff but they just can't bring themselves to admit it. Some know he is downright butt-assed nekkid . . . yet they are desperate not to look, to not finally see the flaccid belly, the drooping, sagging genitals that hang like stretched-out Silly Putty, pressed onto a Twentieth Century cartoon from the funny papers. And I get it. I understand why they can't/won't look. I know from personal experience that it's downright humiliating, mortifying, and a kind of nudity-baring move of your own, to admit you've been methodically and deliberately conned, shown up, double-crossed and double-exposed as a nitwit, a flat-out fool.

Within days of taking office, the media was under attack, full bore—the fourth "branch" of our government, the free press, was basically being told to shut up and go away. If that doesn't send a chill down freedom-lovin' folks' spines, I don't know what would. If it were not so malevolent, it would be absurd, laughable: a big-shot man with miniature-ish hands and a monumentally hideous, orange comb-over, running around nude, genitalia flapping, contradicting his own lies at every turn, presenting himself as God's gift, nanny-nanny boo-booing like a fourth grader, behaving in a way that would be mortifying to most parents *of* a fourth grader, sneering at science, deriding the press, posturing as if playing a game of thrones, and oh, did I mention that he is nekkid?

Words—especially words of fact and thoughtful reasoning—are democracy's nourishment, the peoples' recourse, the enemy of tyrants. Words have the power to right wrongs, embrace the marginalized under-dawgs of society, and call out bullies for the teeny-tiny little humans they really are. And this is a moment in history when the right words are so desperately needed, when anger can be potentially transformed into a deep, calming breath and a sigh of clarity. No grudges, no revenge, no tantrums, no childish choosing up of sides in shunning "the other." I'm certainly willing to try, but I don't think I will ever be the one to hit that high mark of morality.

The cheating former spouse I mentioned? I lied about having a grudge against him—I never had one, in fact, although I did work through a mighty amount of hurt and fury in writing my "fiction." My current husband and I actually have lunch with the ex every month or so, the ex being a kindred spirit and like-minded tribesman, hard to come by in our red neck of the woods. Clearly I'm capable of forgiveness, the release of ill will, a Zen-like inner peace that settles upon my countenance in beatific grace.

As for the conniving, thieving, business associate I have come to see as a con crafter (con "artist" is too high a compliment; the art of the con belongs to The Don), not so much. Ultimately I'll have to examine that filthy-loony little chapter of my life, will have to take a hard look at my pathetic willingness to be bullied and manipulated by a seeming sociopathic narcissist (it is a rich parallel, indeed, that of my life and political life). I'll have to ask what all that says about the deep cracks in my own character, and, even more difficult, I'll have to answer to my weaknesses. No, I have yet to purge *that* reservoir of literary pus. But it is deep in its richness and certain to be exhilarating and cathartic at one and the same time. And once that scab is ripped away, I know that a baptism of peace will wash across my soul and Jesus will like me again.

Would that we—or I—or any artist, for that matter, could come so easily to the baring of the Big Lie, the one that clutches at the spirit of this country, weighing down the soul of the South like a cotton gin fan cast into the murky, murder-worn Tallahatchie River. As Rota says, at the end of "Mixon, Fla., 1962," realizing her wretched station in life at the same time she loses the only real friend she is likely to have for years, because of the color line: "I was . . . afraid of slippin' down deep in the mud forever."

It is my own fear that we, along with our hypocritical outrage and our lack of insight, are quite rightly condemned to life as Mudbugs—at least for the time being. It is our shame and our penance for allowing such a miscarriage of citizenry to be foisted on our freedoms. But as one who clings to that damn half-full glass (preferably bourbon, please) with her sunny outlook all a-glow, playing the "glad game" along with Polly, and insists that hope is always and ever our salvation, I have to believe that good and truth, kindness and redemption, and the grace of empathy are bound to rise and bear us up. It is a rule. It is written in stone, damn it.

"You don't want to piss off a writer." To that well-worn statement I would add, "I tell lies for a living." Let's make sure we understand what this is, this fiction, seeded by life, gestated in pure imagination, born out of deceptively thin air: it is a pack of Big Fat Lies. Hopefully, because I am a decent enough writer, I will occasionally make some gorgeous, *Southern Living*-worthy floral arrangements of lies whose petals fold back to reveal a pistil or two of truth.

But even a liar like me realizes that the better angels of humanity are the moral soldiers equipped to take on the Big Lie—and forge a foundation for victory over the self-deception *within us* that lays us bare to political predators, narcissists nourished by adoration and greed, those who would exploit and use us up, cast us as mere props to generate their own self-crafted accolades. Taking on the Big Lie will be difficult enough, in and of itself, but that moral imperative will never, ever happen until we take on the Biggest Lies, the lies we tell ourselves. And refusing to face those Biggest Lies comes at our peril.

It is incumbent upon writers of fiction to dig down into that reservoir of truth, now more than ever, to "vomit up the anguish," as Baldwin said, in order to reveal larger, insidious truths. Artists of all stripes, of any merit or good conscience, must pull back the curtain on the lies they tell themselves, so that others might look inward to find their own moral chinks and empathetic failings. And those who insist they are free of those deep inner lies—who insist that pure anger, fear, homophobia, xenophobia, fill-in-the-blank-phobia, "alternate facts," racism, sexism, whatever-ism, perversion, and self-adoration are *not* factors in our tainted system—those are the lost souls who are not merely stuck in the mud; they are drowning in the quicksand that threatens to take us all down.

Until that is acknowledged, until a hand reaches back for help, revealing the at-last realization, the profound insight, admission of the lies and confession of the sins, we can't move forward.

Until these words are uttered: "I'm nekkid and I'm about to drown in quicksand," we are, quite literally, stuck. It's time to take a crane to that bog, yank some lost souls out, hose 'em down, throw 'em in a bubble bath, and get 'em into some nice clothes. I have the ever-hopeful feeling that we'll all clean up real pretty.

Deep Water, Dark Horizons

For Wilson

Gary Wright, in his expert, know-it-all way, insisted that what was happening on Turkey Branch was a crime. "A god-damned crime, you stubborn old coot. You can get fined for it. I've done googled it. The county site says $500 a day for every day you let them turds roll down in the branch yonder." The man jabbed his pointer finger with every few syllables.

Yoder Everett ran his fingers through thinning hair, hair that had once upon a time been a thick home to the ladies' painted fingernails that combed through it, now gone limp and thin as he traversed his sixties, alone, but for this one pathetic friend. "You're a goddamned know it all, Gary."

It had finally come to a head, after months of back and forth, after Gary first noticed the oozing fissures in the grass, soil becoming a sloosh of fetid, foul stink. Yoder, tight with a dollar and loath to spend from the thousands he had hoarded over the years, managed to deny, pretend, and scoff his way out of taking any action, until Gary drilled down into something like research. Any fool could find out what was what, it seemed, on the internet.

Now the two men stood beneath one of the massive live oaks that thrust their mossy arms to the summer sky across Yoder's six acres of waterfront on a branch of the Fish River, studying the patch of yard gone to shit swamp. When breezes lifted, along with the undeniable stench, a chorus of clatters and clacks and tinklings and knockings rose and fell from the scores of wind chimes hanging from branches, from hooks on porches, from posts on the wharf and the pier, from the trash can corral Gary had built to keep away the raccoons, armadillos, and 'possums. Gary was handy that way.

The noisy mobiles, though, were all fashioned by Yoder's own hands, inspired by a fragmenting mind, that willy-nilly mishmash of chimes, along with paintings on plywood, palettes of muddy browns, reds, oranges; even murals painted onto the asbestos-shingled sides of his river house. His gnarled yet nimble fingers strung together the cacophonous orchestra of objects tied onto lengths of fishing lines, knotted through the boards of driftwood or stripped sapling limbs or guitar necks or whatever, from which the lines dangled. He used all sorts of materials, too, for the chimes themselves: old costume jewelry, a de-constructed clarinet, wooden kitchen ware, beer cans, women's stilettos, anything at all. "I make art out of junk," he liked to boast. "I'm environmentally friendly that way."

But now here was Gary Wright's dumb ass claiming Yoder was a major polluter, right up there with the goddam BP criminals who had ruined the Gulf this past spring. Now into full-bore summer, the beaches from NOLA to Apalach were so gummed up with the crude that business owners along the coast were yelling bloody murder.

"It's right there in black and white, son," Gary went on. "It's right there on the damn web site. You know, that branch runs out to the river and the river runs to the bay and the bay--"

"Hell, Gary, don't you think I know about geography and watersheds and currents and all? And don't call me 'son'."

"And the bay goes to the Gulf of Mexico, and then out to the whole goddamned world. You're polluting the world with that rusted-out old septic system."

"I told you I've fixed it. I worked on it all day yesterday, down in the bowels of it. Ha!"

"Naw, crawling down in the empty old thing and squirting a hose pipe through it ain't fixed a damn thing about it. You've done broke so many laws I can't count 'em."

"Why don't you google them up, then, the laws?" Yoder shot back. "Google is God now, I guess. Google is the eyes of Dr. T.J. Eckleburg looking down on the Valley of Ashes."

"What the hell?"

"Forget it. Why read a book when you have the google machine to impart life's truths to your dumb ass."

"It's the law, that's all I'm talking about. You can't let a steady stream of turds and piss-water keep rolling down that hill and into that branch. You've got to call a septic service or I'm gonna have to turn you in to the county. You're the property owner. It's *your* responsibility."

Yoder, clench-fisted, tight-toothed, gritted out, "Get off my property, then. I'm a good mind to evict you."

But they both knew it was an empty threat. They had a long history of disputes, even fist fights, going back to when they were young, potent warriors of the gridiron, back when women liked their looks and a loop around the town of Foley, Alabama, from drive-in diners to picture shows in a Ford Mustang, with a make-out chick in the front seat, was the pinnacle of a life promising to be all downhill from there.

They were an odd couple, alright: Yoder, well-educated, creative, once-charming-now-cautious, carrying several DSM-referenced labels; and Gary, of unremarkable intelligence, naïve, spur-of-the-moment. Yoder taught art education in a community college before the mental meltdown that had him on disability by the time he was forty. Gary, no hope of a deferment, found himself, straight out of high school, chasing Charlie in the jungles of Viet Nam. He spoke of it from time to time, though not with enough depth or detail to satisfy the curiosity Yoder kept in check.

"I seen some shit there, over yonder, in itty bitty titty land. Nobody ought to see them things." He would fall silent for several beats, then, "I seen nothing BUT shit all my life," he would repeat, to the air, to the nights, to anybody or nobody, "and shit don't cool for folks like me."

"You think you're the only one that had it so damn bad?" Yoder would toss out, as a challenge, their routine one-upmanship of misery, on twilit evenings when they sat on the dock, working their way through a case of Budweiser. "Hell, my stepmother was cold and wicked and hated my guts," and he would recount tales about how his real mama took the cancer when he was only six, went downhill fast, and how it was clear to everyone that his daddy had "Miss Dinah" waiting in the wings long before the cancer ever even hit.

His memories of his real mama, Janine, were warm and conjured something like reassurance, despite the odd quirks she had, the rituals, a prominent one being the taking of the castor oil, every single Friday evening of every single week. "Folks just believed in it, back then, believed it kept you regular, like it was good for you. Mama was the queen of poop."

Yoder couldn't remember a time in his life, post potty-training, when his mother did not insist on inspecting his bowel movements, to see if his excrement was healthy or if it demanded more attention. He and Gary sometimes had a good laugh about Yoder's fecal foundation. "No, sir, I wasn't allowed to flush, not until mama checked—and she'd say things like, 'oh, that one looks real good, Yodie,' or 'no wiggle worms to be found,' or 'that one's a pretty picture of health'. I didn't think anything about it—that was just how our routines went along, until she got the cancer."

When Miss Dinah took over, her two brats in tow, she showed no inclination to study Yoder's bowel movements. In fact, when, all of seven years old and eager to please his new parent, he finally offered to show her what he had landed in the toilet bowl, she squenched up her face, shuddered, and said, "Why on God's green earth would I want to look at anybody's BM? Let alone, *yours*." And it was the way she said it, "*yours*," that planted her hatred of him in his mind, hardening him to her, young though he was, and by adolescence the reciprocal disdain was set in his soul.

"She was my ruination," he would lament, blaming her for his bad luck with women. "And yeah, I had to call the bitch 'Miss Dinah,' just like my daddy did. He was one goddamned pussy-whipped somebitch. But she sure did pretend-dote on him, waiting on him, baking seven layer cakes and all," and Yoder would recount how the chocolate confections were locked in the china cabinet, locked away from him in particular, locked away in such a way as he would have to see the sheen of the chocolate each time he passed by, lust after it, wish for it, but he never, ever gave her the satisfaction of doing something as brazen or pathetic as, say, to ask for a piece of it. Even when she brought it out as an after school treat for her own two children, his "steps," Yoder refused to ever ask to be included.

"Don't you want a little bit, Baby?" she would sing-song, if his daddy was there, and sometimes Yoder would accept a piece, sometimes not.

The two men shared a bottle of Jim Beam down at the dock that evening, to chase behind the beer, as they typically did of a dusky sunset, having sprayed down with deet, thrown their feet up on foot stools, spending hours swapping memories and disagreements, flicking cigarettes hissing into the low tide, the high tide, the ebb and the flow.

"I'll get some prices, then," Yoder said, finally, his way of acquiescing to his foe in the great septic dispute of 2010. "But you have to kick in something. You gonna take that panhandle gig? The one that gal 'Sissy' or 'Missy' or somebody told you about? Because I'll be wanting you to throw in on the new septic tank. It handles *your* shit just as much as it handles mine."

"It's 'Misty'," Gary said. "Like the song. Like that Clint Eastwood movie, *Play Misty for Me*. And she says disaster money is almost like free money, depending."

Depending on what? Yoder wondered, thinking Gary might need a good lookout on this Misty person.

Gary and Misty had reconnected via the internet, a landscape he had only begun exploring around 2007, when Yoder was threatening to put his desktop out with the trash. Yoder had bought the thing as he entered the 21st Century in a feeble attempt at technology—an attempt that turned into his certainty and fear that the government was spying on him.

"There's a camera on the things you know," he said, disengaging all manner of cables. "Ever since 9-11 they've been watching us all."

"Why don't they just watch them Islams?" Gary pushed back. "It's them Islams that's bombing themselves and all."

"Muslims," Yoder sighed. "Islam is the religion. Muslims are the practitioners of Islam."

"I don't understand. Baptist is Baptist, Cath'lic is Cath'lic, what the fuck?"

"Never mind."

"Okay. Never minding."

But Gary took on the surfing of the nets with uncharacteristic vigor, networking his way through Classmates.com, navigating over to the high schools of some of his old army buddies, reconnecting, flirting his way past a few former girlfriends, then onward to Facebook, where he found Misty again, just after the explosion in the Gulf. She talked him through the skyping process and schooled him on the larger landscape of the internet. When he boasted to her about his artist friend, Yoder Everett, embellishing, "Yeah, he's a big deal around here. He gets big money for his wind chimes—well, he ought to be getting more."

"Is there a web site where I can look at them?" Misty asked.

"Hell, no—Yoder hardly never touches no computer. He thinks they're taking over the world."

"Ridiculous," Misty said. "You *have* to have a web site these days, to advertise, to promote, to sell—you two boys need me. I can do all of that." And that was the springboard for their planned reunion. After they rendezvoused in Florida, after the work for BP played out, they would haul her trailer back to Turkey Branch, and she would barter her promotional work on Yoder's art for something like rent.

Yoder, however, was skeptical. "Normal people don't do that, just pull up stakes, drive off to meet a stranger and start up a new life."

"Aw, she's a good ol' gal," Gary countered, filling him in on how he had dated her briefly when he returned from Nam, during a short, drug-fueled stay on the west coast. "She was one of them hippie chicks—you know, titties flapping and bouncing, hairy pits, the whole deal. Which I ain't minded no hairy pits atall—all I needed was that one little particular patch of hairs, you know? I was fresh out of the army, son. Horny as hell. And she was a wild thing, always into something. Hell, man, she wants to help you sell your wind chimes."

"What the hell? And don't call me 'son'."

"Yeah, she's gonna make you a web site. Says nobody can't do no kind of business without no web site. Says she has real experience in all kinds of business doings, advertising and whatnot."

"Then what's she doing in a doublewide in Arkansas?"

"She's been hiding out from an ex-boyfriend, a mean one, a stalker type. She ran off from him in Portland, changed her looks and all—you know, like that movie, like Julia Roberts in *Sleeping with the Enemy*."

"That's even worse," Yoder said. "All we need is some stalker nut case to come around here. Hell, somebody's likely to get killed."

"Naw, man, you got it all wrong. Her guy can't leave Portland, his job—and last Misty heard he's done took up with a whole 'nother woman. It's cool."

"I don't know."

"Shit, man, think of her like the business manager you never had. Remember you always said the business side of art makes you want to puke? Well, Misty's a pro, knows computers, says she's a real, for sure, 'people person'. Which you ain't, right?"

"Right."

"So let her manage the crap you hate—the crap you suck at—and see if your income gets better. Come on, man."

"Can't argue with that," Yoder mumbled, seeing a few dollar signs gathering in his future. He did, indeed, hate hauling the chimes around to all the fru-fru and she-she and cutesy-cute little galleries and shops in the Foley-Gulf Shores-Orange Beach area, making fake-nice with all the managers and artsy-arts folks. Even though his pieces were popular, unique, and sold quite well, he thought some of those "fancy ladies and gay boys," as he called them, the ones running the shops, might be overpricing and skimming their own special kind of slick off the top of his profits.

It was his mindset anymore, to be wary. The older he got the less he trusted folks, even old friends. He had just about stripped away anyone who ever mattered to him, stripped away by suspicion, always, of ulterior motives. His two children were long estranged, radio silent for over a decade, and the ex-wives did not even bother to try anymore. Gary was all he had. And Gary, like him, had alienated his own set of friends and family, not with paranoia but with his scatter-shot approach to living, his sheer and utter unreliability.

Gary and Misty had skyped throughout May, June, and into July's haze, becoming more and more familiar, gestating the plans that would culminate in their reunion, in mere weeks, the revival of a long-ago, hot second of a romance--all while the Deepwater Horizon vomited its ominous cloud of crude into the cesspit of the Gulf of Mexico, in ever-mounting numbers of gallons per day. CNN had a picture of it on TV 24-7, the live, real-time movie of the slow murder of the Gulf. And the numbers, the volume of the disaster forever ticked upward.

"It's a awful thing," he told Misty's image on the computer screen, "a terrible thing—not just the folks killed but no telling what all else is gonna die. The shrimp, oysters, dolphins, everything. They say it'll kill the coral, even. Hell, I didn't know coral was alive to begin with."

"Well, that's what a lot of the free money is for, to help with that, so I'm going to get there as quick as I can--no later than July's end. Can't wait to see you in the real flesh, sweetie," she cooed.

Gary allowed that she had held up pretty well. She laid claim to the age of fifty-six but looked light of it, with long hair streaked blonde, animated green eyes, and the distinctive laugh he remembered from all those years ago, "kind of a hoarse, horsey laugh," he always called it. And the once braless teeny bopper showed him her relatively new fake boobs. "I was dating a plastic surgeon in San Francisco for a while," she said, spreading her top open, unhooking her bra from the front, spilling them on out, right in his face, giving him the kinds of sexual itches he had not scratched in years. "The doc gave me these, plus an eye job, and a slight nose job—just got rid of that little bump. You remember that little bump on my nose?"

He did not. He was preoccupied with the not-little boobs.

"What do you think, daddy? Nice, huh? It's a D-cup size."

Gary was done for.

They spent more and more hours skyping, which soon became elaborate cyber-sexcapades full of dirty talk and all manner of autoeroticism the like of which Gary had never imagined himself doing. "She sure does know about some variety," he confided to Yoder one humid evening. "But hell," and he took a long pull from the bottle, "why jerk off to a nudie mag when you can see everything right there, just a-writhin' along with you?"

"Can't argue with that," Yoder exhaled his cheap cigarette. "Just seems kind of weird to me, having romantic doings like that."

"You're being old-fashioned, man. This is how it's done these days—everything's on the internet line."

"Can't argue," Yoder said again.

***

Elite Septic Systems sent a "technician" to Turkey Branch the day after Gary headed out for Blountstown, his new, big-boobed love, and the cleanup job, armed with booze and Viagra.

"This one's a doozey, one of the worst I ever seen. Gonna need new field lines, too," Ronny, the self-proclaimed "turd wrestler" insisted. "This thing is a dinosaur, that's all there is to it. We got to put in all new. Run you a few thousand dollars."

"Nothing here to work with at all?" Yoder countered.

"Zero. Zip. You're lucky you ain't had the EPA and the Corps of Engineers and any government regulator you can think of out here. The money you'll save in fines could install a boatload of septic systems."

Yoder seethed and silently vowed to garnish Gary's British Petroleum wages or government money or whatever. And he didn't have to wait long. After only three weeks on the job, sans Turkey Branch commute, not a trailer but a pop-up camper on the back of a Toyota pickup following Gary's own truck came rolling up to his property, which one Misty Smith hit with the force of Hurricane Katrina.

"I'm moving in with Gary," she squealed. "My man. My destiny."

Gary blushed, "If it's no never-mind to you, that is," nodding at Yoder.

"Of course he doesn't mind!" Misty was possessed of grand movements, physically--large swoops of arms, long strides of legs, and she had a booming voice to match, a voice she exercised with the looseness of one who was possessed of few boundaries. "The only way I can get the work done is to set up office space. Not going to happen in a camper, that's for sure. And Yoder, I promise,

I *guarantee* you that I'll get you noticed, get the bucks rolling in. As your agent, I'll negotiate for higher prices, and as your advertiser and web site administrator I'll handle it *all*. My sweetie here explained your dilemma in detail. And it's so typical of artist types. You just need to be left alone to do the art. You deserve to be known, and I'm making your fame my mission in life, along with loving up on this guy," nudging Gary, who blushed again, with her elbow, continuing, "Oh! Where's my camera? Look on the front passenger seat, honey, and grab it for me." But she strode her long legs past Gary, arms flailing a pricey digital camera out of her vehicle and commenced striding, bounding all over the property snapping pictures of individual wind chimes, studying them, making a show of her professional eye. It wore Yoder out already, her energy, but, he told himself, she obviously was a worker bee, and it was, after all, for him.

"What happened to the cleanup job?"

"Aw, man, it was bullshit—walking up and down the beach scooping up tar balls, wearing these dinky, cheap-ass rubber gloves and neon vests. All Misty had to do was hand out water all the livelong day; said she was definitely overqualified for that."

"Can't disagree."

"But after I got hit with that fog a few times I was thinking I had enough."

"Fog?"

"Yeah, man, that shit they been spraying all out over the water from planes. To bust up the oil."

"Dispersant? I saw something about that on the news, I think. Breaks up the oil and sinks it to the bottom of the Gulf." Yoder tapped out a cigarette and lit it. "You say you got hit with it?

"Lots of folks got hit with it—anybody on the beach—'cause the damn planes would be maybe a hundred, two-hundred yards out, and that gulf wind blowed it all up on the beach, in the air, smelling like a bitch, burning our eyes and all. Nasty stuff. It ate clean through them cheap-ass gloves they gave us. And them stupid lawn-mowin' masks ain't no kinda protection."

"Damn, Gary, that can't be good. It's bound to have had some kinds of physical effects on you. Did you get nauseous or light headed?

"Not really. It was just a nasty stink, mostly—my eyes got okay. It's just those damn ate-up gloves, man. That's some toxic shit. Poison."

Gary's utter lack of concern beyond the stupid gloves frustrated Yoder no end. Gary had taken the same, blasé attitude when Yoder had questioned him about Agent Orange, years earlier. "It wasn't no big deal," Gary said, "they used it all the time."

"It *was* a big deal," Yoder said, now, under his breath.

That afternoon, while Misty flitted about the place clicking chiming images and Gary lazed on the hanging bed on one of the screened-in porches on the outbuilding, Yoder drove into Foley, to the public library, and began to sift through the reference section.

***

The septic system was to be installed on October 1st, but the current tank and lines had to be yanked before that. Due to scheduling there would be lag time, so they would have to make do with a Porta Potti in between. Ironically, the Elite Septic System folks scheduled the euthanasia of the tank for September 19th, the very same date that the Deepwater Horizon well was declared "effectively dead" by the National Incident Commander, some admiral or other. And it was on that exact date that Yoder began to move from suspicion to decision about one Misty Smith.

She had, indeed, created a web site, an attractive one, featuring pictures of the wind chimes and some of the paintings on plywood, inflating prices, "just to see if they'll bite," she said. And even though Yoder couldn't argue with that, he was incrementally taking more and more offense to her intrusive, bossy ways. "You need to at least post something personal on your page," was one of the many "you-need-to" remarks he got from her.

"That's *your* job, isn't it? You're the administrator."

"Yes, but if you personalize it more, cultivate some fans, we'll add a Facebook page. The Facebook page is really where you'll find your numbers."

"Fans? Facebook? What the hell? Sounds like you want me to be somebody that doesn't even resemble me. Back off."

"Sure, I'm a pit bull," she allowed, "but you need a pit bull, somebody who will lock their jaws down hard for you—it's for *you*, after all!"

And Yoder would let it be. Gary seemed happy enough, though over the weeks his demeanor gradually became tinged with apathy. "She ain't so easy to live with," he allowed. "Kinda high strung, you know. But she's driven. *Them* kinds of folks—folks that's driven—tend to be high strung is what I think."

"So is it worth it, the sex?"

Gary smirked, "Always, man."

In the meantime, his library research into the benzene component of oil, and into the Corexit 9500 and Corexit 9527 used in the cleanup was causing him to filter government conspiracies through his brain. The toxic brew of Corexit was banned in the United Kingdom, he discovered, and health professionals in general were definitely not fans. Why would the U.S. be willing to put such a chemical into the already poisonous soup that was the Gulf of Mexico? Did President Obama give the okay? If not, then who? Was it not enough to sacrifice the marine flora and fauna on the altar of tourism, but also to calculate how many human lives were worth the salvaging of the sugar-white sands? It gave him a headache, the mulling of it.

Then, on the day of the septic tank killing, Misty rolled out some cockamamie idea about making Turkey Branch an incorporated entity, a move that would require a shared bank account, for business purposes, of course. "I can make this work," she insisted. "I've done it time after time!"

"Like when? Like where?" Yoder pressed.

"What the hell?" she shrieked. "Are you questioning my legitimacy? Do you hear him, Gary? Nobody appreciates a goddamn thing I'm doing around here! You two are a couple of witless idiots—you wouldn't even have a web site if it wasn't for me!" And she strode off into the afternoon. By now both men knew that the snit would last for a few hours, possibly a day, with plenty of passive aggressive behavior to dish out until said snit subsided. But this day, Yoder pushed back. "Exactly what do you actually *know* about this chick?"

"Man, I know she's a great piece of ass. Which, I gotta tell you, I'm not looking to miss out on no nookie. What's *with* you?"

"I'm not looking to have her putting her paws all over my money, that's what."

"She ain't no thief. Come on, this is the first pussy I've had in years."

"Jesus."

"We'll work it out, man," Gary said. "I'll talk to her."

But for someone who was living it up with a great piece of tail, Yoder thought his friend didn't have much fight in him. No, not much fight at all.

It made him wonder, why had Misty insisted on meeting up with Gary over in Blountstown? Why had she pushed so hard for him to sign on for cleanup? What the hell was her angle?

***

October blew in and so did a flatbed truck carrying the brand new, sure enough state-of-the-art septic system that turd wrestler Ronny was so excited to sell him. Forget a rusting metal tank; this concrete one would last at least forty years, probably much longer, long past Yoder's life span.

Yoder set a folding lawn chair out near the work site, brought along a cooler of beer, plenty of smokes, and settled in. He was loath to allow any repairman of any stripe—electrical, carpentry, refrigerator, whatever—to work without being under his supervisory gaze; he trusted no one to do the job "right."

He hollered at Gary, laid out on the hanging bed, for his buddy to come out and join him.

"Naw, man," came a faint response.

"Why the hell not? Nookie time?" he joked, expecting a laugh he didn't get.

"No, Yodie—I'm laying down."

"What's the matter?"

"Nothing, man. Just feeling a little tired, like I'm running out of gas, that's all."

Misty joined him, though. She dragged an outdoor lounge chair up to his, and he offered her a beer. She declined, as she usually did. She rarely drank and never smoked and seemed to like the high moral ground it gave her, though she was never overt or verbal in her self-righteousness. Hell, Yoder thought, she was a goddamn braless, LSD-taking, marijuana-smoking druggie back in the 70s, when she first fucked Gary.

She didn't waste a second. "I wish you wouldn't be so stubborn about forming a real business. You need to look into it. Do some," she enunciated, "*research*."

"Not real thrilled with anybody who uses the words 'you need' with me. *You* need to cut that shit out."

"Well, I know what I know. And I know you *love* some *research*."

"Just like Gary," he said, automatically, "a goddamn know-it-all," certain she had just smugly tossed him some bait. He was baffled, but knew enough that he refused to take the minnow.

She pounced. "I have a limit, you know. I'll only go so far for people who have no appreciation for me."

"Does it count that you're living on my place?"

"Fuck you!" she shrieked, catching the attention of the septic crew. "Tell you what. You like to do stupid fucking research. The old school kind of research. So why don't you research this, for your friend, who's not doing so great. Yeah, research *this*: 'black, tarry stool.' Goddamn research *that*!" She executed her dramatic stride to her camper truck and gravel-slung her way down the driveway.

Yoder took a sip of beer, narrowed his eyes, wondering how she knew so much about his doings, making leapfrogging connections in his head, noting "dark" and "tarry." "Hey, Ronny! You say that concrete tank's going to outlast *me*?"

"Damn right."

"It'll handle the waste?"

"Sure thing. 'Course you got to treat it right. But you'd be surprised what folks put in these things that they ain't supposed to. Hell, tampons, paper towels, dead goldfish, even rodents."

"But it eventually breaks down, huh?"

"Long as it don't get too cluttered. I mean, the solids is gonna go to the bottom, the scum to the top, the liquid to the field lines. It all breaks down if it don't get backed up."

"You're a damn septic savant, Ronny. Not going to argue with that."

***

Yoder watched in fascination over Gary's shoulder as his computer savvy buddy mouse-clicked through a series of websites, a virtual wizard at private investigation. Talk about a savant. He was a little surprised that Gary put up no resistance when Yoder, having abandoned his monitoring of the septic installation, shook him out of the hanging bed, demanding, "Get on that damn computer, right now, ass hole, and show me how to find out about this bitch you've hauled into our lives."

What they found, pretty quickly, was that there was no residence in Portland, ever, as far as they could tell. There *was* a series of marriages, even one to a plastic surgeon, but in Boulder, Colorado, not California. There were hefty divorce settlements, some unimaginative aliases, a few restraining orders against her, a couple of arrests, one for theft of property and another for harassment described as "hacking into a cell phone." She moved often, every year or two at least. Employment records were nonexistent.

"Phone hacking, huh."

"Yeah, you can track a person's whole life, where they are, what they're saying even, just by hacking in their phone. Misty told me she does it all the time."

"The hell you say. Well that explains *that*."

"What?"

"Never mind, Gary."

"Okay," he sighed. "Never minding."

The reality of the whole sorry business settled in on Yoder. "Holy crap, she's a bullshit artist," he said, "only without much artfulness to speak of. She played you, big time. Sorry, Gary."

"Hell, I figured it was too good to last," Gary sighed. He was pale, haggard, and Yoder only now realized just how hollowed-out he was, how that succubus of a criminal bitch had sucked the endangered life right out of him.

"What I don't understand is why you didn't check her out, research her, before you let her come here. I mean, you obviously know how."

Gary sighed, picked up a glass of whiskey. "Age-old story, ain't it?"

"I guess so."

"Well, I had me some pussy for a little while."

"Yes, you did."

"I reckon we're gonna have a knock down drag-out when she gets back." Gary looked down at his hands. "I ain't got much use for that," he sighed. "Outa gas. Damnedest thing."

Yoder studied his friend's profile, the slump of his shoulders, the drop of his chin, his obvious fragility, now. "Don't worry buddy. Don't you worry. You go lie down. I'll take care of it."

"I know. Thanks."

***

Gary slept fitfully that night, images of billowing clouds of smoke in thick jungles, huts ablaze, the screams of women as the planes came in low, misting the vegetation, aiming to strip away Charlie's cover. He half-woke, a few times, and reached to see if she was there, but he was alone with these fever-dreams, racing, like the spirits of dolphins chasing across the waves.

He caught a sleep-soaked glimpse of the moon, hanging like the blade of a scythe in the clouds. It reminded him of the Vincent Price movie, *The Pit and the Pendulum,* of the last, chilling scene, the torture dungeon being locked, the door shut forever on the evil Elizabeth, trapped, all alone yet still alive, in an "iron maiden." Then the dark closed over him, pushing through his consciousness, force-flashing images of dead baby dolphins washing up on the black-blotted sands of the Gulf, seagulls stained slick with poison, and watercolors of pastel children, picking at the tar balls between their toes. And he wondered, in his stormy dreams, if the coral really could die.

Hiding out with Holden Caulfield
Essay (pre-2011 retirement)

Some lawyers are fond of saying that they keep secrets for a living. I am not a lawyer, but I do a whole lot of observing, listening, and keeping my mouth shut—except when I am required to open it. So I'm part spy, part Catholic priest, and sometime tattletale. The workaday world I navigate involves being thoroughly entertained, hearing all stripes of stories, and, for all the toil of it, has a big red cherry on top: staying in touch, on a daily basis, with my inner Holden Caulfield. Neither Holden nor I ever did really want to grow up. Lucky him, with his red hunting hat, to be frozen in fiction as THE adolescent of the twentieth century, commenting on the quality of farts at prep school assemblies and such. Lucky me, to have this job, where farts abide and never fail to amuse or humiliate. I am a grateful and wounded resident of middle school world, having come to the land of public education in a roundabout way.

It went down like this: The not-so-sad fact is that, like Dobie Gillis's buddy Maynard G. Krebs, I was never much of a fan of work and, at college in the 1970s, felt my true calling was to be a professional student and world-famous author—fairly effortlessly, of course. Screw a life of real work and the burgeoning societal desire for the acquisition of all that stuff the Mad Men of the '50s had foisted upon a generation. I was above all that, all the "phonies"

Holden and I disdain. I was an artiste with no bra and the armpit hair to by God prove it; I would live the good bohemian life, thank you very much. However, my parents, the funders of my educational adventure, did not concur, even though I'd actually had some success getting a couple of stories published and winning a writing contest or two. The minor Armageddon that ensued led to that time-honored, age-old question: What the hell do you actually do with an English degree? Answer: get certified to teach, a prospect that kind of turned my stomach, having denigrated education degrees as not very, shall we say, "challenging." Ultimately, though, the humbling of my academic snootiness turned out to be my salvation and made any other job I've held seem like a Dickensian tale of woe and cold gruel.

Having done tours of duty as a cuff clipper on a textile assembly line, a waitress in a college beer joint, a brief graduate assistantship in an English department followed by a year of teaching high school seniors (I wasn't paid nearly enough to give up my personal life for the honor of grading really bad term papers), I finally landed in a place where I truly, truly belonged—a place riddled with stories and peccadilloes and royal fuck-ups to be observed and filed away in my one-day-to-be-a-writer-again brain. Middle school was a land of double-dealing and plotting and subterfuge and intrigue, crawling with denizens eager to engage in all manner of posturing and preening on one end—and slinking away and fading into the background on the other. These beings were unpredictable, impulsive, and irrational, which led to all manner of grand entertainment for me. They also harbored a deep fascination with bodily functions. Old people were gross and anything that was annoying was "gay." I was surrounded by crude, tasteless, base immaturity. I was home. And, over the years, as the job evolved into a career (with four books published, I never quit this, my day job), I gained all sorts of insights—into these hormonally challenged little beings, and into myself. The latter ultimately made it possible for me to write again.

Most sane adult folk see the (sub)human creatures in grades seven and eight as unbearable at best and torturous at worst. And they are correct. Drop an untrained adult into a middle school and its citizens catch the scent of fear very quickly, subsequently gauging where the weak spots are, picking, grinning, circling, and feasting like vultures upon the kill. I've seen many a cocky substitute teacher from civilian world reduced to a tearful, quivering mass of Inner Child by twelve-year-olds who cut their teeth on subs. This pack mentality—even including the onlookers who are too sweet or too shy to join in—is an ugly thing to witness but certainly goes with the territory.

No amount of university schooling can prepare one for the land of the adolescent. Perhaps it is because so many of us have blocked out those traumatic memories of the days when we were tormented by bullies, by the onset of our menstrual periods or our impromptu erections, by our imagined imperfections, or by just the god-awful uncertainty of it all. When I try to coax memories of my junior high days they become a blur of Clearasil, Kotex and the attendant elastic belts, awkward penny walks and bottles spinning, slam books, crushes on teachers, the Beatles, both yearning for and fearing success at getting a boyfriend—because, hey, then what?—Midnight Sun hair coloring, tent dresses, whispered judgments, snapped bras, and Yardley cosmetics.

Once certificated and supposedly ready to be a Giver of Knowledge, I attempted to get my students to be amazed by the wonderful, intricate, scintillatingly complex world of . . . grammar. I was the English Teacher. (I would become the secret-keeping guidance counselor later, like ten years.) Painfully, I learned that no middle school teacher should ever use an outdated film that refers to "grammatical boners"—not ever. "Don't forget your period," an English teacher might sing out as a reminder to punctuate. Not in middle school. And no way in hell could we conjugate the verb "to come." When it came to literature, the "climax" of a plot was territory fraught with snickers, as were any mentions of a "nut" or a "ball." And God forbid that an author of a classic poem or story might have used the words "queer," "gay," or "breast" in some sort of confusing context. Even a seemingly safe vocabulary word like "flagellation" would bring gasps and giggles. In middle school there is not much that is not about sex.

Or about self. And how best to hide that real self.

I accepted that grammar, when held alongside sex, is pretty boring. I began to wish that I had minored in theater since it was becoming clearer all the time that I was going to have to be a goddamned actor/entertainer if I wanted them to take an interest in appositives or infinitives or the subjunctive mood. So I mugged and strutted. I did dialects. I did the hambone, for Christ sake. And I maintain that the fact that I succeeded in taking their minds, fairly often, away from the teeny-bopper drama du jour qualifies me for an Academy Award.

But it was not the parsing of the language that brought me the most joy to impart; it was the smithing of the words that was heady and rewarding. And royally amusing. For middle schoolers do not possess the filters of their older brethren; middle schoolers will write or say anything. Any parental unit who thinks his/her child will be either tasteful or discreet is in a mighty state of denial. For example, ask for an expository or a narrative essay and one might get informed about how Aunt Marcy's toxic farts are known to be akin in stench level to those passed by Spence, the family dog; or told the story of how grandmaw got loose last Saturday and went running the streets nekkid, stopping only to hump light poles and parking meters; or how Cousin Eddie got arrested the other day when he showed his pecker to the little kids on the First Baptist Church playground.

In spite of the great stories, after about a decade spent observing a deteriorating state of parenting, a growing tolerance for disrespectful students, an element of pettiness and small-mindedness among teachers, and an overall system of inflationary grading along with the elevation of mediocre standards, I was burning out. The peripheral shit had sucked the spit and energy from my classroom persona. Holden's exterior world was becoming stale with superficiality while his terrified inner one was beckoning like the Grim Reaper.

And so it was that into the 1990s I marched with a Master's degree in school counseling. I set up shop, determined to listen, nod, question, nod, listen, reflect, nod, empathize, etc. No longer was I in the role of taskmaster, Nazi rule-maker, enforcer of learning and discipline. All of a sudden I was that which only the most egregious of teachers dare attempt to be: the "good guy." Now I got a more up-close look at farting aunts, nekkid grandmaws, and pervertoids like Cousin Eddie—not to mention abusive stepdads, cancer-ridden uncles, evil best friends, bipolar moms, meth-head dads, tormenting older sisters, a cast of thousands. Kids used for Internet porn, rape victims, cutters, children who served as weapons for their warring parents or who had been abandoned or were doing drugs because Mom shared with them. Those stories took on a wash of darkness that had not shown itself so boldly in the classroom and it was beyond disturbing. And of course it was only the tip of the iceberg, too, since the messy, silly, nanny-nanny-booboo trivialities played out most of the time—locker room bullies, girlie-girl dramas, and my-teacher-hates-me delusions. Still, all their stories, whether dark and disturbing or shallow, silly, and trivial, trickled down to the storyteller at my core. I began to miss the writing, and more than just the exercises I once did along with my students in class. I began to feel a need to reach out to that part of me that was twin to my middle schoolers. Writing was the only way I knew.

And then, out of nowhere, the stories took a turn, inside out. An eighth-grade girl defied statistics, put a gun to her head, and pulled the trigger. One of my children committed suicide. Not a girl who was neglected by her parents, or afraid of academic failure, or criticized by her teachers. This was a bright, beautiful young person, a leader among her peers, with a loving family and a constant smile for everyone. The utter tragic dissonance of it all snatched me into the real reason for Mr. Caulfield's tale and how much the surface is such the mirage, especially at an age when you're a chameleon, with the undeveloped brain of a lizard that eats its own tail. It's the flip side of Holden's funny, sarcastic musings. He is, after all, trying to hold together in the face of the most traumatic event of his life: his brother Allie's death. He also has the specter of a former classmate's likely suicide breathing down his neck. He occupies that place where self-destruction and self-awareness cleave, running scared from the truth of his own flawed reality. And that is what we have to always wonder about Holden. Does he make it? Or does he fold in on himself, like my dead student, collapsing under the weight of that youthfully false perception of hopelessness?

Adolescents hide. That is a given, of course, but I mean they really, *really* hide. They change personas sometimes in the space of a day. They only show a few of their cards to that one or to those few who are trusted—or to no one. They hide from every shred of humanity for which they can maintain denial. Sure, some of it pops out—in some children quite frequently. But stripping emotionally naked is not something an eighth grader is likely to do, even behind the closed door of the guidance office.

I had lost other students to tragic accidents, but none self-inflicted, none so accusatory, defiant, and guilt-wrenching as that. It was a death that demanded answers, for the sake of those who might visit and revisit such a choice. Thus began the second-guessing, the what-iffing, the retracing of steps to try to find the moment when such an unthinkable act could have been prevented. But there was no comprehending. The full-bore, scorching sadness dug into me in a way I had never expected—could never have expected—yet, surprisingly but slowly—trudgingly slow—it began to dig me out of the hole that, I was discovering, had been my residence for too long.

I'm sure it's no coincidence that this was around the time I was also in the midst of a fallen-over-the-cliff, smashed-up, twenty-something-year relationship. I had scores to settle, even though I've never looked kindly on the settling of scores. There was a flux of mish-mashed karma riding the ether—a confluence of events coaxing me from that camouflaged perch occupied by the school marm/guidance counselor personas. It began to dawn on me that, like these kids to whom I was drawn, I had been hiding from my own expression, that I had spent a couple of decades as an adolescent. Literally.

But now I set about re-emerging as an author after the long hiatus from word-working. I took a deep breath and "came out," spending two class periods a day, back to back, with one group of students for both English and literature. We called ourselves "The Writers' Block." We read. We wrote. We scorned grammar drills in which students picked out prepositions for an hour and then picked out more for homework. We sneered at templates for formulaic paragraphs that cookie-cuttered the mainstream into an imitation of style. Instead, we masterfully dissected one sentence per day—obliterated it—went grammatically medieval on its ass—then got down to the really important business of books and words.

Those were the most delightful years in my teaching career—when I re-birthed myself and was surrounded by some amazing students who were much braver than their peers in what they shared on the page. A few in the bunch even put me in mind of Holden C., and I put a copy of *Catcher in the Rye* in their hands, even though it was probably on some "banned" list or another in this conservative county where I toil against the tide. Of course, no student to whom I ever gave that book did not love it.

I don't do The Writers' Block anymore. I'm winding down, hopefully into full-time writing mode. A year or so away from retirement, it feels lucky and right and symmetrical that these adolescents, who would rather die than reveal themselves for who they really are, have actually taught me that it's fairly safe to show myself, through the writing. Interesting little critters, these acne-fearing, angst-ridden troubadours, who have told their stories to me and trusted me to really listen. Sure, some of them have been a pain in the ass—some downright disturbing in their skewed sense of reality—and one in particular has become the ghost-voice in my head that begs me to give them all the benefit of the doubt, because the overwhelming abundance of them truly do want to become human, to become themselves.

It has been a dozen years since that ghost-voice was born of a gunshot, and as I write this it is only days since another young lady, a local high school student, died under similar circumstances, but in a murkier atmosphere. In a freakish clustering of events, she was preceded in death this academic year by the suicides of two teachers at her school within the span of a few months, teachers who laid out the blueprint for her and possibly for others. And now comes the collateral damage, the ruined families, the emotional fallout further scattering across the entire community, trickling down to my middle school charges, picking at my own squelched-down guilt and inciting the kind of rage that senseless death taunts out of us. Hearing about such a thing makes the heart of any parent go numb with the sudden severing of possibilities and a story incomplete, unwritten, cut off in a second's worth of irrational role-playing that has no do-over.

We have to think deep and dark, even as we enjoy our inward snickers at the shallow goings-on in 'tween and teen world, grown ever meaner with the folding in of texting, sexting, online communities, and the viral exposure of images and self-expressions that once were deeply private and respected as such. As for Mr. Caulfield: not so lucky after all, to be character-frozen at that point of cleavage between innocence and despair, between humanity and isolation, between protector of children and conspicuously consuming adult. That crazy red hunting hat, with its Elmer Fudd earflaps. That whole '50s vibe of dry martinis and materialistic myopia. Juxtaposed with the electronic age, Holden Caulfield is so very post-World War II, so twentieth century. But his outward bravado and inner uncertainty transcend the subsequent decades since his creation, to expose the sometimes brittle fragility of adolescents everywhere, who, like yours truly, fight to defy the hiding.

Acknowledgements

If my lifelong editor and friend Sonny Brewer had not resurrected Joe Formichella and me at approximately the same time, the turn of the 21st Century, we likely would have never met and ultimately married. As two reclusive writerly souls who had given up writing for a chunk of our lives, the renewed creativity literally brought us back to the Land of the Living, individually and then together. The raising of the dead. The making of the match. Not too shabby, Sonny. Thank you.

Joe did the tireless research for my novels, just because he loves the journey of the digging, which I do not dig. He is also unconditionally accepting of my quirks and phobias and magical thinking and irrational mental meanderings. Paradoxically, in a world of judgement and stereotyping he travels with logic and reason yet still manages to be the most giving and kind person who ever existed. And because we are introverts by nature, have disdain for gossip, chit-chat, and folks who are compelled to fill time and space with spoken words, we can go for hours without uttering a sound. During the COVID pandemic shutdown we were happy as the clams we are. Again, pretty un-shabby. And another solid thank you.

The other Joe in my life, Joe Taylor, he of the resplendent, beaded beard (until he scorched it; no more bonfires for you, Joe) was the first to publish me (post resurrection), and as any author knows, the first time is the one you never forget, the most exhilarating, the highest high of all. And he went on to publish more of my and (my) Joe's work. So a big thank you to Joe and Patricia Taylor, the most honest and decent and above board publishers on the planet and beyond. Another thank you to MacAdam/Cage, which published my first novel, giving it the San Francisco west coast magic that led to a second novel, both books shepherded by Pat Walsh and the late David Poindexter.

It is impossible to name all of those who have been supportive of the solitary art of writing, whether teachers (yes, Florence, Beth, Carolyn, Lloyd, John Craig Stewart, and, and, and, and . . .); friends (yes, Bob, Pamela, Kent, yes, even Stephen [the late], Horrible Karen [who is totally NOT horrible], Ronnie the original re-starter of the writing endeavor and who was always there until the darkness took him, Ira B with lessons [on firing a gun, gutting a deer, along with some super crude turns of phrase], and, and, and, and . . .); movery-shakery folks (Jim Gilbert and Martin and Skip, oh my!); co-workers in public education (yes, LB, Brenda, Vicky, Catherine, the lunch bunch, and, and, and, and . . .); and the writing community (yes, Bev, Tommy, Silas, Karen, Loretta, Daren, Joshilyn, Abbott, and, and, and, and . . .).

The writing community . . . here is a good place to remember friends and fellow writers who are no longer on this side of the Everafter: Terry Cline, Judith Richards, William Gay, Wayne Greenhaw, Carl T. Smith, Brad Watson, and William Cobb.

I have to mention freelance editors like Grammar Guru Suzanne Barnhill (pricey but well worth every penny, as she is a Wizard of Words) and the late Jay Qualey, who charged one hundred dollars plus a large bottle of the cheapest sweet red wine for his "vicious pencil." And my once-upon-a-time agent, Ellen Levine.

There's also a guy who might be surprised by the indelible impression he made with his kind support, back in the day, back in the late 1970s. Paul Bresnick was so encouraging and accepting of this timid little country mouse dipping her whiskered snout into the big ol' world of New York City, not a clue under the heavens how the publishing machine of the 20th Century worked, and who, of course, backed away from it post haste. Paul and I only had a few interactions in the very early couple of years, but come the 2003 NYC debut of my first novel, *In a Temple of Trees* (and thank you to hometown honey Keith Langham for hosting the NYC party), there he was, our first and only ever face to face meeting. It touched me more than just about anything, truly. Thanks, Paul.

There are also writer/reviewers (yes, John Sledge, Don Noble, John Williams, Jay Lamar, Dawn Major, and, and, and, and . . .), READERS (our favorites), LIBRARIANS (our other favorites), along with festivals (yes, Jim Davis, Paul Willis, Greg Herren, and, and, and, and . . .), independent book stores (yes, Johnny, Jake, Tyler, Kathy, and, and, and . . .); and, of course, family, such as it is.

Thank you to my extended family, which has a rich history of fun and humor and service and love and acceptance . . . and depression and addiction and suicide and whatnot, so thank you, family, for all of the great material. Just you wait until I get to the REALLY crazy stuff! What a fun book that will be!

Big love to John & Frances, Nick, Madison, TJ, Ziggy Gene, Melanie, Maverick, Joseph, Lauren, Vinny Maeve, and last but never least, the big brain trust of . . . Sam!

And as always ever-since, in memory of my father Eugene Hudson, and two of my younger brothers, Joe and Wilson Hudson.

My immediate family, here on Waterhole Branch, a tributary of Fish River, at Waterhole Branch Productions, is the most amazing assembled, improvised family unit there can be, even with all the warts and idiosyncrasies. There's my ninety-something year-old mother Booda with her little lap dog, Boo and her evil cat Molly in one plex of the duplex. Also on the property is Jamie Rutan, of the Bonita Avenue childhood neighbor Gardner family. Jamie is Booda's inherited daughter, fellow caregiver (along with the rest of us), and lives in her little house, End of the Line.

The hubs, me, plus our loving dogs Dr. James "Jimmy" Ryan and Frances "Frankie" James Ryan (named for characters in Joe's *Waffle House Rules*) and relatively new cat (not evil, but mischievous) Whomee (named for a cat in Joe's *Lumpers, Longnecks and One-Eyed Jacks*) are in the other plex of the duplex. And having vacated the Rough Draft Cabin on our deck above the

Branch, Over the Transom's Sonny Brewer now resides in his Coda Home, up near the slab, of "Slab Life" (Southern Literary Arts on the Branch) fame.

Our once-upon-a-time Music Shack has a second moniker now, Common Time, a reference to both music and to shared creativity, real collaboration, which springs out of the magically good juju we share in this spiritually special place.

And speaking of music, thank you to the musicians we fell in with for a time—wonderful people basted in talent and something I never had, never hope to have: a singing voice. Here's to Chris, Chuck squared, Corky, Eric, Tim, Erickson, Michael, Suzi, Suzanne, Cliff, and, and, and, and . . . and of course Cindy's Mark, just because. And Grayson Capps! Here's to what coulda, shoulda, woulda, if . . . but, no. Most of all, here is a note of love and remembrance . . . Lari White, whose green-eyed soul and the voice of an angel will never leave this place; her spirit hangs in the Spanish moss that frames the stars.

On less than one hand, way fewer than five fingers, I can count those toxic souls who proved to be the spoilers of creativity, saboteurs of my success, less than artful conners, wedge-drivers among my professional relationships in the writing world (although more than a few were restored—good souls who had their own breakthrough moments), voodoo hexers running on the fumes of selfishness. These wretched folks deserve my appreciation as well. It's all material, the gift that keeps right on giving, fair game, mush to embellish, shit about which to . . . write! And I'm just gettin' wound up. You assholes know who you are. Many thanks!

Finally, thank you to fellow editor (with the Hubs and me) of *The Best of the Shortest: A Southern Writers Reading Reunion*, Mandy Haynes—author, reviewer, and throat-puncher extraordinaire. It was she who, behind the aforementioned Snideley Whiplashes (once purged) burned the sage, hummed a prayerful tune, pronounced the house and grounds cleansed, and hung a protective talisman above our doorway to ward off whatever narcissistically negative traces of dastardly intentions might still be hovering in the ether. Again, good juju.

I certainly believe Mandy's magic "took." After all, this here once snake-bit, semi-sabotaged writer person lives in the Paradise of Barnwell-by-the-River with her sublime soul mate, her chosen family, her sainted dawgs, her creative juices a-flowin', her heart a-*over*flowin'.

And she just got herself a goddamned Truman Capote Prize.

And I will live happily ever after.

Amen.

Previous Publication of Contents (in chronological order)

"LaPrade," *Penthouse* magazine, New York, NY, December, 1977; *Opposable Thumbs*, Joe Taylor, executive publisher, Livingston Press at the University of West Alabama, Livingston, AL, 2001; *The Alumni Grill*, edited by William Gay and Suzanne Kingsbury, Macadam/Cage, San Francisco, CA, 2004

"The Thing with Feathers," *Stories from the Blue Moon Café*, volume IV, edited by Sonny Brewer, Macadam/Cage, San Francisco, CA, 2005; *Red Dirt Forum*, volume I, number 2, edited by Amy Wilson, Red Dirt Press, Shawnee, OK, 2018; *The Best of the Shortest: a Southern Writers Reading Reunion*, edited by Suzanne Hudson with Joe Formichella and Mandy Haynes, Livingston Press at the University of West Alabama, Livingston, AL, 2023

"Yes, Ginny," *A Kudzu Christmas: Twelve Mysterious Tales*, edited by Jim Gilbert and Gail Waller, River City Publishing, Montgomery, AL, 2005; *Red Dirt Forum* (as "Yes, Virginia"), volume I, number 2, edited by Amy Wilson, Red Dirt Press, Shawnee, OK, 2018

In the Dark of the Moon, a novel, Macadam/Cage, San Francisco, CA, 2005; excerpted in *Men Undressed: Women Writers and the Male Sexual Experience*, edited by Stacy Bierlein, Gina Frangello, Cris Mazza, and Kat Meads, Other Voices Books, Chicago, IL, 2011; excerpted in *All the Way to Memphis and Other Stories* by Suzanne Hudson, Rivers Edge Media, Little Rock, AR, 2014

"Opposable Thumbs," title story, *Opposable Thumbs*, Joe Taylor, executive editor, Livingston Press at the University of West Alabama, Livingston, AL, 2001; *All the Way to Memphis and Other Stories* by Suzanne Hudson, Rivers Edge Media, Little Rock, AR, 2014

"Chilling Out," *Opposable Thumbs*, Joe Taylor, executive editor, Livingston Press at the University of West Alabama, Livingston, AL, 2001

"The Good Sister," *All the Way to Memphis and Other Stories* by Suzanne Hudson, Rivers Edge Media, Little Rock, AR, 2014

"See Ruby Falls," *Opposable Thumbs*, Joe Taylor, executive editor, Livingston Press at the University of West Alabama, Livingston, AL, 2001

"Bonita Street Bridge Club," *Southern Bard*, volume II, edited by Thomas Mack Lewis and S. E. Brewer, University of South Alabama, Mobile, AL, 1977; *Opposable Thumbs*, Joe Taylor, executive editor, Livingston Press at the University of West Alabama, Livingston, AL, 2001

"Jesus, Sex, and Sweet Tea," *Opposable Thumbs*, Joe Taylor, executive editor, Livingston Press at the University of West Alabama, Livingston, AL, 2001; *Red Dirt Forum*, volume I, number 3, edited by Amy Wilson, Red Dirt Press, Shawnee, OK, 2019

"The Seamstress," *Stories from the Blue Moon Café*, volume II, edited by Sonny Brewer, Macadam/Cage, San Francisco, CA, 2005; *All the Way to Memphis and Other Stories* by Suzanne Hudson, Rivers Edge Media, Little Rock, AR, 2014; *Belles' Letters*, volume II, edited by Don Noble and Jennifer Horne, Livingston Press at the University of West Alabama, Livingston, AL, 2017

"The Fall of the Nixon Administration," *Stories from the Blue Moon Café*, volume I, edited by Sonny Brewer, Macadam/Cage, San Francisco, CA, 2005; *The Saints and Sinners Anthology*, edited by Amie Evans and Paul J. Willis, Rebel Satori Press, Hulls Cove, ME, 2011; *All the Way to Memphis and Other Stories* by Suzanne Hudson, Rivers Edge Media, Little Rock, AR, 2014

The Fall of the Nixon Administration, a novel, Waterhole Branch Productions, Fairhope, AL, 2019; re-launch (post COVID) 2024 (Louisiana Book Festival, Jim Davis, director); chapters excerpted here: 2 - "Mimi" and 6 - "Lindia"

"All the Way to Memphis," *Delta Blues*, edited by Carolyn Haines; Tyrus Books, Madison, WI, 2010; title story, *All the Way to Memphis and Other Stories* by Suzanne Hudson, Rivers Edge Media, Little Rock, AR, 2014

"Looking for John David Vines," *Climbing Mt. Cheaha: Emerging Alabama Writers*, Edited by Don Noble, Livingston Press at the University of West Alabama, Livingston, AL, 2004; *All the Way to Memphis and Other Stories* by Suzanne Hudson, Rivers Edge Media, Little Rock, AR, 2014

In a Temple of Trees, a novel, Macadam/Cage, San Francisco, CA, 2003; excerpted here: from the chapters titled "August, 1990/ Three Breezes" and "Appomattox"

"Writing the Mud Life," Waterhole Branch Productions Facebook "Notes" (post 2016)

"Deep Water, Dark Horizons," *Alabama Noir*, edited by Don Noble, series concept by Tim McLoughlin and Johnny Temple, Akashic Books, Brooklyn, NY, 2020

"Hiding out with Holden Caulfield," *Don't Quit Your Day Job: Acclaimed Authors and the Day Jobs They Quit*, edited by Sonny Brewer, M P Publishing Limited, Douglas, Isle of Man, UK, 2010; Work in Progress: a *Collection of Excerpts from Some of Our Pulpwood Queen and Timber Guy Authors' Manuscripts*, edited by Mandy Haynes, Three Dogs Write Press, LLC, Fernandina Beach, FL, 2021

"Fools are free."

~Joe Formichella

A native of Columbus, Georgia, with roots in southwest Georgia, Suzanne Hudson (rps.hudson@gmail.com) grew up in Brewton, Alabama, and has been a resident of Fairhope, Alabama, for nearly forty years. A retired public school teacher and guidance counselor, she is also the internationally prize-winning author of three novels, a "fictional" memoir, and her short stories and essays have been widely anthologized. Hudson lives near Fairhope, Alabama, at Waterhole Branch Productions, with her husband, author Joe Formichella (joe_formichella@yahoo.com) and the other denizens of the Branch. She is the 2025 Truman Capote Prize winner.

PGIL2024USA